Praise for the novels of N

MICHELLE SAGARA

CAST IN ETERNITY

mira

ISBN-13: 978-0-7783-8652-0

Cast in Eternity

For questions and comments about the quality of this book, please contact us
at CustomerService@Harlequin.com.

Mira
22 Adelaide St. West, 41st Floor
Toronto, Ontario M5H 4E3, Canada
BookClubbish.com

Printed in U.S.A.

This is for Terry.

Covid has been hard. It leeches color out of the world; it makes the finding of joy much, much more difficult.

Thank you for loving these books anyway.

CAST IN

ETERNITY

01

Corporal Kaylin Neya was thinking about committing murder. She had been assigned her least favorite job: the public front desk of the Halls of Law. Her beat partner had once again been siphoned off to a different department. She tried not to resent either Severn or the Wolves, but it took way more effort than it should.

On paper, the front desk was a shared duty, which passed between the Hawks and the Swords, but Sergeant Keele was in charge of all front desk duties. She was pure Hawk.

If murder was committed in any district Kaylin patrolled, she'd be pulled from desk duty. Murder investigations trumped front desk work. The only downside was the Hawks weren't incompetent enough not to find the culprit, which would mean Kaylin would be out of a job she mostly loved and in jail. Or worse.

For the most part, front desk duty involved a lot of listening and taking notes; it seemed like busywork to her, and she'd been trained by a Leontine who *loathed* paperwork, and often destroyed his desks by clawing his way through the wood when he was forced to actually do any of it.

Kaylin, absent both claws and rank, had dutifully taken out the front desk's mandatory notepad. Records existed for a reason; the Records capture of these so-called citizen reports and queries—half of which were complaints—would be far, far more accurate than simple handwritten notes.

In theory the note-taking was supposed to give the people who came in with their various reports or concerns a sense of comfort; it meant the officer they were speaking with was actually paying attention. Kaylin had seen some of the notebooks others had left crammed in the front desk drawer. Attention. Hah. She wasn't much of a doodler to begin with, and understood on a visceral level that drawing weird caricatures of people who had serious—if completely unhinged—reports was not actually doing her job.

She therefore had a pad that contained written words that could be repeated in public in front of her when Mrs. Erickson approached the desk.

Kaylin's perpetual shoulder ornament had become almost invisible to the Hawks in Marcus's office, because she never left home without Hope. On most days, Hope seemed content to idle across her shoulders like a very inadequate shawl. He evinced no interest in the day-to-day functions of the Hawks.

Only on a few occasions did he deign to lift his translucent head to take a look around, and on even fewer did he consider whatever he saw interesting enough he felt it necessary to actually support more of his own weight by standing. Teela called him a *familiar*, but even her initial sense of caution had faded with time. Hope was Kaylin's—and like Kaylin, the older Barrani Hawk implied—was generally lazy unless the work involved was interesting or necessary. Necessary to Kaylin, that is.

For whatever reason, Hope lifted his head when Mrs. Erickson approached. To Kaylin's surprise, he then muttered the equivalent of a mumbled complaint and pulled himself to his feet.

Mrs. Erickson was a constant—almost daily—presence. A silver-haired older woman with slightly bent shoulders and eyes that were clear as day in a wrinkled network of a face, she never came by empty-handed. If there was an actual Mr. Erickson, none of the officers in the Halls of Law had ever met him. Some were certain he didn't, or had never, existed.

Kaylin hadn't quite managed to work her way up to that kind of deep cynicism yet, although older Hawks told her it was only a matter of time. And while Mrs. Erickson could be difficult to deal with, it was mostly a patience deficit on the part of the Hawks. Mrs. Erickson had never approached the front desk brandishing a knife, a club, a fire iron, or, in one instance, a highly illegal magical device.

Nor had she approached the front desk demanding to see *someone in charge* while looking down her nose at the person who was manning the desk. She didn't consider the Halls of Law to be an extension of her personal fiefdom, and officers therefore her servants. As far as Kaylin could tell, the old lady truly valued the Halls of Law and the services it attempted to provide the citizens of Elantra.

Kaylin had grown up in the fiefs. Old ladies in the fiefs had a kind of grit, a kind of steel to the spine—they'd have to, to have survived for as long as they had, even the ones who appeared sweet in a place where sweetness was the exception, not the rule. It took strength to be sweet—it meant you didn't care if people thought you were a mark. Or a victim.

Kaylin had never been particularly sweet.

But she'd trusted it when she encountered it, or trusted it enough that she didn't immediately pull daggers and back off. Pulling daggers here, at the front desk, would be severely career limiting in any case, unless the visitor had run in heavily armed and obviously intent on causing damage. Even then, it wasn't daggers officers were meant to employ, but the sticks and batons that were part of their beat uniform.

Neither of which would be necessary with Mrs. Erickson. She came armed with a basket, from which the scent of baking emanated. She never came empty-handed, and no one was fool enough to imply that the baking she brought was somehow poisoned.

Also: Kaylin's stomach spoke before she could.

Mrs. Erickson stopped two yards from the desk, her eyes widening at Kaylin. Or, more accurately, at the shoulder ornament. While the rest of the Hawks—and most Swords—had proven that familiarity breeds, if not contempt, then comfort, Mrs. Erickson was not a person Kaylin saw every day. She expected Mrs. Erickson to have words or questions, and was slightly surprised to hear what they were.

Mrs. Erickson smiled and set the basket on the desk. "You're here alone today?"

"My partner has meetings."

"Without you? How odd. But I'm glad you're here."

Kaylin found this mildly confusing because she had encountered Mrs. Erickson only once before, and as far as she knew, Severn always managed to avoid the damn front desk—which was annoying because she was certain he'd be *better* at it than she was.

Mrs. Erickson had baked soft buns with a hint of red at the edges—jam of some kind. She removed napkins from the top of the basket, and then placed two buns on them before offering them to Kaylin. "I should have made cookies instead—these are a bit crumbly and likely to cause a mess on the desk. I'm sorry, dear—I just wasn't thinking.

"But I was told that these would be welcome today."

And there it was. Mrs. Erickson had a ghost problem. Or

a several-ghosts problem. Although not all of her visits involved reports about the doings of said ghosts, most did in one fashion or another. Investigations had been done—this was Elantra, after all, and ghosts were not *quite* as ridiculous as they sounded on the surface. This wasn't to say that the Halls of Law believed in the existence of ghosts; rather, that there were many magical artifacts and echoes of older or ancient wars that somehow lingered, and the residue could cause confusion, panic, and, yes, a strong misidentification.

The Imperial Mages were sometimes interested in ghost reports, but couldn't be fussed to actually sort out which of these reports were the products of too much alcohol at the wrong time, and which were genuinely of interest. The scut work was therefore left to the grunts who manned the desk.

Mrs. Erickson's ghosts, however, had never become part of any case the Imperial Mages would find interesting. For one, they were remarkably mundane in both appearance and behavior; for two, their proclamations often involved the type of things that might annoy or disgust a well-bred Elantran old lady. Rats. An unexpected abundance of insects—cockroaches. Fruit flies.

Sometimes they involved the neighbor's dogs—which the Hawks discovered did not actually exist; there might have been other neighborhood dogs that were causing sleepless nights, but Mrs. Erickson's current neighbors didn't have giant, man-eating dogs. Sometimes the ghosts, however, had led to smuggling arrests, albeit in indirect and unexpected ways. No one expected ghosts to be able to suss out the value of the composition of *fabric*, of all things.

On the other hand, on the tiny chance that Mrs. Erickson was not being advised by one of the many ghosts that haunted her, Kaylin agreed with the reported recommendation. Whatever these were, they were *delicious*.

"You know my partner?" she said, hurriedly swallowing before she spoke. The whole "don't talk with food in your mouth" was a lesson she hadn't learned growing up. There had usually been an absence of food in that mouth.

"He's the dark-haired young gentleman, isn't he?"

Severn did have dark hair. So did Kaylin. Kaylin nodded, wondering if she should save the second pastry for later.

"He wears that very unusual belt; it's striking and so bright. I think it's lovely, if possibly slightly inappropriate for normal office wear. Oh, don't mind me," she added, slightly flustered. "My thoughts were elsewhere."

Belt? Kaylin decided against saving the pastry and bit into it while she thought. So far, so good: no ghosts. Kaylin privately suspected that Mrs. Erickson was lonely. As far as anyone in the department knew, she lived alone, and if she had ever had children, none of them visited. Not that background checks of average citizens who were not in any way considered a threat were common—but Mrs. Erickson was, if slightly frustrating on busy, chaotic days, nonetheless well-liked.

Two years ago, the old woman had failed to enter the office. People had been slightly surprised at her absence, but thought little of it. But she failed to arrive the next day, and failed, again, on the third day. In a row.

Since Mrs. Erickson wasn't young anymore, mild relief gave way to concern, and one of the Hawks finally went round to check up on her; her reports were filed with a clear address on them, and the address hadn't changed in all the years she'd made her trek to the Halls of Law.

She had fallen down the stairs to the basement and had injured her leg. Not her hip, which Red said would have been far worse for a woman of her age, but her leg. It was sprained, not broken, and the Hawks had gone round to dredge up money to buy actual crutches, which they then took to her home—along with a basket of various kinds of food, similar to the food that she generally brought with her.

But in the investigation, they learned that she was, and had been for decades, living alone in the small house. She had no pets—she said she liked both cats and dogs, but cats refused to stay in her home because it was haunted, and dogs required more physical energy than she had these days, where *these days* had been the case for as long as Kaylin had been with the Hawks.

People living alone for that long could find the isolation very difficult if they lacked either health or the energy to go out and socialize. Or the money. Going out and being social required money. Money for drinks, money for food, money to go see the open-air plays that were the only plays Kaylin had ever watched. There was very little that was free in the city. Kaylin wasn't certain what Mrs. Erickson did for money; she suspected it had something to do with sewing, knitting or similar activities, but hadn't actually asked. Mrs. Erickson was of a generation in which talk of money and money problems was considered socially very rude. Or so Kaylin had been told by one of the older Hawks who didn't mind manning this desk.

Kaylin was fine with lonely old women who brought baked bribes. It was better than people like Margot.

"You've noticed his belt, haven't you?" Mrs. Erickson asked.

Kaylin, mouth full, nodded. She was good at swallowing food in a hurry, which would be considered an essential life skill by most of the Hawks. "It's actually not a belt."

"Well, no, I didn't think so, given how much it glows. It's magic, is it?"

The belt did not glow in Kaylin's vision. "I think it must be. But it's attached to two weapons on either end of the chain, and it can be used—in an emergency—as a shield against magic."

"Against magic?"

"Sometimes criminals are armed with magical devices. Illegal devices," she added quickly. "A shield against magic can save lives."

"I see. Well, I'm sure he's an excellent partner, but I made note of him because of the...weapon." She sat in the chair in front of the desk, not as if she owned it, but as if she was honored to be a guest. "But I'm glad you're at the desk today, because I have a report to make, and it involves your partner.

"Some of my friends have noticed him, and I believe they're concerned."

Kaylin struggled not to ask obvious questions. As she reached for ink, she brushed crumbs off the desk. Mrs. Erickson offered a rare frown.

"You'll get mice if you do that," she told Kaylin, her lips slightly thinned—as if mice were worse than crime. Kaylin didn't understand the visceral hatred some people had of mice. They were tiny vermin, and generally harmless; up close they were even kind of cute.

She mumbled an apology and promised to clean up later. Under the weight of Mrs. Erickson's silence, later became now, which at least took her away from the desk in search of a broom and a dustpan.

Mrs. Erickson was waiting, with a much more usual-for-her expression, when Kaylin returned from her mission and the hilarity it caused. She cleaned up before she once again sat, pad in front of her, messy handwriting in the immediate future.

"I shouldn't actually say they're *friends*, as it feels quite presumptuous," Mrs. Erickson then confessed. "These are not the ghosts trapped in my house." Mrs. Erickson had tried to let those ghosts out, but nothing she had done had met with any success. But the ghosts hadn't harmed her, and in one or two cases, they'd actually helped. Although Elantra was not the fiefs and crime wasn't a way of life, an elderly woman living alone in a house she actually owned had—for some elements of society—marked her as the perfect victim.

It was those elements that Kaylin was paid to discourage.

"These are new ghosts?"

Mrs. Erickson nodded. "Well, not new precisely—they seem to be free to roam the streets at will, but as I'm certain you're aware, most people can't see them." She hesitated, and then asked a variant of the question Kaylin had expected to hear first.

"Are you aware that you appear to have a small ghost sitting on your shoulder?"

Kaylin realized, only belatedly, that Mrs. Erickson was talking about Hope. "Oh, he's not a ghost—everyone can see him. It takes more skill *not* to notice, especially when he's squawking."

"I see." She sounded as dubious as Mrs. Erickson ever managed to sound. "I'm sorry, I was just curious. Where was I? Oh, yes. The city ghosts. They seemed to take an interest in your partner."

"Corporal Handred," Kaylin said. "My partner is Corporal Handred. What kind of interest?"

"They drifted toward him, and followed him to see what he was doing. But that's not the point of concern—I mean, they aren't really bothering anyone, and they can hardly be credible spies if they can't report information to other people, can they?"

Kaylin agreed that no, they could not. Had the target of this particular report not been Severn, she wouldn't have given Mrs. Erickson's words much thought. But...Kaylin didn't see Severn's weapon chain as magical. She saw it as a belt, and sometimes as a grossly inconvenient set of weapons. Severn only brought them into play when magic—and magical attacks—were almost certain to be involved.

Mrs. Erickson didn't come across as a liar. She didn't come across as sound of mind, either—but Kaylin was willing to give her the benefit of the doubt, probably because she seldom worked the front desk *and* she'd just been fed. If it was true that Mrs. Erickson saw Severn's weapon as brilliantly glowing, what did it mean?

"They wanted me to tell you—or perhaps to tell someone— that your young man might not be what he seems."

"What do you mean?"

"They're worried about him; they think the belt is a dangerous weapon that shouldn't be here."

Kaylin knew she should think before opening her mouth, but it was still a bit of a struggle if she didn't feel the consequences for failing would lead to immediate death or injury. "I'd like to speak to your friends."

"But you can't see them."

"No. And I can't speak with them—but you can. If you'd be willing, I'd like you to be an interpreter. A translator." She almost felt guilty when Mrs. Erickson's face lit up from within as she smiled. Mrs. Erickson often smiled, but her normal smile and this one were miles apart. Countries apart, metaphorically speaking.

"Now?" she asked, with almost naked eagerness, which did nothing for Kaylin's growing guilt.

"I can't leave the desk until the end of my shift—but when I'm done, I'll head over to your place. You're still on Orbonne Street? Number fourteen?"

"It's fourteen and a half. There is no fourteen." At Kaylin's expression, she added, "I don't know why houses are numbered the way they are. But I could wait until the end of your shift, if you want."

"It gets pretty noisy in here, but if you'd rather not have Halls of Law visitors on your doorstep, you can. It's entirely up to you."

"My neighbors were a bit concerned the last time Hawks showed up at my door."

But not concerned enough that they had checked up on an elderly woman, living alone, when they hadn't seen her for a couple of days. Not concerned enough that they wouldn't have ignored her injuries and her sudden disappearance. Kaylin knew nothing about the neighbors but instinctively disliked them.

"I'll get you a better chair."

"You want permission to do *what*?" Marcus growled as his claws drummed against his desk.

"I'm finished Sergeant Keele's assignment, and I'd like to walk Mrs. Erickson home." This was true; it was the stuff that she wanted to do before heading to that destination she left out.

"Mrs. Erickson has turned anyone who sits at the damn desk into driveling—"

"Sergeant," Caitlin interrupted. "There's an incoming mirror call."

"It had better be important."

"It's the Hawklord. Private channel request."

Marcus rose, Mrs. Erickson—and Kaylin's pathetic request, as she was certain that was where the tirade had been going— forgotten. Hawklord mirror messages were generally taken in a room with an audience of exactly one: Marcus himself. Only after he'd vacated the office did Kaylin turn to Caitlin, the Hawks' godlike secretary.

"Mrs. Erickson is a lonely woman," that secretary said. Marcus's disapproval was nowhere to be seen; Caitlin clearly approved.

"I know."

"But she doesn't generally require an escort to her home; the streets there are considered safe by our standards." There was a tonal rise in the last few words although on the face of it, Caitlin hadn't asked a question.

"She came in with an odd report. Yes, I know she always does that, but this one was less about lost shoes, lost puppies, and lost bits of sentimental jewelry."

"You have crumbs on your clothing, dear."

Kaylin reddened. "I want to actually do a tiny bit of investigating, and when I suggested it, she seemed really happy."

Caitlin nodded. "Don't get her involved in trouble." The fact that Mrs. Erickson had come to the Halls of Law, and not the other way around, wasn't lost on Caitlin.

"I know. I'll try." Kaylin turned on her heel, and then turned back. "She's waiting for me, but—I need to ask an Imperial Mage a question or two as well."

The gentle look of approval vanished from Caitlin's face. "I mean it, Corporal. Don't involve her in trouble she cannot handle."

"That's why I want to talk to an Imperial Mage. I'm not certain she's not already in something that could be trouble she can't handle."

"I look forward to seeing your report."

"It'll be on Sergeant Keele's desk by the end of the week." Sergeant Keele didn't like paperwork any more than Marcus did, but she understood the necessity of it and wanted it out of the way as soon as humanly possible. For the Hawks that was "end of week."

⋆ ⋆ ⋆

Kaylin retrieved Mrs. Erickson from the waiting room adjacent to the front office. She noted, with a pang, that the basket the older woman was carrying was a lot lighter than it had been when she'd first set eyes on it. She knew this because she offered to carry it, and Mrs. Erickson agreed, thanking her.

Mrs. Erickson smiled. "I couldn't fit everything I baked into one small basket," she said. "And if you're walking me home, I have a few more goodies you could take with you to share with your friends."

Mrs. Erickson was dotty in the minds of most Hawks, but it was an affectionate term. It was certainly more affectionate than *psychotic* or *delusional*. Or drunk. While Hawks could, and did, get plastered while off duty, they generally tended to trust themselves not to allow drunken fury to lead to murder, attempted murder, or in one case, arson. At least, not for fellow Hawks or, in the latter case, the Halls of Law itself.

Home, however, wasn't going to be the first stop. Kaylin walked Mrs. Erickson out of the building; she paused to say hello to the on duty guards, and then quietly led the way.

Kaylin discovered that a twenty-minute stroll through the streets of her own city could take much, *much* longer than twenty minutes as she accompanied Mrs. Erickson. Clearly Mrs. Erickson was surrounded by the type of friendly strangers who knew her on sight. They might not know where she lived, and they might not be close enough to actually check up on her if she somehow failed to make an appearance—but she knew about them.

Or their children. Or their husbands or wives. Or their grandchildren. Or the trouble they were having with foreign merchants. She clearly remembered snatches of earlier conversations, and she clearly remembered small details—

like children's birthdays. Not only did she remember those, but she remembered which birthdays, which meant the age of those children.

Some of those people probably approached Mrs. Erickson because she was walking beside an obvious officer of the Halls of Law and they were concerned. But the conversations that unfolded in spite of Kaylin's presence, and the very natural way Mrs. Erickson engaged with them, either put them at ease or made them decide that Kaylin's role here was not a threat to the old woman.

No one, on the other hand, was as friendly with Kaylin as they were with the old woman whose mostly empty basket she was carrying. Mostly became empty; Mrs. Erickson clearly had reserved some of that baking for chance meetings with younger children. Their parents did not seem to be suspicious at all of the contents.

An hour and forty-five minutes later, having run the gauntlet of friendliness, Mrs. Erickson stopped walking without also readying conversation. "It's here," she told Kaylin. She frowned. "Sometimes they aren't here, though, and I didn't make any arrangements to meet with them."

"Do you ever make arrangements to meet with them?"

"Not often," Mrs. Erickson confessed. "It tends to make people uncomfortable if they see me, because they assume I'm talking to myself."

Since this was a reasonable assumption by any measure, Kaylin nodded.

"Sometimes I do it anyway, though. If I feel the need to visit the Halls of Law to make a report, it does help to have details."

It didn't really, but Kaylin kept this to herself.

"And you're here with me, so it's less likely to cause people concern if I'm speaking with you. Ah, there he is."

Kaylin stared at the spot in the street which Mrs. Erickson seemed to be indicating. She'd come to a stop near one of the public wells. Everyone Kaylin could see was carrying a couple of buckets, some on sticks suspended across their shoulders to balance weight, some by hand. Most weren't concerned with anything but their place in line or the companions who had come to the well to get water of their own.

She saw no people, none of the ghosts to which Mrs. Erickson so often referred.

Mrs. Erickson's smile was touched with a hint of sorrow, possibly at the thought that the invisible people with whom she interacted were dead. "And there she is—she tends to be more chatty. I'm not sure if they are—or were—married, but they really are a lovely couple."

Kaylin nodded, which seemed safest. But she was curious. She assumed—they all assumed—that Mrs. Erickson was delusional, but not in a way that caused harm to others. Given the delusions that did, they accepted hers. What if she wasn't? What if she was seeing things that others simply couldn't see?

She had seen Severn's weapon chain in a way that Kaylin had never seen it. Maybe she wasn't the first, but she was the first to mention it.

Kaylin, who had not taken a step forward when Mrs. Erickson had gone to greet her invisible friends, poked Hope, who had remained more or less standing on her shoulder. Hope lifted a translucent wing and smacked Kaylin's face with it to indicate his annoyance, but left it across her eyes.

Mrs. Erickson was not, as Kaylin and the rest of the Hawks had assumed, harmlessly delusional. Or if she was, Kaylin had just fallen into the well of the older woman's delusion.

She could clearly see, through Hope's wing, a young man and a young woman.

02

As Mrs. Erickson said, the young man was with a young woman. They were both dark-haired, the hair color itself bright and natural; their eyes at this distance appeared to be brown. Were it not for Hope's wing, Kaylin would have assumed they were oddly dressed but otherwise normal humans. She couldn't hear them yet—she was uncertain that she'd be able to hear them at all—but could see that Mrs. Erickson had also been right about which of the two was chattier; it was the young woman who was now talking animatedly— she was one of those people who tended to use their whole body, especially their arms and hands, when speaking.

Remembering Mrs. Erickson's reluctance to reply when alone, Kaylin, face masked in wing—which would probably draw attention here—quickly joined the old woman, standing by her side but a half step back. She didn't want to frighten the ghosts.

It was clear that the ghosts could see Kaylin, and equally clear that they hadn't expected to be seen by anyone who was not a friendly old woman; the girl stopped midmotion, which is to say her arms froze, when she glanced in Kaylin's direction and their eyes met. To Kaylin's surprise, all conversation stopped, and the young man immediately stepped between Kaylin and the young woman who had fallen silent.

"She means no harm," Mrs. Erickson said, her voice soft, even soothing. "She's the person I told you about—she's the partner. She works for the Halls of Law. Look, you can see the tabard she's wearing. It's the Hawk. You might see similar tabards on other officers—usually Swords. It's only the Wolf you might want to avoid."

It bothered Kaylin that Mrs. Erickson was, in her gentle way, bad-mouthing the Wolves. If she'd been answering a question the young woman asked, it would be different.

Severn wouldn't have cared. He certainly wouldn't have corrected a harmless old woman. Given it was Severn, if his opinion had been sought at all, he might have agreed, or offered that friendly smile that never appeared to be the wall it actually was.

From Severn's point of view, the Wolves being bogeymen was probably for the best; they were the Emperor's final resort in dealing with dangerous criminals—criminals beyond the abilities of the Hawks and the Swords to safely and legally handle. The patina of fear or distrust the Wolves often engendered underlined their role: they were the last expedient of an angry Emperor. His executioners.

Except they were called his assassins. They were part of the reason people distrusted the Emperor. Well, that and if the Emperor truly lost his temper, he could set half the city ablaze without breaking a sweat. She considered the latter to be far more of a threat. The Wolves were the option before the Emperor really lost it. As such, they were the thin wall between Draconic fury and the people who, mostly mortal, occupied the city streets. They were *valuable*.

You didn't like them either, that I recall. Severn had always been like this.

What, people aren't allowed to change their minds? Kaylin *did* care about respect or, more pertinent, lack of respect. She had struggled most of her life to change that, to become more like Severn. So far, the attempts hadn't been a raging success.

They are. You're right about everything else. I know what we are and what we do—or did—and I see no reason to demand respect from people who don't know.

Mrs. Erickson had, in the meantime, turned to Kaylin, a frown changing the contours of the lines time had etched in her face. The frown inched up her face as her silver brows drew together. "What is your pet doing?"

Kaylin lifted a hand to cover Hope's mouth before the stream of squawking invective started. "He's not exactly a pet," she told Mrs. Erickson. "He's a companion. A partner." The squawking lowered in volume.

Mrs. Erickson's expression changed to one of concern, which was ironic, given how often the old woman was on the receiving end of exactly that look. "Why is he holding his wing across your face?"

Kaylin exhaled. "It's a kind of magical thing. Sometimes I can see things through the wing I can't see otherwise."

The old woman's eyes rounded briefly as the implications sunk in. "You—you can *see* them?"

"I can see them—but only with the help of my companion." She then turned toward the two, the girl still halfway hidden behind the young man. "I'm Corporal Neya, of the Imperial Hawks. You are?"

The man looked to Mrs. Erickson, but Mrs. Erickson was

momentarily at a loss for words. It was clear he intended to wait until she found them again.

"As I told you, she's a Hawk. It's her job to look out for people like me." Mrs. Erickson's voice was quavery. "I…didn't realize she'd be able to see you. No one else has ever been able to see any of the friends I've made who are…like you."

This didn't seem to comfort the young man; the young woman, however, had inched out from behind his back and was now more visible. What Kaylin heard in the older woman's voice, she also heard, and her expression was complicated. If the young man didn't care all that much for Mrs. Erickson, it was clear his friend did. She turned to look at Kaylin.

"I'm Amaldi," she said quietly, in soft High Barrani. "It's a pleasure to make your acquaintance." Kaylin could hear her. Her voice was soft and yet somehow deep; if aural tones had been something as mundane as money, hers would have been worth a fortune, it was so rich in texture.

"I'm Corporal Neya, as I said."

The man turned to look back at Amaldi, the line of his shoulders tense and slightly drawn in.

"Please," Amaldi said, more edge in her tone. "If we had never been willing to take risks at all, we wouldn't have Mrs. Erickson as a friend."

"Mrs. Erickson obviously means us no harm."

"Yes. And she brought the corporal to meet us."

"Oh, no, dear. I didn't expect she would ever be able to see you. The corporal wanted to ask a few questions, and she offered to accompany me. I was meant to be an interpreter or a translator—but I see I'm not needed."

"What did she want to ask?" This was the young man again, his voice deeper than Kaylin would have expected, given his appearance—and exactly as friendly as he appeared, otherwise.

"I told her about the young man."

Both Amaldi and her friend stiffened.

"I mean, I told her that you were worried about him. Corporal Neya is his partner. I'm not sure if you're aware, but the Hawks always have a partner. Hers is Corporal Handred. She seemed surprised that I knew who he was."

Amaldi's expression had shuttered, as if windows had been closed to fend off a coming storm. But she met Kaylin's gaze and held it. "He is a...friend?"

"He's my partner. Mrs. Erickson is right. Hawks don't operate solo outside of the Halls of Law." Instinctive trust warred with learned caution for one long breath. "Mrs. Erickson was the reason I came. When she was talking about my partner, she described his weapon chain as a belt. That's fair—from a distance it looks like a decorative belt. It's not normal beat issue for a Hawk."

"I would hope not," the young man snapped, entering a conversation he clearly thought should never have taken place. "Do people honestly think of it as a *belt*?"

"If they've never seen it in action? Sure they do. What else could it be?"

Amaldi winced, but this time, she stepped on her companion's foot. It was an extremely familiar gesture. "You were concerned for Mrs. Erickson, then?"

"Yes. Mrs. Erickson made clear that what she saw when she looked at that belt wasn't what anyone else sees. It's clear she sees a lot of things that other people can't, but I don't want to get her involved in things that might be dangerous."

"Then turn heel," the man snapped, "and go back to wher-

ever it is she found you. Leave this entire line of question-
ing alone."

Amaldi's expression was grim, but there was no fear in it;
she was annoyed. "Darreno." The syllables were a snap of
sound that would have been at home in a sergeant's throat—
even Kaylin's Leontine sergeant. "Please forgive my friend.
He is concerned for Mrs. Erickson as well, but he's entirely
too clumsy when it comes to expressing it.

"It is true we noted your partner. We cannot, as we are,
commit crimes that would be of concern—or even of note—
to you. Or so we assumed. Mrs. Erickson is, we thought, singular. And if we have each other, it is hard to exist as a simple
observer. There are advantages to our...condition, but we
have had time to dwell on the disadvantages.

"We did not expect that any of you might be able to see
us. But...Mrs. Erickson could. And she could speak with us.
We took an interest in her because she could. She's the only
friend we have made..." She trailed off. Kaylin noted that
the young woman's Barrani was accented, but she couldn't
pin down the woman's original language, assuming ghosts
had one. She was definitely human in form.

Mrs. Erickson said, "It's very difficult to be unseen. It's difficult to see what no one else can see—on bad days, it makes
me feel a bit dotty." Her smile, however, belied that. "And
you've always been so pleasant, dear. I think I might have
felt lonely and entirely irrelevant if not for meeting people
like you."

The young woman turned to Kaylin. "Please accept my
apologies for my companion's manners."

"He can apologize himself if he cares. I don't find his protectiveness or caution offensive—I said a lot worse in my
childhood."

"I am not a child," the man snapped.

Kaylin offered a very Hawk-like nod in response, which didn't seem to improve his mood any. She hadn't intended the comment to be an insult, but could see why he'd take it that way—and frankly, she wasn't overly concerned. What was he going to do? File a report?

Mrs. Erickson cleared her throat in that particular way that immediately reminded Kaylin of Caitlin in the Halls. To the man Kaylin said, "I'm sorry. That didn't come out the way I thought it would. I don't think you're a child; I only meant that I've done worse so I won't take offense."

He seemed to relax at what was, on the inside, a very grudging apology.

Kaylin understood why Mrs. Erickson felt self-conscious talking to ghosts in public, because Kaylin was drawing the kind of attention that usually caused people to give a person a very wide berth. Then again, some drew closer because of the familiar. On Elani street, the regulars had grown accustomed to Hope, and those that approached usually had money in hand in an attempt to buy him. They went away disappointed—or in one case, in high dudgeon because the young woman had offered *so much money* to a grubby Hawk, which had both angered Kaylin and slightly amused her.

Here, no one would likely have that kind of money to front; they might be thinking of stealing Hope. That wouldn't work out well for them, and Kaylin had been told, in no uncertain terms, that even if the attempt was made it was *Kaylin's* job to make certain they didn't die after trying. She thought it unfair, but Marcus had made clear that petty theft wasn't a capital offense. Kaylin privately thought that stupidity was—but she wasn't in the fiefs, now; she was in Elantra.

The young man was staring at the familiar, youthful brow

creased with lines that would melt away when his expres
sion shifted. Almost against his will, he said, "What's that?"

"His name is Hope, and I've been told he would have once
been called a familiar."

The young man blanched.

The young woman, however, frowned. "May I approach?"
she asked, voice soft.

Kaylin, curious to see whether or not ghosts had the ability
to actually touch anything, nodded. Hope squawked loudly
in her ear, but it was a grumpy or annoyed squawk. More or
less an echo of the many voices in her daily world, except he
didn't bother with actual syllables.

Amaldi walked through someone. They didn't notice. She
didn't appear to notice much either, she was so focused on
Hope. Darreno, had he required breath, would have been on
the verge of passing out, he seemed to have held it for so long.
He watched as she reached out, very slowly, to touch Hope.

Hope squawked again, and when her hand was in range,
he bit her finger. She gasped and instantly drew back. Hope
had drawn blood.

As far as blood went, it was about as deep a cut as a cranky
cat who hated to be touched would make. Kaylin, however,
knew that cat bites could cause a lot of problems for the bitee.

"I'm sorry," she said, immediately lifting a hand to hold
it between Hope's small jaws and anyone else's appendages.
"He doesn't usually do that."

Amaldi smiled. She turned to her friend. "Darreno, look!"

He hadn't looked away once. "You're bleeding."

"I'm *bleeding*!" she repeated, in an entirely different tone.
Maybe being dead drove people crazy. She sounded as if she'd
just been given an unexpected and miraculous gift. Darreno
gave her a look that probably matched Kaylin's.

The crowd that had gathered—moving slowly as if minding their own business—also stared at Amaldi.

Mrs. Erickson noticed immediately. "Amaldi," she said, her voice just above a whisper.

Amaldi caught it anyway, and turned.

"People are staring. At you."

Amaldi blinked, her arm frozen in midair, the shock of being bitten—and the delight in it—suspended. She blinked rapidly as Darreno rushed to her side, stepping in front of her as if to protect her from the curiosity—or the hostility—of strangers. No one could see him. Kaylin considered telling Hope to bite him as well, but Hope had never been the most compliant of companions.

If Kaylin thought the slowly moving stream of witnesses were surprised—and annoyed—by Amaldi, it was nothing compared to what happened next. Hope, with no word from Kaylin, withdrew his wing; she could no longer see Darreno, but could still see Amaldi clearly. She could therefore see the moment when Amaldi began to shimmer in place, limbs becoming translucent, transparent, and then nonexistent, followed swiftly by the rest of her body. People shouted, some screamed, and if milling witnesses were a bit annoying, panicked witnesses who now tried to run away *through* the rest of the people were far worse. She wasn't a Sword, and technically, she wasn't a Hawk either, being off duty and without a partner.

Mrs. Erickson was almost sent flying by someone who had come too close to Amaldi; Kaylin caught her before she went down on the cobbled street. She kept an arm around Mrs. Erickson while raising her voice.

I'm on it, she heard. Severn was close.

Hope replaced the wing across Kaylin's eyes—this time

without smacking her face with it first. Darreno had an arm around Amaldi; she was pressed against the side of his body, and he was glaring out at a world that could no longer see her.

As the crowd had been small, panic had lesser immediate effect. Kaylin's tabard—and Severn's—had more of one. They weren't Swords, and they hadn't had the Swords' extensive training in crowd control, but Severn's voice and presence had an almost immediate calming effect, something Kaylin's hadn't managed to achieve on its own. She tried not to resent this, which wasn't as hard as it might otherwise have been, because she was thinking about how much trouble she was going to be in if things got further out of hand.

Hawk starts riot.

Amaldi's utter absence wasn't noted by newcomers or people who had failed to see her momentary solidity, and panic was replaced by a lot of head scratching and mutters about kids these days, even if some of the runners had been old enough to be Kaylin's grandfather, whoever he was.

Severn came to stand by Kaylin's side; he was also wearing his tabard. "Sorry I took so long."

"Meetings always run long."

He shrugged. Not a meeting he could discuss, then. He turned to Mrs. Erickson and extended a hand. She took it, but her expression was four parts worry to one part good manners, as she called them.

It was clear why. Both Amaldi and Darreno had frozen in place, as if so afraid to draw Severn's attention they had chosen to mimic statues in the hope of being overlooked. He couldn't see them.

"What happened?"

"I came to ask a few questions of Mrs. Erickson's friends."

His expression was perfectly neutral, as if Mrs. Erickson's friends weren't a matter of Halls of Law gossip. And Records.

"I came with her," Mrs. Erickson said, as if attempting to defend Kaylin from Severn's ire. Kaylin would have found it amusing had the older woman not looked so strained.

"She had to come. I can't see her friends. Or I couldn't without Hope."

Something in the focus of his gaze changed. "You can see her friends?"

She nodded. He could, if necessary, see what Kaylin saw; he could listen—and clearly he had, because he'd come to join her. But she was never certain that he knew what she knew, the way the Barrani whose names she held did or could. "I can't see anything if Hope removes his wing."

There's more, she added, afraid to spook the two not-actually-ghosts.

I know.

I think they recognize your weapon.

He nodded. "Have you asked the questions you came to ask?"

Not yet—I don't think they'd answer anything even if I did. They seem terrified of you.

He didn't find this as surprising as Kaylin had. It made her wonder what he did in the meetings he couldn't talk about.

The two ghosts weren't going to be engaging in dialogue now. She recognized the look; they were afraid of Severn. It was normal—if not useful—to have people be afraid of Hawks, especially if those Hawks were Barrani. The Barrani Hawks *did* play by the rules the Halls of Law set out—but no one trusted Barrani, and if Kaylin were honest, she considered this rational and intelligent. But Barrani in Hawk tabards were *Hawks* first, Barrani second.

Regardless, they viewed Severn as if he were Barrani, and at that, a powerful Barrani Lord with the usual regard for the lives of others.

Kaylin exhaled. "He can't see you. He can't hear you. He can't touch you."

Hope squawked.

"Fine. He can't touch you without deliberate intervention on the part of my familiar—an intervention I give you my word will not happen again without your consent. My partner's not here to hunt ghosts. He's not here to...do whatever it is you're afraid he'll do. He's mortal, like I am, and like you appear to have once been.

"I came here because Mrs. Erickson knows Severn is my partner. We're both Imperial Hawks. We work at the Halls of Law. The Halls of Law enforce Imperial Laws. If the law is broken, there are consequences."

"What are your laws?" Darreno demanded.

"Do you have five hours?"

Almost bitterly, Amaldi said, "We appear to have all the time in the world."

"You've been people watching for a long time, haven't you?"

Amaldi nodded.

"So—you're aware that you're a ghost in an Empire—and a city—ruled by a Dragon, right?"

"Ghosts are dead people," Amaldi replied. "We're not dead."

There had been functionally no difference for a long time, in Kaylin's opinion. But she didn't argue because Hope had bitten the young woman, and for a single moment, she had been as solid and real as any other citizen on the street. "I wouldn't have guessed that. Neither did Mrs. Erickson. Mrs. Erickson sees ghosts," Kaylin added.

"We know. Sometimes she talks to people neither of us can see—but we aren't sure if they're…in the same situation we are. We don't know. And we don't want to cause trouble for her."

Kaylin nodded. "You don't need to eat or sleep?"

"We don't need to eat. I think we sleep, sometimes? But if we do, time passes beyond us. No, we didn't know the Empire is ruled by a Dragon." She shook her head. "That's going to take some time to get used to—which, as I mentioned, we have a lot of." As she spoke, she walked straight up to Severn. And put an arm through his chest.

This seemed to satisfy her in some fashion—possibly because it made clear to her that Kaylin's claim about Severn's inability to see or interact with them was true.

"Mrs. Erickson was curious about your interest in my partner. She trusts the Hawks, so she didn't entirely understand it—she thought possibly you were worried *for* him." They were clearly worried in the other direction. "What exactly do you see when you look at him? Is it the weapon?"

They exchanged a glance. Amaldi was now offering her words with more care and far less animation. "How long have you known him?" she asked, countering Kaylin's question with a question.

"I met him when I was five years old."

"And how old was he then?"

Kaylin's expression must have made clear that the question made little sense to her. She answered the surface of the words. "Ten. Or as close to ten as any orphan can determine. Why?"

"He was ten? You're certain?"

"As close to certain as I can be."

Darreno leaned over and whispered something to Amaldi that Kaylin's strictly normal hearing couldn't catch. Amaldi then turned to look at the crowd, which, given it was nearing end of day, was sparser. "Like that?"

"Like that, but a boy, yes."

"And you saw him grow? The normal way?"

They noticed me for a reason. They're clearly afraid. I've done nothing of note that should scare people I can't see and can't interact with.

Mrs. Erickson said they followed you; she asked because she could tell they were interested. I don't think she realized they were afraid of you; I think she thought they were worried for you.

Mrs. Erickson is a trusting soul. Ask them about the weapon, if you can.

Kaylin wanted to know what in the hells they thought Severn was, but relented, as she'd come here to ask—through Mrs. Erickson—about the damn weapon.

"I saw him grow the normal way, yes. It was the way I grew but I started out younger." Before Amaldi could speak, she continued, trying to keep the edge out of her voice. "My mother was my only parent. She died when I was five years old. If it hadn't been for Severn, I'd've followed. He kept me safe from Ferals and from lack of a home. We struggled, but we struggled together." She had folded her arms, and then loosened them.

Amaldi considered Kaylin, her gaze intent. "You trust him."

"With my life." Kaylin felt no need to make any possible exceptions clear, and besides, it wasn't a lie—she trusted him with her life. But there had been things she'd valued more, things she'd have died to protect, and it was *her life* that had been his concern.

"Did he always have that weapon?"

"Not when we were growing up, no. That came later."

"Do you know how he came by it?"

"No."

"And he's never told you?"

"I've never asked. Look—I trust him, but I don't *own* him. He has responsibilities that aren't mine. If he wanted me to know, he'd tell me; if he didn't want me to know, he didn't think it would cause trouble for me."

"Then he hasn't made something clear to you."

"I just said—"

"He cannot be what you are and wield those weapons. They were not meant for people like us."

03

Kaylin tried hard not to interfere in Severn's life—both to protect herself, and to protect him. But she'd developed an instinct when dealing with witnesses, and that instinct told her no matter how much she shied away from it— that Amaldi was telling the truth as she knew it. The young woman spoke with grave certainty.

"Clearly that's not true," Kaylin finally said, although her words and voice were now softer. "Perhaps what you were told wasn't complete, or perhaps people like us weren't allowed to touch them?" She knew that the weapons had come from the West March; knew that the Barrani there weren't best pleased with Severn's acquisition of them, but also knew they were forced to accept it, however grudgingly.

Kaylin thought of the people trapped in the Academia, and thought of how long they'd endured there before the Academia had once again rejoined the real world. She'd assumed most hadn't been aware of that captivity, but knew at least one had. And the building itself had been half-aware and injured.

These two were definitely not buildings. If it weren't for the fact that they were clearly invisible to most people—she'd have to investigate Mrs. Erickson far more seriously after today—she would have assumed they were slightly oddly dressed people who'd traveled here from a different country.

But she believed they recognized Severn's weapon, and to be fair, having seen it once herself, she'd never mistake it for any other weapon.

"Have you actually seen it in use?" she asked.

Amaldi nodded. Darreno was silent.

"When?"

The two once again exchanged a glance. Amaldi spoke. "It was not wielded by your...partner. Not then."

Did you catch that?

I did, through you. But...in theory the weapons take shape based on their wielder, in some fashion.

Kaylin snorted. *So the weapons thought you* wanted *that unwieldy chain with sharp bits attached?*

She felt his brief amusement. *I believe my teacher felt that my will was not strong enough to force the weapons to conform to my personal ideal, yes.* The amusement faded. *Mrs. Erickson's "ghosts" imply heavily that the weapon conformed to the ideal of some prior wielder. I don't know a lot about the history of these weapons, and I know nothing about the other hands that wielded them.*

What do you know?

Barrani who wanted to wield them came and went; none succeeded; most survived.

Most, she thought. Not all.

"Do either of you experience the passage of time in the way you might have when people could actually see you?"

They exchanged a glance. It was, to Kaylin's surprise, Darreno who answered. "Not entirely. We're aware that time has passed. Amaldi told you that we sleep sometimes, but when we wake the world around us has shifted. Sometimes the shifts are simple: the buildings are slightly altered. There are more—or fewer—people.

"Sometimes the shifts are far greater. We recognize almost none of the buildings, and the people are...different."

Amaldi immediately leaped in. While Darreno continued to be cautious—he seldom looked away from Severn—her natural gregariousness was clearly difficult to keep suppressed. "This time, when we woke, there were so many people. People like *us*. We can still see Barrani, and we can see the Barrani High Halls—but most of the streets are full of people.

"This would have been paradise for us, once. There's so much here, so much to see and do—and people like us are doing most of it!" She glanced at Darreno, who had given up on attempting to keep her in check. "There are winged people as well—mostly like us, but not quite—I love to watch them. Sometimes I chase their shadows across the ground."

Kaylin might have once done the same were it not for the very real people in the streets—but Amaldi wouldn't have that problem.

"Where do you live?"

Some of the light in her eyes dimmed. "Here," she said. "We don't have a home, if that's what you're asking. Any home we might have had was destroyed long before our birth, and the crèche we grew up in was destroyed in one of the Barrani wars."

"With the Dragons?"

Amaldi shook her head. "I don't think it was the Dragons. We didn't ask. Some of my people were used as subordinate soldiers to their masters; Darreno and I were considered too weak or too young. We had been trained to other things, and our master considered our deaths on the battlefield a waste of all her cultivation efforts."

Kaylin was silent for a long beat. She glanced at Mrs. Erickson; Mrs. Erickson nodded.

"Can you travel anywhere you want?"

"What do you mean?"

"Can you leave the city?"

Amaldi's expression clearly said, *Why would we want to?* But Darreno shook his head. "No. If we attempt to move outside of the confines of the city, we sleep. There are streets within the city we cannot follow. There seems to be a specific radius to the area we're allowed; we can trace a large circle.

"At the center of it is the High Halls."

"The current High Halls?"

They both frowned at the question. Darreno turned toward the High Halls, although technically they were obscured by the taller buildings that housed multiple families close to the well. "What do you mean when you say 'current' in that tone?"

"The current condition of the High Halls is new. For most of my life that's not what the High Halls looked like."

They traded another glance. "Do you mean it has changed recently?"

She nodded.

"It…looks the same, to us. But brighter or newer. Amaldi wondered if we had somehow gone back in time."

"I was quite happy to know that we hadn't," Amaldi added. "But it's true I wondered. I wondered if somehow this city with all these *people* was like this before all the wars and the—" She shook her head.

Are you thinking what I'm thinking? Kaylin asked Severn.

Severn, silent, nodded slightly. *Do you mind if I intrude?*

No. I don't hate it, it just tickles a bit. Severn slid into the space behind her eyes. She hadn't lied. He almost never did this because it felt so uncomfortable to both of them. Severn wasn't used to seeing out of two sets of eyes and Kaylin wasn't used to having Severn in particular look through hers. She was too aware of his presence.

He studied their clothing.

"I'd like to ask a couple of questions about your clothing."

"Our clothing?"

"Yes. It's not like the clothing most of the people here are wearing." Amaldi was wearing a brightly colored silk, which appeared to be a single length of cloth wrapped about her body in a way that emphasized color; laid over that was a necklace that matched the delicate strands of her earrings. Darreno was dressed in almost exactly the same silk, but it was a bit more standard: arms, legs—the legs a darker shade, but looser in fit than the present norm.

"Oh. This is what I was wearing when we…left."

"You can't change?"

"Into what? We didn't bring clothing with us—or if we did, it became solid enough that we couldn't touch it. I didn't wish to disrobe and have no way to reclothe myself, and… we don't have problems with dirt here." This last was said self-consciously. "Which is good because we couldn't bathe if we did."

Got it, Severn said, retreating.

"Can you walk to Mrs. Erickson's house, or is that too far?"

Darreno said, "We can, but we didn't wish Mrs. Erickson to feel uncomfortable."

"I would never feel uncomfortable inviting friends to my house," Mrs. Erickson replied. Given her expression she meant it, too.

"If you're safe now," Severn said out loud, "I will return to my duties."

Kaylin nodded; they were in theory off duty, which meant the rules governing partnering didn't apply. She thought

Amaldi and Darreno would be more comfortable if Severn was anywhere else. Besides, she had an inkling of what he now considered his duties to be: research into Amaldi, Darreno, and the clothing they wore.

If what they had said was true, they had woken this time when the High Halls had changed, becoming the building it had once been before Shadow had started the war between Dragonkind and the Barrani. She wondered if the master Amaldi spoke of was Barrani at all, or if it was one of the Ancestors that had, woken, nearly destroyed the High Halls for no reason at all that Kaylin could understand.

They had been surprised by Hope; they had recognized the word *familiar*.

"I'm certain this isn't how you imagined you'd be spending your evening," Mrs. Erickson said, dragging Kaylin's attention back to the present. "But if you'll let me do a little bit of shopping, I'll make you dinner."

"Don't worry about feeding me."

"I'm not, dear. Most of my friends can't eat, and cooking for one can be a bit lonely."

A bit of shopping later, Kaylin carried a much fuller basket—she insisted—as she followed Mrs. Erickson home. Amaldi and Darreno walked to one side of the old woman, Kaylin to the other.

"I'm going to go quiet for a bit," Kaylin told the two. "Hope is probably getting a wing cramp." Hope immediately retrieved his wing, folded it across his back, and fell across her shoulders as if greatly fatigued.

"Poor dear," Mrs. Erickson said, with genuine sympathy.

Kaylin considered pushing him off her shoulder, especially when he started to snicker.

★ ★ ★

The first thing Kaylin discovered about Mrs. Erickson's house was: it was an actual small house. It was narrow, and to either side larger houses had been built in place; they were both obviously newer than Mrs. Erickson's, and if not in better repair, then at least constructed in a way that implied they should be.

Mrs. Erickson had a small lawn. Kaylin wondered if this was the remnants of a coach house, but the houses to either side weren't an indicator of the kind of wealth required to own one's own horses and carriages. Admittedly she didn't know a lot about horses, and what she did know generally caused horse people to frown or lecture her.

Regardless, this was where Mrs. Erickson lived. Until Kaylin's first home—an apartment—had been destroyed by a large arcane bomb, Kaylin hadn't dreamed of an actual house. She now lived in Helen, in one of the swankiest of neighborhoods, and still felt residual guilt about it.

Kaylin didn't like at least one of Mrs. Erickson's neighbors, because at least one of the neighbors ventured out of their own house onto her lawn, rather than using the narrow walk that led from the street.

"What did the old biddy do this time?" he asked. He was a broad-shouldered man with a very irritating grin.

"Mrs. Erickson," Kaylin replied, emphasizing her name, "came to the Halls of Law to report something. As many citizens do." She was aware that many of those citizens lived in an alternate reality, often augmented by far too much alcohol or other items of questionable legality. But the man's question set her teeth on edge.

Worse, however, was Mrs. Erickson's polite smile. "I'm sorry if we made enough noise to disturb you." There were ways of delivering such an apology that made an insult of it.

Condescension was a prized social weapon for most of Kaylin's Barrani friends or acquaintances. But that wasn't what Mrs. Erickson was doing, here. Her shoulders had dropped, her back curving as if to ward off unwanted notice. Which never worked.

Hope sat up, catching the man's attention. "Hey, what's that you got on your shoulder?"

Kaylin saw Hope open his jaws, the ruby interior of his mouth in stark contrast to the translucence of his body. It took her longer than it should have to insert her hand between Hope and the neighbor.

"An exotic pet," Kaylin replied. "Now, if you'll excuse us?"

"Where'd you get it?"

Ignoring him, Kaylin turned to Mrs. Erickson. "Lead the way."

Mrs. Erickson's entire tell was one of gratitude, and this made things worse. She was afraid of her neighbor. One of the two who'd failed to notice her absence, and who'd failed to check up on her. If Mrs. Erickson had relied on the aid of her neighbors, she'd probably have starved to death.

"Hey, I asked you a question," the large man snapped.

"I heard it," Kaylin replied, her voice a particular kind of neutral that would have immediately caused any Hawk who knew her to step in. Being off duty, none of those Hawks were here. She didn't bother to look in his direction, but did lower her hand.

"Answer it."

"Mrs. Erickson?" Kaylin's smile was probably a clear indicator of her emotions at the moment.

Mrs. Erickson, being Mrs. Erickson, was now worried. For Kaylin, of course. Kaylin could see the patina of guilt shift the old woman's expression. She struggled to remember that Mrs. Erickson, not Kaylin herself, lived here; Mrs.

Erickson—not Kaylin—would have to deal with the consequences of this man's displeasure. Yes, there were Hawks and there were laws, but so far no laws had been made that made being an unpleasant waste of space illegal.

And there *were* laws on the books that made decking a jerk a crime. A minor crime. Which Hawks weren't supposed to commit.

"I said, I asked you a question," the aforementioned jerk said, in a much lower tone. He stepped forward, hand raised, as if he intended to grab Kaylin's arm or shoulder. Or worse, grab the familiar that rested on one of them.

Kaylin was fine with this. Neither Hope nor Kaylin could be hurt by this man without very bad luck on their part. But Mrs. Erickson could. Kaylin wondered if part of the reason the old woman made the daily trek to the Halls of Law was the temporary safety provided by the presence of so many Hawks.

None of the other Hawks had mentioned the neighbor, not even the ones who had gone to Mrs. Erickson's to check up on her when she failed to show up for her daily incursion. But those Hawks had probably come during business hours, as it were; they had come in pairs.

And Kaylin was admittedly not the largest or most instantly intimidating of the Hawks. Maybe he felt safe, stepping closer so he could loom over both of them. Maybe he thought his presence enough of a threat that Kaylin would buckle and fold, just as Mrs. Erickson—an older, frailer woman—clearly did.

She had daggers.

She drew her baton instead. "And I said I heard you. Unless you're in front of the Imperial Court or the Emperor himself, failing to answer questions isn't a crime."

The man's brows—streaked gray—rose; his skin darkened. "Is this how you were taught to show respect?"

"I was taught," Kaylin replied, "that respect is earned."

The man raised an arm. Kaylin was ready for him.

What she wasn't ready for was Mrs. Erickson, who stepped between Kaylin and the large, odious man, although the space between them had closed enough, her back bumped into Kaylin.

"She's a new Hawk," she told the neighbor. "She's young."

"She knows the law," Kaylin said, voice lower; she had to look over Mrs. Erickson's shoulder. "If you hit Mrs. Erickson, the one who'll be visiting the Halls is you. If you hit me, your visit will be much longer." She reached out with her free hand and attempted to move Mrs. Erickson safely out of the way.

Mrs. Erickson's determination was greater than her slight weight implied; she didn't budge.

"Go and get your things," Kaylin told the old woman, coming to a decision. "We can conduct the rest of the interview at my house." The ghosts that occupied Mrs. Erickson's house were forgotten. Kaylin wanted to remove her from the vicinity of the neighbor.

"Come with me," Mrs. Erickson said, without moving.

"I will. If you have no other business," she said, to the neighbor, "we'll be seeing to ours." She had, until Mrs. Erickson had stepped between them, been spoiling for a fight. If the jerk touched or attempted to hit her, any action she took that didn't break every bone in his body was likely to be given a grudging pass—especially if he opened his mouth.

But she was afraid now that he'd hit Mrs. Erickson instead. If not today, then tonight; if not tonight, then tomorrow. She shouldn't have pushed him if she wasn't the one who would bear the consequences. Cursing internally she once again turned toward the front door of Mrs. Erickson's home.

If Hope leaped off her shoulder and bit the man's nose, could she somehow fudge the report she was certain she'd have to make in a way that still allowed Hope to be her shoulder ornament during a working day? Highly doubtful.

He looked as if he'd object; his arm lowered, but his hands—both of them—were fists—large fists, which implied incoming pain. Kaylin couldn't force herself to back down with any semblance of grace—and it was humility and groveling the man wanted. She'd seen his type before, admittedly not nearly as often on this side of the Ablayne.

She stepped out from behind Mrs. Erickson, baton clenched in fists that were just as white-knuckled as the stranger's. Mrs. Erickson, no longer a shield between Kaylin and her neighbor, immediately turned toward the closed door of her house, as if this was the only way she could somehow avoid a confrontation between the neighbor and the Halls of Law. This was because Mrs. Erickson wasn't stupid.

The man watched Mrs. Erickson as she scurried for the door. Kaylin watched him, her breath deliberately slow and controlled. She wasn't angry. She was teetering on the edge of enraged.

Kaylin.

Severn, in his fashion, came to her rescue. He didn't insult her by saying he should have come with her, either. He knew she could handle the man she now faced if violence started.

If I'd accompanied you, he wouldn't be out on the lawn.

It was true. But Kaylin wanted to teach him enough of a lesson that the tabard of the Hawk would be a deterrent even if a five-year-old was wearing it.

That's not respect, Severn said softly. *It's fear.*

I'll take fear. Mrs. Erickson—

Yes, I know. But she's not a child. Turn and follow her. She's waiting and you don't want her to come running back to the lawn armed with a frying pan.

She wouldn't. Kaylin inhaled slowly. The old woman would return, because to Mrs. Erickson, Kaylin probably *was* a child.

If you have to hit him, you know the drill: wait until he tries to hit you first. You should probably plan out where to let him connect to avoid actual injury. But that's not what you were thinking.

It is.

She could feel Severn shake his head. *It isn't. If you kill him, you'll lose the Hawk.*

I wasn't going to kill him. But she stopped arguing. Let Severn's calm anchor her because she had almost none of her own left, and holding on to it had become increasingly difficult.

If you skin him alive, Severn said, *Mrs. Erickson will be traumatized.*

More than she already *is?* She didn't tell him that she had no intention of skinning the man alive. She knew what Severn meant. And she knew the deep, visceral fury she could barely keep under lock had echoes of the one time—long before she was officially a Hawk—that she'd done exactly that.

She turned toward Mrs. Erickson.

Hope squawked.

She shook her head, exhaling. There were some fights you had to walk away from. This was one of them—for now. She turned toward the door, showing the neighbor her profile. She didn't speak, and made no further attempt to provoke him.

For his part, he husbanded his demands as well, which she hadn't expected. She wasn't certain why. Maybe it was because he wasn't entirely stupid and he'd seen, clearly, the certainty that lurked beneath Kaylin's momentary, but murderous, rage. If her size made her an easy target in the eyes of people like the neighbor, her anger added weight and gravity, as did the Hawk.

Not even the neighbor could consider a physical altercation with an Imperial Hawk to be an entirely safe bet—not when the Hawk knew exactly where he lived.

Mrs. Erickson wasn't holding a frying pan when Kaylin reached the door. She didn't appear to be holding a weapon at all, but there was something both tremulous and martial in the older woman's expression.

"It's such a pity he turned out like that," the old woman said, holding her door open to allow Kaylin entry. "His mother was such a sweet soul."

Kaylin glanced at Hope, who was rigid on her shoulder. He lifted his wing, placing it almost gently across her face, as if her visceral fury was terrain to be carefully navigated.

You should have let me eat him, he said. At the sound of comprehensible words she understood two things: the first, he was almost as angry as Kaylin had become, and the second, that he probably could.

"I don't see why you should have fun when I'm not allowed to have any."

His reply was a very loud squawk.

Amaldi and Darreno were standing in front of Mrs. Erickson, and given Darreno's expression, he wasn't any happier with the neighbor than Kaylin. He might even be angrier, which she would have bet was impossible.

It was Amaldi who said, "The worst part about our condition is the helplessness. We can see everything. We can do *nothing.*"

"He isn't your problem, dear," Mrs. Erickson said, her voice gentle. "And we have laws in this city that are meant to help people like me. If you *could* interfere, and you killed the man, you'd suffer for it—and I would feel guilty for the rest of my life. He's never hit me."

"He'd better not," Kaylin snapped, simmering. She turned

on her heel, but the man had retreated into his own, much
larger, house. She wondered if Hope could set it on fire.

I could.

She reached out and clamped his legs to her shoulder.

"He wasn't always like this," Mrs. Erickson said, as if Kaylin hadn't spoken.

"I don't care if he was a saint when he was a child," Kaylin replied, more tersely than she'd intended.

"Well, I wasn't," Mrs. Erickson said, in a far kinder tone. "There's no point in regrets, but I don't think you can live as long as I have without finding some anyway. They're like burrs. They cling. Sometimes you don't regret a thing until far later, when you can see it in a different light. Come in, come in." She glanced at Amaldi and Darreno.

Both shook their heads. Darreno was only barely paying attention; he was glaring at the neighbor's house, as if the walls were transparent and he could focus on the man inside them.

"They never come into my house," Mrs. Erickson said. "I can't offer them much in the way of hospitality."

"You've offered them friendship—or what friendship you can. At this point in their lives, I don't imagine they think of normal hospitality the way the rest of us do." Hope kept his wing up over Kaylin's eyes.

"Haven't you ever had those days when what you can offer someone in need never feels like it's enough?"

"Sure." Often. "But you're offering everything you can."

Mrs. Erickson nodded in a way that indicated she'd heard the words, considered them, and found them both true and wanting at the same time. She headed down the hall, indicating with a hand that Kaylin—heavy basket in arms—should follow.

Kaylin set the basket down on a battered but clean table—

a small one, meant to seat two, or perhaps three in a pinch. It was very similar to the first table Kaylin could call her own. That table, along with the apartment, had been destroyed in the explosion of the arcane bomb. Which had in turn given energy to hatch Hope.

But the destruction had led, in the end, to Kaylin's current home: Helen, a sentient building.

"I don't see anyone else here," she said, as Mrs. Erickson set about putting food into cupboards. There was too much of it, but she'd offered Kaylin a meal, and Kaylin had the vaguely guilty feeling she was eating Mrs. Erickson's food budget. It wasn't a thought that would have occurred to her a year ago, but she'd now spent some time figuring out what a budget was, and how to stay within it. More or less.

But she'd lived hand to mouth for years, and when it came right down to it, she had trouble walking away from people in need—they reminded her of who she'd been for half her life, and she was accustomed to having nothing anyway. She just...didn't want to take things away from an elderly woman if it wasn't necessary.

"The ghosts aren't in the kitchen yet," Mrs. Erickson replied. "They're a bit shy." Something fell in the distance. "And sometimes a bit petulant."

"Are they like Amaldi and Darreno?"

Mrs. Erickson shook her head. "Amaldi and Darreno are outside ghosts. They don't really have a home—I think they've come to terms with that. My friends are indoor ghosts. They can't leave this house."

"Is that why you stay here?"

"No. This is my home. I was born in it. It's not large and it's not fancy—but it's served us all well." She hesitated. "Help me cut those vegetables?"

Kaylin nodded. She was handed what Mrs. Erickson no

doubt thought of as a knife; it was so dull Kaylin could have done a better job cutting things with her baton. "Do you have a sharpening stone?" she asked, grimacing.

"Not as such, but I don't generally need a sharp knife. And sometimes the children get a bit unruly, so sharp knives might be a bit of a hazard."

"They're ghosts, right?"

"Yes, dear."

"How can sharp knives be a problem?" Another crash sounded, this one closer. "Never mind. Forget I asked the question."

"That'll be Jamal." Mrs. Erickson reached for an apron, as if falling objects of decent weight were an everyday occurrence. "He can throw things when he loses his temper. Oh, no—that sounds far worse than it is. I think he throws things to prove that he can—that he does exist, that he can somehow still make his presence felt. He doesn't really like it when I go out, but we've reached an agreement."

"So…he throws things around because he's having a tantrum in your house, and you call that an agreement?"

"No—he's throwing things because he doesn't like that I have a guest." Her smile, as she turned it toward Kaylin, was almost affectionate. "I don't have many guests."

Kaylin could see why. She pulled one of her own long daggers. She'd just sprain her wrist if she continued to use Mrs. Erickson's knives. "I imagine Jamal scares most possible visitors."

"A bit, yes. If they could see him, they'd be less frightened, but they can't. I try not to explain too much, because it makes visitors even more uncomfortable. On the other hand, the neighbor has never tried to enter my house again."

Kaylin froze. "Again? You mean he tried to force his way in here before?"

"He visited with his mother as a child. But yes, he's only made one attempt as the adult he's become."

"I don't imagine Jamal cared for him."

"He's even objecting to you, dear."

Fair enough. Kaylin finished cutting what she thought of as broccoli, although it was the wrong color. "Do you mind if I speak to Jamal?"

"Not at all. You might even be able to see him."

Kaylin rose, wiping the blade before resheathing it. She couldn't decide if that would be bane or blessing. But as she headed toward the arch—not door—that led from the kitchen, Mrs. Erickson almost shrieked.

"Are you all right?" Mrs. Erickson asked, her worry obvious.

Kaylin frowned in confusion. "I'm fine." She then looked down at her arms: the marks that adorned her unexposed skin were glowing through the cloth of her sleeves.

04

Mrs. Erickson left off whatever cooking she'd intended to do. She seldom moved quickly, but made an exception; she was by Kaylin's side in an instant. "Your arms!"

"They're fine," Kaylin replied.

"But they're—they're on fire!"

"No, it's not fire. It's like magic." Which wasn't a lie. "I don't love it, either. But...your ghost, or one of your ghosts, seems to have set off my defenses." She spoke as if this was totally normal, even mundane, which calmed Mrs. Erickson down—but not completely.

"He really isn't dangerous," she said. "He's just—"

"Lonely and possessive." Both of which could cause severe danger when mixed in with the wrong personality. She hoped that Jamal was as much a child as Mrs. Erickson thought he was—if age of death mattered to the dead at all.

She put Mrs. Erickson firmly behind her. "I have no intention of harming him—how could I, if he's a ghost? I'd just like to stop him from breaking things or driving visitors out of your home."

"I've tried that."

"Yes, well. You're a civilian." Mrs. Erickson's expression made clear that Jamal didn't differentiate.

Kaylin's marks were glowing brightly—a brilliant blue-white that would have caused Kaylin to squint had they not been so much a part of her skin by now. Kaylin had never fully understood what made them light up; she only knew that when they did something was significant.

A ghost that could pitch things across a room was significant, if that's what was happening. Kaylin had been haunted by the usual regrets and memories; she'd never expected to be haunted by an actual ghost. If there had been ghosts, if they chose to haunt people, she knew whose faces she would have been terrified to see, in part because she would know she deserved their pain and rage.

Not a happy thought. She reminded herself that Jamal—if that's who it was—had somehow driven out the next-door neighbor the one time he'd entered Mrs. Erickson's house. Jamal was probably the reason he'd never returned. She exhaled. If Mrs. Erickson intended to follow anyway, she might as well get this over with as quickly as possible, and only in part because she was hungry.

The halls were narrow—everything about the house was. Kaylin listened for any more sounds of objects hitting things, but none came. She hadn't heard anything shatter, so maybe he'd chosen things that *could* be retrieved and returned to their proper place.

She found the room down the hall. It was a small parlor, similar to the one that Helen opened up when there were guests, but a lot smaller. There were books on the floor, some facedown, some closed; it depended entirely on how they'd landed.

She didn't see Jamal. She glanced at Mrs. Erickson, but Mrs.

Erickson was looking around the room, so the old woman didn't see him, either. Maybe he'd gone into hiding because he was aware that he'd behaved badly. If so, Kaylin could sympathize.

But the marks on her arms were still glowing brightly. "Does he usually stay in this room?"

"No, not usually. But here is where he usually shows the most displeasure."

"Probably because it's a room meant for guests."

"Don't judge him too harshly. Amaldi and Darreno at least have each other. Right now, I'm all he has—and he knows I'm not getting any younger."

"If he's afraid of losing his time with you, there are way better ways to spend the time he does have."

"Loneliness can do terrible things to people."

Jamal wasn't in any of the rooms on the first floor. Kaylin therefore headed up to the second floor. She tried, twice, to convince Mrs. Erickson that food was more important, but Mrs. Erickson clearly thought Kaylin was just being polite.

They trudged up to the second floor. There were three rooms—a bedroom at either end and a room she referred to as the family room. "But we don't use it much anymore." The door was closed, but Mrs. Erickson continued toward the room at the end of the narrow hall that faced the back of the house.

"This used to be my room, when my parents were alive," she said quietly. "He's probably in there."

Kaylin followed the older woman, and waited for her to open the door. The marks of the Chosen were now almost white. Jamal—whatever he was—was here.

Hope lowered his wing, which she hadn't asked him to do,

but he'd probably done it because he realized that his wing was entirely unnecessary.

Kaylin, without Hope's intervention, could see Jamal clearly.

Jamal didn't look like Amaldi or Darreno, neither of whom she could see without Hope's wing. Something about him was familiar, though; she couldn't place what immediately.

"Corporal?" Mrs. Erickson's anxious voice came from behind.

"Call me Kaylin. I'm off duty." She was certain she'd never seen the child before; was certain that his image hadn't graced the missing persons files she'd perused over her years as a Hawk, or as a Hawk's mascot. She was missing something.

She set it aside, for now. "Jamal?"

Jamal's eyes had widened so much they might have fallen out of their sockets had they not been somehow attached.

"Wait. I just want to have a little chat with you." Not exactly the most comforting of words, but she realized this only after they'd already left her mouth. "I can see you, just like Mrs. Erickson can.

"She can't touch you, right? She can't hurt you."

This caused him to solidify, his expression folding into lines of anger. "She would *never* hurt me. She wouldn't even hurt a spider." He paused and then added, "Flies don't count."

At any other time Kaylin would have laughed. "No. She wouldn't hurt anyone, given the choice. But you've been throwing her things around and scaring any possible visitors she might have, and that should stop."

Anger compressed into a more familiar sullenness. "She doesn't need them."

"Do you know what happened a couple of years ago? You were here when she fell, right?"

Silence. Sullenness gave way to something else—fear? Guilt? Helplessness? They were all mixed together.

"If it hadn't been for people like us—the Imperial Hawks—she might have died here. She couldn't move properly, and she has no friends who could visit and check up on her. She's living alone, as far as most people know—and that gets risky when you get older. You understand that, right?"

"I tried to lift her," he said, his voice much smaller and much less defiant.

"You shouldn't try—sometimes when people are hurt, that can make things worse. Or that's what I was taught when I was training to be a Hawk."

"But you guys came anyway."

"Yes—because she comes to the Halls of Law almost every day, and she missed three days."

"I brought her water."

"I know you care about her. I'm glad you were here. I'm sure she's glad you were here, too—but there's only so much you can do."

"I've been practicing. To try to be able to do more."

"Jamal, you're a kid. I've been a kid, too. There's only so much I could have done when I was your age. I don't like to depend on others, but sometimes we have to accept that we have no choice." She walked toward him, and he stood, waiting for her; his eyes were on her arms, and she could almost see the reflected glow of their light in his eyes.

"You can see me, too."

She nodded. As she did, she remembered the Arkon, his private collection, and a piece of armor that had evaporated on touch—her touch, sadly, given the way the Arkon viewed his collection. She remembered the way the marks had glowed then, too.

"Jamal, why are you here?" She asked without anger. As

she waited for his reply, Mrs. Erickson peeked in through the open door.

"I don't know. I was here when I woke up. I'm here now. I can't leave the house." He turned toward the open door, his expression a mixture of happiness and guilt. "She was here, too. I'm sorry about the books."

Mrs. Erickson nodded. But added, "You can't keep doing the wrong thing and apologizing for it afterward—sometimes you have to learn not to do the wrong thing first."

He nodded, hanging his head. Kaylin thought him between the age of ten and twelve, although he might have been older when he'd been alive. "Jamal, do you see any of the other ghosts that live here?"

Jamal shrugged. Kaylin couldn't tell if this was a yes or a no.

"He can see the others," Mrs. Erickson said.

"How many are there? I don't see any others now."

"Three more," Mrs. Erickson replied. "But they're not here, right now. They don't tend to stay when Jamal is in a bad mood."

This didn't surprise Kaylin. If she couldn't stop Jamal, she wasn't certain she'd stick around while he was having a tantrum, either. "Were they always here as well?"

"Pardon?"

"Were the ghosts in your house always here, or did some of them drift in later?"

Mrs. Erickson blinked. "I...think they were always here, like Jamal. But they aren't as forceful."

"When did you first notice them?" Kaylin backed up. "Sorry, let me start again. How long have you lived in this house? Were you born here?"

Mrs. Erickson nodded. "My family wasn't wealthy, but we had the house. It's been my only home. When I married, we lived here."

Kaylin was a bit surprised that Mrs. Erickson had actually been married; the Hawks had never met Mr. Erickson and many privately believed he had never existed. She was then ashamed at the surprise. "Your husband died here?"

Mrs. Erickson nodded. "Don't look like that, dear. It was a long time ago, now. Long enough that the good memories aren't overwhelmed by the sense of loss. As for the ghosts? I always saw them. As far back as I can remember."

"And your husband?"

She shook her head. "When he died, he didn't return."

"Do you know who owned this house before your parents?"

She shook her head. "It never occurred to me to ask. It was home, it had always been here. Is this an interrogation?" Her tone was bright, her smile genuine. Her eyes seemed almost to sparkle with delight.

Kaylin, however, reddened. And her stomach growled.

Jamal immediately pointed at that stomach and burst out laughing, which didn't help.

"I'll go downstairs and finish making dinner if you want to talk to Jamal for a bit."

"So you knew her when she was a little girl?"

Jamal nodded. "When she was a *baby*." The emphasis on the word was childlike. He was young, and decades hadn't changed that essential fact.

"She could see you then?"

He nodded. "I used to play with her. I mean—I'd pick up rattles or toys when she started to cry. The others can't."

"There are four of you?" At his nod, she continued. "Were they always here when you...woke up?"

He nodded again.

"Can any of you leave the house?"

"No."

"Do you know how long you've been part of the house?"

The question seemed to confuse him, which is what she'd expected. She tried again. "Did you see Mrs. Erickson's mother and father?"

He nodded.

"Did you see the mother—or father—when they were babies, too?"

He shook his head. "They came later. They were older. They couldn't see us. Only she could." He frowned. "And you. You can see me. I don't know if you'll be able to see the others." He hesitated, and then hung his head. "She's going to go away soon." He lifted his head. "Can you help?"

"I can't give people youth."

Jamal shook his head. "We're okay being here now—we like Mrs. Erickson. But if she goes away, there won't be anyone here, and we can't leave."

Oh.

"We thought Curly would join us, and that would have been good."

"Curly?"

"Her husband."

"His name was Curly?"

"It's what we called him. She called him Davos. His hair was curly, especially during the summer. It was funny. But he died, and she was sad, and he didn't come back. I'd've come back for her, if I were him."

"When did you come to the house?"

Silence.

"You must have come here when you were alive."

Jamal's eyes widened; his mouth half-open as he stared at Kaylin. He didn't answer. He vanished.

★ ★ ★

When Mrs. Erickson called Kaylin down for dinner, she went, but it took her a couple of minutes to shake the Hawk-investigator frame of mind. She was certain that Jamal had died in this house. He had died before Mrs. Erickson's parents had purchased the house, because he was dead when they arrived.

Kaylin felt certain Jamal's death was no accident.

Her arms were no longer glowing. Hope was spread across her shoulders as if he were boneless.

Mrs. Erickson placed two plates on the table, one in front of Kaylin and one in front of her own chair; the smell of cheese wafted up from the hot food, causing Kaylin's stomach to grumble again. She ate, in part to prevent further embarrassment and in part because she was hungry.

Jamal appeared to her left. "You're sitting in my seat, you know."

Mrs. Erickson said, "Jamal, she's a guest."

"Can't she sit in a different seat?"

"I only have two chairs."

He sat on the table, instead. Kaylin thought about what her now-dead mother would have done if Kaylin had tried that, and winced. "I'll move once I'm finished eating," she offered. "But you don't need to sit."

"You don't, either! You can eat while you're standing!"

"It's harder," a new voice said. A girl, she thought, although at that age it was hard to tell. She was younger than Jamal, her clothing similar: loose-fitting tunic, leggings. Both were in decent repair, but not new. Her hair was gold-tinted, her eyes bluer; Jamal was ruddier, his eyes a more familiar brown.

"So what? We *live* here. She's just visiting."

"I think we're supposed to treat visitors better."

"Why?"

Mrs. Erickson sighed. "Please accept my apologies on their behalf," she told Kaylin.

"Nope. If Jamal is behaving badly, it's up to him to apologize and *fix his own behavior*. He's not a baby. He's closer to my age than yours."

Jamal's eyes narrowed. "It's my chair."

"Would you rather that Mrs. Erickson give up hers and eat standing up instead?"

"No!"

"Then let me finish eating and I'll give you back your chair." She wanted to add a few Leontine words to the mix, but wasn't certain Mrs. Erickson wouldn't understand them.

Another child joined Jamal, and then, shortly after, a third. These were Mrs. Erickson's ghosts—and Kaylin could see them all. The marks on her arms were glowing faintly. She was both annoyed by Jamal's demand, but also sympathetic. She did finish eating quickly—but she always ate quickly. It was a reflex from childhood and she had to work *hard* to eat as slowly as most of her friends did.

She did leave the chair as soon as she'd finished, with apologies to Mrs. Erickson.

Mrs. Erickson didn't seem unduly upset. Kaylin wondered if the old woman had had children with her husband, but didn't ask. If she had, those children were not among these ghosts, and these ghosts had come with the house; they weren't haunting Mrs. Erickson for any reason other than isolation. Hers and theirs.

Kaylin then stood to the side of Jamal's chair, and Jamal immediately pounced on it and sat, hard. He wasn't actually sitting on the chair, but he was pretty good at mimicking it. He watched Mrs. Erickson eat, content. Mrs. Erickson might be lonely, as most of the Hawks assumed she was, but she wasn't alone.

* * *

After dinner, Kaylin helped wash up, taking a bucket of water from the rain barrel and heating it while Jamal and his friends spoke with Mrs. Erickson. She told them about Amaldi and Darreno, and about Kaylin, Severn, and her visit to the Hawks today.

"I always tell them about my day," Mrs. Erickson said, over her shoulder. "I'd take them all with me if I could, but they've never been able to leave. We tried for years," she added, voice softer. "So I leave, and I try to come back with stories."

Stories. Stories made up of her activities—her mundane activities—for the day. Kaylin revised all of her assumptions about Mrs. Erickson. She had assumed that the old woman came to the Halls of Law because she was isolated and lonely. That wasn't the right story, or the whole story.

These children weren't hers, but they had been here, if Kaylin understood what she'd heard, for the entirety of Mrs. Erickson's life. She wasn't getting younger. She knew she'd be leaving them behind when she died, trapped in this house. Maybe other people would move in—but the likelihood that they could see the dead was very low.

No wonder Jamal hated visitors.

"Hey," he said, looking past Mrs. Erickson to where Kaylin stood. "You can sit. I'm done." His tone was grudging—but it seemed to please Mrs. Erickson, and that was probably the intent.

None of the children told Kaylin their names, but she picked them up as Mrs. Erickson addressed them. Jamal was the oldest, Callis next, followed by Esmeralda; Katie was youngest. Of the four, Esmeralda was the most transparent; she was also mostly silent. Kaylin couldn't tell if that was because a stranger was present or not.

But had Kaylin been dead and trapped in the house, she'd've probably been far more like Jamal than Esmeralda. She had questions she wanted to ask, and she sat on most of them. Jamal, the boldest of the four, had disappeared when she'd started, and she didn't want to chase them all away.

She was also worried about the neighbor. The neighborhood itself was considered both good and safe, in the usual Hawk sense of the word, which didn't mean murder didn't happen in them. Still, she couldn't camp out here tonight. She couldn't spend the evening standing guard outside—she had work in the morning.

But she intended to get herself put on the front desk everyone tried to avoid—because she could ask Mrs. Erickson questions there that she couldn't bring herself to ask in front of the children they concerned.

"You're here early today, dear," Caitlin said, as Kaylin's jog came to a stop at the desk that all Hawks had to pass to enter Marcus's branch of the Hawks' offices.

Kaylin nodded.

"You saw Mrs. Erickson home safely?"

"I did. I want to run a check on one of her neighbors. And I want to run a check on the house she's living in now. Oh, also: if Severn's still out with meetings, I want to be put on the front desk again."

Caitlin's brow furrowed as her expression shifted into concern about the state of Kaylin's health.

"I'm fine," she said, although Caitlin hadn't actually asked. "But the neighbor appears to be perfectly happy to trounce across her lawn to bully her—even when she's accompanied by a Hawk."

"And the house?"

Kaylin winced. "You know those ghosts she's always talking about?"

"Yes, dear."

"I met them."

Caitlin didn't get involved in office business but she wasn't
oblivious. She glanced at Hope, who was flopping out across
Kaylin's shoulder.

"Sort of."

"Severn should be in meetings this afternoon."

"Great. I'll take front desk from whomever it was handed
to. Can you let Sergeant Keele know?"

Kaylin had a to-do list that was impressively long, considering her lack of active, ongoing investigation. Mrs. Erickson,
and things tangential to Mrs. Erickson, occupied almost all of
it. Mrs. Erickson could see the dead children and—if Jamal
was right—had always been able to see them. She could see
Amaldi and Darreno, two people who Kaylin felt instinctively
weren't actually dead. She could see Severn's belt. Or rather,
could see that it was magic, and a strong enough magic that
it made her squint. Mrs. Erickson had probably never been
tested for magical aptitude.

"Caitlin, do you know Mrs. Erickson's actual name?"

"I believe it was Imelda. Imelda Swindon Erickson."

"Thanks."

On the off chance Mrs. Erickson had, at some point in her
early life, been tested, some information would be in Records. In Records as well would be information about the
former owners of that house. And the current owner of the
house one over.

She had the first names of the four children. She knew
they were dead—long dead by this point. She knew where
they'd probably died: the house itself. Who had the previous

owners been? Whoever they were, they were dead and out of the reach of Imperial justice. But the children were still trapped in the house.

She needed to ask questions about Severn's weapon. Amaldi and Darreno had been terrified at the sight of it. Enough that they had trouble believing Severn was human.

"Records: Missing Persons. Date range: one hundred years ago, to eighty years."

"Search criteria?"

"Children, age eight to twelve. Also: Esmeralda, Jamal, Callis, and Katie."

"Full names?"

"Those are the only names I have." She frowned. Many people avoided the Halls of Law; not all missing persons became the subject of reports. Those that didn't wouldn't appear in Records at all—but she had four names, and one of them might. They didn't look like they were the children of the wealthy, or the reasonably well off, given the clothing they wore—but she didn't know enough about the dead because, until yesterday, she mostly hadn't believed ghosts existed.

No, that wasn't completely true. She just hadn't believed *human* ghosts existed. "Time?"

"Seven forty-five."

She had to reach the front desk in fifteen minutes, and while the front desk was possessed of a mirror, searching Records in front of civilians was heavily frowned on.

Sergeant Keele wore an expression very similar to Caitlin's, but with an added dash of deep suspicion. People didn't volunteer for front desk duty; they were assigned it, and they went with minimal—but obvious—grumbling. Severn was still unavailable, which meant Kaylin was off her beat, and in any other circumstance, she would have stayed quiet and hoped to be passed over.

"I need to speak with Mrs. Erickson," Kaylin told the sergeant.

"Mrs. Erickson."

The younger Hawk nodded. "I saw her home yesterday, and we had a spot of trouble from her neighbor."

"We? As in the both of you?"

"He didn't seem all that impressed with the Hawk, no."

Sergeant Keele's lips compressed, but she nodded; this was an acceptable reason to volunteer for a duty one usually avoided like the plague. "How did she react to this?"

"She tried to make excuses for me, and to point out that I was young and didn't mean to be disrespectful."

The sergeant's eyes narrowed. "Fine. Desk is yours."

Mrs. Erickson tended to visit the Halls of Law in the early afternoon; Kaylin was certain she spent the mornings baking in preparation for that visit. She wondered if the children crowded into the kitchen while she worked; she suspected they did.

That meant that Kaylin was at the front desk when other, less amiable civilians visited. She dutifully wrote—by hand— the gist of their complaints, and forced herself not to doodle in the margins. Some were property disputes, which was difficult. Some demanded protection from...well, Kaylin wasn't exactly sure what. She tried her best not to be judgmental, and that lasted about an hour.

Some were serious complaints, one involving domestic violence and children. Those she forwarded immediately to the Hawks whose investigative beat it was. And some were complaints from obviously well-heeled people who had thought it would be a lark—or a test of courage, if not a test of stupidity—to have a party in the *warrens*.

There was nothing outrageous enough to be humorous, and humor was one of the few rewards of the public desk— albeit a humor that sprouted from outrage and disbelief.

But Mrs. Erickson did make her way to the front desk. Only when Kaylin caught sight of her did she relax. The presence of the neighbor weighed far more heavily on her mind than she'd expected.

Mrs. Erickson was smiling. She carried her usual basket, and when she opened the lid, the smell of her baking filled the small room; it obviously extended past it, because some of Keele's people appeared in the doorway behind Kaylin's back.

Kaylin got up from her chair behind the desk and replaced the chair in front of it with something that was both more solid and more comfortable.

"It's not necessary, dear." But she took the chair as Kaylin relieved her of the basket. "Thank you for yesterday. I know Jamal wasn't exactly friendly, but thank you for accepting that."

"It's his house, too," Kaylin replied, lowering her voice. If she now believed in Mrs. Erickson's ghosts, she also believed most of the Hawks would think she'd gone crazy, and she wanted to avoid that for as long as she could. She hesitated and then said, "I think Jamal's worried for you."

"Children sometimes worry when they shouldn't." She smiled. "I'm not a child anymore; I worry about them. I don't suppose you need a place to live?"

Kaylin shook her head. "I have a very large place to live; I'm sure it could accommodate a couple of ghosts—but not if we can't move them."

"If you're wondering about how to free them, I'm not sure

there *is* a way. I did spend some time looking. I've spoken to priests, even the Renunciates of Life."

Kaylin frowned. "I'm not sure I know that one."

"It's a small religion that deals far more broadly with the concept of death and permanence—but I had hoped that they might have answers for me, or at least for the children."

"I take it they didn't."

"They couldn't see the children. The man in charge even insulted me until Jamal started to throw things at his head. You are the only person who's entered my house since I was born who *could* see them. And you're younger than I am. I'm a bit afraid to abandon them—I'm not getting any younger."

Kaylin nodded, unsurprised. She didn't know a lot about ghosts; she knew stories, but stories were an echo of imagination and fear. Especially if the ghosts were vengeful ghosts. What she knew at the moment was that her marks had reacted to Jamal.

Ghosts, however, were only one part of the equation.

"Mrs. Erickson, have you ever been tested for magical aptitude?"

05

Mrs. Erickson's shoulders dipped. Her face, which was usually expressive, became more of a mask. She failed to answer the question, which was answer enough: Yes, and it had not gone well.

Kaylin didn't press for the *yes*. "How old were you?"

"Thirteen."

"Did your parents take you to get tested?"

She nodded.

"Did they go to the Imperial College of mages?"

She nodded again. "It's so long ago," she said, her voice low. "I know it shouldn't bother me all these years later."

Thirteen. That meant whoever was responsible for her testing was probably dead, which was a bit of a pity, as Kaylin wanted the opportunity to punch them in the face. Which would be the definition of career limiting. She reined in her immediate reaction.

"It was because of the ghosts, and a few other things," Mrs. Erickson continued. "My mother thought I might have what she called 'the gift.' She didn't, but her grandmother did."

Kaylin nodded. She had set aside the scratch pad; she had no intention of entering this discussion into any formal report.

"We were lucky," the old woman continued. "We had a roof over our heads, and we had enough food for the table. We didn't have a lot of money left over. But we weren't dressed in rags. We had to make an appointment, and that was difficult; my mother had to answer questions about my 'education.'" She enunciated the last word in a very different way.

"I knew how to read by then, but we didn't have much time for other lessons. Practical lessons—cooking, laundry, cleaning—took most of our time. I don't mind the outcome for myself, you understand. But my mother was so *hopeful*. And she was crushed by the results. I had no magical aptitude."

"I'm sorry, I don't believe that."

"Pardon?"

"Whoever was responsible for the assessment had their head up— I mean, I think they were wrong."

"That's kind of you."

"And I think we should visit again."

Mrs. Erickson shook her head. "The Imperial Mages are very busy people."

"Yes. And this is one of their responsibilities, according to the *Emperor*."

"I don't want to be a bother."

"You won't be."

"Corporal, I'm old now. I am too old to change. I am too old to plan or build a new life. All that would happen is I would waste a day—or several days—of a mage's time. I'm not certain why you think this is a good idea—most people think I'm a bit dotty."

"You've never worked with actual mages," Kaylin replied.

"They're way more than a bit dotty. You probably have more common sense than the rest of them combined."

Mrs. Erickson smiled, but also ducked her head as if to avoid the heart of the compliment. "Let's pretend that you're right. That I somehow do have magical aptitude, and that the mage who dismissed me decades ago was wrong. What do you expect that to change for me?"

Kaylin hadn't been thinking about the future life Mrs. Erickson might lead; she'd been thinking about Severn, his weapon chain, and Amaldi and Darreno. She was fairly certain the ability to see ghosts wasn't couched in magical talent, or rather, wasn't couched in normal magical talent, if there was such a thing. Her own ability to see Jamal and his compatriots was almost certainly due to the marks of the Chosen.

She knew that Jamal was probably more important to Mrs. Erickson than Severn's weapon chain or Amaldi and Darreno. But Severn wasn't a ghost, and his weapons weren't theoretical. Amaldi and Darreno weren't ghosts either, in her opinion.

"If you'll agree to it, I'll make arrangements with the Imperial Mages. I'll go with you as escort."

"You have work."

"I do, but this is part of that work." Hopefully, Marcus would see it that way as well. "The ability to use magic is like perfect pitch—or so I've been told. It's rare."

"But why do you believe I can?"

"Because you could see—and interact with—Amaldi and Darreno. They're not like Jamal and his friends."

"No—they aren't trapped in a particular building."

"Mrs. Erickson, I don't believe they're dead at all."

Cookies—Mrs. Erickson had brought cookies for her daily afternoon visit—were spread among the lurking Hawks. Sergeant Keele surprised Kaylin—she came out to the front desk.

Keele wasn't all that interested in baking. She might take a cookie, but she seldom ate them. Keele was the type of person sugar was probably allergic to, rather than the other way around.

"You're wanted by your sergeant," Keele told her.

Marcus hadn't called for Kaylin, as she discovered when she stopped by Caitlin's desk. Caitlin was the early warning system for every Hawk who set foot in the office, because Caitlin knew pretty much everything Hawk-related that happened within it.

Still, it allowed Kaylin to head to her mirror. What she'd had to say, she'd said, and Mrs. Erickson hadn't said no. She hadn't exactly said yes, either. Kaylin had some magical ability; she could certainly see magic and magical traces just as well as the best of the Imperial Mages. She couldn't use magic the way they used it, but had never had a strong desire to learn. There were no Hawks that were Imperial Mages, after all.

But she knew that no two mages saw magic—or the aftereffects known as signatures—the same way. What they saw, their minds interpreted in unique ways. Kaylin didn't see magic when she looked at Severn's belt. She'd never really surveyed anyone else to see if they saw—or more accurately, didn't see—what she did.

Teela and Tain were out patrolling, so she couldn't ask them.

But first things first. "Records, I'd like to speak with Lord Sanabalis. The Arkon," she amended, wondering how long it would take her to get used to the change in title.

The mirror flared to life, although it remained mostly reflective. She waited, wondering if this was a request that should have been forwarded through Hanson in the Hawklord's office instead. She had a sneaking suspicion the answer was yes, but also knew it might take a while to arrange an appointment to speak with Sanabalis, and she turned her attention to the old missing persons Records, because Records had some information for her.

As she'd suspected, the children weren't, for the most part, entered into Records as missing. They were physically different enough that they might have been adopted, in which case any abuse or damage was unlikely to be reported by the abuser. But she suspected, given the difference in clothing styles, that they weren't, or hadn't been, part of a family.

They were a family of necessity now.

Only one of the four children was listed as missing: Esmeralda. Esmeralda Noachin. Kaylin checked the date of the report: ninety years ago.

Mrs. Erickson was seventy-one as of this year, according to Records. Kaylin was surprised. She knew Mrs. Erickson was old, but not *that* old. No wonder the kids—or Jamal, at least—were worried. Ninety years ago, Esmeralda was reported missing. But her case wasn't in the open log, which meant she'd been found.

Kaylin began to read the report more carefully. Esmeralda had been found. Records capture usually included images of corpses, if the corpse, not the living child, was recovered instead. There was no corpse. According to Records, Esmeralda had been found and returned—alive—to her family.

Kaylin had definitely seen a ghost named Esmeralda. Was it possible they'd returned the *wrong child*? No. No, that wouldn't be possible—the family would have recognized the difference, surely?

"Records, further files associated with Esmeralda Noachin."

Records began a gentle ding. There were files associated with Esmeralda. One looked to be long and complicated.

"Records: location Esmeralda was found."

A map appeared in the mirror's surface. It was the wrong map; closer by far to a common well than it was to Mrs. Erickson's home, where the girl was in theory trapped. Somehow, a girl whom her own family accepted as Esmeralda, had been found alive in the wrong place.

Kaylin went back to the missing persons report, to the sketch made of the girl in her clothing—clothing that matched what the ghost wore.

"Records," she said. "Search for reports related to Mrs. Erickson's home. All time periods. Any report." Mrs. Erickson's house was, in Records, at 14 1/2 Orbonne Street. Why *half*, Kaylin didn't know. It's true the house was smaller than either of its neighbors, but half?

"What are you muttering about, kitling?" Teela's voice drifted over her shoulder.

"I thought you two were on patrol."

"We were. There was some trouble and we had to bring a couple of very, very inebriated young men in to cool their heels in a cell."

Kaylin winced. "How bad were they?"

"We could incapacitate them and dump them in the cells for a day or two, or we could kill them in self-defense. They were, as mortals say, armed to the teeth." Teela sounded vaguely bored, which meant the inebriated criminals were most likely human. "What are you looking at?"

"Missing persons report."

"That's real estate, not missing persons." Teela frowned. "Mrs. Erickson?"

"I escorted her home yesterday."

"Why?"

Kaylin hesitated. Before Teela could lean in, she said, "Mrs. Erickson was worried about Severn."

Teela blinked. "Do go on. Was one of her ghosts concerned?"

"Two of her ghosts."

"And because he's your partner you decided to check it out?"

Technically, this was accurate, and Teela might forgive her because the Barrani lived in the margins of technicalities—it was why all the laws and most of the lawyers were steeped in Barrani minutiae, although the lawyers themselves were, by and large, human. Teela, however, was less patient when others attempted to rely on technicalities where Teela was concerned.

"Yes. But it wasn't just that. Tell me, what do you see when you look at Severn's weapon chain?"

"An unusual belt."

"So…it doesn't glow when you look at it?"

Teela stilled in a way that indicated Kaylin now had what she didn't really want: all of her attention. "No. I assume you aren't referring to enhanced magical investigation."

"I'm not. To me—and you know I'm sensitive to magical signatures—it looks like a belt made of chain."

"And Mrs. Erickson's ghosts see it differently."

Kaylin shook her head. "It's not her ghosts—well, maybe her ghosts do as well—it's Mrs. Erickson. She knew who Severn was because she vaguely knows who I am, and he's my partner. Him and his painfully illuminated belt."

"Painfully?"

"She has to squint sometimes when he's too close."

Teela's eyes were blue, but they usually were; she was concerned, but not worried. Not yet. "And that led you to investigate Mrs. Erickson's house?"

"Oh—no, that came later."

"And that's why you *volunteered* for front desk duty today?"

"Pretty much. I had a couple of questions I wanted to ask Mrs. Erickson. I think we should have her tested for magical aptitude, but I wanted to know if she'd been tested before."

"Judging from your sour expression, she had."

"Yes, but probably by an idiot. I'm sure the Imperial College will have some record of it. I think she should be tested again, regardless."

Because Teela wasn't mortal, she didn't say, *At her age?* "Did you want to tell me the rest?"

Not particularly, but Kaylin knew this offer of a listening ear wasn't actually an offer.

Teela was clearly bored enough that everything Kaylin told her—and she kept nothing back—was of interest. To Teela, Amaldi and Darreno were the most pressing concern because they recognized the weapon itself, and Kaylin couldn't actually see them without her familiar's wing. They had clearly had some experience with Barrani in the past—and that past was distant enough Teela might have been a child when it had happened.

Mrs. Erickson's possible magical talent was of interest because it appeared to allow Mrs. Erickson to see the two. Mrs. Erickson's ghosts were of interest only because Kaylin could see them without the familiar's help, and their presence seemed to engage the marks over most of Kaylin's skin.

"Don't you have a report to write?"

"Tain's writing it. Records: Esmeralda Noachin."

Esmeralda Noachin's final report was gruesome. She had been executed seventy-four years ago, having been found guilty of a series of very gruesome murders. The victims: her family. Three family members, mother, father and younger brother, and one cousin. Four victims.

She hadn't spoken a word in her own defense; she had refused to answer any questions. She had not reacted to the verdict the court handed down: she was guilty of murder, and she would pay the ultimate price. Even on the day of her execution, she'd been expressionless and silent.

Prior to the murders, however, there had been minor misdemeanors, breaking and entering, attempted theft.

No motive for the killings could be found; one lawyer felt there might be answers associated with her disappearance as a child. But she had always denied being kidnapped; she had claimed that she had gotten lost and couldn't remember what happened afterward.

"Do you have family names for the other three ghosts?"

Kaylin shook her head. "I only have Esmeralda's because of Records searches." She felt a chill take the air around her spine. "Records: search for Jamal, capital crime files."

Jamal hadn't been reported missing. There was no information about his disappearance in Records. Many families didn't trust the Halls of Law; some were involved in petty crimes they didn't want revealed to officers of that law. But the lack of a missing persons report didn't mean he wasn't in Records.

Jamal Rayan had been convicted—and executed—for a series of gruesome murders that had taken place over a century ago, one hundred and fifteen years to be more precise. He had, at the time, been twenty-five years of age. The image Records offered was an adult male, broad shouldered and tight-lipped, hair long and braided down one side. Forty-one years before Esmeralda's murders. He had killed his family, but his family lacked a father. His mother, his two sisters, and his half-brother—a young child—had been his victims.

Kaylin noted the number of victims, and wondered if four was significant; he'd killed the same number of people as Esmeralda before he'd been sent to his death.

But before his death, he had also been arrested for petty crimes—breaking and entering, attempted theft. His life had not apparently been kind.

"Are you betting that the other two ghosts will have somehow not been dead until they reach a certain age? And that their eventual death leads to the executioner?"

Kaylin nodded.

They were interrupted in their third name search, Callis Creekson, by the interoffice Records gremlin: Kaylin had an incoming call. She didn't immediately recognize the chime, which was a relief: it meant the Hawklord hadn't inserted himself into the call for a possible Records meeting.

She shuffled the report on Callis Creekson to the figurative side as a familiar face loomed large in the mirror's frame.

"Corporal," the new Arkon said, his voice a Draconic rumble. "You wished to make an appointment to speak with me."

Kaylin nodded.

"Is it urgent? I have become, regrettably, a far busier man than I was before Lannagaros chose to accept the Academia's chancellorship."

"I want you to either personally examine a possible candidate for the Imperial College of mages, or to personally select someone whose oversight and ability you trust to conduct the examination."

Lord Sanabalis blinked. "Pardon?"

She repeated her request.

"Then the appointment would not involve you in any way?"

"I intend to accompany the candidate; I believe she'll be too nervous to go, otherwise."

"And you somehow believe that a Dragon examiner will put her at ease?" His eyes were orange, but flecked now with gold; he was amused.

"Well, you're not allowed to go full Dragon without Imperial permission, so I'm not entirely certain she'll know that you *are* a Dragon."

"Technically, I *am* allowed to go—as you so inelegantly put it—'full Dragon.' I'm the Arkon."

"Wait—the old Arkon was allowed to do that?"

"The position is a position of trust across the whole of our race. We are, and were, trusted to do so only in situations of dire necessity. And no, I imagine meeting one human would not warrant it. Why, exactly, do you consider one possible mage—a profession about which you complain almost as often as you breathe—so important you insist that I conduct the interview myself?"

"She's a bit unusual."

Sanabalis's eyes became a darker orange. "This had better not be a waste of my time."

"What do you mean?"

"Exactly what I said. Very well. It is my hope that she is a far better student than you've proven yourself to be. I have time in two days. If you arrive at the palace before the early dinner hour, I will see you then."

Teela was drilling figurative holes in the side of Kaylin's head by the time Sanabalis's face faded from view. Callis Creekson was waiting for their perusal.

"Records, pause," the Barrani Hawk said, over Kaylin's shoulder. "You intend to take Mrs. Erickson to see the Arkon."

"To see Sanabalis, yes. Could you do me a huge favor, by the way?"

"Probably not. I try not to accept requests from the almost criminally insane."

"Very funny, Teela."

"The Arkon?"

"First, it's Sanabalis. Next to Emmerian he's probably the least scary of the Dragon Court. Next to the old Arkon, he's the most competent in magic, ancient and new. He can't be bribed—that I know of. He can't be bought. Any decision he makes, for whatever reason, I can trust."

"It might have escaped your notice, but Mrs. Erickson is old for a mortal. Much of the aptitude testing the Imperial College engages in is in the service of finding new Imperial Mages—mages who can be trained to be useful."

Kaylin groaned.

Teela cuffed the back of her head. "Even if your suspicions are somehow correct, how is that of benefit to either Mrs. Erickson *or* the Imperial College of mages?"

Kaylin shrugged. "That's the other reason for Sanabalis. Even if she's too old to teach, he'll find her interesting."

"That's almost like an answer," Teela said.

"You don't find all of this odd?"

"I find it odd, yes. It will remain odd. If her magical aptitude is confirmed, what will that change?"

Kaylin shifted. "It's not the ghosts that are my biggest concern. It's her two outdoor ghosts. I doubt you'd see them, even if you were looking. Mrs. Erickson didn't have to struggle. You know I'm allergic to magic."

Teela snorted.

"She wasn't using any. She's gifted, I'm telling you. But she was tested when she was much younger, and sent home as a waste of time by someone in the Imperial College."

"Ah."

"Ah?"

"You want to know who."

"It was probably fifty-five years ago, give or take a few. But yes, if that person was somehow still alive, I'd like to have a few words with him."

"And Sanabalis can give you that information."

"If he feels like it, yes. But more important, he'll probably remember the mage, even if the man is dead. And he might be moved to investigate other candidates that that person has written off. It'll help the Imperial College, even if they don't know."

"What if she fails the various tests again?"

"Then he'll know the tests are outdated, narrow in scope, and just plain wrong?"

Teela chuckled. "It would almost be worth forcing myself to visit the Imperial Palace to watch the outcome. Almost."

Barrani Hawks seldom went to the Imperial Palace. In theory, they were welcome. In theory so were Lords of the Barrani High Court. Given the Draco-Barrani wars, and the permanence of Immortal memory, it almost never happened.

"Could I ask you to force yourself to visit the High Halls, instead?"

"Why?"

"I want any information you can find about Severn's weapon. I'm going to visit the chancellor of the Academia. Well, no, I'm going to ask permission to visit his library, and possibly one of his teachers."

"Tread carefully, Kaylin."

"I think there's a good chance Larrantin would be interested."

"In the weapons? I highly doubt it."

Kaylin shook her head. "In the displacement and entrapment of living people."

"I'd suggest you're going to be spreading yourself far too thin. You should concentrate on the task you've set Records. Callis Creekson."

"It's the same," Kaylin said. "Four murders. Twenty-five years of age."

Teela nodded. She had, as she often did, commandeered Kaylin's mirror instead of returning to her own desk. Kaylin was grateful that she was still allowed to sit in her own chair, because when Teela got That Look, it wasn't guaranteed.

Katie Holdern had also been executed for a series of gruesome murders. She, too, had killed four people, although the Records report indicated the possible ritualistic nature of those murders, a detail that had been missing from the prior three.

"Your real estate Records have arrived," Teela said, while Kaylin carefully read the final ghost's report.

Kaylin nodded. Fourteen and a half Orbonne Street filled the mirror's frame. Kaylin had expected a visual record of the house she'd visited, but Records had decided that the floor plan was more important. Kaylin's brows bunched in minor confusion.

"You don't recognize the floor plan."

"I don't recognize the house, no. Mrs. Erickson's house is half the size—and I would have said the lot isn't anywhere near wide enough to accommodate the floor plan here."

"Records," the Barrani Hawk said, "lot size." Records coughed up a number. "According to our taxation Records, the lot *is* wide enough."

"Records: lot size 12 Orbonne Street and 16 Orbonne Street. Overlap with fourteen and a half."

Teela rose. "Are you going to be visiting Mrs. Erickson again anytime soon?"

"Three days from now, at least. You could volunteer for front desk duty if you wanted to speak with her—she comes in every day."

"Barrani are never put on front desk duty," Teela replied, a hint of smugness intertwined with her usual smile.

"I'll see her in three days—I'll be going to the Imperial Palace with her. If you want you can meet us after the assessment, because I'm going to escort her back to her house. Why, by the way?"

Teela shrugged. "These Records don't align. The house at fourteen—if there ever was a house at fourteen, as opposed to fourteen and a half—should have a wider frontage than either of the two houses that stand as its neighbor."

Records rippled, and 14 Orbonne Street came into view, although neither of the two Hawks had specifically requested it.

Kaylin stared. There was, in theory, a house number fourteen—there was certainly a lot for it—and that house had not changed hands in some time. The problem, of course, was that the house didn't exist.

Mrs. Erickson's parents, Stacia and Collin, had purchased fourteen and a half a few years before Mrs. Erickson's birth.

"Is an owner listed for the missing fourteen?" Teela asked Records. To Kaylin she added, "This is why good record keeping and competent bureaucracy is essential."

Records coughed up a name. Teela's frown froze on her face, but her eyes became a midnight blue. The name was Barrani, or at least styled as Barrani names were styled—some of the more pretentious human families chose names that were as close to Barrani as they could legally be.

Given Teela's reaction, that wasn't the case here. Kaylin took note of the name: Azoria An'Berranin. "Arcanist?"

When Teela failed to answer, Kaylin glanced at her profile; it was rigid and pale. "So I guess you're going to visit the High Halls."

Teela's nod was so rigid it was a wonder she could move her head.

You will be expected to accompany An'Teela, a familiar voice said. Ynpharion inserted himself into her thoughts through the bond they reluctantly shared.

Kaylin was never going to understand Ynpharion. She held his True Name. He hated the fact; he found it both lowering and humiliating. The taking of that name had, in the end, saved lives—one of them, Ynpharion's. But Ynpharion seemed to be one of those death-before-dishonor Barrani. Ah, no—all Barrani evinced that position, but in her opinion, few actually believed it.

Ynpharion did. His home was now the High Halls; he served the Consort personally.

Did you recognize the name? Azoria An'Berranin?

No—but the Lady does, and she is…unsettled by it. The Lady is desirous of your company.

Because of the name?

I think it is more than that, but I at least have a modicum of patience. And a ton of condescension.

It is not condescension, it is frustration. *You have tools available to you that you do not wish to use. There are other people to whom you can turn for information; I suggest you consider them. I have no intention of doing* all *of your thinking for you.*

"Kitling?"

"Sorry, I was talking to Ynpharion."

Teela frowned, a reminder that Kaylin's name bonds were supposed to be a deep, dark secret that she carried with her to the grave. Lack of secrecy simply meant the grave might be a more immediate destination.

"Did he have anything useful to say?"

"Not a lot, and all of it was condescending."

"Ah. He is frustrated with you?"

"Always. But at least he's consistent." She hesitated and then said, "He thinks the Consort wants to talk to me. Or us—he told me I should accompany you when you go to the High Halls."

"I am not taking you to the High Halls dressed like that."

"Like a Hawk?"

"Indeed." Teela contemplated Kaylin's outfit. "You have the assessment with Mrs. Erickson in three days. We'll visit the High Halls in four days. You have suitable clothing, and you had better be wearing it when I drop by to pick you up."

"I'll trade. Tell me about Azoria."

Teela glared at her and walked away.

Kaylin knew—from Mandoran—that the Academia was setting up mirror access to the rest of the city. Mirrors were a part of daily life in Elantra. They were very seldom used in the fiefs of her childhood. But Helen didn't like them, and allowed access only in what she termed a "safe" room. Tara, the Avatar of the Tower of Tiamaris, didn't like them either, and made the same choice Helen made. Had her lord, Tiamaris, not required mirror network access, she wouldn't have allowed them at all.

The former Arkon—Lannagaros—was accustomed to mirror use; Kaylin would have expected mirror functionality to be one of the first things the new chancellor of the Academia instituted.

Apparently, she would have been wrong.

She looked up at the sound of the internal office clock—its cheery, friendly voice giving tired Hawks information they actually wanted: time to go home. She had far too many things on her figurative desk at the moment; her mirror feed now looked like an extremely unartistic collage. It was hard to focus on just one thing; she had the instinctive sense that many of them were somehow connected.

Home was Helen. Kaylin had the privilege of being tenant to one of the very few sentient buildings in Elantra. Helen was an oddity, even among sentient buildings. She didn't have masters, she had tenants. Kaylin would have felt more insecure about this had she not known that most of Helen's tenants had remained her tenants until their deaths. Helen was waiting for Kaylin as she set foot across the property line; she stood in the open door of the front foyer, where she always stood when Kaylin came home. Kaylin had been fond of her old apartment, but not in the same way. Having someone to come home *to* made a big difference.

Today, however, not so much.

"What were you doing at the office today?" she asked. While she generally asked about Kaylin's day at work, there was usually less concern in Helen's tone.

"Research and initial investigations into possible murder cases."

"Ah."

"What's wrong?"

"Teela was shocked or upset enough by the mention of a Barrani individual that she failed to entirely mask her reaction from the rest of the cohort."

"Oh." Kaylin exhaled. "Sedarias?"

"She is concerned, yes."

Great.

06

Kaylin entered the foyer. She wasn't particularly surprised to see Mandoran at the height of the stairs that led, in the end, to the rooms all of Helen's tenants and guests occupied. He was usually the bridge between Sedarias and everyone else.

"If it weren't for Teela's reaction," he said, folding his arms and half sitting on the stair railing, "no one would be concerned. Whoever Azoria was, she isn't the only person to own human domiciles."

"And by *person*, you mean Barrani."

He winced. "Yes, I did. Sorry."

"Never mind. When you say Sedarias is concerned, I take it you don't mean she's sitting in her room fretting."

"Oh, she is. But that's not all she's doing."

Kaylin very much wanted Sedarias to be Teela's problem. Or anyone else's. She and Sedarias didn't have business which overlapped often, and at the moment, Kaylin was grateful for that.

"She wasn't in her room this morning. Two guesses where she went."

"Can I maybe have the rest of this discussion in the dining room? I'm hungry."

"Fine."

The dining room was almost uninhabited; the table was therefore much smaller than it was when the cohort—or those parts that could be bothered—were in full attendance. Mandoran and Terrano had joined Kaylin.

"Teela's on the way," the latter said cheerfully.

Mandoran rolled his eyes.

"Is Teela on the way to speak to me, or Sedarias?"

"Does it matter?"

"Kind of—I have to work with her."

"Both, I think. She's not happy."

"Figures. I want to note for the record that I've done nothing wrong."

"Neither has Sedarias," Mandoran said, his tone more serious than Terrano's. "She visited the Mellarionne rooms in the High Halls, and spoke with a few of her family's supporters."

"This would be after Teela's surprise?"

Mandoran nodded. "Teela didn't wish to discuss Azoria An'Berranin. Sedarias did. She therefore chose to approach those who serve her line with a request for information. Those she tasked with investigation weren't familiar with the name."

"But Teela is."

Mandoran nodded.

Kaylin chewed on both food and thought for a bit. "Which means Azoria is old."

"Very, in my opinion." This was Terrano. "I don't think Sedarias was counting on ignorance. Now she's annoyed."

"Annoyed?"

"She dislikes being ignorant of significant events, and Teela's reaction made clear that some significant event surrounds this

Azoria. Don't worry—if Teela won't talk about it, we will."
He winced. Sedarias clearly didn't agree.

Neither did Teela.

Although Teela wasn't one of Helen's guests, she'd stayed with Helen before, and she was part of the cohort. It would never occur to Helen to keep Teela out. Nor would it occur to her to give much in the way of warning, given the presence of Mandoran and Terrano.

The Barrani Hawk walked into the dining room. Before she took a seat—if she intended to—she said, "Drop all parts of the investigation that have anything to do with Azoria." When Kaylin failed to answer, she amended her previous demand. "Drop the investigation entirely."

Mandoran grimaced. "Not the way to go about asking, Teela."

Teela ignored him, her gaze welded to Kaylin's as Kaylin leaned back into her chair and folded her arms.

"I can't."

"It's a cold case—a *very* cold case, given the age of Records. It's not part of your job. It's not a duty assigned you. You can drop the investigation, and it's in your best interests to do exactly that." Had anyone else spoken the words, they might have been a threat. There was no threat in Teela's voice.

"I can't," Kaylin repeated. "The ghosts are children."

Teela raised a single brow. "Children who are already dead."

Kaylin nodded, as they wouldn't be ghosts otherwise. "They've been trapped in Mrs. Erickson's house since before Mrs. Erickson was born. She saw them when she was a baby, a child, and an adult. She saw them after her husband died and she was left a widow. She's old, and she's the *only* person who could see them, until now."

"Until you."

Kaylin nodded. "I think it's the marks, but it doesn't matter. They can't leave the house, and I'm not moving in there when Mrs. Erickson dies. Jamal—the kid who can physically throw things when he's having a tantrum—hates visitors because he knows Mrs. Erickson isn't going to be around for much longer, and he wants whatever time she has left.

"Part of the reason she visits the Halls of Law is to have stories about her day she can tell the kids. And I think the reason she's afraid of dying is the kids. They're trapped there.

"Look—I have these marks. I've seen a dead person before. I think the marks freed him. I think the *reason* I can see the kids is…I'm meant to free them. And it would bring Mrs. Erickson peace of mind, which she deserves."

"Fine. That has nothing to do with Azoria. Figure out how to free the ghosts. Leave Azoria out of it. Azoria is dead. Her entire line was excised."

Terrano whistled, which did nothing to lighten Teela's mood.

"Dead? You're certain?"

"As certain as I can be, yes."

"How long ago?" Given the ignorance of Sedarias's Barrani agents, it had to be a while. Which, given her name on Imperial property taxation Records, didn't line up.

"Long ago," Teela replied. "Long enough that the second Draco-Barrani war hadn't started yet."

"So—when you were a child."

"Yes."

"How do you even know the name, then?"

"I was a child in the High Halls," Teela replied, her expression a wall.

"But I think Azoria *is* somehow tied into the fate of those children. If not Azoria, then *someone* who somehow made use of whatever it was she was studying. And I think whatever it was was not *good*."

"You are making entirely too many intellectual leaps based on almost no information."

Mandoran said, "How's that different from what she usually does?"

"I wouldn't make the leap at all if it weren't for two facts. One: Azoria owned 14 Orbonne Street. Not fourteen and a half. Two: number fourteen is *missing*, Teela. It doesn't exist. It's not just the renumbered neighbor's house on either side. It did exist; it was in the city tax Records. It doesn't exist *now*. Instead we have fourteen and a half. Which is where Mrs. Erickson lives. And the children who are ghosts who somehow didn't die until fifteen years after they theoretically escaped the damn house."

"They escaped fourteen and a half."

"We don't *know* that. According to Records, fourteen and a half didn't exist when any of the four were executed. I might be able to ignore things if it weren't for the disappearance of a house and its lot. But *if* she was a dangerous Arcanist, and *if* she was doing her research in the human part of town, *then* the children may well have had something to do with the ill effects of that research.

"And I can't do anything until I know whether or not that's the case. I can't determine whether or not that's the case without more information." Kaylin folded her arms. "And I'm not going to give up or look the other way. If I could think of some way to free those children without any research at all, I'd do it."

Teela was utterly silent.

Mandoran said, out loud, "She's the *Chosen*. You all go on about how she doesn't do anything with her marks—"

"I heal."

"—and it seems clear to some of us that this *is* something she's supposed to do with the marks. This is part of being the Chosen." Mandoran grimaced; Teela turned a very dark blue glare on him. He was clearly more comfortable with this than Kaylin would have been. "What? She's here, and she's the one it involves and *someone* won't let me share *my own name* with her so we could avoid the whole talking-out-loud-in-person thing. She's going to keep doing research unless Teela can convince her boss to nix it.

"Even if she can—and I allow for the possibility—she's just going to move the investigation to her personal time. If the Emperor forbids the investigation, she'll be stuck—but I'm not thinking the Emperor is someone any Barrani of note is going to approach. It makes more sense for us to help her figure it out—quickly—so that we can put it all behind us." He turned to Kaylin. "I don't suppose you've got anything else you shouldn't be investigating?"

"Not yet. But some of Mrs. Erickson's ghosts aren't actual ghosts, in my opinion."

Mandoran smacked his own forehead. "Can we forget I asked that question?"

"Kaylin probably can, given a decade. You know the rest of us won't." Teela slowly relaxed, the tension leaving the line of her jaws and shoulders. "You might as well tell them the rest, kitling. Terrano—at the very least—will make a pest of himself otherwise."

"That's unkind, dear," Helen's disembodied voice said.

Teela stayed for dinner. The cohort—those in residence—came down to eat. The table elongating made it clear they would. But the table was silent; the cohorts' shifting facial expressions made clear that arguments were ongoing regardless.

Teela was perhaps the only member of the cohort accustomed to keeping—and maintaining—her own counsel; she could listen and join in, but her thoughts weren't immediately on the table, as it were. She turned to Kaylin as dinner was winding down, interrupting the sparse sounds of chewing.

"What are your plans for tomorrow?"

"I'll be on the front desk, I think. Severn's almost finished whatever it is that's pulled him out of the Hawks' roster."

"And after?"

"I'm heading to the Academia. I have a couple of questions to ask."

"You've received the chancellor's permission?"

"Do I need it?"

Several eyes turned in her direction. "Terrano says no," Teela replied, "if that tells you anything."

It did. "Helen, can you try to reach the Academia by mirror?"

"Serralyn says you can check in at the desk as a visitor," Mandoran told her before Helen could respond. "What? That's exactly what she said."

Kaylin turned back to Teela. "I'm going to the Academia tomorrow. After work."

Sergeant Keele was still suspicious when Kaylin—without complaint—volunteered for the public desk again. Unlike most of the Hawks, Keele kept any possible sentiment out of the office. Far enough out, in fact, that most of the Hawks assumed she didn't have any. She did partake of Mrs. Erickson's offerings, but only when there were obvious leftovers. And she didn't forbid the Hawks under her jurisdiction from interacting with the old woman, or checking up on her if she failed to show up.

But she considered Kaylin's interest to be bordering on the

seriously unprofessional; Kaylin was certain Marcus would hear about it.

"If Corporal Handred were let out of the stupid bureaucratic meetings he's tangled up in, I wouldn't be here," Kaylin told the sergeant, with a more or less straight face.

Less, Severn offered.

Keele had the same love of that tangled bureaucracy that Marcus did, but didn't destroy her desks when frustrated, lacking the very large claws of the Leontine sergeant. "You're getting too attached," she finally said. It wasn't what Kaylin was expecting. "You're an officer of the Halls of Law. Mrs. Erickson is a civilian. She's not family. Your responsibilities to her lie in the enforcement of Imperial Laws. Do not forget that."

Kaylin offered a clipped nod—necessary because she was standing stiffly at what was called attention.

She thought better of her choice after the first four hours of the long morning. Three reports of vampiric activity—in different parts of the city—hit the desk, along with reports of hauntings and in one case, ghostly Dragons. One report of talking buildings—but not the type of talking that Kaylin was familiar with, as the building in question wasn't so much talking as shrieking.

There were reports of missing people, and those, Kaylin passed—gratefully—to Missing Persons. Most of those reports sorted themselves out without legal intervention; some didn't. Kaylin was mulling over one of them when Mrs. Erickson arrived at the front desk.

Her face was swollen, and the darker skin implied that the bruise that was coming up would be large. She was, however, carrying her basket.

"Sit down, dear," she said. "I'm fine. I tripped while coming down the stairs—I hope the contents of the basket aren't too damaged."

All of the blood rushed out of Kaylin's body; she was frozen for one long moment. She had no idea what her expression looked like to the outside world, but it clearly looked bad, because Mrs. Erickson moved quickly, setting her basket down on the front desk, and reaching for Kaylin's hands. Which were balled in fists.

Blood rushed back in at the contact, and with it, fury.

"You fell down the stairs." This was not the first time Kaylin had heard this sentence. It wasn't the first time she'd assumed it was a lie, either.

"Corporal."

Kaylin froze, years of training coming to the rescue as Sergeant Keele entered the space behind the front desk and the actual office she ran. Mrs. Erickson immediately withdrew her hands.

"Sergeant," she said, her voice containing a smile that Kaylin couldn't otherwise see.

Sergeant Keele nodded. "Imelda."

"You don't come out of the office much anymore."

"I'm a sergeant now. Babysitting the Hawks is more than a full-time job." The tone of Sergeant Keele's voice pulled Kaylin the rest of the way out of blank, all-encompassing rage; the expression on her face did the rest.

She was actually smiling. Like a human being. At another person.

"They are so lucky to have you," Mrs. Erickson said, beaming.

"I'm sure Corporal Neya has opinions about that. As do most of my roster."

"I've never heard them speak disrespectfully," Mrs. Erickson began.

"I hope you've never heard them speak about me at all."

Mrs. Erickson smiled. "Well, now I can't embarrass you

by telling you about the positive things they've said. You've come a long way since we first met."

"Since things are slow, what did you bring us today?"

Mrs. Erickson's smile deepened; she lifted the lid of her basket. "Small cakes," she said. "I thought the corporal might be tired of cookies."

"You expected her at the desk?"

"Yes, dear—I know her partner has been on active solo duty."

Sergeant Keele nodded, and accepted the small cake she was offered. "She told you that, did she?"

"Oh, no—it was my friends. The outside ghosts. The corporal isn't allowed to discuss her partner's work."

The sergeant's expression barely flickered—but if it was true that Keele had served on this desk when she was a lowly private, she expected to hear about Mrs. Erickson's ghostly friends. No one who worked the desk expected her to talk about anything else—it was the theoretical reason she visited, after all.

Kaylin decided then and there to go through the reports generated by Mrs. Erickson's other visits.

"You didn't report that," Sergeant Keele said. This caused a different kind of shock: it meant Keele was actually *reading* the reports Mrs. Erickson generated.

"Well, no. I know we're not supposed to discuss those things. My friends do because they can't really interact with other people and they want *something* to talk about. But I almost never share."

"Almost?"

"Well, I'm speaking with you right now—and with the corporal."

"The corporal and I will speak about this after she's escorted you home today."

"I hope she isn't in trouble." Mrs. Erickson looked, with worry, in Kaylin's direction.

"Most of my job is this kind of trouble," Kaylin said, smiling. "Why don't you take a seat. Tell me what you came to report—you have to have something to tell Jamal."

07

As it happened, Sergeant Keele asked to speak to Kaylin privately before she could escort Mrs. Erickson home. Mrs. Erickson looked worried.

"I won't bust her down a rank, and she won't lose her job," Keele told the old woman. "But I do want her to check your stairs. Your house is old. If the stairs need some carpentry work, she can help arrange that."

Silence.

The stairs were in perfectly good condition, as both Keele and Kaylin knew. So, apparently, did Mrs. Erickson.

"I'm just getting on in years, Bridget."

"As am I," the sergeant replied. "Corporal?"

Kaylin followed the sergeant into the interior office, but turned to offer Mrs. Erickson what she hoped was an encouraging smile. She said nothing because sergeants had ears and eyes in the backs of their heads.

Keele closed the door once Kaylin had walked through it.

"What did I tell you about sentiment?"

"Sentiment bad, sir."

The sergeant's eyes narrowed. Her eyes remained a steady brown because she was human.

"Is Mrs. Erickson having difficulty? Is that why you escorted her home yesterday?"

"No, sir."

"Speak freely. I don't have time to play twenty questions."

"I don't think Mrs. Erickson's ghosts are imaginary, sir. I offered to escort her home because I wanted to confirm the suspicion. I didn't expect to actually see the ghosts."

Keele froze. "You saw her ghosts."

"Yes, sir."

"The front desk is crazy enough we don't need any more of it. You're sloppy but I know you don't drink on duty."

"Too many Barrani in my department for that."

Keele snorted. "Her fall down the stairs?"

"Her neighbor to the left is hostile."

"We can't send her home with an escort every day."

Kaylin cleared her throat. "We can't ask her to stop coming in. Even if she could avoid the neighbor by remaining mostly at home, she still needs to leave to get water and food. She comes here daily because the ghosts in her house are trapped there—they can't leave."

"You're certain you saw these ghosts?"

"Yes, sir. Four. All children between the ages of eight and twelve at best guess. Only one of them was in missing persons Records."

"Which one?"

"Esmeralda Noachin. Mrs. Erickson comes here with her vague reports because it gives her something to talk to the children about. She considers them her responsibility. To be fair to her, one of those ghosts is what keeps the neighbor out of the house. I believe he crossed the threshold once, and never again."

"Where is this going, Corporal?"

"I don't know, sir. But…I like her. She sure beats the vampire reports I've been logging."

"You should look into those."

"Vampires, sir?"

"You can see ghosts," Sergeant Keele replied.

"True, but it's not Mrs. Erickson making the vampire reports."

"I have some Records searching to do myself."

"Mrs. Erickson's?"

"Related," was the terse reply. "You know the sentiment I told you has no place in the Halls of Law?"

"Yes, sir."

"There's a reason I gave you that advice. Mrs. Erickson has been coming to the Halls of Law for as long as I've been part of them. Green-behind-the-ears private, and she was old to my eyes, even then. We all thought she was dotty, but never dangerous; she's almost part of the department by this point. She remembers names, remembers details—she takes an interest in a person, and it's genuine. She was unfailingly encouraging, and she knew how to listen. Also: baking." The almost gentle expression drained from the sergeant's face. "I want information about the neighbor."

Kaylin nodded. "If the neighbor comes out again?"

"I ask only that you escort her home in civvies."

How long should I remain off the schedule?

Kaylin jumped at the sound of Severn's interior voice. *What do you mean?*

You're pursuing information about Mrs. Erickson now. You're worried about her. But you won't be at the front desk if I'm on the active roster.

Wait, you're finished?

No. But I could be.

Can I answer that after I see if the neighbor is lurking on the lawn? He has to wait for her—he's too cowardly to try to enter her home.

The sergeant is right—we can't escort her home every night.

I can, if she waits. I was off duty the last time; I'll be off duty this time as well.

Severn said nothing.

I'm heading to the Academia after I see her safely home.

Amaldi and Darreno were nowhere in sight in the streets that led to 14 1/2 Orbonne Street. Although Kaylin offered to carry her basket, Mrs. Erickson didn't stop to shop this time. She had other things on her mind.

"I'm worried about Jamal," she said.

"What did he do?"

"He was upset this morning. I'm almost afraid to see what he's broken."

Kaylin had a word or two to say to Jamal. She could guess what had tipped him over into rage, and if her guess was right, she *strongly* sympathized. But breaking Mrs. Erickson's things as a response to that rage? No.

"It's very frustrating for him. Please understand that."

"Oh, I assure you, I do." The house came into view. Hope squawked, quietly this time, in her ear. She nodded, and he sat up, lifting a wing to place it gently across only one of her eyes.

She could see Mrs. Erickson's house—and the steps that were old but in obviously decent repair—through both eyes. She could see the next-door neighbor's door open through both eyes. Not even the presence of the neighbor, however, could distract her from the building she could see only through Hope's wing. It wasn't Mrs. Erickson's house. It wasn't the neighbor's house, either—both of those were present in the exact same locations they'd been in the day before.

A wider, taller building rose above the two more mundane buildings she could see without Hope's help. Its height suggested a tower, or towers, had been part of its construction, but it quivered in the vision, like the rare mirages that occurred during horrible heat weaves in the city; it wasn't solid. Kaylin knew there were vestigial traces of its existence in Records. She'd have to dig. She was almost certain that anyone living close to a building of this size would remember it—it wasn't anywhere near the usual architecture found in the neighborhood.

If, in fact, the Records information still existed.

It does, Severn said.

You were looking?

I thought it best to protect those that could be quietly preserved, yes.

You think the Barrani might interfere with it?

It's happened in the Hawks before.

"Fourteen Orbonne," she said as she looked up.

"What, dear?" Mrs. Erickson said, turning toward Kaylin, her brows folding into far less familiar lines. "Fourteen?"

"I see you're back again, *Officer.*" The neighbor's booming voice interrupted whatever Mrs. Erickson might have said. Kaylin wouldn't have heard it anyway. She turned toward the neighbor, who was grinning in that extremely fake, jovial way.

Kaylin's lips turned up at the corners. "I am. I see you're still minding everyone else's business."

The smile on the man's face stiffened, but didn't fall off. "Old lady's my neighbor. We're neighborly—we look out for each other."

Kaylin stepped between the neighbor and Mrs. Erickson. "What's your name, neighbor?"

"Why do you need to know?"

Kaylin shrugged. "It's not an official question—yet. I'm here as a friend. Of Mrs. Erickson's. Name's Kaylin Neya."

"I didn't ask your name."

"No, you didn't. Some people have no manners, but I'm a Hawk—I'm used to bad manners. I'm also used to criminal behavior and assault. Bad manners are free. Assault, not so much."

"What are you talking about? Did the old lady say I assaulted her?" The smile, which was repulsive, went away. What was left was anger. Kaylin could see the man's hands curl into fists. "She tripped. I even helped her up."

Kaylin said nothing. She did, however, meet—and hold—his gaze. "Mrs. Erickson, why don't you head inside. I'll join you in a minute." Her tone was calmer than the neighbor's, although she was certain she was at least as enraged. She'd learned a few things in her years with the Hawks.

Mrs. Erickson hesitated.

"Don't go anywhere," the neighbor snapped. "I'll want a witness."

"To what? You getting the crap beaten out of you by a girl half your size?" Kaylin glanced at his girth. "A third your size?"

His fists tightened.

Kaylin's didn't. She knew he had the advantage of reach, size, and muscles, but her training had always taken that into account. What she most hated about him in the moment was his hesitation. She wasn't afraid. She couldn't mimic fear.

And he didn't want to touch someone fearless. Maybe if she turned her back on him, he'd attack then. But facing her? No. Mrs. Erickson, Kaylin noted, stayed rooted to the spot until the moment something flew out the window. Clearly, Jamal was watching.

The neighbor lowered the fists he'd involuntarily raised. This time, there was fear in his expression. "We'll sort this later," he told Kaylin, under his breath.

"I'm sure we will."

★ ★ ★

Day two of needing to punch the neighbor in the face and failing to find the right opportunity left Kaylin with more adrenaline than ideal. She did turn her back on the neighbor, on the off chance he'd try to push her or trip her, but Jamal—she assumed it was Jamal—had killed the mood entirely.

He'd also broken a mug, by the look of the ceramic shards at the foot of the stairs. Kaylin stopped to pick up the larger pieces, and then went into the house to find a broom.

"You don't have to do that," Mrs. Erickson began.

"I'll let you talk to Jamal first. I'll clean up the shards while you do."

"You shouldn't antagonize him."

Kaylin smiled; she knew *him* referred to the neighbor. "I should be more adept at it, yes. He's clearly a coward, and I wasn't acting intimidated or terrified enough."

"She's right," Jamal said, coming into view. He was, no surprise, ferocious in his youthful rage.

"That doesn't mean," Kaylin then said, "that you throwing things out the window is helping anything."

"He ran away," was the sullen reply.

"Before I could hit him *back*, yes."

"Why don't you just hit him first?"

"I'm an officer of the law," she replied. "Hitting him first is assault. Hitting him back isn't."

"You're mad."

"I am. Did you see what happened to Mrs. Erickson this morning?"

Jamal shook his head, grim now. "Esmeralda says he slapped her. He's afraid of us."

"Maybe we should invite him in."

"Corporal," Mrs. Erickson said, the word an admonition.

Kaylin tried to remember she was talking to a child, and

grudgingly relented. "What exactly is his problem? Was he always like this?"

"Not until he lost his wife. He started to drink."

"Was that recent?"

Mrs. Erickson said *yes*. Jamal said *no*. The latter was far, far angrier than Kaylin, and Kaylin was pretty angry. She took a breath and fell back on the training that had allowed her, in the end, to be a Hawk. "When did he start to harass you?"

Mrs. Erickson was silent.

Jamal was not. "Two years ago, give or take a few months. We're not great at keeping track of living time. He hammered on the door and forced himself into the house—not that she was trying to keep him out."

"What did he do?"

"He wanted to look for something. He accused her of stealing it. From him."

"Did he say what it was?"

"No. Mrs. Erickson doesn't *steal*. She's probably never been anywhere near his house!"

It was Esmeralda who continued when Jamal's words tailed off into sputtering curses. Kaylin hadn't seen her arrive. "He had a peculiar look, as my nana used to say. We thought he'd been drinking, but it's harder to tell—we can't really *smell* anything, either. But he pushed her out of the way and forced himself in.

"I think he would have hurt her if he couldn't find what he was looking for."

A third child joined the other two. "He was never going to find it." Callis was quieter and less obviously certain than either Jamal or Esmeralda. "But he was going to destroy a lot of things while searching." His voice implied that this was the best case, and Kaylin understood this.

He'd probably demand that Mrs. Erickson produce a thing she couldn't produce, and if she failed...

"Jamal hurt him. Jamal started to throw things at his head—he's a pretty good aim. He got scared, and he ran out of the house screaming about ghosts." Esmeralda smiled. Had Kaylin seen that smile at any other time, she would have assumed it was friendly, if mischievous.

Given what she now knew of how each of the four children—or their bodies—had died, she felt a bit of a chill. It took the edge off her anger. She turned—more calmly—to Mrs. Erickson, unwilling to hear any more about children trying to murder an abusive wreck of a neighbor. "Has he been demanding that you give him whatever it is he thinks was stolen?"

Mrs. Erickson nodded.

"Did he happen to say *what* it was he was missing?"

"No. He seems to believe I know. I've asked," she added, her voice soft. "I thought maybe I could scrape together enough money to buy a replacement. But asking just angered him; it didn't give me any answers. I haven't—"

"We know. You didn't steal anything from him. Have you ever been in his house?"

"A decade ago—maybe a bit less—when his wife was still alive. She was a lovely young woman."

"She never came here," Jamal added. He was obviously skeptical about Mrs. Erickson's claim.

"Did you see her?"

"She'd come to the door when she was ready to have guests, and she'd escort Mrs. Erickson to her home—but no. She didn't come in."

"Did you invite her?"

Mrs. Erickson nodded. "We went to her home. I think she wanted her husband to get used to me."

Kaylin couldn't criticize Mrs. Erickson because she seldom had guests in her house. On the rare occasions she did, Helen took over, and Kaylin was happy to let her. But given various idle conversations in the Halls of Law, it seemed a bit strange.

"When did his wife die?"

"Three years ago in two weeks. I attended her funeral. She was a lovely young woman, but there were very few attendees. I felt terrible for her husband."

She probably still did. Kaylin exhaled slowly. To Jamal, she said, "I'll be walking Mrs. Erickson home for the next little while. If the neighbor shows up, do *not* interfere again."

"He went away."

"Yes. And as I said earlier, he went away before we could... resolve the issue."

"Before you could hit him, you mean." Esmeralda was clearly not shy about making corrections.

"What is the neighbor's name?" When no one immediately volunteered the information, Kaylin frowned. "I can look it up in Records back at work."

Jamal offered a choice word or two as if it were a name.

"I doubt that's what his legal name is."

"Brennan Oswald," Mrs. Erickson said. "His wife was Alisa, but I think that was a nickname."

"Her full name?"

"Annalisa Oswald."

Kaylin nodded briskly. "I'll leave you with the kids."

Esmeralda looked mutinous at the word. "We're older than either of you," she snapped.

"Fine. I'll leave you with the octogenarians."

Kaylin exited Mrs. Erickson's house, glaring at the neighbor's much larger abode as she made her way down the stairs. She did stop to check the condition of the stairs, although it was a waste of time; there was nothing wrong with them.

They were old, they'd worn slightly in the middle, but without inspecting closely, they looked in decent repair.

She then rose, grinding her teeth. She disliked people who assumed they could physically intimidate her. She hated people who picked on little old ladies. She might have been able to clear up both problems had the neighbor led with his fist.

She exhaled. Poked Hope. Hope lifted a wing to her face, and this time she saw a ghostly building rising between the Erickson residence and the Oswald residence, although it overlapped Mrs. Erickson's home. The passage of time had robbed that building of solidity; Kaylin thought if she attempted to view it again at a later hour, she would see nothing there at all.

All of this was worrying. She made a mental list of questions that she wanted answered, paring it down to essentials; other questions would no doubt arise when the few on the list had been answered.

But to get answers, she needed to do her research on foot. She therefore headed to the Academia.

Severn met her on the way; he, too, had left the Hawk's tabard behind. He wore his weapon chain, and he no doubt carried at least a decent dagger or long knife, although it wasn't immediately visible. Both indicated his level of comfort.

"Are you done with whatever it is you've been doing?"

"Not entirely, no."

"Good. I need you to be busy for the next few days."

"How few?"

"Maybe a week? I've been part of Sergeant Keele's desk for the past couple of days, and I need to continue for a bit. I'm worried about Mrs. Erickson."

"Teela said you arranged to have her tested for magical aptitude."

"I did. We talk to Sanabalis tomorrow."

"You're taking her?"

"It's the palace. I think she'd be more comfortable if we went together."

"Does she know about this?"

"Sort of." Kaylin shrugged. "She was tested when she was young; she was judged a waste of time. I want Sanabalis to assess, and *if* she does have magical potential, I want him to turn the jerk who dismissed her to a pile of ash."

"He's probably dead, given Mrs. Erickson's age." Severn offered a half smile and a shake of the head. "Lose the rage," he advised her as Kaylin marched toward the bridge across the Ablayne.

"I am. I'm walking it off."

The Academia was unusual in a number of ways. First and foremost—at least from this remove—was its geography. It was almost impossible to add the Academia to a regular map because it overlapped every fief, while being part of none of them. Anyone could, if they knew the road, reach the Academia— from any fief. Choose the wrong street, and the Academia was practically invisible.

Kaylin chose to enter the fiefs through Tiamaris. She trusted the Dragon fieflord. Or perhaps she trusted his Tower. Tara was a friend, and Tara had made choices to make Kaylin's visits more comfortable—for Kaylin. Tiamaris accepted this; the cohort felt it was beyond stupid. There were no portals to bar entry to the Avatar's heart for those who had not been invited, because Kaylin's magic allergy rendered portal use a nauseating agony.

The Tower watched its borders; it was sensitive to intrusion.

This didn't mean that the Tower always reacted to Kaylin's entry; sometimes she was busy gardening. Given the emptiness of the streets across the bridge, this was probably one of those days. Kaylin didn't need a guide to find the street that led to the Academia, and she was, as Severn guessed, still angry. No one approached her.

She started to work to lose anger as she headed down the winding street. The buildings on either side of the road became larger and in much better repair. She was certain some of those buildings were now occupied by the fieflings who, as Kaylin herself once had, found themselves homeless. Homelessness was not something that was safe in the streets of the fief.

It probably wasn't safe in Elantra either, but it wasn't an immediate death sentence there. Tax laws and the ownership of property were built into Imperial Law, which didn't exist in the fiefs. Kaylin wondered, briefly, if these new buildings had landlords, if the Academia owned them, or if squatters had moved in, hoping they wouldn't be noticed and evicted. She wondered how long it would take for petty criminals to become those squatters, becoming in the process de facto landlords to people who had no recourse.

People like Kaylin and Severn in the streets of Nightshade in their childhood. She was certain that children very like them still existed, struggling to find shelter, food, and a safe place to avoid Ferals.

In that bleak mood, Kaylin lengthened her stride; Severn had no trouble keeping pace with her. He was accustomed to the small burst of speed she gained whenever something annoyed her, and if he wasn't annoyed himself, he knew her well enough to accept it.

The streets passed by, and turned at last into what she

thought of as the main campus of the Academia itself: multiple large buildings, arrayed around a circular road which encompassed a green park. Students between classes occupied that park, lying out on the grass beneath the clear sky, some alone and some in small—and louder—groups.

Kaylin wasn't terribly surprised to see Serralyn. She was alone, and she rose the instant Kaylin came into view, making a beeline toward the two Hawks.

"Yes," she said, before Kaylin could ask. "Sedarias wanted me to keep an eye on you."

"How closely?"

"I have a class in two hours. If you take longer than two hours, you may have Valliant—but Terrano might show up instead. Technically, he's not supposed to, but the chancellor mostly ignores him. Killian the Academia's Avatar—likes Terrano, but Killian sometimes gives him the boot if Terrano's in his experimental *how does this work* mode."

"Why doesn't he apply as a student?"

"It's Terrano. He gets hives—is that the right phrase?—being confined to someone else's schedule. Among other things." She cringed. "He got into a really long argument with one of the newer teachers here; I thought they were going to burn down the class just to shut him up."

"A class you're in?"

Serralyn nodded. "Mostly he just listens in through either Valliant or me—but if he hears something he thinks is ridiculously stupid, he just...ports in."

"I'm amazed Killian lets him do it."

"Killian's really quiet, but he has opinions. And...it's hard to keep Terrano out."

Kaylin felt a pang of sympathy for Killian.

"So where are you heading first?"

"The chancellor's office," Kaylin replied. "Oh, no, wait— I'm supposed to sign in, I think?"

Serralyn nodded, and turned toward a familiar building— the first building Kaylin had actually entered when the Academia had not been fully awake. "Do you know if Larrantin is teaching now?"

"He is." Serralyn placed a palm against the door of the administrative building. "Valliant's in that class." The door opened inward as Kaylin grimaced. Door wards. Ugh. "You wanted to speak with him?"

"If he doesn't have another class immediately after—and if the Arkon doesn't turn me to ash—yes."

"You really have to stop calling him that."

"Right. I'm trying."

"Sedarias says: *very* trying. Teela agrees." Serralyn's eyes were green.

"Is anyone on my side?"

"Terrano. And Mandoran says at least you're not boring."

There were three people at the long desk Kaylin thought looked very much like a bar—but without the bottles, glasses or stools. "Serralyn," one woman said; to Kaylin's surprise she was a gray-haired human.

"Matilda, this is Corporal Kaylin Neya—she's an Imperial Hawk. Her partner, Corporal Severn Handred."

"We're not yet under the auspices of Imperial Law," the woman said, voice brisk. "But the chancellor has had several meetings with the Emperor. You're welcome here, but you won't have the authority of the law behind you."

"It would be pointless—the boss of the Academia is a Dragon."

Matilda smiled, exposing a dimple on the left side of her

face. "That he is. You can sign here. We don't have mirror check-in or Records in the Academia—more's the pity."

"You probably won't get them," Kaylin replied, picking up the quill she was offered. "Most sentient buildings consider their use a dangerous security risk."

"Those that don't have to do this kind of work can feel that way—it'd make *our* job a lot easier. I think the chancellor might be expecting you, though."

"Oh?"

"I've got a note here that says you're to come to his office before you visit anyone else. It's his handwriting—he's got very distinctive handwriting."

"Oh."

"I haven't *done anything yet*," Kaylin told Serralyn as they walked toward the building that housed the chancellor and almost all of the classrooms. And the dining hall, which Kaylin privately considered far more important.

Serralyn glanced at Severn, who nodded.

"The chancellor doesn't usually send notes like that."

"Might've heard from Sanabalis."

"So you *have* been doing something. Teela's worried about Azoria. Or that's what I think."

"I haven't been doing anything but desk work and visiting one little old lady's house because her neighbor is harassing her."

Serralyn clearly didn't believe this, but held her peace. It had never been her job in the cohort to bring up difficult subjects or demand answers. She accompanied Kaylin to the chancellor's door. "It's not warded," she told Kaylin, who then knocked.

The door rolled open. If it wasn't warded, magic was nonetheless in use; Kaylin could feel her skin start to tingle.

"Of course," a familiar—and disembodied—voice said. "I believe I would be considered almost entirely magical in nature." Killian had arrived. "I've been with you since the administrative building," he corrected her, still failing to physically appear. "Hello, Hope."

Hope squawked. The squawking, while quieter than usual, was also longer. Suspiciously so.

"Are you waiting for an escort?" A low, rumbling voice came from the inside of the room.

"We have to go," Kaylin told the invisible Killian.

The former Arkon occupied his desk as if it were very oddly shaped personal armor, his eyes a steady orange—not a terrible sign, but not a good one, either.

"How did you know I was coming?"

"Things have been too peaceful in the last fortnight," was his deadpan response.

"Sanabalis?"

"*The Arkon*, and no. Why are you here?"

"I wanted to speak with the librarians, and I wanted to speak with Larrantin."

"About what, Corporal?"

"Well, I think I've met a couple of people—humans—who seem out of phase, the way the students in the sleeping Academia were. They can't be seen by anyone except one little old lady, and me if I'm wearing Hope's wing as a mask."

"And you weren't drinking at the time."

Kaylin rolled her eyes. "No. I mostly don't drink unless Teela and Tain go out tavern hopping and drag me with them."

"Where did you meet these people?"

"Near the well closest to Cross."

"And you spoke with them?"

Kaylin nodded.

"Which means they could see you."

"They could. I could understand them. I thought of the Academia, because it was locked down for so long, but…people like Larrantin sort of existed, as did Killian. Everything was here, but…not quite real. Larrantin knew a bit about it; Killian knew about it. I'm sure it's not the same thing, but there could be some information that could be relevant to the two people I met."

"How so?"

"Well." She hesitated. "I think they might have been stuck wherever it is they are before the first Draco-Barrani war."

Heavy brows rose; the chancellor's eyes paled into a silver or an orange-white. Kaylin hadn't seen that color before. "What makes you say that?"

"Killian—and the students trapped here—didn't age. They were separated from the passage of time and from what we call reality in almost all ways. I think the same has happened to these two, because—" she inhaled "—they recognized the High Halls. As they are now.

"They hadn't seen the High Halls as they existed for all of my life prior to that. I think they were put into this place as a way to preserve their lives; they seem very familiar with Barrani things, and it's highly likely they were slaves."

"And you wish, no doubt, to free them."

Kaylin nodded. "They've gotten used to being invisible, and they sleep—but not the way the rest of us do."

"Those who need sleep," Serralyn added.

"But I think they've been trapped there for a long time, and yes, I'd like to figure out how and why, because if we know that, we might be able to open their cage door."

Killian cleared his throat.

"Please," the chancellor said, voice edged in very familiar sarcasm. "*Do* join us."

Killian immediately materialized. "I believe that what was done to your humans was not what was done to the Academia. Our survival was linked to the Towers. In some fashion, the entirety of the Academia resided in the small corridors of the outlands in which those Towers are partially rooted.

"The survival of the students was linked to the Academia; they were caught in the time frame of the Academia itself. But the Academia, and the strength of it, resides in those students. You think I am a sentient building, like unto your Helen."

Kaylin nodded.

"It is more complex than that. I am not a Tower, but the chancellor is the captain of whatever it is I am. His power in your world and my power in mine is dependent on the interest, on the frisson of intellectual possibility, the students bring. I believe our students were preserved because they were, in some basic way, part of me.

"That will not be the case with your displaced or out-of-phase humans. There is a risk."

"What do you mean?"

"If you attempt to break the enchantment that imprisons them, you may open the door to death—for them. There is no guarantee that the time that has been suspended will remain in abeyance. That is not, to my mind, a great concern.

"But in doing so, with no understanding of the actual spell, you may also open the door to things that were not meant to exist in your world at all."

08

Kaylin had always had difficulty seeing different worlds as separate. If she could see something with her own eyes, it was part of reality. The fact that others couldn't—or the fact that she couldn't without Hope's intervention—didn't change that reaction.

She attempted to disentangle it now.

"It is less difficult for those of us who were removed from what you consider reality," Killian said, a smidgen of sympathy in the observation.

"I'm just trying to get a sense of what *not meant to exist in my world* actually means. It's clearly not a matter of judgment or there wouldn't be Ferals. The Shadows that come from *Ravellon* are clearly part of my world—the entirety of the fiefs were created to cage them. The Academia clearly exists in my world—but it can't be properly mapped as part of the fiefs because it somehow exists beside or on top of... every other fief.

"Releasing the Academia—allowing people like me to reach it—didn't release anything so dangerous it would be best if it remained trapped the way it was." She folded her arms.

The former Arkon rolled his eyes.

"I mean it," Kaylin said. "I need some clear sense of exactly what the danger is."

"You recall the Devourer?"

She stiffened.

"He entered this world, consuming everything on his path between this world and the worlds he destroyed utterly."

"But nothing *we* did called him here. Nothing we did would have changed his path."

"That is not true," Killian said.

Severn wasn't entirely happy, although none of the unhappiness showed in either his posture or his expression. She wondered, then, if she would have noticed it without the unusual name bond that mortals didn't, in theory, have the ability to share.

"It is."

"No, it isn't. You chose not to make the attempt because you were concerned about the fate of the Norranir; if the Norranir were to remain homeless and isolated, it is likely the Devourer would have remained safely outside of our borders. And yes, Severn is concerned; this is not a topic that has come up, and the stray thoughts that you constantly—*constantly*—have, should not, in his opinion, have touched upon the subject. But as you ask for a possible risk, I feel compelled to speak of that one."

"But it worked out." Her arms tightened.

"Yes. And it has caused some permanent harm to your relationship with the Barrani Consort." Killian didn't need to sigh, although his expression would have otherwise accompanied one. "Let me examine something that is closer to your literal home."

"Go ahead."

Killian turned to Serralyn. "You were trapped in the Hallionne Alsanis for centuries."

Serralyn's eyes were now the regular Barrani blue. She nodded.

"Tell me, what might you have done had someone thought to immediately unlock the Hallionne's doors?"

Serralyn shrugged.

"Would you have perhaps visited your home and the family that sent you to the green to be influenced by the ceremonial *regalia* hoping for power for their line? Would you have let it be known that being thrown away had consequences?"

"That's enough—" Kaylin said, stepping toward Killian.

The chancellor growled; she froze in place.

"Oh, probably," a new—and familiar—voice said. Terrano was, if not visible, in the chancellor's office. "We weren't a threat to the stability of the *world*, just Barrani high society. And they deserve the enmity."

"Sedarias *wanted* to go to the green," Kaylin pointed out.

Terrano slowly became visible. Given his expression, it wasn't entirely his choice. "Mellarionne was so messed up, it wouldn't have mattered if she'd gone home to make her opinion known. Most of the line would have probably been delighted."

Killian ignored this. "Alsanis contained the children until they could control their impulses and their power. Or most of their impulses," Killian said.

"She opened the door for us," Terrano replied, although in theory Killian was speaking to Kaylin.

"Yeah, and some days it doesn't seem like it was a great idea."

Terrano rolled his eyes. "He's trying to point out the dangers that exist."

"You can't argue that you weren't of this world, though."

"Actually," Killian said, eyeing Terrano, "I believe I could make that argument, academically speaking. I will refrain from doing so. You did what you did because you value An'Teela so highly, and you had come to understand both her grief and her self-loathing. I will not argue that you did the wrong thing.

"But spaces such as the spaces in which the Academia were confined are not subject to the same rules that govern your existence."

"But the Academia is free now."

Killian nodded. "From a purely selfish perspective, I am grateful for your efforts; I am certain the chancellor shares my sentiment."

"The chancellor," the chancellor said, in full Draconic rumble, "is wondering how much safer things would have been if the corporal had somehow remained in the outlands—an exchange, of sorts."

Terrano grinned.

Kaylin didn't. To her surprise, neither did Serralyn. She glared at Terrano instead.

"What? I didn't say it." He grimaced; clearly other members of the cohort had opinions, and were sharing. "Fine. There's one thing here that catches my attention."

"And that?"

"You said the two phased mortals recognized the High Halls as they are today."

Kaylin nodded.

"And they didn't see any marked difference between the now and the very long centuries of then."

She nodded again, this time more slowly.

"Don't you think it odd that they're here now, when the High Halls are finally what they once were?"

★ ★ ★

The silence that greeted the question was full of thought, or at least Kaylin's part of it.

Everyone's thoughts, Severn then said. *This didn't occur to you?*

I was kind of thinking about what it might be like to be trapped for centuries in noncorporeal form, she snapped back, pride pricked.

"You believe their entrapment was somehow rooted in the High Halls itself? Or the sentience that once governed it?" The chancellor directed the question at Severn, with far less rumble and annoyance than most of the questions he threw at Kaylin.

"I have no beliefs, at the moment; too little is known."

"Can you introduce me to them?" Terrano asked of Kaylin.

"I'm not sure you'll be able to see them."

He once again employed the rolling of eyes. "If I can't, I can't. But I'm pretty good at detecting boundaries—I have to be if I'm going to find cracks."

This wasn't why Kaylin had come to the Academia, but... it made sense. She was hesitant only because Terrano could be so unpredictable.

"He is reckless with his own safety," Killian agreed.

"He doesn't really pay attention to anyone else's, either." This was Serralyn.

Terrano was probably going to sprain his eyeballs, given the amount of rolling they were now doing.

"Is this something you could do?" Kaylin turned to Killian, brows slightly furrowed.

"As I have not met your phased people, I cannot answer the question. I would think Helen would encounter the same difficulty, but she is more accustomed to the way you think."

"You can hear everything I'm thinking."

"True; your thoughts tend to be very loud. But I do not hear them unless you come to visit, and my exposure is not the equal of hers. I can imagine situations in which I might achieve what was done to your friends—but I cannot imagine, having done that, that they would somehow be freely roaming the streets of your city; what I could achieve would be confined to the Academia itself.

"I believe your Helen would have the same difficulty. We have almost total control of what occurs within our physical boundaries—but those are transcribed with words. The High Halls as they once were was a sentient building; it, too, had control over only its immediate environment.

"You wished to speak to Larrantin, and to the librarians." Kaylin nodded.

"Chancellor, with your permission?"

"Larrantin is teaching now. Perhaps visit the library first." He looked down at his desk. "Dismissed."

The library was both part of, and separate from, the rest of the Academia. Killian had no control over what occurred within the library's confines. He could forbid students from attempting to enter, as the door was on Academia property. She often wondered if the librarians were happy to surrender that responsibility to someone outside of their purview.

"Not always, no," Killian replied. "But they were also once professors, and they know what students can be like. They accept that, inasmuch as it is possible, I will keep the library safe from external enmity." He looked up at nothing Kaylin could see. "There appears to already be a visitor."

"It's a library," Kaylin said, shrugging.

"It is, indeed. But it differs greatly from the Imperial Library. Ah, forgive me. By *visitor*, I mean they are not part of the Academia."

"Did they have to sign in?"

"Of course. In theory, they don't require the chancellor's permission to visit the library, merely to reach it."

"I can," Terrano said.

Killian sighed.

Serralyn swatted her cohort member across the back of his head. Her eyes, however, were green. She desperately wanted to visit the library, and she hoped her presence here would be overlooked—she could enter as part of Kaylin's party. Kaylin intended to speak up for her if Killian attempted to divert her and send her back to classes.

To Kaylin's surprise, Killian's lips curved up in a slight smile as he glanced at Serralyn. Killian had led them to a wall, a smooth stone face that was curved into the shape of an otherwise empty alcove. "Please wait here," the Avatar said, the smile fading. "There may be some difficulty among the newer students." He vanished, the last syllable echoing against stone.

The library doors appeared perhaps five minutes later, laid against the shape of this wall; they were curved, as was the frame. It looked wrong, but Kaylin had given up expecting things to conform to her concept of correct. The doors opened inward, the curve of the wood flattening.

Standing in the doorway was a familiar giant spider. Kaylin had almost gotten used to Starrante's nightmare-inducing appearance. He opened his mouth and emitted a series of clicks, stopped, and tried again, those oddly clicking sounds now wrapped around Barrani.

"Please, enter, Corporal Neya. We are pleased to see you again, Corporal Handred." Arbiter Starrante then paused. "I see you brought trouble with you."

Kaylin nodded. "We call him Terrano, if that helps."

"And the student standing beside him?"

"She lived with me and Helen until she became a student

here. I'd really appreciate it if you'd allow her to attend as an aide."

"Killian agreed?" Starrante sounded dubious.

"He didn't disagree."

"Very well. As you cannot keep Terrano out even without a door, I shall not place responsibility for his actions or their consequences on your shoulders." Which heavily implied that she was responsible for Serralyn's. That didn't worry her.

"I heard you had a visitor?"

"Have," he replied. "Bakkon is visiting." Starrante paused for a long beat. "I am truly grateful for your intervention on his behalf. It gives me hope. He feels indebted to you, and I am willing to carry some part of that debt."

"How does he find living in Liatt's Tower?"

"Confusing, in part. He also feels that the Wevaran who live there do not get out enough."

Kaylin winced. She hesitated, and then said, "Liatt's citizens might consider the Wevaran a fact of life—but no one in any other fief will, and outside of the fiefs, Bakkon walking through the city streets would cause a *lot* of panic."

"Ah. Yes, Robin has been attempting to explain the mortal fear of spiders. He brought one here. We have nothing in common; they are small and helpless."

"Some are venomous," she pointed out.

"Avoid getting bitten. Robin believes, however, that they will look at us as if we were insects, without pausing to attempt to converse."

She nodded. "It's not fair, but fear makes people dangerously stupid. And the Emperor has a rule for Immortal citizens."

"Oh?"

"He asks that they appear before him, in the throne room,

to pledge their oath of allegiance. I'm pretty sure the Wevaran are Immortals—like the Barrani or the Dragons."

"We are. I am uncertain that Bakkon would desire to offer such an oath. Do the Barrani?"

"Each and every one of them—but it isn't a blood oath and they don't take it seriously."

"The Barrani were ever duplicitous."

"That is harsh," Arbiter Androsse said, joining the conversation as if he were a more responsible version of Terrano. His smile, slender, was all edge. "We considered their attempt at duplicity as charmingly transparent." Androsse looked Barrani, to Kaylin; he was not. He was a member of the race the Barrani called the Ancestors. She knew very little about their civilization and their culture—and had zero desire to learn more.

Ancestors had almost destroyed the High Halls, and far worse in Kaylin's opinion, had been responsible for the deaths of fellow Hawks.

"Harsh, but not inaccurate," a rumbling voice added. The third of three Arbiters, Kavallac the Dragon, joined the other two.

Terrano rolled his eyes.

Serralyn, however, did not. Her eyes narrowed as she looked at the three Arbiters, as if she could see something Kaylin couldn't. But her eyes remained green and her gaze drifted toward the shelves that carried the library's many books. There was no visible end to the shelves; there were alcoves along the sides of the walls that also contained shelves, and therefore books. Books heading into eternity.

Books that Kaylin was almost certain Serralyn couldn't read. Yet.

"It is delightful," Kavallac said, the Draconic rumble softened, "to see a student who is so excited. If you wish to peruse the books while we listen to Kaylin, please feel free to do so."

"But I can't?" Terrano demanded, clearly annoyed.

"Your interest is not in the contents of the library itself; you consider the library a puzzle to be solved, a lock to be picked. Your compatriot has made no attempt to enter this library through anything but the channels provided to students— but of course, being a new student, the permissions required to visit have not yet been formally established." She spoke to Serralyn. "You have, however, proven yourself of aid to Kaylin Neya, and we are indebted to her. If Killian did not prevent your approach, we will assume he considers it acceptable.

"Do not, however, tell all of the other students in your year. No one likes to be forced to say no, even old Dragons."

"I thought they turned the askee to ash," Terrano said.

"In the library? Fire? Don't be ridiculous." She then turned to Kaylin, her eyes gold-flecked orange. Terrano had amused her. Somehow.

Serralyn turned to Kaylin, as if seeking permission. And maybe she was, if she was here because she was Kaylin's escort. She nodded and Serralyn wheeled on foot, tracing a jittery circle as she looked at books in all directions. She finally closed her eyes and started walking because clearly, she couldn't choose, and she knew her time was limited.

Bakkon met her halfway to wherever it was she was blindly heading, and navigated carefully around her. His eyes—all of them—were up on stalks, and he was clicking excitedly. He came to a stop as he noticed Kaylin, and switched languages.

"My apologies, Lord Kaylin—there are books here that even I have never encountered. I cannot, of course, know every book ever written—but so much has been lost to history. It is good to see you again. You have been well?"

"I've been well, but... I've been having a bit of a ghost problem."

Starrante and Bakkon froze. "A...ghost?"

Kavallac answered. "In mortal terms—and Kaylin is mortal—they are the...remnants of the dead. Things that remain behind when the body has died."

Clicking started immediately.

"Clearly there is more to your difficulties than that," Androsse said. "You would not have been given permission to even approach the library if you meant to speak of mortal children's bedtime stories."

"We don't tell ghost stories to children at bedtime." Kaylin folded her arms. She'd gotten used to Barrani condescension, understood that Androsse wasn't actually Barrani, and still felt annoyed and a bit defensive.

Androsse compounded this by ignoring her correction, because clearly being accurate was beneath him.

Kaylin ignored him, turning instead to the two Wevaran. "What do you think *ghost* means? Why are you reacting that way?"

"All races have always had superstitions," Bakkon replied. "Our ghosts are not your ghosts; they are enemies that can cause great damage, but are impervious to any defense we might mount. But we are also aware that we will have very different stories, and I am interested in your ghosts. They are all human, yes?"

Kaylin nodded. "Some of them *are* dead. But my concern today is mostly about the ones who aren't—the ones I think are just trapped out of phase." She hesitated, and then said, "The ones that are dead are... I'm not sure why they're trapped, but I know if they weren't, they wouldn't be here anymore. They're not alive.

"I saw something—entirely through my familiar's wing—

that might be associated with their captivity. A building—I don't think it used to be a sentient building—seems to be out of phase in the way the non-dead ghosts are."

"You feel that this building is related to the non-dead ghosts?"

"Ummm, no. Sorry. There's too much that's tangled together, and I don't understand a lot of it."

"Or most of it?" Androsse interjected.

Can I kick him?

Severn chuckled. *I imagine Kavallac would appreciate your attempt, but I wouldn't.*

Kaylin exhaled. "Let me tell you what my week has been like."

Starrante and Bakkon listened; Bakkon interrupted only to make certain he understood what Kaylin was saying. Androsse and Kavallac were silent, the latter curious but unconcerned.

When Kaylin spoke about the ghostly building, the Dragon's eyes narrowed, shifting from orange-flecked gold to pure orange.

Androsse's, however, shifted to a midnight so dark, they were black; the pupils became invisible. "Please repeat that name."

"Orbonne Street?"

"No. The former owner of the ghostly building you cannot see without intervention."

"Azoria. Azoria An'Berranin. She was Barrani."

Kavallac turned to Androsse, her eyes reddening. She did not interrupt Androsse.

"It is not a name I have heard recently."

"But it's a name you recognize? A person you recognize?"

"Indeed."

Kaylin was silent for a long beat. "You met her."

"Indeed."

"When she was a student?"

"Yes."

"But—but that would make her *ancient*!"

"She *is* Barrani, and if the Barrani are in all ways lesser than my kin, they are nonetheless Immortal; the truth of their names is as eternal as the truth of ours."

"I was told she's dead."

"Ah. I had not heard that—but we have been closed to visitors for a very long time; it is not unlikely that someone as dangerously ambitious as Azoria would have failed to survive, but she was not considered bold by others."

"But by you?"

"Very bold," he said, smiling. The smile was cold.

The two Wevaran were chittering in the background. It was Bakkon who spoke. "Starrante believes he, too, had experience with the student you have named."

Kaylin found Starrante far friendlier than Androsse, spider or no. She turned toward him. "Did you consider her bold?"

Starrante did not answer. To Kaylin's surprise, Bakkon lifted a forelimb and poked Starrante's body.

"You have Terrano," Starrante said, obviously reluctant to speak.

Kaylin wanted to object, but couldn't. She nodded instead; it seemed safest.

"Azoria was, in personality, nothing at all like Terrano. She did not have the excuse he has to be what he is."

"Excuse?" Terrano said, brows rising.

"She was not subject to the power of the ancient green at an age when she did not have experience to ground her. That is what happened to you—to all of you, except perhaps An'Teela. Azoria was far colder, far more certain of herself."

"I'm certain of myself!"

"We are all certain you are, Terrano," the Dragon librarian said, her voice less Draconic and far warmer than usual. "We are cautious because you can do harm without intent. You are not malicious."

"And Azoria was?" Kaylin asked, attempting to wrest control of the conversation back.

"I believe you would consider her somewhat malevolent. Androsse did not, but you have had experience with those of his kind before."

Androsse was not amused, but Kaylin noted he didn't disagree. "She was not like Terrano in feckless personality; she was ambitious. She had seen a greater world than the one she was born to occupy, and she wished to reach it. Surely you are not implying that she should have known her place? I find that very authoritarian of you, Kavallac. I am surprised."

He was, of course, lying.

Yes, Severn said. If all other eyes were on Androsse, Severn's attention was more subtle.

"There is a strong difference between accepting limitations that are not yours except by social consensus, and despising what you actually are. Azoria crossed that line, denying both kin and race," Kavallac snapped.

"And Terrano? You do not seem to consider him a similar threat." Androsse's smile was thin; the wonder was that it existed at all, given Kavallac's mood.

"Neither do you. I will not play these pointless, verbal games—but I am highly displeased to hear that name spoken in this place."

"She did not do a great deal of damage."

"Not for lack of trying—and this is not the time or place to speak of that. But if we are not to accept our *limitations*," she continued, her voice dropping into the rumble of Draconic form, "we are nonetheless responsible enough to accept our *duty*. What is yours, Androsse?"

Androsse was now annoyed.

A hairy limb tapped Kaylin's shoulder. She could hear Bakkon's chittering voice somewhere near her right ear. "They will, according to Starrante, continue in this fashion for some hours. But if you wish to discuss things without the heat and the history of near disaster, he asks that you withdraw to the chancellor's office, where we are unlikely to be interrupted by the—" Kavallac's roar drowned out the much quieter Wevaran voice.

"I think that's a great idea." Kaylin mouthed the words, because whatever Kavallac was saying didn't stop in time for normal speech to be heard.

She backed away from the two angry Arbiters. Only Terrano seemed rooted to the spot—but it wasn't with terror; he was listening. Carefully.

"Terrano—go get Serralyn. We're leaving."

The floor shook as Androsse spoke, and Kaylin remembered that Dragon against Barrani Ancestor was not nearly as certain a fight as Dragon against Barrani.

When the library doors closed at her back—authoritatively and perhaps a touch too forcefully—she tried to relax. Starrante's eyes were not the indicator that Barrani eyes would have been to Kaylin, although she was certain that Robin would know what they meant. Spiders had a lot of eyes, but in Starrante's case, they were mostly retracted into his central body.

"Are they always like that?" Bakkon asked, in Barrani.

"No. But when they disagree—and this is a fundamental disagreement about the nature of study and research—it can be quite loud, and perhaps intimidating to those who are not accustomed to the built-in protections of the library. I do not believe the Arbiters *can* kill each other, and I am not entirely certain they will try."

"But you're not certain they won't?" Kaylin asked.

"When they are very loud, the more vulnerable races can be swept up, to their detriment. But I wish you had not mentioned that name. It was a point of contention when the Academia was at its height—a bitter point."

"Is there any chance that Larrantin once had this Barrani woman as a student?"

"A very high chance." Starrante paused. The pause went on for a bit too long. "I am not certain that mentioning her would be in your best interests."

"Oh, it likely won't. I've already been asked to drop the investigation in regard to her."

"I am not certain Larrantin will not choose to take the same approach."

Bakkon chittered.

Starrante clicked at Bakkon before resuming Barrani, although his reply was clearly to the Wevaran. "Well, yes. But they will not harm the books, and they are unlikely to kill each other. Understand," he added, to Kaylin, "that it is difficult for any three people to be the only source of company for centuries without break."

"You're not in there fighting with them."

"No, that is true—but I fail to see how such conflict would resolve anything. I have come to understand that in some fashion it does, but I would rather not be part of it. Our people do not weather isolation as poorly."

Kaylin glanced at Bakkon. He had spent far longer enclosed in his library—alone—than the Arbiters had, together.

"If Starrante feels it is unwise, perhaps you should reconsider your questions," that Wevaran said. "Larrantin is of the younger races, and he may react in a hostile fashion."

Kaylin shrugged. It wouldn't be the first time a teacher had verbally attempted to flay her alive. "Killian won't let him kill me. Or injure me too badly."

"Larrantin is perfectly capable of leaving the Academia at this point," Killian pointed out, materializing behind the two Wevaran. "The chancellor is willing to allow you the use of the conference room—and he suggests that you ask Larrantin to attend you there. Having students witness a professor losing his temper would not, in the chancellor's opinion, be good for morale."

"Does the chancellor recognize the name?"

"In passing. I do not believe he had direct interaction with the student in question."

Student. Kaylin slowed as the word sunk roots. "If she was a student here, you must have information about her in your own internal records."

Killian said nothing.

"Helen remembers all her tenants."

"And does she speak about them to you?"

"Sometimes?"

"She speaks of her own responses to them—but they are dead, and cannot be hurt. Even so, she does not speak of their personal matters."

What were personal matters to a building that could read the minds of anyone who happened to be standing inside of it?

"I believe Helen will be able to clarify. Yes. I knew Azoria—but only as well as I know you, Terrano, or Serralyn. Understand that students have their own reasons for desiring residence in the Academia—but they seek knowledge. Their search spawns new searches, illuminates new corners, adds to the history of research and learning.

"Why they seek that knowledge is not for me to judge; it is why chancellors exist. Do not ask me what Azoria wanted.

I cannot answer. I am willing to discuss her grades, her promotion, the avenues of her study—but that is all. And even those I will disclose at the discretion of the chancellor, alone." His expression was somber. "I am sorry, Lord Kaylin.

"This is the way I was built."

09

The chancellor was only barely of a mind to allow them the use of his conference room, and Kaylin was almost certain he did so only because Starrante requested it; had Kaylin been on her own, she was fairly certain Killian would have been asked to see her to the figurative door. Lannagaros's expression was thunderous. It was still more friendly than Kavallac's had been at the end.

Starrante waved his forearms at the chancellor. "If there are appointments granted to the older students for library privileges, I'm afraid they will have to be delayed."

The chancellor froze, his eyes shading to a dark orange. "Why?"

"Young Kaylin asked Arbiter Androsse about a former student. Arbiter Androsse and Arbiter Kavallac...disagreed about that student, and they are engaged in a colorful—and very loud—argument at the moment. I am almost certain some of your Barrani students could weather that storm, but it is not a risk I would take. It is not her fault."

"You do realize that I will have a handful of very argumentative and aggrieved students in my office if I cancel these privileges?"

"Yes. I consider the possible alternative outcome to be more regrettable."

"Very well." He turned his orange-eyed glare on Kaylin. The former Arkon was being as fair as he generally was. Kaylin wasn't stupid enough to share this grumbling thought. "Serralyn, however, has classes. Valliant could stand in for her, but I am not of a mind to allow students to take unnecessary liberties with *my personal space*."

Serralyn looked disappointed, but didn't argue.

Which probably meant Terrano was once again invisibly nearby.

Larrantin came to the conference room an hour later. He was, as Barrani were wont to be, blue-eyed when he entered the room. "Someone has put the chancellor in a very bad mood."

Kaylin winced.

"That would be Arbiter Androsse and Arbiter Kavallac," Starrante said.

"Are they fighting again?"

"Some things don't change," Starrante replied.

"What set them off this time?"

"Ah. That would be Lord Kaylin."

Larrantin frowned and turned to said lord, his brows folding as if he were attempting to understand how a mere mortal could have such effect; his eyes cleared as he whispered the word *Chosen*.

"No," Kaylin said, slightly annoyed herself. "Imperial Hawk."

"You cannot possibly accuse the Arbiters of petty crime."

In Larrantin's view, all of the Halls of Law were clearly absorbed in the investigation of the petty.

"No. I came to ask Arbiter Starrante about the use of portals in regard to physical displacement—in this case the displacement or suspension of the entire Academia. Which doesn't actually exist on maps because there's no sane way it should."

"I am uncertain that Starrante would have much information about that, although he is the expert on the use of portals. There is nothing in that question that should have provoked disagreement between the Arbiters."

"No. But I asked about—I mentioned—the name of a former student."

Clearly students were also considered petty in Larrantin's view. This, Kaylin thought, is why she disliked the Barrani. "There are no students currently studying who could provoke that ire."

"The student in question is not a current student, and I've been told that she is dead. Along with the rest of her line."

"You asked about a student who existed before the Towers rose?"

"I had no idea she was that old—she was the owner of a building that doesn't seem to be completely in phase with the rest of the city. Which...is like the Academia."

"Name?"

It was Starrante who answered, although the answer was a series of clicks and whistles.

Clearly, Larrantin understood the Wevaran tongue; his eyes darkened from the usual blue to a much, much deeper color. Arrogance and boredom drained from his features as he turned all of his attention to Kaylin.

"Why did you think it necessary to ask about this person?" This person. Not Azoria.

"Because her name is listed as owner of record for a house that no longer exists. It doesn't exist in any current map in Records—and in the Records to which I have access, it hasn't existed for at least a century. If not for the taxation office, I would never have stumbled across the name at all."

He held up one hand. "You will now go back to the beginning and you will explain."

For the second time in as many hours, Kaylin detailed the travails of Mrs. Erickson, Mrs. Erickson's two flavors of ghosts, and the house she could only see through Hope's wing.

"I fail to see the purpose of this investigation. The strangeness you have encountered has nothing to do with our former student."

Kaylin, however, shook her head. "That's not the way this works. And I'm less and less certain she has nothing to do with what happened to the indoor ghosts."

"They are not trapped in the nonexistent building; were they, you would not have encountered them."

"Well, that's the thing," Kaylin replied. "Fourteen doesn't exist anymore. No one remembers it. But fourteen and a half didn't exist prior to that century-old map, at least according to taxation Records. It exists *now*, and it existed eighty years ago, but eighty years is a long time for us; it's just part of the street that's always been there to people who live on that street."

"You don't believe it's always existed," Killian said.

"I know what I saw—there's no way that that building became the other, much, much smaller house. And the house is small for the street—it looks slightly out of place. But if Azoria was somehow involved there might be a reason she chose to abandon the building she originally owned. If she was involved, it would be at least a century ago, which is when the children started to disappear. Which would imply that she wasn't dead, as has been claimed."

"I did not claim she was dead."

"No, that wasn't you. Given Androsse's reaction—"

"*Arbiter* Androsse." Larrantin's eyes narrowed.

"—Arbiter Androsse. Sorry. Given the Arbiter's reaction, I wouldn't be surprised if I found out that she was still, somehow, alive. I mean, look at you. You stayed here when the Academia was, in theory, obliterated with the rise of the Towers, and you're demonstrably not dead."

"She has not been seen in the High Halls?"

"Probably not. I have an upcoming meeting in the High Halls, and I will certainly be bringing this up there."

"You have a meeting in the High Halls?"

"I was invited to attend a meeting with the Lady, yes."

"It is to be hoped, given your deplorable manners, that the meeting is a private one."

"Mostly private. An'Teela has also been summoned."

"Expect that your questions will not be greeted with any great joy," Larrantin said. His eyes weren't indigo yet, but it was close.

"Azoria was a student here before the Academia's long hibernation. Was she a student of yours?"

Starrante chittered; Larrantin lifted a hand, palm out, in the Wevaran's direction. "She was a student of mine, yes. But she was predominantly a student of the Arbiter Androsse."

"The Arbiters take students?"

"No. That is why it was considered significant. I would guess that the conflict between the two Arbiters stems from his decision in the distant past."

"Was she a good student?"

"She was an excellent student: very focused and very driven. She was, in Barrani terms, a woman of astonishing ambition."

"Ambition to do what?" Kaylin tried to keep any accusation

out of her voice; when Barrani were said to be ambitious it usually meant bad things for anyone who was not said Barrani.

"To learn, of course. To absorb any and all knowledge not already in her possession. She was an impressive talent, magically speaking; she was considered the only natural choice for heir of her line."

"I assume a head of line already existed."

Larrantin rolled his eyes. "Of course. But not all families decide inheritance by careful assassination; I did not have the sense that there was anything but amity between Azoria and her father, An'Berranin of old."

"Her line was wiped out," Kaylin then said.

"Ah. I see that I have been remiss. I am less aware of the changes in familial lines than I once was."

"Did you know him?"

"He came to the Academia to visit Azoria from time to time; this was also considered unusual. He was not pleased when she chose to take up residence here with the rest of the students—she was well within her rights to come to classes during the day and return to the High Halls when those classes were finished.

"But she felt the travel time diminished the time she could spend on her research, and in the end, her father agreed. She was unusual for a Barrani—she felt the passage of time almost as keenly as mortals do."

What had Berranin done?

What had Azoria done? Kaylin was certain that Azoria was at the center of the downfall.

"What did she study with you?"

"A better question would be: What did she *not* study? I told you, she was voracious; she wanted knowledge she didn't have. The knowledge itself could be anything; she could learn new languages or dead languages with the same focus and dedication she learned to control her power for the more usual martial purposes. Remember that the Barrani have never been far from war, whether it be with Dragons or each other. The desire for dominance is, in the end, rooted in the desire for safety; if we rule everything, if we have the *power* to rule everything, we assume that we will be safe."

"Not a good assumption," Kaylin replied.

"I did not say it was intelligent; I merely described the impulse. She did not, however, speak of rulership. I believe she was, inasmuch as a Barrani of power can be, fond of her father. It was certainly due to her presence that he retained his hold upon his line."

"And her mother?"

Silence.

"Did her mother survive?"

"No one in Berranin, if you are being accurate, survived."

"Did her mother survive her birth, her existence? Was she set aside, was she assassinated?"

Larrantin smiled; there was nothing friendly about the expression. "As I was not aware that Berranin had been utterly excised, I cannot answer that question. As you would surmise if you were actually listening to my words. But I will offer you this: knowledge is power. You have no doubt heard that before in your extremely brief life; attend to the truth of it.

"The reason those who seek knowledge frequently fail to rise to positions of power is they seek only avenues of obvious power. They are focused solely on things that will grant them martial superiority, and they fail to learn enough to understand the subtlety of something as irrelevant—to them— as a dead language.

"I was considered an expert in certain fields—but I have fallen behind, and must myself become a student." His smile became a wall. "If you should encounter Azoria—in whatever form she has taken—please send my regards."

"You don't believe she's dead."

Larrantin did not reply.

Starrante was silent until Larrantin had clearly finished speaking. "She was interested in portals, and in particular in the way we spin them. She could not spin them herself in the same way—there were biological limitations, and apparently your kind frequently consider the spinning of portals... socially rude?"

"It's because it looks like you're spitting," Kaylin replied.

"Yes?"

"It's usually considered a sign of contempt or disgust, at least among mortals. And Barrani manners are famously restrictive, so I imagine it was even more so for her. But you taught her?"

"I could not teach her to do what we do; she was not born to it. It frustrated her, but she accepted facts she could not—at that time—change. What we attempted to teach her was the underlying concept of the web itself."

Bakkon chittered then; the chittering lasted for much longer. Kaylin didn't understand the language, but she took some hint from the way he'd drawn his limbs toward his body. And the volume of the unintelligible words.

I would guess that what he attempted to teach is not taught. Clearly Starrante is cringing, Severn offered.

How can you tell?

Body hair, and the direction of the one eye he's lifted from his central core.

"Bakkon is not pleased."

"It was a long time ago," Kaylin offered the angrier Wevaran.

"There is a reason," he said, practically hissing, "that the web cannot be traversed or manipulated by outsiders—it is the heart of our people, the place from which we are born, and to which we return upon death."

Kaylin immediately held up a hand as if she were still a mostly despised student in the Halls of Law.

Bakkon lifted a limb and waved it, which she assumed was an invitation to ask her question. "Is that like the Barrani Lake? Is that where you get your names from?"

Silence. Wrong question.

"Sorry—I know Dragons aren't born with the entirety of their names; they're not like Barrani, who can't wake unless a name is bestowed upon them by someone who is not their mother. I didn't mean to ask a question that's somehow offensive."

Starrante chittered in Bakkon's direction. "He is old," Starrante then said, almost apologetically, "and has always been somewhat... I believe Robin would call it 'stuffy.' Your question does not translate well; it is almost a threat."

"Not what I intended. At all." Kaylin spoke in emphatic High Barrani. "We don't need True Names to wake. We don't need True Names to exist. True Names are like magic, to us."

"Technically speaking, they are indeed magic: so much power and so much that is unknowable. Even the so-called spells of the young are, to us, a scratch upon the surface of the power they are actually touching. We are born in very inhospitable circumstances. Many, many hatch—we have more young than the Dragons, when we survive to breed.

"But most of the children don't survive. In the dark, we kill each other in a frenzy of hunger and fear. This has long caused...discomfort in other races, although we do not interact with any other people until we are fully adult. Once, perhaps, that might have been possible—but it would not be safe.

"We were not raised to value safety; our imperative was survival."

Bakkon chittered again.

"Bakkon appears to have forgotten his manners," Starrante said. "He does not like the direction any answer to your question might lead; it is the heart of his angry criticism of me. I will therefore not answer that question."

Kaylin nodded, and chose to ask a different one. "With what you taught her, would it have been possible for Azoria to reach that place?"

"She would be highly unlikely to survive it."

"That's not an answer."

"She was bright and difficult, driven and proud. I see some of her in your Terrano, but he lacks her ferocity of focus, instead approaching things as if the entirety of creation is a puzzle game created just for him to play. It is a striking combination of personality and competence."

"Striking because you think he should amount, in the end, to very little?"

"It is often the fate of those who descend into self-indulgence—but not always. It is possible that Azoria could have found a way to enter our birthing spaces, but she would then be faced with the hunger of our young." He hesitated. "Adults do not remain within that web, and they do not return to it."

"Could they?"

Bakkon shrieked.

Kaylin decided, given the rising of all the hair—and eyes—on the older Wevaran's body, that she had no more pressing questions that needed answering.

Severn, however, disagreed. "If—and this is entirely hypothetical—Azoria had learned enough that she might enter your birthing place, what might she find there that she could use?"

Bakkon's voice grew loud enough that Killian intervened, dampening the noise. "My apologies, Lord Kaylin, but the place of their birth is the place from which they eventually emerge as adults. It is not something that should be spoken of publicly—and to Bakkon, speaking of it to anyone from any race that is not Wevaran, is public. Barrani might respond in exactly the same fashion should you begin to carelessly discuss the Lake of Life in a fashion that might allow someone to reach it."

Kaylin was silent for a beat, but that silence was filling with a growing discomfort.

Starrante was watching Kaylin, not Bakkon.

Kaylin had always been accused of being an open book, which could be a problem in more delicate investigations, and was the primary reason Marcus or the Hawklord didn't send her to investigations that involved the monied and the powerful.

"There are things I should not speak of," Starrante said. There was no anger in his voice; it seemed to Kaylin there was a mixture of sorrow and guilt. "It has been so long since I emerged I forget—and Bakkon reminds me that I have no excuse.

"But at the time, I felt it likely that there would be no more young—none of my kin, emerging from darkness into light. I wished the knowledge not to be lost. It is why, in the end, I am Arbiter and Bakkon could not be. I cannot see how Azoria could take what little information I could share and use it to her advantage—but the application of knowledge once considered harmless has oft been surprising.

"She could not use the birthing place to become what we are; she could not—to my knowledge—derive any power from it."

Bakkon chittered, his voice more subdued.

"Yes," Starrante replied, still speaking in Barrani. "If there were a clutch of young again, and she could somehow reach the birthing place and survive them, she could *possibly* derive power from that; Bakkon is afraid that she would become the Devourer, rather than the devoured; that it is not one of our kind who would emerge, but Azoria.

"But as I have told Bakkon: there are no young. The birthing place is empty of all words, all power, all life."

Kaylin, who had decided that questions were a bad idea, nonetheless raised her hand.

"Yes?"

"Are you saying that the power to become adult is derived in its entirety from devouring your clutch mates?"

Starrante did not reply.

Kaylin was uncertain that she'd gotten what she needed from this visit to the Academia; she had questions—more questions—and distinct unease.

Larrantin, however, had taken hold of the question Kaylin probably shouldn't have asked; he had questions of his own, and he asked them without apparent shame or delicacy. "You are implying that those of you who emerge have words at their core, just as the Barrani do, but they gain those words by devouring each other.

"Which implies—heavily—that in some fashion each of your clutch mates is born with a...fragment of a word? And that the devouring of the fragments somehow *becomes* a True Name?"

"I told you!" shrieked Bakkon, in the highest of pitches Kaylin had yet heard him use.

"Perhaps it is why we do not view our birth or our fight in the same fashion other races do," Starrante conceded. "We feel we are *all* of our clutch. In some fashion, we are. Our birth is not your birth; it is not the hatching of the Dragons. It is certainly not the birth of the mortals, who live without necessary words and die so quickly, consumed in almost an instant by the ravages of time. There is no amity, no friendship, between any individual element of the clutch—and on occasion, not one, but two might emerge from the birthing place, although that is very, very rare.

"I am of the belief that Azoria could not benefit from any act of destruction she might attempt—but there is no evidence to bear that out. Arbiter Kavallac fears that Azoria attempts to become what Androsse's people were—to rise above the truth of her existence as Barrani and to become more or other."

Kaylin turned to Larrantin. "She was your student as well. Do you concur?"

"She did not speak to me of her ambitions in a general sense; as I said, she was interested in *all* knowledge that she did not herself possess. But if you ask my opinion? Yes, it is possible. She did not like barriers or boundaries; nor could she rest easily accepting them. You have, I am certain, heard tales of those mortals who attempted to become Immortal."

She'd also had experience with them; it was always ugly.

"You were raised in the fiefs," Killian said, which surprised Larrantin.

Kaylin nodded.

"You do not live there now. Had you accepted your station in life, the lot to which you were born, you would have remained in the fiefs. You would not have crossed the Ablayne."

"It's not the same thing."

"Why? In both cases you attempt to rise above the circumstance of your birth."

Kaylin was frustrated because this was true. But the question Larrantin asked seemed genuine rather than dismissive. "I accept that I'm human. I don't consider being human to be a weakness or a sin. I have a full range of the possibilities available for humans. One of them isn't becoming something other than mortal.

"We can make choices that defy social custom—any of us, from any race. But if we hate what we *are*..." She shook her head. "It's not the same."

"Perhaps. Perhaps not. I will not argue. I have never felt an overwhelming desire to be something I am not, although I am certain many of my relatives had an almost overwhelming desire to mold me into their version of what I should be."

Killian, thoughtful, surprised Kaylin. "Azoria did not accept her limitations. If you wish to understand all the things that might have gone wrong, I believe you will find better possible answers from Terrano and his friends."

Terrano once again became visible. He didn't look annoyed; he was too deep in thought for that. "I wasn't trying to ignore our limitations," he finally said, to Killian, the one person who could easily eject him from the premises, even if he couldn't be certain he could keep him out.

"No. But I believe you—and all of your friends—were fundamentally altered by the green itself. Some part of you desired to return home."

"Not me."

"And some did not. You had years of experience existing to one side of the True Names that give the Barrani life, but that name was, nonetheless, yours. And you carry those names within you now, but your experience being almost nameless could not be unmade. What you are, now, is not what you were. You have leveraged that to do things that should not be possible, and would not be had you followed the designs laid out by your creator."

Terrano shrugged. "You have no idea how boring it is to be stuck in a cell. It's not that we wanted to be something more or other—we wanted to be free. And over the passage of centuries, we began to look for, to see, the cracks in the cage walls. Azoria wasn't trapped as we were trapped, was she?"

"No, not to my knowledge. But perhaps she felt ignorance and the limitations of her personal power were as much a cage as a Hallionne. Regardless, you have what answers you might find in the Academia at present. Should the two Arbiters come to an armistice and decide there is information of relevance, I shall ask the chancellor to send you a letter."

Kaylin knew a dismissal when she heard one.

"Yes, I'm sorry. I would be delighted by your company, but the chancellor now desires my attention—and the privacy in which to receive it."

Serralyn, sent from the office, met them as they were leaving, somewhat out of breath.

"Sedarias says she's found some information about Azoria." The Barrani student's eyes were dark blue. "She asks that you return home so that we can discuss it in safety, and she further asks that you…stop talking about her anywhere other people can hear you."

Kaylin turned to Terrano. He looked, to her surprise, uneasy, but after a pause, he nodded. "I'm to accompany you on your way home."

"You think some Barrani would be stupid enough to throw his life away trying to end mine?"

"Personally? No. But Sedarias is being Sedarias; she sees assassins everywhere."

"She has her reasons," Serralyn added. "And she's right more often than she's wrong. I admit your visit today has filled me with doubt. You caused a huge argument between the two Arbiters, and I think Bakkon is going to get cramps from the rigidity of whatever shock he received. Maybe this really isn't a good idea."

"If Azoria has nothing at all to do with the trapped ghosts, I'll drop it, okay?"

Terrano snorted. "Sedarias points out that the ghosts are dead. It's not like you're saving their lives."

Serralyn winced. "Please ignore that," she said. "Mandoran agrees with you—he points out that we were trapped for a lot longer, but at least our cage was sentient and predisposed to actually care about our welfare."

"I take it you agree as well?"

"I don't want to start a fight—or join one—but yes, since you ask, I agree with Mandoran. But I also agree with Sedarias. If lords of power decide that your investigation is a genuine threat to their interests, you're being too careless with your own safety.

"Terrano is pretty capable, even if he doesn't look it."

"Oh, believe we're fully aware of that," Kaylin replied.

Serralyn flushed.

Terrano grinned. He was clearly willing to let bygones be bygones, but he would be: Kaylin hadn't made any attempt to kill *him*. On the other hand, the Consort had forgiven him, and appeared to have forgotten about the actions that had been such a threat to her. Kaylin loved some of the Barrani, but admitted she would never fully understand them.

Then again, she could sympathize with Terrano's goals at the time, and could understand why everything had happened. So maybe she could.

Severn was quieter, but she noticed that he didn't branch off to return to his own home.

"You're coming with us?"

"If you have no objections."

She didn't. She wouldn't have minded having Severn under Helen's roof; Helen could make a home within that home for anyone of any race, and besides, things were almost too quiet since Bellusdeo had taken on her Tower and become absorbed in her new responsibilities. Kaylin had offered once or twice; Severn had never accepted. She understood that his need for privacy, for space of his own that did not magically shift beneath his feet when it felt change was necessary, was completely valid. It was, until Helen and the cohort, what she thought she'd wanted for herself.

Severn smiled and shook his head slightly. He didn't speak.

As there were no waiting assassins of any stripe—and Kaylin and Severn paid attention at street level and everything above it that seemed like a likely place for assassins to park—they made decent time. Helen was, as she always was, waiting at the door from the moment Kaylin stepped across the fence line. All of it—fences, manicured lawn, garden, and house were part of Helen; once you crossed that line, you were in her territory.

If you intended harm to her tenants—or their guests—you were in for a world of pain.

Still, no one mentioned Azoria or the Academia outing until they had entered the house—Kaylin pausing to accept a welcome home hug that was not extended to anyone else, although Helen did beam happily at Serralyn—and the door had shut behind them.

"I feel that you should all eat first, and dinner is on the table."

Kaylin, hungry, agreed. She therefore headed to her room to change out of her work clothing and wash up. Her home clothing on most days looked a lot like her work clothing—she didn't like to fuss about clothing, but made allowance for weather; it was the only time clothing had truly mattered in her childhood.

There was too much information, and it was too tangled to properly assess; she'd reached the point where she needed more in order to untangle the mess. Given all of the reactions to the name Azoria, she hoped that that one thread could be understood and put firmly aside.

Hah. Who was she kidding? She'd never been that lucky.

She dressed and headed back down the stairs to the dining room, where she paused in the doorway. Sedarias was seated to one side of Kaylin's normal seat, which wasn't unusual. She was wearing a very elaborate gown—with edges that seemed to be made of solid metal, none of it warm gold—and her eyes, when she turned to meet Kaylin's, were almost black.

10

A quick glance—when she could tear her gaze away from Sedarias—showed that most of the cohort hadn't chosen to dress up for dinner. Mandoran and Terrano in particular; Terrano hadn't bothered to change his clothing. Serralyn hadn't bothered to change hers, either.

To her surprise, Teela was seated at the table. She wore green, a resplendent, bright color that reminded Kaylin, conversely, of the long, long imprisonment of the rest of Teela's friends. This didn't, in Teela's case, mean Teela supported Sedarias, but it did indicate that she considered Sedarias's information to be of formal importance.

Allaron wore his usual clothing, but Torrisant was dressed in very similar fashion to Sedarias—as were Fallessian and the usually utterly silent Karian. Torrisant had chosen more formal wear, but it matched Teela's choice, not Sedarias's. Clearly battle lines had been drawn before she'd set foot in her home. She was grateful that Serralyn had chosen to stay, and envied Valliant, who remained in the safety of the Academia.

But Severn had chosen to remain as well, and he occupied the seat directly opposite Sedarias's. Kaylin walked into the dining room, heading toward the chair that was farthest from the door. Teela rolled her eyes. "We are not going to eat you. Sit down."

"Why are you dressed like that?"

"Clothing does not define the meal."

"No. It just destroys the appetite." She dragged her chair out and sat in it. Since her ability to eat wasn't dependent on her appetite, Kaylin decided to clear the air immediately. "So why did you call a meeting?"

"We lack necessary information. I therefore approached allies of Mellarionne and asked that they seek that information. Two of the informants have failed to report in. A third is dead. Our assumption, in the absence of bodies, is that the two are likewise deceased." This might explain the color of her eyes. "When information presents a danger to Barrani, caution is required in its pursuit—but if three of those allied with Mellarionne have been killed it implies the killers either have no fear of Mellarionne or their fear of Azoria, or someone of rank in the High Court, is stronger."

"In theory she's dead," Kaylin said.

"Yes. Regardless, some response on the part of Mellarionne is now required. Had the interested parties approached me first, I would not have considered this action one that deserved reprisal. This did not happen."

Kaylin had a headache. A Barrani-sized headache. But she understood Sedarias's anger now. She understood the clothing of those members of the cohort who had chosen, in their own fashion, to stand behind her, and lifted a hand, palm out. "If you have information that's going to get me killed, I'm not certain I want to hear it right now."

"That's unfortunate. For you. At this point, it seems the use of the name merits—in the eyes of an as-yet-unknown enemy—death to Barrani; I imagine the laws of exemption would make your otherwise certain death far more complicated. Our people do not call upon the laws of exemption in life or death. Any retribution from Mellarionne is therefore entirely outside of your remit—and it will *stay that way*. Mellarionne, as any Barrani family of note, has no wish to fall afoul of those laws."

"I concur," Teela predictably said. "This is a Barrani matter."

"If Azoria was somehow involved in the death of those children—or the kidnapping—it *isn't*. You said Azoria is dead, as is the whole of her line. The implication was that her death has been fact for a long time.

"But either that's inaccurate, or some other person chose to purchase land in an area entirely occupied by mortals—by humans like me under her name. The building that she bought doesn't exist anymore."

"It was destroyed?"

"No. It never existed, except in tax Records. In its place, a much, much smaller building does. That building was either built or bought some eighty to ninety years ago—by mortals." Kaylin turned toward Teela. "Mrs. Erickson's parents."

"Mrs. Erickson's parents are the only owners in taxation Records."

"And the location of fourteen and a half?"

"It appears to have been built when, or just before, the Swindons assumed ownership and tax responsibilities," the Barrani Hawk continued. Kaylin wondered if she were lying.

She isn't, Severn said. *What Records contains is the information she is now offering.*

Could those Records be tampered with?

Almost anything can, but tampering with Imperial Records requires upper level intervention or permission. Or turning a blind eye at a very specific time.

Or the Emperor's direct command?

The question surprised Severn, but it also amused him. *Or that, yes. Is that what you suspect?*

I don't suspect anything yet. But…I don't believe that Azoria is dead. Her family, maybe. I think it would be hard to hide an entire family line if most of it hadn't been wiped out. But Larrantin implied that the father—An'Berranin—had no real interest in Azoria's studies; he encouraged her and supported her.

Teela cleared her throat. Loudly. Kaylin reddened. "Sorry. Is there any land grant recorded? Any transfer from the former owner of the lot?"

"As you no doubt suspect, no. The land itself was transferred in its entirety to Mrs. Erickson's parents, the Swindons, and upon their deaths to the Ericksons."

"From who?"

"From the Imperial office. A government stamped transfer."

"A transfer's an interaction between two parties. It goes *to* the senior Swindons, but it has to come *from* somewhere."

"Indeed. It comes from the Imperial Palace; it is a land grant."

"But the taxation Records…"

Teela nodded again. "Those were not altered. There does not seem to be a codicil to the ownership. The record—the one that mentions house fourteen and its owner—appears to be a Records artifact. It has no bearing on the Records related to property, ownership, and the laws created to cover them.

"There is no legal reason that a Barrani—lord or no—could not own property in the city of Elantra should they have the money to legally purchase a property. It is not done, of course—to live as a mortal among mortals would be considered a social disgrace."

"Tain does."

Teela's smile was cool. "Indeed. But *Lord* Tain was considered a disgrace when he declined to take the Test of Name, and in truth, I admired his conviction. He joined the Hawks when I did; he joined, I believe, because I did. His adoption of what you consider a 'normal' abode was his way of making clear—to anyone who might question him—that he served me and my interests, no matter where they might lead.

"Most Barrani would be far more willing to commit murder than to lose public face. Tain, however, is not most Barrani."

"But Azoria—a woman whose name strikes dread in powerful Barrani Lords—was perfectly willing to buy a merely mortal dwelling."

"Be careful," Teela said, voice soft, eyes dark. She meant that as a warning; it wasn't a threat, but a request.

"I'm always careful."

Mandoran choked on what he was drinking, causing a spray of liquid—and coughing—that did not amuse Sedarias. It did amuse Terrano, but he was outside of the spray radius.

Teela ignored it. She did, however, choose to speak in High Barrani, not the Elantran with which she usually addressed Kaylin. "I would tell you to abandon this inquiry, but I know you too well. Perhaps, if the trapped children were adults, you could do it—it would spare many lives in the end."

"You think there will be more deaths?"

"Don't you?"

Sedarias remained silent, leaving the discussion in Teela's hands, which wasn't like her.

"If you cannot leave it be, let me accompany you," Teela continued.

Kaylin froze. She felt Severn's amusement, although it was a quiet, black amusement. *She's always kept an eye out for you.*

The Barrani aren't supposed to investigate this—they're not supposed to mention her name at all—and Teela isn't subject to the laws of exemption if she's killed in action.

I wouldn't be so certain of that; she's an Imperial Hawk. I'm cer-

*tain, given her history as An'Teela, that she will not be approached
with the cold-minded carelessness that the Mellarionne allies were. If
she were, the assassins would be the ones to die.*

"I won't be going anywhere immediately."

"You've been escorting Mrs. Erickson home when you've
finished desk work." Not a question.

Kaylin nodded. "Not because of Azoria, whoever she was
or is, but because Mrs. Erickson's neighbor is—" She paused
and then pulled out a Leontine obscenity for good measure. "According to Jamal and Esme—Esmeralda was her
full name—he's forced himself into the house at least once.
They made him leave. Jamal can...interact with physical objects, but as he can't be seen, the neighbor believes the house
is haunted."

"So the neighbor isn't entirely stupid." This, in Elantran.

"I wouldn't say that."

"You generally dislike acknowledging the strengths of people you otherwise despise, yes."

"No, that's not what I mean. He thinks Mrs. Erickson has
something that belongs to him—that she maybe stole it or
something. And he's hell-bent on getting it back, which is
why he tried to force himself into the house the one time."

"What exactly does he think she stole?"

"She has no idea. He never said. I highly doubt he'd tell
us, either."

Teela's answering frown was much more familiar—and
oddly comforting—to Kaylin. "You want to get into a brawl
with him."

"He almost hit me," Kaylin replied, which everyone present took as *yes*. "But Jamal scared him off."

"I will accompany you when you escort Mrs. Erickson
home."

"She's harmless. I don't want you intimidating her."

"Why would you think I would do that?"

Kaylin snorted. "You're *Barrani*. You intimidate people just by breathing in their direction."

Teela raised a single brow. "I will, of course, be wearing the tabard of the Hawks."

"It's *after hours*," Kaylin snapped. "We're not on duty."

"Oh. And you therefore went in civilian clothing?"

"I will be, today. Look, she's a harmless, gentle old lady who brings us food. I mean, we all thought she was a bit dotty, but if she is, so am I."

"No argument there," Mandoran cheerfully added.

Sedarias, eyes far too dark, said, "We are trusting An'Teela and ask that you do the same. You are Lord Kaylin, but you are not Barrani."

"I approve of that," Mandoran said. "Most Barrani are boring if they're not trying to kill you—present company excepted, of course."

"I might consent to be less boring if you do not stop interrupting me." Given the color of Sedarias's eyes, she wasn't joking. Mandoran rolled eyes, but fell silent. "Teela understands what will—or will not—cause political difficulty, both for us and for the Barrani.

"But we don't expect that this is entirely political; there is too much cohesion of approach. Azoria is not a name that is spoken aloud among those of our kin who did not spend centuries jailed in a Hallionne. If Teela judges whatever it is you can, or cannot, see to be truly dangerous, she will ask you to stop your investigation as it touches upon Azoria.

"She won't stop you from attempting to somehow free the dead. The mortal dead are not our dead; they are—or were, to our minds—children's stories. We are willing to believe that you—who bears the marks of the Chosen—can see them; we are therefore willing to believe that they exist. But if they can be somehow set free without perturbing or terrifying the rest of the Barrani, please, *please* do so."

"If it can't?"

"If it can't, we will at least have forewarning and we can plan our own defenses at that time."

"There's only one thing."

"And that?"

"Tomorrow I'm not escorting Mrs. Erickson directly home."

"Oh?"

"I have an appointment with Lord Sanabalis."

"The Arkon," Teela added. "You should learn to use the title."

"Fine. The Arkon. I have an appointment with the Arkon. I've asked him to assess Mrs. Erickson for magical potential."

After a brief silent pause, Sedarias grimaced. "I would hardly think that would be worth his time, given both her race and her age."

"Luckily, I haven't asked the cohort to assess."

"It's Sedarias," Mandoran said, earning a glare from Sedarias herself. "She thinks about things in a purely utilitarian way."

"If I did that, I would have gotten rid of half of you already!"

Terrano snickered. "What? I'm allowed to laugh—I'm part of the half she'd ditch. Sedarias likes a smooth and obedient chain of command."

"It's a wonder she never strangled you."

"To me, too. But I was the most…flexible of all of us. I was the first to be able to escape Alsanis."

Since his escape had caused a lot of damage, Kaylin wasn't certain this was a good thing. But if he hadn't, the cohort wouldn't be here, and that would, in the end, be a loss. "Fine. I'll take Teela. I *don't* want Terrano to tag along."

Terrano's smile was bright and almost childlike. "Well, sucks to be you."

"Terrano," Sedarias snapped.

"You can't stop her from being Kaylin, and she's mortal. What makes you think you can stop me?"

"I can beg Helen for a favor."

"Not that one." He grinned. "I wouldn't mind if Helen tried to keep me trapped here; it would be a bit of a challenge. Assuming she wouldn't just kill me."

"I would not," Helen's disembodied voice said. "Nor would Sedarias truly wish for your death."

"Could I perhaps wish for his silence?"

Terrano laughed.

Serralyn said, "I'd vote for that, if it were possible."

"Helen, they're ganging up on me." Terrano's eyes were green.

Helen materialized physically; Kaylin suspected it was because she wanted the gentle smile on her face to be seen.

Kaylin spent the morning at a busier-than-usual front desk. Six of the reports were about ghosts. There were often reports about hauntings of various kinds, but perhaps because of her recent experiences, she was tempted to take them seriously. There were another two reports of vampire sightings, and she made a mental note to check for bodies in the morgue; sometimes people came up with unusual explanations for deaths they'd heard about in the rumor mill.

Her facial muscles were cramped by the time Mrs. Erickson made her appearance; it was hard to treat every complaint with respect when the people who were making those complaints were hostile. Politely accepting overt hostility had never been one of Kaylin's core social strengths, and it was theoretically a requirement of this desk.

Her smile, however, was genuine when Mrs. Erickson—basket over arm—came into view. The old woman took a seat, as she did when there were people who had arrived before her. Her clothing today was more staid, more stiff, and she actually wore bits of jewelry; if Kaylin had wondered if Mrs. Erickson remembered that they were going to the palace, she had her answer.

Mrs. Erickson was vastly more patient with the passage of time than Kaylin—and neither had a patch on angry, busy Dragons. But there was no one else that Kaylin could wave over; most Hawks avoided front desk duty as if it were contagious. And deadly.

She was therefore in a bit of a rush when she was finally finished. She barely looked at the basket Mrs. Erickson was carrying. But everything smelled *good*, and after the day she'd had she deserved a bit of a treat.

The sergeant appeared as if summoned the moment Kaylin opened the basket. On most occasions, this would have given rise to humorous comments, not that Bridget was terribly forgiving of them. Time, however, was a problem now. Kaylin said, "We have an appointment with the Arkon at the Imperial Palace. Today."

"We?"

"Mrs. Erickson and me. We have to leave now or we're going to be late."

Bridget nodded. "Can you leave the basket here today, given that Kaylin's 'or' should be replaced with 'and.' No one wants to be late to meet a Dragon; they have bad tempers and notorious memory."

Mrs. Erickson nodded. "I have three others at home. I'll pick that one up when I come by tomorrow."

Teela was waiting for them on the safe side of the public office door, arms folded, shoulders against the nearest wall. Barrani could do this without appearing to slouch. She peeled herself off the wall. "I thought you said your appointment was at 4:30."

"It is."

"I thought so. I've taken the liberty of calling for a carriage." To Mrs. Erickson, she added, "I'm Corporal Teela, a friend and mentor of Kaylin's. You must be the Mrs. Erickson she talks so much about."

"Oh, dear. I hope she hasn't said anything bad."

"About you? Not at all. She is not, I'm afraid to report, impressed with your neighbor."

Mrs. Erickson winced, and in an effort to change the topic, added, "Are you going to introduce the young man beside you, or is he not with you?"

Kaylin stared at the empty space to Teela's left. "The young man is Terrano. He's one of my housemates."

Terrano looked flummoxed, an expression he retained when he materialized so that Kaylin could see him; she was certain Teela had been aware that he was present.

"I'm sorry—have I said the wrong thing?" Mrs. Erickson asked Terrano.

"Sort of?" Terrano replied. "Kaylin couldn't see me."

Mrs. Erickson winced. "I'm sorry, dear—I didn't realize you were trying to be invisible." She apologized as if invisibility was a condition one could achieve by wishing for it.

Terrano's glance at Kaylin said, *Is she for real.* Kaylin glared in response—safely behind Mrs. Erickson so the old woman couldn't see her expression.

"Kaylin talks about you a lot," Terrano then said. Kaylin's glare became a death glare. "So I wanted to see what you were like."

"Oh."

"She's right, though—you're definitely different. No," he added quickly, "it's a good different, not a bad one."

"You mean I can see ghosts."

"And not just ghosts," he replied. "Because I'm definitely not dead."

"I'm sure something could be arranged," Kaylin muttered.

"Not by you," Terrano shot back, having regained equilibrium. "So...we're going to the Imperial Palace?"

Kaylin was certain her brows had disappeared into her hairline. "No. *We're* going to the Imperial Palace."

"The Imperial Guard won't see me."

Kaylin cleared her throat. "Mrs. Erickson will."

"I'm accustomed to pretending I can't around most people," Mrs. Erickson said, in a tone that implied she felt sorry for Terrano, or at least for his exclusion.

Before Kaylin could speak, Teela said, "No."

Given Terrano's expression, she wasn't the only member of the cohort to say so. Kaylin was fairly certain that Terrano would make the attempt regardless, but sometimes he surprised her; he listened to Sedarias. Given that Teela, a member of the cohort, intended to escort Kaylin, Terrano's presence wasn't required; Sedarias would be able to see and hear via Teela. And none of the cohort really wanted to anger a Dragon.

Teela did not drive the carriage, so Kaylin and Mrs. Erickson arrived at the palace in one piece, without losing anything they'd had the time to eat before the ride. Teela was giving Kaylin the stink eye for much of the ride because Kaylin's attitude toward Teela driving was well-known. It was also well deserved in the cohort's opinion, although Mandoran and Terrano were more ambivalent; Teela driving was never going to be boring, after all.

The palace steward's face was made of stone, given his expression, but he did check his appointment book, and he did call for a page to escort the trio to Sanabalis's office. The office itself hadn't changed location; Sanabalis clearly hadn't chosen an out-of-the-way room with a door that appeared by magic but couldn't otherwise be seen. The former Arkon was famously grouchy when interrupted; Sanabalis wasn't.

Given his expression when he opened the door, however, that was probably likely to change.

Kaylin didn't understand the function of an Arkon within the Dragon Court. Given that Immortals had perfect memory, a keeper of history seemed almost irrelevant.

"Come in. Or stand outside in the hall while I close the door on you." Sanabalis was speaking Elantran, not the High Barrani generally used by Imperial bureaucrats. Given how suspicious they were of Barrani, Kaylin had often wondered why High Barrani was the language used for almost all legal or bureaucratic work.

Then again, given how much she hated both, maybe that was the answer.

The orange-eyed Dragon looked at Kaylin, the gaze pointed.

"This is Mrs. Erickson of Orbonne Street. And this is Corporal Teela of the Hawks."

Sanabalis turned to Mrs. Erickson. "I am Lord Sanabalis, Arkon of the Dragon Flights."

Mrs. Erickson tilted her head as she studied the Dragon. She looked intrigued, not intimidated.

"Might I ask a question?"

"Certainly," he replied. "You are the reason I allowed the corporal to interrupt my day's work." He smiled, and the orange in his eyes lightened.

"Is it not uncomfortable to contain quite so large a form in a body our size?"

His brows rose slightly; this was not the question he'd expected. He recovered quickly. "It is not uncomfortable at all; it was, when I was very new to adulthood."

Mrs. Erickson nodded, as if that had answered a question. Kaylin guessed both that it had, and that the question hadn't originated with Mrs. Erickson; she suspected Darreno was the original source. If Darreno was to be believed, he had been born during a time before the first Draco-Barrani war, but the antagonism between the two Immortal races had had long roots prior to that war's start.

"Did Kaylin tell you why she wished me to meet with you?" the Dragon asked.

Mrs. Erickson looked down at her feet while she answered. "She wanted you to assess my magical potential." She lifted her lined face and added, "I did tell her that I was tested for magical ability when I was a child, and the Imperial Mages said I had no potential, but she didn't believe their assessment was accurate."

"Indeed. Did she perhaps tell you why?"

At this, the old woman seemed to shrink about three inches. She glanced at Kaylin; Kaylin nodded in what she hoped was an encouraging fashion.

"She believes that my ability to see ghosts is somehow related to magical potential."

"I see. Do you believe she's wrong?"

"I don't know. She's the only other person who has ever seen my friends—I mean, my ghostly friends. But she thinks she sees them because of magic, and if that's why, she thinks I..." She trailed off. Her hands curved into half fists; were it not for her wrinkles and her frailty, she could have been a much, much younger woman.

"It is possible for Imperial Mages to be mistaken in their assessments. If they were unaware of your ability to see things that others can't see—or if they perhaps considered it a childhood conceit or fancy—they may have rushed through very, very standard tests.

"For how long were you assessed?"

"It was a long time ago," she replied. "But I recall it being most of a morning."

"*Very* standard tests. Do you wish Kaylin to remain while I personally assess your potential?"

"If it wouldn't be too much of an imposition."

"And the other corporal?"

"She's one of Corporal Neya's friends, and she's a Hawk." A long way of saying yes, which Sanabalis did not misinterpret. He walked to the door, opened it, and held it open for Mrs. Erickson. "Come with me. Most of the tests will be conducted in a location other than my office; there are too many interruptions and I dislike interruption when I am attempting to give a task my full concentration."

Sanabalis led them past Imperial Guards toward a familiar set of doors: the Imperial Library. He opened the doors himself, which meant Kaylin didn't have to touch them. The door wards on the library doors were special, and frequently raised an almost deafening alarm when touched by Kaylin; the Arkon had never chosen to make adjustments to the wards.

Kaylin wasn't surprised to see the librarians behind the main desk; nor was she surprised when Sanabalis walked past them. He slowed his walking speed to accommodate Mrs. Erickson because she—like any first-time visitor to a library such as this—was glancing from side to side at the height of towering shelves, all of which contained books.

He walked past those books, and from there, past the shelves that, less impressive, contained fragile fragments of historical interest. This part of the collection was seldom seen, and never without appropriate permissions; the librarians were not allowed entry without them, either.

Beyond this were small halls and smaller doors, but Kaylin had a suspicion that the hall they would eventually take would not lead to any of the usual rooms the Arkon—Lannagaros—had occupied. Sanabalis passed them by, as expected. He then opened a door that led into a much darker space, gesturing light into being, as light was needed here. "I should make you do it," he told Kaylin.

"It's not my fault you've been too busy to teach me recently."

"No. But your lack of practice can be laid at your feet; I feel at this point that consistent and constant practice would at least allow you to create a small light that would ease passage in darker spaces."

"You're learning magic?" Mrs. Erickson asked.

"She is fighting tooth and nail not to learn it," Sanabalis replied, his voice a critical rumble.

"I'm allergic to magic," Kaylin told Mrs. Erickson, feeling slightly guilty because she'd dragged the old woman here. "It makes my skin hurt."

"Oh," Mrs. Erickson replied, with a sympathetic tsk. "Are you going to be all right here today?"

"I wasn't certain you'd want to come here alone. I mean, Sanabalis—Lord Sanabalis—the Arkon." Gods, Kaylin hated titles. "The Arkon is a Dragon, and most people don't interact much with Dragons."

"He seems like a perfectly polite young man," Mrs. Erickson said, as if to reassure Kaylin.

Sanabalis coughed. He was, in comparison to Mrs. Erickson's lived years, beyond ancient. But Mrs. Erickson was hard to dislike, and almost impossible to find offensive unless your entire outlook on life depended on the ability to take offense.

Kaylin had met a number of people like that, and she avoided them like the plague, which would probably be preferable.

"If you'd prefer we wait, we can do that, but I'm curious about the testing, and I'm almost certain the Arkon is going to have questions for me after the results are in."

"Well, if it's all right with you, I'm happy to have you there. It is all right?" she said, slightly anxiously, to the Dragon who'd be administering the test.

"It is. It is always helpful when the applicants are relaxed, and it appears that the corporal is here to offer support. In many cases parents would fill her role; we are accustomed to having observers."

He continued down the dark hall, his voice echoing off the uneven walls.

The door opened into a familiar cavern—familiar, that is, to Kaylin. Teela, almost expressionless, was nonetheless looking around the cavern with genuine interest; this room was not a room she had ever seen before, and she seemed to be slightly surprised that she was allowed to accompany Kaylin into it.

Kaylin was almost positive the former Arkon would never have allowed it, and wondered if the Emperor knew Teela was here. She didn't ask.

Sanabalis, however, was—as always—ahead of her. "I am certain," he said, in High Barrani, "you are wondering why I have admitted you into this room."

Teela's nod was respectful. She didn't have the cohort's visceral fear of—or hatred for—Dragons, but she was always going to approach them with caution.

"There are two reasons. The first: you serve the Halls of Law. The second, more relevant, is your knowledge of both magic and Corporal Neya. It has not escaped the notice of *any* of the Dragon Court that the corporal is frequently at the center of highly unusual—and frequently dangerous— magical anomalies."

Kaylin bit back any words she might have offered in return, because Mrs. Erickson was here and she didn't want to even imply that all of the anomalies were the old woman's fault. She watched Sanabalis carefully; he made no move to find the ladders that were used to reach the very large stone altar toward the back center of the room.

That altar was the Ancient's version of a mirror. To invoke its use, the Dragons had to speak in their native tongue. Kaylin wasn't certain what polite *Draconic* language was—but to mortal ears it all sounded like fury and imminent death. Possibly to Barrani ears as well.

To her eyes, that altar seemed to be shedding light. She frowned, but said nothing, turning her attention to Sanabalis and Mrs. Erickson. Sanabalis's tests for magical potential—at least in Kaylin—were the tests usually administered by the Imperial College of mages. She suspected similar tests were conducted in the Academia, although magical potential there was not a prerequisite to entry.

Sanabalis clearly intended to skip all of it. Because of Kaylin. Was she nervous? Yes, a bit. But she knew what she'd seen, and she knew Mrs. Erickson wasn't, as most assumed, crazy. She wasn't hallucinating. Yes, she might be lonely, but her visits to the Halls of Law weren't about *her* loneliness; they were about the isolation of four young ghosts.

Ghosts of children who had, in theory, died at the age of twenty-five.

"Mrs. Erickson, please stand here, in the center of the cavern." She did as bid immediately.

Sanabalis began to chant, the words low and sonorous, the voice tinged with a hint of Draconic rumble. The hair on Kaylin's arms began to rise as her magic allergies kicked in. She kept the usual grimace off her face because Mrs. Erickson—in the presence of a Dragon—continually glanced at Kaylin to make sure Kaylin was all right.

When the light at the top of the altar flared to life, becoming an almost blinding white, Sanabalis's syllables broke in what Kaylin assumed were the middle of words. He turned from Mrs. Erickson toward the altar itself and exhaled a steady stream of smoky breath.

"Corporal," he snapped, "go get the ladders."

There was no question about which corporal he meant.

11

The ladders in the cavern were against the walls—but the light, which hadn't dimmed at all, made them easily visible to Kaylin's vision. Teela had probably seen them instantly. Kaylin trudged across the cavern's stone floor. The ladders had wheels—Kaylin wasn't entirely certain she could have lifted them, given their heavy construction. Even rolling them across the floor here was a struggle because the floor wasn't entirely flat.

She might have resented it more, but Hope snapped to attention on her shoulder. He squawked *loudly*.

Sanabalis wheeled then, his eyes passing from orange to red—never a good sign in Dragons. Teela's eyes were indigo, although they weren't glowing, so they were harder to see at this distance.

"What is it?" Kaylin demanded. "What's wrong?"

In reply, Hope lifted a wing and slapped it across her face. Kaylin, attached to the ladder, froze.

Mrs. Erickson was standing in front of Sanabalis. The altar above them continued to glow a blinding white. But with Hope's aid, Kaylin could see that that light was not the simple illumination it had first appeared. There was form and shape in the bright miasma, lifting itself from the surface of an altar that remained, without the positioning of ladders, invisible.

Kaylin's arms began to glow; she was certain her legs, her back, and every other inch of her skin covered with the marks of the Chosen, were glowing as well.

Teela stepped toward Mrs. Erickson—or the altar; it was hard to judge because the older woman stood between Teela and the large stone structure. Sanabalis had turned toward the altar itself but, at Hope's squawking, turned toward Mrs. Erickson instead.

Mrs. Erickson was shining as well. Given the radiant brilliance of the altar light, Kaylin might have otherwise missed that glow—but as she watched through Hope's wing, she could see that it was steadily increasing in brightness.

"Oh, dear," Mrs. Erickson said, audible even though the texture of her voice was soft. She was looking up, as Teela looked up, at the altar. Kaylin was certain that what she now saw through Hope's wing was naturally visible to the older woman.

Teela came to stand to Mrs. Erickson's side; she placed a staying hand on the older woman's shoulder. The Barrani Hawk gestured quickly and sharply; Kaylin felt Teela's magic as if something had walked by and peeled off a layer of skin. She could see a barrier rise in front of Teela, Mrs. Erickson, and Sanabalis; it was Teela's magic.

Mrs. Erickson winced. "I don't think it means harm," she said, raising her voice as if to be heard. "It's a...ghost."

Kaylin knew—or thought she knew—that the liquid that occupied the surface of the altar wasn't the water that occupied the surface of Tara's pool; it was the blood—the golden blood—of an Ancient, those beings who had once been the creators, the gods of this world. The Ancients were gone, although their work endured: the Towers that guarded the fiefs, the Hallionne that provided shelter and defense as one approached the West March, the sentient buildings like Helen, whom Kaylin called home.

It hadn't occurred to her that gods could die.

But Darreno and Amaldi weren't dead, and Mrs. Erickson considered them outside ghosts—and friends.

"I don't think it's a ghost," Kaylin said, keeping her voice even.

"If you could stop babbling and join us," Teela said, "that would be safest."

"I have Hope," she replied. She would have joined Teela regardless because the circumstances had grown strange enough that Teela served as her partner here, and Hawks were forbidden to work alone. But she felt it urgently important that the ladder be placed against the rise of the side of the stone altar, and she put her weight behind that ladder, pushing it as quickly as she could.

Only when she heard it smack stone did she turn toward Teela and the barrier Teela had raised.

"Sanabalis!" Kaylin shouted. "Can you see it? Can you see what Mrs. Erickson can see?"

The Dragon, eyes red, roared in response; Kaylin instinctively reached up to cover her ears, not that it helped. But she remembered that sometimes Dragons spoke their native tongue when interacting with ancient things. This altar was that. She closed the eye that Hope's wing covered as a demi-mask. She could see light, and perhaps a subtle hint of movement at its base.

But through Hope's wing she could see something like mist or fog, something attenuated and dispersed struggling to take shape, to don form. She was certain that this was what Mrs. Erickson herself saw, and given Sanabalis's eye color, the Dragon was aware of it as well.

It was to Mrs. Erickson that Kaylin turned, and to Mrs. Erickson that she ran. Teela had drawn sword—which was not part of the Hawk's official uniform, but she'd worry about that later—and Sanabalis had stepped outside of the radius Teela's protective circle traced. Kaylin could see the barrier through Hope's wing.

Even though the physical distance was a warning, Kaylin was surprised when Sanabalis, new Arkon of the sole remaining dragon flight, began to shift in place, his scholarly appearance spreading into a shape that was far, far larger. She looked away, as she often did when Dragons shed their human appearance; there was something disturbing about the way the body transformed, because each element of the transformation was visible; it looked, on the outside, like some form of hideous magical torture.

When Sanabalis roared, the cavern shook—or at least the parts of it beneath Kaylin's moving feet. She sprinted toward Teela and Mrs. Erickson, skidding to a stop beside the older woman. When she had asked Sanabalis to personally assess the old woman for magical potential, this was *not* what she'd expected.

Mrs. Erickson was pale; clearly this wasn't what she'd expected, either. But while she glanced at Sanabalis in full Draconic glory, her eyes were drawn, once again, to the moving, writhing light she had called a ghost. Her expression was not one of awe, and she surprised Kaylin because, in the growing brightness, she could see the trails of tears nestling in the folds of Mrs. Erickson's lined face.

Mrs. Erickson took a step forward and faltered—Teela still gripped her shoulder.

"Tell her," Mrs. Erickson told Kaylin, "that I'm not in danger."

"If the altar itself is not a danger," Teela said, in a voice meant to carry even over a Dragon's roar, "the Dragon may be. The cavern is large enough to accommodate a Dragon in this form—but it is not so large that the Dragon can move freely as danger necessitates. Here, you will be as safe as it is possible to be where a Dragon is raging."

"I am *not* raging," Sanabalis said in rumbling, guttural Barrani. "But An'Teela is correct—I am uncertain that there will not be danger. Please remain by her side."

"Should we leave?"

"I am not certain that that is now possible. There is a reason this room exists where and as it does, and in the event of catastrophic change, the door will not open for anyone or anything. I am included in that," he added, before Kaylin could ask. He pushed himself up, toward the cavern's height, his wings spread and moving. She had never understood how flight in creatures the size—and weight—of Dragons worked, but remembered hazily that Dragons required a world with certain levels of magic to do so.

This one clearly had enough.

"Corporal," Mrs. Erickson said, far more urgency in her tone, "I will be safe. The ghost does not intend me harm. Kaylin—please, talk to her."

Hope squawked as Sanabalis reached the height of the altar. To Kaylin, he added, *What I can allow you to see is not all that Mrs. Erickson can see.*

"Should we let her go?"

I believe that is wise—for you, and for your friends.

"But will she be safe?"

I do not know. I cannot see what she sees. Understand that. But there is movement in the miasma I can see, and it is not friendly.

Kaylin turned to Mrs. Erickson, who was now wiping her eyes with her sleeve. "Please, Kaylin. Trust me."

Kaylin couldn't say no. Teela could, but the marks on Kaylin's arms were glowing, and the color of the altar's light was the color of the marks. "Teela," she said quietly, "keep the shield up."

Kaylin—don't. It was Severn.

She didn't ignore him, but she couldn't obey him; she could not turn away from what she saw in Mrs. Erickson's face. She held out a hand to the old woman, and the old woman took it. Kaylin's marks rose from her arms, from her legs, forming a sphere around them both—a sphere Kaylin thought only she could see.

And Severn, her partner, who was at a safe distance and could see what occurred only through Kaylin's eyes.

Sanabalis didn't come to land on the altar; he hovered there, his wings almost metallic. Kaylin couldn't see his eyes from her position on the ground. The ladder was wide enough that both she and Mrs. Erickson could climb it together, if it came to that—it had been built with the density of Dragon weight in mind.

She wasn't certain it would come to that, because as Mrs. Erickson, hand in hand with Kaylin, approached the base of that altar, the light above spread and changed; Kaylin thought she could see the amorphous form of wings—wings raised as if, somehow, the light could break free of the stone that anchored it or contained it.

Mrs. Erickson's hand tightened. "Can you hear them?" she whispered.

Them. Hope squawked, but there were no words—no words for Kaylin—in the sound. If he spoke to either Teela or Sanabalis, neither chose to respond.

"Sanabalis?"

The Dragon was utterly silent. Kaylin frowned and looked up; he seemed frozen, his neck curved down, toward the altar's surface. The wings of the ghost were, Kaylin suddenly thought, the width and breadth of Dragon wings. "Hope. *Hope.*"

Yes, the familiar said, his voice attenuated, as if he were speaking from a much larger distance than beside her ear.

"Go to Sanabalis. Go now."

Hope was silent; he did not move.

"I'm not in danger!"

Hope didn't reply, but his claws pierced cloth to prick the area beneath her collarbone.

Kaylin was horrified, but not surprised, when the light emanating from the altar's unseen surface enveloped Sanabalis; diaphanous wings like shadows composed of light fell across Draconic wings, traveling up the neck of the Dragon Lord until it enveloped the Dragon's face.

Only then did Sanabalis, suspended and weightless in Draconic form, turn away from the altar. His eyes were white, and his teeth, as he opened his great mouth, white as well, but luminescent, almost opaline. Kaylin's hand tightened enough that Mrs. Erickson winced.

He opened his mouth on a roar—or the physicality of a roar, absent all sound.

Mrs. Erickson, however, took a step back—as large a step as she could while still attached to Kaylin by hand.

"What do you hear?" Kaylin asked her, trying—and failing—to keep panic out of her voice. The marks of the Chosen—the floating marks—responded to her panic more quickly than Mrs. Erickson did. They rose instantly, to form a revolving shield, their colors so pale they might have been part of the illumination shed by the altar's light.

When the Dragon that she could no longer think of as

Sanabalis roared next, she could hear its voice—it was echoed by the marks of the Chosen. She lifted her free hand to cover her ear, as she often did when Dragons started their conversations; Hope bit her hand hard enough to draw blood. As he had a mouthful of her hand, he didn't speak, but his meaning was clear.

She was to listen, just as Mrs. Erickson was listening.

Her concern at the moment was not the elderly civilian, it was the Dragon. Any force that could possess a Dragon was beyond dangerous. Should whatever inhabited Sanabalis decide to kill them all, they were dead—and it might not stop there. The Imperial Palace was full of people who stood no chance against a Dragon, and only a handful who did, none of whom were in the immediate vicinity.

Mrs. Erickson didn't seem to be concerned about surviving a Dragon. She lifted both hands, dragging the one locked in Kaylin's up, as if beseeching. Kaylin looked at the Dragon's eyes.

"Hope—can you bring Sanabalis back?"

No.

"Can't or won't?"

Cannot. Not even if you were willing to pay the price of it. There is power here with which I cannot interfere. I am not a god, Kaylin.

At any other time, Kaylin would have been interested in the statement. Now she was too worried about other things: Sanabalis. Mrs. Erickson. Even herself. Teela was present, but anything Kaylin and Mrs. Erickson could survive had no chance of killing the Barrani Hawk. She could say the same about Sanabalis; her fear for him was different.

Mrs. Erickson's eyes were wet.

The not-Dragon roared with Sanabalis's throat—but the roar was attenuated, the echo of a Dragon's voice, not the sound itself. She wondered if Sanabalis was somewhere behind the white eyes that were focused almost entirely on Mrs. Erickson.

"Mrs. Erickson."

The older woman failed to hear.

Kaylin's arms hurt. Mrs. Erickson stood behind a moving shield of True Words, and Kaylin didn't have the time to attempt to read them. She glanced at her arms. All of the marks on both had lifted themselves from her skin to form this shield of words, this moving cage.

"Mrs. Erickson! *Mrs. Erickson!*"

The old woman attempted to walk through the words; Kaylin wasn't certain whether the thing that stopped her was Kaylin's hand, or the words themselves. Those words shivered in place as Mrs. Erickson attempted to move toward the possessed Dragon.

Something was terribly wrong—which was a ridiculous thing to think because it was so obvious. Kaylin tightened her grip on the old woman. Whatever now inhabited Sanabalis probably didn't *intend* to harm her, given Mrs. Erickson's tears and the expression that transformed her face; there was no awe in it, no joy, just a kind of bitter recognition. Whatever this ghost was, Mrs. Erickson appeared to instinctively grasp some greater part of it.

Kaylin understood that Mrs. Erickson and the Dragon had to remain separated.

Yes, Hope said. The awe that Mrs. Erickson lacked, Kaylin heard in the voice of her familiar. *It is a ghost, Kaylin. You should not have brought her here.*

Mrs. Erickson spoke, lifting a quavering voice to be heard. She had always been soft-spoken, but a thread of steel underlay the syllables that left her mouth now—syllables that Kaylin herself couldn't understand.

The Dragon replied.

Kaylin understood Amaldi and Darreno. She understood the children trapped in Mrs. Erickson's home. She could not understand whatever it was that now inhabited the Dragon. Dragon voices—even attenuated and distant as this one was—lacked nuance or subtlety. This one didn't.

Mrs. Erickson was speaking the same language, modulated by an entirely human throat.

"Hope—can you understand a thing either of them are saying?"

Hope was silent for a long beat. *Stop her. If you value the Dragon, if you value her as she is, stop her.*

Kaylin looked once at Sanabalis, silver light emanating from his open eyes, his moving jaws. She then turned fully toward the old woman whose hand she held.

"Imelda! Imelda Erickson!"

For the first time since the light had enveloped Sanabalis, Mrs. Erickson, tears still dampening her cheeks, turned toward Kaylin, her brows raised in surprise, not sorrow. She blinked.

"Imelda," Kaylin said, voice softer. "I need to know what you see when you look at my friend."

"Your friend, dear?" Her voice was weaker, probably because she'd been shouting, or as close to shouting as Mrs. Erickson ever got.

"The Dragon. Lord Sanabalis. The Arkon. The man who was supposed to be testing you for magical aptitude. Remember?"

Kaylin heard sound at her back; lighter steps. Teela, in all probability.

"How strong are these symbols?" a familiar voice asked. Not Teela. Terrano. Of course it was.

"I don't know. I think they'll protect us from...whatever it is that version of Dragon exhales; I doubt it'll help much against his jaws." She couldn't turn to face Terrano; she was too afraid to lose what she'd only barely managed to get: Mrs. Erickson's attention.

"How much of a risk are you willing to take?"

"Do *not* do anything stupid."

"You should seriously join us in the asylum," he snapped. "You'd fit right in." He muttered the only Barrani curse words she knew, and then added, "You can't see what your friend can see."

"You can?"

Hope squawked. Loudly.

"I can see what you can't." Terrano's reply was terse.

"What exactly—"

"Not the right time for this," he replied. "If I make it out alive, we can argue about it then."

The steps Kaylin had heard were Teela's; the Barrani Hawk reached out and grabbed Terrano as if he were an errant pickpocket clever and fast enough to rob her, but not fast enough to get away with it. She was silent; whatever she had to say wasn't meant for Kaylin's ears. Her expression made clear that Kaylin should probably be grateful for it.

Mrs. Erickson turned to Terrano, of all people, her eyes widening again, her mouth open but silent. She found her words. "Don't hurt them," she said, her voice a whisper. "They have been hurt enough. Don't hurt them."

Terrano's brows rose, briefly, into his hair. "Me hurt *them*? You might not have noticed, but they're sitting inside a *Dragon*."

"They don't mean harm. They don't. They're upset, they don't mean harm!"

"When a Dragon has a tantrum, it *causes* harm," Terrano told her. "Look—you can talk to the ghost all you want *after* we pull it out of the Dragon's body. The Dragon has done nothing to deserve possession."

Kaylin looked, briefly, at Terrano. "Imelda," she said, voice soft, "we can't hurt a ghost."

Mrs. Erickson shook her head. "You can. He can."

"And you?" Teela asked, abandoning whatever conversation—if it could be called that—she was silently having with Terrano.

"I never would. I *never* would." The words were louder.

Hope squawked. The possessed Dragon had alighted, and he now stalked toward them. Had he been Sanabalis, he could have covered the distance with ease; he appeared to be struggling to walk now.

Sanabalis was still there, and Sanabalis did not want to reach them. Or rather, didn't want whatever was in control of him to reach them.

Hope exhaled beside Kaylin's ear; it was the wrong ear, the one she couldn't cover. When he lifted his voice, when he spoke, Kaylin heard...nothing. It was a long nothing, given the tension in the claws that gripped her shoulder.

Whatever it was he said, Mrs. Erickson flinched, and the possessed Dragon halted in its tracks. Its eyes remained white. Kaylin noticed that the inner membranes had been lowered. When it opened its jaws, it spoke.

This time, Kaylin understood the words; she heard them in Elantran.

Help us. Help us. Help us.

Mrs. Erickson flinched. "I'll try. I *promise* I'll try. You don't need the Dragon to speak with me. I can see you. I could see you before you approached him. We need the Dragon back, if you can release him."

Help us.

"Yes," she said, her voice softer, her tears once again falling freely. "I will do everything in my power to help you. To help you all. But…leave the Dragon. Please." The last word, low, was emphatic. A request, not a command. But Kaylin recognized it as a negotiation. Mrs. Erickson didn't believe that Sanabalis would return to them on his own.

Hope squawked, this time very, very loudly. It was almost comforting because it was normal.

Sanabalis's eyes remained white.

"Corporal. Kaylin. You have to let go of my hand now."

"Not a good idea," Teela snapped.

"Trust me. Jamal is strong—you said that yourself. Jamal is a kitten in comparison to them. I know you can't see what I see—but you can see something. If you want your friend back, you need to let go of my hand."

Kaylin shook her head as Hope squawked.

"If you're worried about me, don't. If I'm possessed—as your Dragon is possessed—I can do far less harm. Far less."

"Do. Not. Let. Go. Of. Her." It was Sanabalis. Sanabalis's voice, broken and strained.

"They don't mean to harm you," Mrs. Erickson said, recognizing Sanabalis's voice although she had heard it so seldom. "They have been here, waiting. Waiting in the dark. Waiting to be released."

"Who are they?" Teela asked, her voice less sharp.

"I don't know, dear. I won't know until they tell me. I can see ghosts, but they're like any other stranger when we first meet; they have to tell me who they are, and I have to listen." Before Kaylin could speak, she added, "Jamal has been part of my life since I was born. I know those children as well as I know myself.

"But Amaldi and Darreno I met as strangers. We've become friends, who might not have been had they been able to interact with anyone else. You must let go of my hand."

"Kitling."

Kaylin glanced at Teela. She read the Barrani Hawk's expression and shook her head. "Sanabalis will turn me to ash."

"Terrano will be there," Teela replied. "Terrano will accompany her."

Kaylin shook her head again. "If Mrs. Erickson needs to approach the…ghosts, she and I will go together." To Mrs. Erickson, she added, "Would that be all right?"

Mrs. Erickson nodded; she did not once look at Kaylin.

Severn was in the back of Kaylin's head, his concern deep but wordless, as it so often was. She knew he considered this a poor idea. Teela was bristling, but Terrano was clearly less certain; his gaze drifted to Sanabalis's occupied body, and then returned to Mrs. Erickson as if she was the answer to a puzzle he had not known, until that moment, he was trying to piece together.

He had no intention of being left behind, but he made no attempt to reach for, or touch, either Kaylin or Mrs. Erickson— as if the words that encircled them both were a barrier through which he couldn't safely pass.

Kaylin had been in this room before. She had looked into the altar at the top of a far-too-tall pillar. She understood that what might have been considered water by those who viewed it was actually the spilled blood of the Ancients—blood that was not, as the blood of even Dragons or Barrani, red.

She had had no sense at that time that the Ancient had bled to death, which made the blood itself something that was alive in some fashion. The Ancients weren't mortal, but they weren't Immortal as Kaylin understood immortality, either.

There was no guarantee that the ghosts trapped here— just as Jamal and his friends were trapped—were in any way related to the Ancients. But Jamal had not possessed Kaylin, either.

"What do they look like to you?" Kaylin asked Mrs. Erickson.

"People, dear."

"People like Amaldi and Darreno?"

Mrs. Erickson shook her head. "We can talk later," she said, in a much quieter voice. "It's rude to talk about people as if they aren't here when they are."

Chastened—which was, on the surface, ridiculous given the possessed freaking *Dragon*—Kaylin shut up.

Together, the old mortal woman and the young mortal Hawk approached that Dragon, hands entwined. Kaylin wished, for a moment, that she could be Mrs. Erickson—that she could focus her concern and her compassion on the dead.

But the dead were clearly dangerous if they could possess and inhabit a living Dragon, and if they weren't content to leave, things were going to get ugly.

The marks of the Chosen enveloped both mortals as they walked, centered around Kaylin, but encompassing Mrs. Erickson, the unofficial baker of the Hawks, or at least Bridget's section.

The ghost that possessed Sanabalis had stopped its plaintive, desperate roar; it stood on four feet, neck folded almost to ground, when it realized that Mrs. Erickson—to whom it had been speaking the entire time—intended to approach, not retreat in the terror anyone else would have.

Only when it was clear that she would reach the possessed Sanabalis did the possessor fold fully to ground, placing the whole of its lower jaw against the stone floor. Mrs. Erickson nodded, her smile tinged with regret. As she reached the Dragon, she reached out with her free hand, and placed it—with no hesitation whatsoever—against Sanabalis's nose.

"I'm here," she said, voice soft. "I will stay here until I understand why you're here. If possible, you might come with me when I leave."

"Not a good idea," Terrano said.

Kaylin glanced back at him; his skin was distinctly green-tinged.

"I don't know if it's possible," she continued, as if Terrano hadn't spoken. "But I'm willing to try. That's the important part: I'm willing to try. But the Dragon is not, and he has many, many responsibilities that an old woman doesn't. Will you please let him go?"

The ghost shook the much larger head, but very carefully—as if it were a child.

"But you'll have to if you're going to come with me. A Dragon this size won't fit in my home, and I need a home—it keeps me dry when it rains and warm when it snows. Come. Come on out."

The ghost spoke. Kaylin couldn't understand it; she wouldn't have heard it at all had the marks of the Chosen not responded, as if they were wind chimes in the breeze of inaudible voice.

Mrs. Erickson didn't have that problem. She held her palm steady against Sanabalis's face as if Dragons were giant, unhappy puppies.

The marks that surrounded Kaylin began to glow, a golden color rising from the core of each word to saturate its outward appearance.

Chosen, Hope said, his voice reedy, *you have done this before.*

Kaylin was pretty certain she'd remember if she'd been in this position before, but was unwilling to argue with Hope while the ghost and Mrs. Erickson were somehow conversing. She found herself holding her breath.

"Kaylin, could you let go of my hand?"

Kaylin shook her head.

"Then you will have to extend a hand of your own. I'm just not sure it will be helpful if you can't see the person you need to reach out to." For the first time since she'd approached the possessed Dragon, she looked at Kaylin; seeing Kaylin's expression she nodded. "We can try. My free hand is, as you can see it, touching the Dragon. But it isn't the Dragon I feel."

"What do you feel?"

Mrs. Erickson's smile was soft. Sad. "I can't feel anything. I can't touch ghosts. You could touch Amaldi and Darreno—and that shocked them. I don't know how you managed; I never have. I did try, with the children. They're lonely—they're people. But they're children—and children should be hugged or held or comforted. I only have words and expressions."

"Then…how do you think you're going to pull the ghost out?"

"The same way I do with Jamal and others. There are many ways to reach out, and many ways to listen. I'm not certain if this ghost is trapped the way the children are—but I have to assume so." She hesitated, and then added, "Maybe you can touch them."

Kaylin shook her head. "I couldn't touch any of the children who live in your house—and I don't think Amaldi and Darreno are actually dead."

"But this ghost is?"

Kaylin nodded.

Mrs. Erickson began to talk, her voice soft, her words gentle. Kaylin could understand all of them, but was forced to infer the other half of what was clearly a conversation by the words Mrs. Erickson chose.

Almost without thought, Kaylin reached out; as she did, the shield of words shrunk until her arm was ringed by the sigils; all were golden, but the golden light was warm and gentle, just as Mrs. Erickson's tone was.

She was shocked when something lay itself against her upturned palm.

12

It didn't feel like a hand, although it retained the warmth of living flesh; it was too hard for that. Kaylin ignored her first instinct—to yank her hand back—in part because she was standing beside Mrs. Erickson, a civilian who wasn't terrified by anything but the possibility that she wouldn't be able to help.

Warmth filled her palm; she kept the hand as relaxed as she could, although her arm was tense. "Hope, can you help me out here?"

No.

He'd skipped the usual lecture about cost or price. Whatever she could see through the wing he had fastened across her eyes was all that he could see. "Can you lower the wing?"

That, he could do. Without the wing, she expected to see nothing: no light, no illumination, possibly normal Dragon eyes. She was wrong. Whatever it was that now lay across her hand was solid, hard; her fingers closed slightly at its weight, because the weight was increasing.

But what she saw without Hope's wing was…a word.

It was a word very like the words that now spun slowly

around her arms. Whatever Mrs. Erickson saw, Kaylin didn't expect to see—but she hadn't expected this. The word in her hand, heavy as it was, was very like other True Words she had touched before. It matched the color of the floating marks of the Chosen almost exactly.

"Whatever you're doing," Mrs. Erickson said, "keep doing it."

"I'm just...holding out a hand."

"You must be doing more than that. I can see..." She shook her head. "I think we'll have your Dragon back soon." She then looked away. "You mustn't do to Kaylin what you've done to that poor Dragon Lord. She is trying to help you. We both are—but none of us know exactly what's needed."

The word shivered against Kaylin's palm. Kaylin glanced past the word to Sanabalis. "Hope?"

He returned his wing to her face with a little more force than necessary; she looked through that wing to Sanabalis's eyes. They were murky now, but the white that occupied their center was less brilliant, less all-encompassing. As she watched, color returned to the eyes—a crimson, unlidded red, moving from the edges until it once again covered everything but pupils.

The weight across her palm didn't increase during this transition. The number of words did. They were similar in shape and size, but didn't seem connected to her eye. They had an unusual complexity, very different from most of her own marks, as if they were meant to describe entire worlds. Tiny, delicate worlds.

"Are they—are they still talking to you?" Kaylin asked the old woman.

"Yes, dear—but very quietly now. They aren't crying or screaming anymore."

Kaylin had her eyes on an enraged Dragon. "Sanabalis?"

His voice, when it came, was an unintelligible rumble.

"They're very sorry," Mrs. Erickson said. Had Kaylin let go of her hand, she would have moved to stand in front of Kaylin.

"Teela?"

Teela stepped forward, inserting herself between the Dragon and the civilian. Terrano, however, moved to stand in front of Kaylin's outstretched hands, his brow wrinkled in a blend of curiosity and confusion. "What do you see?" he asked.

"Words," she replied. "I think they're the same language as the marks of the Chosen, but they're far more complicated. The only time I saw something close was..." She stopped. "Never mind."

"I'm listening."

Kaylin shrugged, uncomfortable now. The Devourer's name had had form and complexity like this. So had the outcaste Dragon. In neither situation was the owner of those words in any way welcome, and she was afraid that similar conclusions might be drawn.

Because they should be.

Ah, Ynpharion, his voice laced with the usual frustration and disgust. It was almost a comfort, although she failed to respond.

Kaylin continued to speak to Terrano. "I'm not sure what to do with the words."

"Have you done something like this before?"

"No." Pause. "Yes. Maybe?"

Disgust in Ynpharion grew deeper and stronger, but it was less comforting because too much of it was aimed at himself. She wasn't ever going to be his biggest admirer, but she thought there should be a limit to self-flagellation.

Except when you do it? the Barrani Lord asked. She ignored that, too.

Terrano rolled his eyes. "Let's go with yes, to start."

"Someone had a word on their brow and I...took it."

"You took it."

"Yeah—it was during the time when you were causing serious trouble for the rest of us."

Terrano winced. "Okay, so maybe we start with the maybe."

Teela glared at him. "What did you do with the word?"

"If I remember right, I stuck it on my forehead. On my skin. It— I think it was a Barrani True Word."

"There are no Barrani True Words," the Dragon said, the crimson in his eyes slowly fading into the more normal red that indicated anger. "There are True Words."

"Can you see them?"

"No. Not without interference." He exhaled smoke and ash, but had the grace to turn his head to the side before he did. "I believe magical interference is inadvisable at this juncture." His form slowly dwindled into the far more familiar Lord Sanabalis. Kaylin knew that Dragons *could* wear magical clothing that somehow survived the human-to-Dragon transition and back; he appeared to be wearing it now.

"Mrs. Erickson, I have a few questions to ask."

"Of course. I'll answer the ones I can—but people often don't think my answers make enough sense."

"They would. I do not believe I will have that problem. And I believe that the corporal may now safely let go of your hand."

Kaylin's hand was numb, except for the parts that were painfully tingly. She attempted to force her fingers to move enough to let go of Mrs. Erickson's hand; she knew an order when she heard it.

"So...you think Mrs. Erickson has magical potential?"

"I am uncertain that you would call it potential in the tra-

ditional sense that either the mortals or the Barrani employ,"
Sanabalis replied. "But if the events of today were entirely
unpredictable—and believe that they were—there is a reason that I asked her to come here for the possible tests we
could administer.

"The mage responsible for her first test is dead—of old
age, I hasten to add. But he was not fully apprised of how
unusual her circumstances are; there are tests that might have
been performed that he would not have considered relevant."

Kaylin rolled her eyes.

"They are old tests, and they have fallen much out of fashion. I admit it likely that it would not have occurred to him
to provide those tests."

"Because he wouldn't have known of them?" Teela asked,
voice level.

"Perhaps. The Arcanum spends more time delving into schools
of magic that would not be considered entirely practical—but
would be considered dangerous or forbidden in the Imperial
school."

Mrs. Erickson blanched. So did Kaylin.

"Ah, forgive me. I criticize the Arcanum, as is our wont;
I am not in any way implying that Mrs. Erickson was engaged in illegal, forbidden arts. At one point in the history of
what has become the Imperial Collegium, such tests could be
conducted, but they were not considered as relevant because
while potential could be indicated by elements of those tests,
that potential could not be *taught*. It could not be schooled."

"Is becoming a student here free?" Kaylin asked.

"I am certain there are times when you will not think about
monetary aspects of most things," was the severe reply—a
reply which suggested now would be a good time to start.

Kaylin said, "I need to eat. I'm not a Dragon Lord. I might
be considered a Lord of the Barrani High Court, but it's not

like they're paying me—and without money, I starve. Or freeze." She folded her arms as Teela sighed. Loudly.

"You will forgive her, I hope," she said in High Barrani. "She is young, even for one of her kind."

"I am well aware of both her youth and her predilections, and I have not yet reduced her to ash—although on some days it has been tempting. To answer your question, yes. In cases where becoming a student would cause financial hardship, we teach without fee. I would imagine that we will see fewer students in the immediate future, given the rise of the Academia." His eyes had paled to orange with red flecks, which was about as good as could be hoped for.

"Mrs. Erickson, I believe you are what was once called, in various mortal cultures, a shaman. In the opinion of the learned, mortal shamans did not actually exist. The promise of communication with the beloved and departed was a way to part people from their money."

"And now?" Kaylin asked, her temper in check because she immediately thought of Margot the Elani street charlatan, which always soured her mood.

"There is no question in my mind. I have never met a mortal shaman—but in my existence, I have met only one who would qualify as a shaman at all. The purpose was not to seek the spirits of the departed—that is not the way our kind, or the Barrani, work. The words that are our breath of life return to where they were first placed by the Ancients who were responsible for the creation of our race.

"But where there is thought and will and even fear, there is study. This would not be considered auspicious."

"Among Dragons?"

"Ah, no. You mistake me. Among Dragons it would be considered impossible. As such, the mages of the Imperial College may well have considered the information they were given highly suspect—many are the students who desired a place in the College in Mrs. Erickson's childhood. But I cannot doubt what I have seen. If Mrs. Erickson is amenable, I would like to conduct those tests, but perhaps in a less... fraught...environment.

"And now, Corporal, I must ask the obvious question."

Kaylin knew what it was, but waited.

"What will you do with the...words you now carry?"

"Take them home," she replied. "If they agree." She glanced at Mrs. Erickson. Mrs. Erickson nodded and began to speak, asking questions in Elantran, but receiving answers in a language no one present could understand.

"When the Ancients provided their blood to activate this mirror," Kaylin began.

Sanabalis lifted a hand. "We will not discuss that here. While the room is secure, there are cracks in the protections; I believe you are aware of at least one."

"But the Arkon said—"

"The Arkon says," Sanabalis rumbled.

"Yes, sir." She hesitated. "I don't think the words are dead. I mean, I don't think they're whatever ghosts are for gods."

"And I'm certain you have very solid reasons for that," he replied, in a tone that implied the opposite. "I do not see what you see, and I am reluctant to begin the magicks that would allow me to apprehend True Words, given the events of the day."

"Were you aware of them?" Terrano asked, interrupting them, the question meant for the recently possessed Dragon.

"Yes."

"And Mrs. Erickson's interpretation is right?"

"I find it exceedingly gentle, given events—but it is clear to me that whatever possessed me could hear her—and only her. I do not think Kaylin would be in possession of new words were it not for Mrs. Erickson. I envy you, ma'am," he added to the older woman, his voice softening.

"And not fear?" Teela asked, her voice soft in an entirely different way.

"There is an element of fear, yes—but I consider that pragmatic. I will need to confer with the Dragon Court."

"And what happens to Mrs. Erickson?" It was Teela again, speaking quickly as if she intended to interrupt before Kaylin could.

"Mrs. Erickson is free to return to her home," he replied. "I assume that the corporal will escort her. It is not Mrs. Erickson that is my current concern, or rather, not my sole concern; I am far more disturbed by the...ghosts. They are not echoes or attenuations in the way they might once have been in the distant past; we do not, as I said, have ghosts in the sense that mortals fear them."

"I've seen mortal ghosts."

"Yes. That is a concern. But if what you said was correct, those ghosts—"

Kaylin immediately stepped forward and interrupted the Arkon. There were things she didn't want to share with Mrs. Erickson, and the eventual fate of the children trapped in her house as ghosts was one of them.

"If you want to escort me, or want me to go with you to talk to Lannagaros, I'm free."

"I wish you to stop by your home first and discuss the situation with Helen," he replied. "I will reach out to you when I have fully digested the events, and I will speak separately with Lannagaros; I believe he would—in other circumstances—find it fascinating." He said this with a twist of lips, but turned at last to Terrano. "Young man, I do not believe it wise for you to attempt to either see or hear as Mrs. Erickson does. Your existence is far too tenuous.

"If you wish to make the attempt, I ask that you have An'Teela present; she is far more grounded, and far less likely to fall prey to the trap that almost consumed me."

Terrano looked highly disgruntled; he opened his mouth, but snapped it shut again, wincing. Kaylin was certain that he was now getting an earful of Sedarias—and Sedarias was on the Dragon's side.

"Fine. Fine. But I live with Kaylin, so I'll be accompanying her home."

"Perhaps I might suggest that Corporal Neya visit her home before she escorts Mrs. Erickson to hers," Sanabalis then said.

Kaylin looked to Mrs. Erickson, who fidgeted. "I need to check in with Helen," Kaylin said. "And I'm sure you'd like her."

"Helen is your roommate?"

"Ummm, no. It's a bit complicated. Terrano is my housemate. He and his friends. Helen isn't my mother," she said quickly; she felt it likely that would be Mrs. Erickson's next question. "She's my home."

This didn't appear to make things any clearer. "I'm just worried about leaving the children at home alone," she confessed. "They fret."

"We won't stay," Kaylin said quickly. "But...if these... ghosts can possess a Dragon, they're dangerous."

"There's no guarantee they won't be able to possess Helen," Terrano cheerfully said. Given his expression, he didn't consider it a credible risk, but felt the need to point it out.

Kaylin almost blanched.

"I don't think they'll do that again," Mrs. Erickson quickly said. "But I can't promise. Could you maybe bring them to my house instead?"

Sanabalis growled. There was only one answer, and Kaylin dutifully offered it. "No." To the Dragon she added, "Mrs.

Erickson can talk to them; they can hear her. I'm not sure they'll be able to hear me. Or us. They couldn't hear Terrano, and he's the most flexible of all of us."

"And Mrs. Erickson cannot remain with you?"

"I'd love it if she could—I think Helen would enjoy her company. But the children are trapped in Mrs. Erickson's house, and we can't ask her to abandon them."

"The children don't appear capable of possessing people."

Kaylin nodded. "Mrs. Erickson is a civilian. I can't order her to leave her house. Neither can you."

"That is true."

Kaylin exhaled.

"The Emperor, however, can."

Kaylin switched immediately to High Barrani. "That is not a good idea. Mrs. Erickson has done nothing wrong. She has broken no Imperial Law. Taking her into custody for her own safety is something she has to *request*."

"If she is considered a threat to the safety of civilians, that is not the case."

"She's not a threat—your private, hidden room powered by the literal blood of the Ancients is!"

"Kitling," Teela said.

Kaylin inhaled, lowering her chin briefly. When she raised it again, she said, "Mrs. Erickson is not a threat. If her presence gave desperate hope to the dead, that is not her doing. No warning was given to any of us."

"Had we been in possession of that information, I assure you we would not now be in this chamber."

"Which was your decision, not hers. She has been terrified enough for one day. I will return to Helen, and from there, escort Mrs. Erickson to *her* home."

Mrs. Erickson wasn't Kaylin or Teela or Terrano—who was no doubt always doing something dangerous, both to himself and others—she was a civilian. A lonely old woman who happened to bake for the Hawks who listened to her outlandish ghost stories. Well, no, her very mundane ghost stories, but still.

Kaylin was a Hawk for a reason.

"Perhaps you wish to speak with the Emperor yourself."

"Perhaps I do," Kaylin replied, standing her ground. "The chain of command doesn't allow the Emperor to break the law."

"The Emperor *is* the law."

"That's not the oath we swear."

"An'Teela?" Sanabalis continued to glare at Kaylin as he spoke.

"She is, of course, correct. But I am Barrani; I do not expect simple words—written or spoken—to have true weight. I will note, however, that most of the people who have sworn the Imperial oath are mortals without the necessary experience with legal treachery."

Sanabalis exhaled a stream of smoke. "I see." He then turned to Mrs. Erickson, switching into Elantran. "Mrs. Erickson, you have shown evidence of an ancient magical ability today. It is not well understood by the Imperial College, but I am not solely a student of that modern college. I am uncertain what caused the events of today—events I am sure you will agree were not entirely safe."

She nodded.

"Kaylin is concerned about the disposition of the ghosts you see. If they attempt to possess someone again, they might cause damage in the attempt. As a matter of concern, we would ask that you either remain within the palace—where rooms will be provided for you—or remain within Kaylin's domicile. We are given to understand that you have responsibilities to children in your care. Are they of an age to understand the concern?"

"Understand it? Yes. I'm not sure they'll accept it so easily."

"Then you must decide whether your responsibility to the pathos of the dead outweighs your responsibility not to add to their number."

Kaylin was outraged, and turned to Mrs. Erickson.

Mrs. Erickson met—without evident fear—the eyes of the Dragon Lord. "I understand," she said. "Yes, if Kaylin can escort me both to her home and to mine, I will—if it is acceptable to Kaylin—remain in her custody."

"You're *not* in my custody. My house is *not* a jail."

"Your house was the only home considered safe enough to house Bellusdeo," Sanabalis replied, his eyes once again losing their red. "It is both for her safety and for ours that I ask this of both of you."

"Corporal," Mrs. Erickson said, "he is not attempting to bully me. He asked, and it is a reasonable request. I have agreed. You can, however, refuse."

Terrano snorted. "She can't. She's just mad because she wanted to have a screaming fight with a Dragon." To Kaylin he added, "Sedarias says you can have a screaming fight with her if it will make you feel better—she's outraged."

And not on Mrs. Erickson's behalf, either.

"Fine."

To no one's surprise, Sanabalis chose to join them in their walk to Kaylin's home. He chatted with Mrs. Erickson; he could be charming, an adjective she would never have thought to use before. Mrs. Erickson was polite, but clearly charming Dragons were not an impossibility in her experience, given how little she actually had.

But she often turned to Kaylin, and in particular to Kaylin's cupped hands; she offered those hands an encouraging smile. If she was self-conscious about talking to ghosts in public, none of that showed; she had chosen possible embarrassment over social fear.

On the other hand, Teela—who accompanied them—and Terrano, who was on the way home as well, knew that she wasn't talking to nothing.

Sanabalis couldn't drop back to speak privately to Kaylin; he looked like he wanted to, but Mrs. Erickson's presence prevented that. Kaylin wasn't certain whether or not to be grateful. Although Sanabalis was shockingly charming, his eyes remained predominantly orange; Kaylin wondered if it took effort to keep the flecks of red there to a minimum.

Most humans had no interaction with Dragons, but red eyes always looked slightly threatening.

Helen was waiting at the open door; she came out the moment Kaylin crossed the threshold. From a distance, it should have been difficult to see the color of Helen's eyes; it wasn't. They were obsidian. She did, however, wear her normal clothing, and her expression, if you didn't notice her eyes, was gentle and welcoming.

She offered Sanabalis a nod—not a bow. "Welcome, Arkon."

"Yes," Sanabalis said.

Helen's eyes did not revert to their normal color. "Please, come in." She then turned to Mrs. Erickson, her expression far less welcoming than Kaylin had expected, which, given Helen's welcome of the cohort—one of whom had arguably tried to kill Kaylin—came as a shock.

The expression did soften. "Please forgive me," she said, voice soft. "I...heard a cause for alarm on the perimeter, and you catch me at my most wary. Please, come in." She moved out of the doorway. When she glanced back at Kaylin, her eyes were their normal brown, and her expression, careworn but warm. "Hello, An'Teela. It is approaching dinnertime—will you stay?"

Teela nodded, her eyes midnight.

Helen wasn't human. She had never been human. She turned to Kaylin. "What do you carry?"

"I...I think they're words."

"They are," Helen replied. "But what do you intend for them? They are old words, Kaylin, and even when my memory was not so fractured, I do not think I would have been able to speak them, to read them."

Kaylin glanced at Mrs. Erickson. "Mrs. Erickson thinks they're ghosts."

Helen's brow furrowed, but it was brief; Kaylin knew she had given up on polite questions and was, instead, shuffling through Kaylin's memories, looking for what *ghost* meant. Her brows rose, and she turned to Sanabalis, who waited.

He nodded.

"Oh, my dear," Helen said to Mrs. Erickson. The Avatar held out both of her hands, palm up, and almost without thought, Mrs. Erickson placed hers over them. "I am so terribly, terribly sorry. Come in. Here, unless you desire it, you will not hear their voices."

Mrs. Erickson looked almost shocked, but beneath the veneer of surprise was something infinitely sadder. "These voices," she said, "I have to hear. They—they possessed Lord Sanabalis. If it had happened in the streets people would have been hurt."

Helen nodded.

"Can you hear them?" Mrs. Erickson then asked, her voice shaky with, Kaylin realized, hope.

"I can't. Not the way you can. No one present will be

able to do that, although Terrano is likely to give himself a monthlong headache trying. He does believe you. He can sense something—but he is a very unusual boy."

"Can you safely contain what Kaylin now carries?" It was the Arkon who asked.

Helen nodded. "I believe the High Halls could do so as well. But I do not believe these words should be brought anywhere near the Barrani Lake of Life. Nor do I believe that they should be brought anywhere near the words at the heart of any building such as I, any building constructed by the Ancients, who have long vanished."

"What do you fear will occur?"

Helen shook her head. "I have no specific fear; it is at best a guess made from a position of caution. All of us have methods of protecting those words, but when those protections are breeched, we are easily lost. Mrs. Erickson said you were possessed by these ghosts—do you understand the mechanism?"

"Ah, no."

"Were you aware of the possession? Were you aware of yourself?"

"This is not a conversation I am willing to have in such a public fashion," Sanabalis said, after a long pause. He shook his head. "I am old for this, and I, too, operate from the dictates of caution. I cannot trust you as Kaylin trusts you." He exhaled a thin stream of smoke. "But I came this way for two reasons. If you feel you can safely house these guests, I will take some comfort in that."

"That is one reason."

"I wished to know if you could hear or see what Mrs. Erickson can."

"Of course not," Helen replied, looking genuinely confused.

"Of course?"

"She was born with the gifts she now possesses. It is as much a part of who and what she is as your breath, your ability to transform, is to you. But hers are far rarer and far more complicated. Kaylin is Chosen, even if she does not fully understand the weight of the power and responsibility that comes with it. Mrs. Erickson's gift—if it can be called that—is as rare, in my limited experience, as the marks of the Chosen. It is not nearly as well-known."

"How came you to know of it?" Sanabalis's voice was soft, but the orange of his eyes deepened in color.

Helen was silent.

It was a silence Kaylin recognized. "She can't answer you."

"Can't?"

"Won't. It involves a former tenant."

Sanabalis searched Helen's carefully neutral expression. "My apologies," he said. "My concerns are not the only concerns present; they are pressing to me for what I hope are obvious reasons."

Helen smiled. "Mrs. Erickson might speak to you more about her experiences, if you have the time; I am not certain those experiences will answer your questions." She lowered her chin for a moment. When she raised it, the line of her shoulders tensed. "But I believe Mrs. Erickson has a rare gift, and a much stronger one than any I have encountered.

"I cannot move, as you well know; my knowledge has therefore been secondhand, if my observations were my own. It is possible that I am mistaken; that there are others who have the same strength of gift, and about whom information never reached me." To Mrs. Erickson, she said, "If you would speak with the spirits Kaylin now carries, it is safe to do so here. It is safe to do so in the presence of Lord Sanabalis—or any other person of power you might encounter.

"It is not, in my opinion, completely safe for Kaylin to

carry what she has carried—but Kaylin is my tenant, and my concern for her well-being is perhaps coloring that opinion." To Kaylin she said, "I have a room for your guests, if you would follow me. Mrs. Erickson, if you wish to see them safely housed, you may also join us."

She notably did not include anyone else in that invitation.

Sanabalis wasn't foolish; he took the hint. He looked only slightly nonplussed when Helen split in two. To be fair to him, Kaylin found it surprising as well, although she shouldn't have. Helen was not her Avatar; there was no reason that her Avatar could not exist in as many places as she desired. It's just that Kaylin had never seen one version step out from the other.

"Allow me to offer you refreshments, Lord Sanabalis. I will find a quiet parlor in which we two might converse."

Terrano immediately grimaced.

"Yes, dear. I feel that it is best for the moment to be able to fully focus on my answers to Lord Sanabalis's questions without constant interruption or correction."

"A moment, Helen," the Arkon said.

13

"At what age did you first encounter ghosts?" Sanabalis's question was softly voiced.

"I've always seen them," Mrs. Erickson told the Dragon.

"Always? You have no memories of a time when the ghosts did not appear before you?"

"No. I don't remember a time when they weren't part of my home. My memory isn't what it used to be," she added. "But I can remember incidents from my childhood. My mother in particular was angry—at me—because Jamal had thrown a vase across the room, shattering it. She was certain I'd done it, and she didn't believe in Jamal. I can still remember her disappointment that I would lie to her."

"If she took you to the Imperial College, that must have changed."

Mrs. Erickson nodded. "With time, yes. There were too many coincidences, too many things I had heard of that had nothing to do with our family."

"And your father?"

"I always thought, as a child, that he believed me. As an adult, I'm less certain. He wanted me to know that he loved me, that he would support me. I think he was afraid of what the ghosts meant to me, and of what it said about me.

"When I was a young child, I asked them if I had had brothers or sisters who had died." She winced, even at the remove of decades. "They said no. But I could see Jamal. It was Jamal's idea to prove his existence to my parents." The grimace became a slight smile. "I'm not certain they believed a ghost existed, but his trick—to be in the room with them when I was not, and to report what they'd said or done—caused concern. In the end, my mother chose to have me tested for magical potential."

"And you were assessed as without talent," Sanabalis said.

She nodded. "I think my mother was disappointed. We weren't wealthy, and she worried about my future. I was odd," she added. "So odd. I might have made friends had I understood that, but... I was young. Children are not unkind, but they are not always accepting; I think some of the people I met felt I was lying to gain attention.

"As you can imagine, it didn't make finding friends easier. My mother hoped that if I had talent, I might find company among the mages—mages aren't normal to begin with." Sanabalis raised a brow, and Mrs. Erickson actually chuckled. "Dragons would definitely not have been considered normal; I'm certain my poor mother would be beside herself with anxiety if she could see me now."

"Perhaps not," Helen said. "You are healthy and you have friends—I think she would be far more at peace."

"You didn't know my mother."

"No. But I have known many parents in my life. I confess I did not always understand their fears; to me, they seemed largely needless or misplaced. But I am not as you are, and I did not consider the worries pointless; I considered them an element of life that a sentient building could not experience."

Mrs. Erickson seemed surprised by this. "It's our way to worry when we have some responsibility. I worry about my invisible family. I'm not getting younger, and they've...never aged. They can't be seen. They can't be heard. And it's important for children to be seen and heard. I know that—I was one. I still remember the pain of not being believed. Their entire existence is something no one believes in.

"But even the children my age who were willing to believe weren't accepted. Jamal drove them away."

"Did he not understand what that did to you?"

"He's a child."

"So were you. His age does not excuse his behavior."

"I don't think ghosts age. They're trapped, and these ones are trapped in the house. They can't wander. They can't watch other people, and even if they could, they can't talk to them. They can't *be heard*."

Helen lowered her head, as if in respect. When she raised it, her expression was complicated. "What do they look like, for you?"

The question was not the one Mrs. Erickson was expecting. "The children? They look like children of about ten years of age—possibly younger, possibly older. So much depends on environment. I was small for my age until I hit my growth spurt."

She was small now. Kaylin failed to say this, but Helen heard it anyway.

"No, I didn't mean the children. I meant the ghosts still cradled in Kaylin's hands." She smiled as she said it.

Mrs. Erickson blinked. She looked at Teela, at Sanabalis, and then at Helen herself. Last, she turned to look at Kaylin's hands, her eyes narrowed, some confusion in her expression.

"They look like children, to me."

"Mortal children?"

"Children. Children of all races look like children to you, no? This isn't different. They're smaller than I am, their voices higher and weaker when raised. They remind me most of Jamal, not in physical appearance, but in feel. I think they've been trapped for a long time—longer than Jamal. Longer than Darreno and Amaldi—although the young corporal tells me she doesn't think Darreno and Amaldi are actually dead."

"We cannot see what you see," Helen said, a note of mourning in her voice.

Helen could; she could read minds. She could read thoughts. Mrs. Erickson was not a Barrani Lord, nor an ancient Dragon. Kaylin highly doubted that she was shielding her thoughts against Helen; she probably didn't know what Helen could do.

"No. But she is a shaman, and what she sees, as she sees it, I cannot translate, for want of a better word. I see as Terrano sees. And no, dear," she added, to the aforementioned Terrano, "try as you might, you will not see what she sees."

"If it keeps him occupied and out of trouble, the attempt itself is useful," Teela told her.

"Terrano is incapable of remaining out of trouble, and his attempts might cross boundaries none of us wish to see crossed," was the very reasonable reply.

"I'm actually standing right here," Terrano told them both.

"We know, dear."

Helen shook herself and began to lead.

"Arkon?" the second Helen said to Sanabalis.

Sanabalis shook his head. "You will forgive me, but I would take great comfort in seeing your new visitors properly housed. It is your ability to house disparate elements in safety that swayed my decision to allow Mrs. Erickson and her new ghosts to leave the palace."

Helen frowned, but nodded, and the second version of her quietly faded.

The hall to which she led Mrs. Erickson was not the hall the cohort—and Kaylin—otherwise occupied; nor was it the end of that hall, with its door that led into an outside that wasn't part of Elantra. She walked past it. Kaylin hadn't been aware that there was a way to walk past it, probably because there hadn't been, until now.

"It was here," Helen said, voice gentle. "But it was not of relevance to you—and you don't really *like* big, open spaces, even in a home. There's a reason Sedarias has such extensive, expansive quarters while yours are much smaller and more cramped." To Mrs. Erickson, she added, "I am Helen. All of this—the halls, the rooms in which Kaylin and her friends live—are part of me. They are part of what I was built to offer guests—the part I wished to keep when I finally had the choice.

"Kaylin has not seen all of the rooms that exist within me, but with the coming of the cohort, as the others are called, she has seen more of them than most of my tenants ever saw. This, too, is an aspect of me." And so saying, she gestured, and a new hallway appeared at the far end of the gallery, railings to one side, walls to the other.

"I cannot guess what your ghosts see when they walk here; I cannot guess what they might expect of a home. But we can only offer what is ours to offer. Come. You might stay with them, were it not for your other children; I understand that they need you at home. If you are not as I am, you give them something that no one else can give them.

"With your permission, I will attempt to understand what it is Kaylin has brought into her home."

"I don't think you need my permission for that," Mrs. Erickson said. "This is such a lovely home." But if it was, the home itself was not where her gaze went. She paused once, and spoke to whatever Kaylin now cupped in her palms. "She won't hurt you." Her voice was soft. "She won't use you. All she hopes to offer you for the moment is someplace to rest."

Helen nodded. She then led them down the new hall; it was unadorned by anything as common as doors, except at the far end. The doors there were similar to the doors that terminated the hallway in which Kaylin's room—and everyone else's—was situated.

She then opened the doors, gesturing rather than touching them, which was unusual for Helen. The doors rolled to left and right, and as they did, a gray light filled the hall, brighter than it should have been, given its color.

Kaylin frowned. "Helen—that's…"

"Yes, dear?"

"It looks like the outlands. Almost."

Sanabalis's eyes were narrowed, as if he, too, were forced to squint. But his eyes had lost their orange tinge at some point between the foyer and this hall; they were gold, but flecked with a color the light made impossible to catch.

"Does it? It has been long indeed since I have seen the many paths between us. Ah, I forget myself. It does not look like that to my eye, but I understand the confusion. All of the rooms the cohort call home begin here. All of the rooms I have offered my many guests over the centuries begin here. And when those rooms are no longer wanted or necessary, they return."

Kaylin didn't understand the difference between this place and the words at the heart of Helen.

"It is the difference between brain and heart. You might ask Red in your morgue about them, if this is a bad analogy."

Kaylin shook her head. She understood the point.

"Come," she said. "The only reason you are seeing hospitality—my hospitality—in its nascent form is that I cannot see your guests, cannot read them or hear them. I do not know what they want or need. But if they rose in the presence of Mrs. Erickson, if they somehow inhabited Lord Sanabalis, they are clearly looking for something."

"I'm sorry," Mrs. Erickson said. "It's hard to hear their voices, and they seem to be talking over each other. Mostly, they're anxious. Excited, but anxious. I really do think they're like Jamal, at heart."

Jamal was mostly anxiety; if he'd been excited—ever— Kaylin had missed it beneath anger and possessive resentment.

Terrano, on the other hand, was excited. Teela grabbed him by the shoulder, as if to keep him pinned in one place. Not that that would work if he was determined.

The odd words in Kaylin's hand quivered in place, as if straining to move toward whatever it was they could see in the pale, luminous fog. They didn't leave Kaylin's hands. It occurred to her that they couldn't; that somehow, she contained them. It was probably the marks; they were glowing, their color now similar to the color of the fog.

"I think I have to carry them there," Kaylin told her home.

"I think so, too. You will be safe should you choose to enter the room; if they are willing to leave you— if they are capable of it—it will be there. I would suggest you leave as quickly as possible, if that proves to be the case; I am uncertain what the room itself will become, and it may be inhospitable."

Kaylin nodded. "Can Mrs. Erickson come?"

Helen's hesitance was an answer.

"Stay on the hall side of the door," she told Mrs. Erickson. "You can speak to them from there—but Helen's concerned that you might be injured."

"And she isn't concerned about you?" The question was asked with no edge or ego; Mrs. Erickson was genuinely curious.

"Not in the same way. I have special marks that offer some protection."

"The marks of the Chosen," Mrs. Erickson agreed.

Everyone turned to look at her, and she reddened slightly. "Amaldi mentioned them. I'm sorry for interrupting you."

"Everyone does. I'm used to it. You can't expect a lack of interruption if you live with Terrano."

"Hey!"

Kaylin grinned and then turned once again to the open door. She couldn't see anything as solid as floor on the other side of the doorjamb, but she'd run through the outlands without any visible ground beneath her feet. She was worried, but it was a nebulous worry; she had brought…something into her home that could possess a Dragon. Something that had somehow been trapped or attached to an altar in a hidden room in the bowels of the Imperial Palace.

"Yes. They responded to Mrs. Erickson. If she has spent her life quietly, she has great power."

"She doesn't know how to use it," Sanabalis said.

"It is not something that is easily taught by those who do not have a similar power," Helen replied. "It is not magic as the Arcanum understands it; nor is it magic as the Imperial College does. But I would argue that she has used that power, unbeknownst to her, since she first opened her eyes. Whatever these are—ghosts or spirits as she calls them—they could see her, and she could see them. They understand her when she makes the effort to speak. No one present can do the same.

"But Kaylin is very fond of her, and I understand why. She intends no harm."

"Harm can be caused, regardless," was the sober reply. "But yes, I agree; if harm is to be caused with intent, there will be no harm. Corporal?"

Kaylin nodded and took a step over the threshold.

★ ★ ★

In the odd light of this gentle miasma, Kaylin could see the words more clearly; they grew more solid, and they gained an unfortunate weight. She was by no means weak, but she knew that carrying this weight in her palms, arms partially extended, couldn't be done for long. She turned, slowly, toward Mrs. Erickson.

Mrs. Erickson's eyes were luminous, wide, almost unblinking; the color of the fog itself was so strongly reflected in those eyes, they seemed to be one and the same for a disconcerting moment.

It was Teela who caught Mrs. Erickson by the shoulder, her grip on the older woman almost the same as the grip she maintained on Terrano. Kaylin could see that much before the fog rolled over her eyes, obscuring anything as mundane as a doorway. The marks on her arms were glowing more brightly, gold at last coming up through a sheen of silver gray.

She closed her eyes, the landscape that emerged from the fog was painfully disjointed to look at, the colors that she could perceive clashing like a visual screaming match at a volume that would deafen the unprepared. Into the reddened darkness of closed eyes in bright light, came physical sensation: the ground beneath her feet—which in this case wasn't so much ground as puddle. She could hear words being spoken, words being repeated, in a language she didn't understand, but nonetheless recognized.

Words, like the marks on her arms.

"Is it safe to open my eyes?" she asked, assuming that the door was still open and the rest of the people she'd come with were still bearing witness.

"It is safe," a familiar voice said. Only one.

"Helen?"

"Yes. I am here. I could not guarantee Mrs. Erickson's safety, but I can guarantee yours."

Kaylin opened her eyes.

She realized, belatedly, that the burden she'd carried no longer resided within her cupped palms; her hands were empty. Instead of lowering them, she stretched out both arms, up and to the side, regaining normal movement absent heavy weight.

She was standing in a pool, but the liquid the pool contained wasn't water; her feet weren't wet. Or soaked. She would have stepped onto dry land, but there wasn't any in sight as far as the eye—or hers, at any rate—could see. She was surrounded by shallow, still liquid. The color was golden.

"That is not what I see," Helen told her. Her voice was measured, but it wasn't entirely calm.

"Is everyone else on the outside of the room?"

"They are. The doors closed when the fog began to clear."

"You closed them?"

"It was a precaution. The room itself is secure for now; I believe even Terrano would have difficulty breaching the protections; they are not entirely of my design."

"The occupants?"

"I do not believe they are what you would consider ghosts."

"Are they like Amaldi and Darreno, then?"

"From what you have witnessed, no, they are definitely unlike the two. I do concur with your belief that the two are displaced or trapped—but I am not certain what will happen to them should they somehow be freed. Come away." Helen reached out with a hand, indicating Kaylin should take it. "You will not be able to reach the door the usual way, but a door does exist."

"Can you hear them, now?"

Helen shook her head. "No. But I can see what was built to provide them comfort and a sense of safety."

"Does that give you any clue as to what they are?"

"Perhaps. But you perceived them as words, and that is not entirely inaccurate. These words I cannot hear, cannot speak; I perceive them only because you carried them and they came...here. But they spoke to Mrs. Erickson." Helen's eyes were obsidian. "You have not asked my advice, and the advice I give is therefore without weight, but..."

"But?"

"Mrs. Erickson is mortal. Her gift, such as it is, has never been detected until now. She is as you perceive her—and as you suspected, I do like her. But she is nonetheless dangerous, Kaylin, if Lord Sanabalis's possession did not make that clear."

"She had nothing to do with that!"

"She did not possess him, no. Nor would she, in my opinion. But they would not have woken were it not for her presence. In your stories, you speak of ghosts. In my experience, there were mortals who could see the echoes of those who had passed on, they called themselves shamans. But there were others that spoke with the dead; others who could command them."

Kaylin stared at the Avatar of her home.

"I believe they were called Necromancers."

"Necromancers don't exist! And they weren't about talking to the dead or freeing them or comforting them—they were about raising an army of mindless undead!"

"Is that what you've been told?"

"I haven't been *told* that—they're *stories*, Helen."

"Would you like to hear the stories I heard, long before I found my freedom?"

"Do you actually remember them?"

"I do. The loss is not entirely predictable, and I retained

more than I feared I would, although I accepted the possibility of a greater loss. What I protected—what I tried to protect—were memories I made with those few who saw me as Helen. As you do." She smiled then. "Necromancers were not like the Sorcerers of old. If your stories now speak of those who raised the dead—as shambling monsters, meant to terrify mortal armies—some of those stories have roots in the truth.

"But Necromancers were far more subtle in the stories I was told. As you suspect, I did not get out of the house much, and the information I retain came to me through visitors. But some of those visitors were my first lord's servants and accomplices. And among them was one who could, as Mrs. Erickson does, see the lingering echoes of those who once lived.

"I do not understand what causes those echoes; nor do I understand how the dead persist, because most do not. But if my tenants were somehow trapped here as ghosts, it would grieve me. Ah, it starts."

As Helen spoke, Kaylin could see the pool beneath her feet begin to shift, as if currents were struggling to rise to the surface. What she had thought of as liquid was more viscous than simple water—or blood, if it came to that; it was thick, more molasses than water.

No, not molasses; that didn't rise the way this pool was now rising: in spikes, in columns, in strange shapes that seemed to echo the human form without ever truly cohering completely.

"What do you hope I can do here?" Kaylin asked her home.

"I'm uncertain. If it were safer, I would ask to invite Mrs. Erickson in. But perhaps it's better this way. She woke them, somehow."

Kaylin wanted to argue, but couldn't. "But I could somehow carry...whatever they are...because of the marks."

"Yes, I believe so. But I also believe they would not have come to you were it not for Mrs. Erickson's presence."

"So…Necromancers."

"She can speak to the echoes that linger. I would have said mortal ghosts couldn't exist," Helen added. "But I am certain in the darker places and ancient recesses, ghosts of Immortals do. Sometimes words echo, and the words at the core of the first races are enough to support a life that would, without war or accident, continue for eternity.

"Those echoes have some hints of the power the living once possessed, but that power is irrelevant to any who cannot somehow bespeak it; who cannot hear the echoes. Mrs. Erickson could. I do not understand how," she added. "If you could, it would not surprise me."

"I can see the dead children trapped in her house."

"You have the marks of the Chosen; were they absent, I do not believe you would have seen them at all. Even with the marks, you did not see what rose from the ancient mirror at the heart of the Imperial Palace." Helen fell silent for a moment, and then said, "Perhaps they could not hear you; perhaps it is not that she could hear them, but that they were aware of her.

"Once aware, they panicked."

"That…didn't seem like panic, to me."

"No. But they were afraid when they arrived."

"And now?"

"Cautious. Possibly hopeful; I sense no rage, no malice. But I cannot hear their thoughts as I hear yours or the cohorts'. I cannot speak to them the way I speak with any of you. It is, I admit, a challenge."

Kaylin wondered if it was safe. If they could possess Sanabalis, what could they do if they could possess Helen?

"It is not without risk," Helen admitted. "But it is a risk

I choose to take. It is…a challenge to my hospitality. If they cannot speak to me as you do, they speak to some part of me—it is why things are taking shape in this room. I believe Terrano might have some chance of actual communication should he choose to try—but I also believe he would be at the most risk. He made choices in his captivity in the Hallionne that allowed him, in the end, to escape what the Ancients built—but he has difficulty at times retaining his form. His connection with the cohort helps in this regard—Teela is the anchor, there. She spent most of her life as the Barrani you now know.

"But I believe it is time to leave."

"Why?"

"Because they are waking fully, and I am uncertain that I will be able to keep enough of a separation between you and whatever it is they are or were. You may be safe, regardless; the marks of the Chosen may protect you. But I am unwilling to risk your safety until I have learned how to listen, to hear, and to speak with them."

Kaylin nodded; the landscape was now shifting constantly, and she found it hard to watch as up became down and down turned sideways. Closing her eyes helped, but not enough.

"This way, dear," Helen said, her voice coming from Kaylin's right.

Kaylin nodded, which was a mistake. "Helen—is this a portal?"

"Not in the traditional sense, no. Does it feel like that to you?"

Kaylin didn't answer; she was trying to hold on to her last meal.

"I'm terribly sorry," Helen then said, in the softest of her voices. "We will be out of the room soon. You didn't feel this way when you entered?"

"No."

"When did it start?"

Later, Helen. Just—get us out of here first.

"Wow, you look terrible," was the first thing Kaylin heard when she could safely open her eyes again. She didn't need to see the speaker to recognize him.

"Don't be rude," Helen said to Terrano. "She is not feeling well."

"What was rude about that? She does look terrible."

"I look about as good as I feel."

"What happened?"

Kaylin was seated in the parlor, in a chair that was more cushion than structural furniture, which suited her at the moment, as she didn't have the fortitude to sit up straight. She found deep breaths helpful, and took a few before she tried to answer.

"I went into the room Helen created for our new guests. It was fine—I mean, it looked like an oddly colored pool of honey or molasses. Helen didn't see it the same way."

Terrano grimaced. "She wouldn't let me enter, so I couldn't check. Sedarias was against it, given what purportedly happened to the Dragon."

"How was Sanabalis?" Kaylin asked Helen.

"You can ask him yourself; he's been waiting for you to recover. I believe, given the color of his eyes, he is somewhat concerned, but he is far more adept at hiding his thoughts than most of your guests."

"He's still here?"

"He has—and I quote—'canceled all appointments for the rest of the evening,' one of which includes the Emperor. Are you feeling up to speaking with him?"

"He's not leaving until we talk, is he?"

"I don't think so, dear—unless you wish me to forcibly eject him."

Kaylin grimaced. "I like my job." Her legs were wobbly, but she rose. "And I'm feeling better—portal nausea doesn't usually last."

"No. But, Kaylin, there was no portal. It's possible the protections I put in place to keep you safe caused the same reaction—they are not protections I have employed until now."

Terrano, bright-eyed and interested, bounced between Helen's Avatar and Kaylin. "What protections?"

"Terrano, now is not a good time." Kaylin's jaw was slightly clenched. She knew she had as much chance of getting rid of Terrano as she did of getting rid of Sanabalis. Or less.

"I can create a space around Kaylin—and only Kaylin—due to the nature of our contract. It is expensive, in terms of power; should I come under attack, it would be difficult to properly defend myself while maintaining it. I did not expect she would be attacked, but it is clear to me that these guests are impulsive, given their possession of Lord Sanabalis." She emphasized the title.

"The Arkon," Kaylin said, trying not to feel petty.

"But those protections were in place for the entirety of your time in that space; you did not react to them until the guests began to influence the space."

"No. I didn't notice them at all until then. It might just be visual—the entire landscape was spinning and transforming from second to second."

"You don't believe that."

"It really *felt* like a portal tunnel."

"That is interesting, and I will keep that in mind."

"Is Mrs. Erickson with the Arkon?"

"She was, but she had become somewhat worried about the children. Teela and Mandoran offered to escort her home—

with the Arkon's very reluctant permission—and she eventually accepted their offer. She was also worried about your new guests, but understood my explanation."

Kaylin was surprised Sanabalis had let Mrs. Erickson leave. "Which explanation?"

"They need time to establish comfort in their new home. I do believe she will return if you allow it."

"Do you think she'll be safe?"

"I think she is the only person in this house who will be."

Terrano clearly felt mildly insulted, which Helen gracefully failed to notice.

"She did speak with the Arkon for some time. He is concerned, but he does not believe she intends harm."

"Because she *doesn't*."

"Indeed."

Kaylin sighed loudly. "Let's go face the Dragon. Unless you've invited him for dinner, I won't get to eat until he leaves."

14

Sanabalis was orange-eyed, but flecks of red persisted. He had been ushered into the parlor by Helen's Avatar; he was offered a drink, which he refused, and food, which he also refused. He sat heavily in the chair offered, his forearms across the chair's rests, his hands a little too white-knuckled.

"I would ask, in future, that you not ask favors of me. It has been a very trying day."

It had been a trying day for Kaylin as well, but she kept this to herself.

The Dragon glanced at Terrano. Terrano, usually not one for taking hints, vanished. Sadly, he didn't bother with the door. Kaylin suspected he'd remained in the parlor.

"I've been conversing with Helen on the topic of Necromancers," Sanabalis said. "And I have sent a message to Lannagaros. He will, no doubt, be annoyed by the interruption; the duties of chancellor take every waking minute of his time, and he was never full of cheer when interrupted. Mrs. Erickson is a danger."

"Is *in* danger? Because she's a little old woman who likes to bake and feed people, and she only gathers ghosts because they're lonely and she can see them." Kaylin had to force her arms to remain at her sides.

"I do not believe there is anything wrong with your hearing. Helen made clear that Mrs. Erickson's influence—such as it was—was benign; the very disturbing possession occurred at the whim of...her ghosts. She is therefore being escorted to her home, but you will forgive us if we place her under surveillance."

Kaylin looked down at her lap. "You have Records of tax collection and tax law."

"We do."

"Mrs. Erickson lives at 14 1/2 Orbonne Street."

Sanabalis nodded.

"There used to be a 14 Orbonne Street. It doesn't exist anymore. I'm not sure the lot exists, in the traditional sense—which would be strange. But I've been asked not to continue to investigate that house because of the last known owner. The Records we have access to in the Halls of Law show number fourteen only in one place: tax Records. Teela thinks the mention of fourteen is an artifact—an error in Records."

"You don't."

"I don't, no. Mrs. Erickson's home was bought by her parents; the land transfer indicates that the previous owner was the Emperor, or whoever makes those decisions on behalf of the Emperor. But the artifact in Records implies that 14 Orbonne did exist a century ago. And that would make sense, given the street numbering."

Terrano cleared his invisible throat loudly.

"I've been asked not to pursue the parts of the investigation that involve the missing fourteen, given the name in Records."

"And that name?"

"Azoria An'Berranin."

Terrano coughed.

"My ears are not mortal ears," Sanabalis said, exhaling smoke. "Children's games of this nature do not prevent me from hearing what the corporal has to say."

Terrano, becoming visible, turned to Kaylin. "You told Sedarias—"

Sanabalis roared; Kaylin could swear it shook the floor beneath her chair. "Records have limited access from the Halls of Law. I will look into the issue when I return to the palace. I expect you to keep an eye on Mrs. Erickson; research is now being done elsewhere, and I will inform you of any results that are relevant." He fell silent, brooding. "I was aware during the possession. I concur with Mrs. Erickson; there was panic. But panic or no, I have never experienced such a loss of control—not since I was a hatchling, and at that time, rage was the driver, not...ghosts."

"Echoes is what Helen called them."

"Regardless. It was disturbing, and I trust you understand why. Should echoes, if that is the preferable word, control most mortals, the harm they can do is minimal."

Not to other mortals. But Kaylin concurred; a single Dragon was infinitely more destructive than even a mob.

"Could you hear them?" she asked.

"Hear them?"

"Mrs. Erickson could hear their voices. She spoke to them the way she speaks to Jamal and the rest of the children she cares for."

"No."

"Me, either."

Sanabalis rose. "I will speak with you, should it be necessary, on the morrow, or perhaps the day after."

"I've been summoned to the High Halls tomorrow," Kaylin said. "Teela and I will attend the Consort after work."

"Very well. If she has anything of relevance to contribute, I expect to hear of it."

"Yes, sir."

"You should have said no," Terrano said, well after Sanabalis had departed, the door had closed behind him, and he had left the perimeter of Helen.

"How stupid do I look? No, don't answer that. Helen will be upset if we start a food fight."

"She certainly would," Helen said.

"I'm not the one saying it. No, okay, I did say it—but I wasn't the one who was thinking it. You can blame Teela."

"Who conveniently isn't here."

"Seems safest to me—that way you're not starting a fight with anyone in arm's reach."

"If Barrani had normal memories, I'd consider it. Sanabalis understands the political dance of the High Court and its interactions with the Dragon Court. He won't demand information I am not authorized to give."

"He already did."

"He didn't. That's just the way he talks." Kaylin folded her arms. "Look, Elantra is difficult enough as is. Delivering information from one of the rulers of the *High Court* is above my pay grade."

"And if he demands to know what the Consort said?"

Kaylin shrugged. "I'll let Teela handle it."

Terrano broke out laughing. No one else at the table did. Sedarias smiled, but it was a ferocious expression. Kaylin felt that it deserved an entirely different descriptive verb. She'd personally feel safer with a knife at her back than she would Sedarias if she was sporting that smile.

"Tell Teela *very funny* for me."

"You're certain it was Teela?"

"I'd bet money on it."

Terrano frowned.

"What is it?"

"I'm not sure. Teela's at Mrs. Erickson's. A belligerent mortal is also at Mrs. Erickson's. Someone you know?"

Kaylin rose from the table. "Not personally, no. He's the neighbor who believes Mrs. Erickson stole something important from him. He doesn't believe it enough to report whatever it was stolen; he just believes it enough to threaten her."

"How stupid is he?"

"How would I know? Not stupid enough to be lured into punching—or attempting to punch—an officer of the law."

"He's not attempting to punch Teela," Terrano said.

Kaylin glanced around the table. All of the cohort, except the visiting Serralyn, looked slightly vacant-eyed; their attention was on whatever it was Terrano could see. Serralyn, on the other hand, looked as if she was concentrating on something no one else was paying attention to.

"What exactly is he attempting to do? Is he stupid enough to threaten Mrs. Erickson when Teela is right there?"

"No, but..." Terrano grimaced. "How long would it take you to get there from here?"

"Twenty to thirty minutes."

"If you were running?"

"Terrano, what's going on?" When Terrano failed to answer, she looked to Serralyn. Pointedly.

"He...seems to have mistaken Teela for someone else," Serralyn said. "I've been spending some time with Robin; he's been explaining various mortal interactions, and I've been trying to observe the few mortals on campus to see how well his explanations align. I mean, there are so many of you."

"The neighbor would, sadly, be one of them," Kaylin snapped.

"Sadly? You want the neighbor to be Immortal?"

"I'd like him to be some other race's problem, yes."

"It doesn't work that way. I mean, I suppose you could fiddle with caste courts and maybe the caste courts could elect to grant someone racial status? But that's not what you meant."

"What is he doing?"

"Well, weeping, if you must know. He's weeping very, very loudly. Mrs. Erickson is worried. Teela is disgusted. Mandoran has sauntered up the stairs, but has made no attempt to enter the house. He doesn't like tears—they make him feel useless."

"Funny how he doesn't feel that way when he's actually being useless," Sedarias snapped.

"Ummm, something just flew out the window. The window was closed. Bits of glass are now rising and falling—I think whatever's inside is trying to hit Teela. No chance it'll work—she's too far away. They should aim for Mandoran instead."

That would be Jamal. "Helen, I need to leave."

"I know, dear." Her house sounded worried. "I think—from the sounds of things—Teela might actually appreciate your company."

Kaylin didn't manage to get out of the house alone; Terrano followed her like an unwelcome shadow. His expression, however, was serious enough that she didn't bother with the pointless argument she'd otherwise have started; he was coming—for Mandoran's or Teela's sake, or his own—and she wasn't going to be able to stop him. She saved herself minutes trying.

Terrano kept pace with Kaylin, who started out at a fast jog. He floated along beside her, as if he were a balloon she was pulling. When she slowed a bit to even out both pace and breathing, she snapped at him.

"Could you at least *pretend* this is taking some effort on your part?"

"It is—just not sweaty effort."

"Sedarias's eyes are always blue—why are yours?"

"Something's wrong with the neighbor. With the house. With this entire situation. Teela knows it, but she's not telling the rest of us anything."

"So when you said Teela would appreciate my company—"

"That was Helen, not me. I thought the exact opposite, which is probably why Helen asked you to go. If it won't disturb you too much, Serralyn thinks the neighbor thinks he's in love with whoever he thinks Teela is."

"And if it would?"

"Would what?"

"Disturb me?"

"Sucks to be you."

Kaylin made it to Mrs. Erickson's with time to spare—but only if she wanted to be witness to a weeping grown man.

Severn arrived three minutes later.

Kaylin stared at him. *Why are you here?*

He shrugged. *Things involving Mrs. Erickson have become dangerous enough I thought you'd want backup.*

This isn't Halls of Law business, though. I won't get demoted if I don't have a partner on-site.

The Arkon is likely to make the investigation Halls of Law business—but that's not why I'm here. You feel it, too. Things are too chaotic; it's like something is about to give. He wore his chain, but had not yet unwound it.

Teela glanced at him and nodded; in that brief glimpse of her face Kaylin could see the color of her eyes. Disgust was generally Barrani blue; it implied distaste without any element of fear. This color implied either implacable rage—highly unlikely—or a worry that had blossomed, exposing the heart of fear.

Kaylin headed toward Mrs. Erickson, who seemed stricken at the sight of her bully of a neighbor weeping. The older woman knew better than to attempt to offer comfort, but not by much; she was caught between retreat and approach, as if she knew she should be doing something—anything—but couldn't figure out what.

Fair enough. Kaylin had the same response to open weeping. "Mrs. Erickson," she said, loudly but in a more Hawklike fashion.

Mrs. Erickson immediately turned toward the sound of Kaylin's voice. "The corporal didn't do anything to him," she said, the words tumbling out as if they were necessary to protect Teela from a charge of misconduct.

Kaylin nodded. "I'm not worried about the corporal; she can take care of herself. And anyone else in the immediate vicinity. I'm worried about Jamal."

"He broke another window," she said.

"Yes—but I'm pretty sure it's not just the window that's broken. He didn't even notice Mandoran—who was closest to the door. I think he might be trying to hit the corporal."

Mrs. Erickson's brows rose. "She's wearing her tabard."

"Technically she's off duty—she probably wore it because she intended to escort you home if you were unwilling to stay with Helen. In most cases it keeps people like your neighbor at a safe distance."

"It doesn't seem to be working very well, does it?"

"You can say that again. But we need to go in and talk with the kids. I think...they're more worried than jealous."

Mrs. Erickson nodded and headed toward her front door, Kaylin by her side, Severn pulling up the rear.

Jamal was in the front hall. Kaylin could see him without Hope's wing. Hope had been so silent throughout dinner and the race to Mrs. Erickson's house, Kaylin almost forgot he was on her shoulder.

"Jamal—stop. You've broken a window, and Mrs. Erickson isn't so wealthy she can afford to have windows constantly replaced."

He looked straight through Kaylin, as if she were the invisible one. He had eyes—through the open doorway—for only one person: Teela.

"Jamal. *Jamal.* Listen to me." Kaylin kept her voice soft.

"Jamal," Mrs. Erickson said, joining her plea to Kaylin's. The old woman's voice reached him. To Kaylin's surprise Jamal attempted to throw himself into the old woman's arms. He passed through her.

Kaylin crouched to bring her face in line with his, as Mrs. Erickson had. "Jamal," she said quietly, "An'Teela is my friend. She's a Hawk." She took her first chance. "She is not Azoria."

Silence then. Or silence from Jamal.

"She's not? You're sure?" Katie asked, her head and shoulders jutting out from a wall.

"I'm absolutely certain." Kaylin hesitated, and then said, "I know the Barrani are very, very similar to look at—but she's a Hawk. She serves the Emperor. There's no point in breaking windows. Nothing you could throw—nothing *I* could throw—could hurt Teela."

"Will it annoy her?" Esme asked, coming through the same wall that Katie had half appeared through.

"It depends on her mood."

"She doesn't look like she's in a very good mood right now."

"No. But her mood might improve if you could get Jamal to stop throwing things out the window."

"I doubt it," Katie said, fully emerging as well. "He's not going away." *He* referred to the neighbor. "Do you think he thinks she's Azoria as well?"

"I'm not sure," Kaylin replied slowly, as if considering the question. She was. Azoria, if she were truly the occupant of a home that no longer existed in Records, except as an artifact—a ghost—had not been in the neighborhood since well before the neighbor was even born. If he had made the same mistake the kids had, there had to be a reason for it. She didn't like the possibilities.

Teela didn't make the immediate connection, the man didn't speak a name as he wept and groveled. He *did* appear to be apologizing for losing her special gift—but also begged her to punish Mrs. Erickson for the theft. That much, she could glean from what Severn could hear, because Severn had remained between the house and Teela, as if intent on extricating the Barrani Hawk should things become messy. Or messier.

"Jamal, why don't you guys head into the kitchen?"

Jamal shook his head. He couldn't actually touch Mrs. Erickson, but could he, Kaylin was certain he'd have a death grip on her sleeve. Mrs. Erickson, for her part, smiled at him, trying to be encouraging.

"Are you sure she's a Hawk?"

"Yes, dear. I see her from time to time in the front office." Kaylin's word was clearly suspect; Mrs. Erickson's was not.

"Sorry."

"No one was hurt."

"I broke the window."

"Yes, yes you did. Please try not to do it again—I'm old enough that I don't have much work, and I won't be able to afford to replace the window that often." The words had the feel of rote to them.

Jamal's nod, while genuine, had the same feel.

Kaylin cleared her throat. "I know it's upsetting, but I need to talk to you guys."

Jamal was instantly suspicious. The other three, the two girls and the boy, who seemed paler and more silent than his friends, were not. They exchanged looks.

"Mrs. Erickson?"

"Maybe we should talk in the dining room. It's not large, but there's no front-facing window."

Interrogating children in the midst of an investigation was never an easy task. Kaylin was better at it than the Barrani Hawks, and she'd spent much of her early days as Hawk mascot under the figurative wings of Teela and Tain. She'd started to intervene on the rare occasions children were considered witnesses, because some of the children were scared enough she could practically see them try to calculate what Teela wanted to hear, that being the smartest choice if one wanted to survive.

But she'd never tried to talk to children about their own murders. Or half murders, given their official dates of death—and the reasons for it.

"What do you want to ask us?" Jamal demanded, taking point. He stepped in front of Mrs. Erickson, keeping her behind him.

Esme wasn't as suspicious as Jamal, but she didn't seem to be as possessive, either. Or maybe she had, over the decades, come to accept that there wasn't very much she could do.

Katie and Callis were the quiet two, but they watched Kaylin with caution, not fear.

"You're aware that you've been in this house for all of Mrs. Erickson's life."

Esme smiled brightly. "She was *such* a cute baby. And when she started to walk? It reminded me so much of my own baby brother!"

The baby brother she had murdered as an adult.

"Do you have memories of this house before Mrs. Erickson was born?"

"What do you mean?"

"Did you see her mother and father? Did you enter the house—somehow—when they bought this house?"

Jamal blinked. These weren't the questions he'd been expecting. He glanced at Esme, who shrugged. "I don't remember how we got here," she finally said. "I… When I think about it, I've always been here, you know?"

Callis looked at his feet. Katie looked at Callis. She nudged him, and Kaylin noted that her hand passed through him, just as it would through a living person.

"Callis?"

He then turned to Jamal. "You tell her."

"Does it matter who tells her?"

"If it doesn't matter," Katie snapped, "why can't it be you?"

"Because it's not my story."

"But you know it, right? You can tell her."

"You could tell her!"

Kaylin watched them; they were children, dead or not. They were afraid of looking either stupid or worse, and they wanted someone stronger to take the risk. Judging from the way Jamal had attempted to leap into Mrs. Erickson's arms, Jamal didn't see himself that way.

"It's all right," Mrs. Erickson told them. "Kaylin is a friend.

She can see you, she can hear you—she means you no harm. If her friend Teela is scary, remember that she can't see or hear you at all. If Jamal could avoid throwing things at her, she wouldn't know you existed."

"She could see us," Callis whispered. Kaylin knew he wasn't speaking of Teela.

Patiently, she shifted her legs, coming to sit cross-legged on the floor. "Callis, I won't tell anyone else unless you give me permission."

"Dear, you're a Hawk—"

"There's a statute of limitations," Kaylin replied cheerfully. "Your children are older than those limits—there's no crime that persists that long. Not among humans. The Immortals have their own laws and punishments, but the Imperial Laws were created, in some ways, for those of us with fleeting lives. If you don't give me permission, I won't tell anyone else."

"But Mrs. Erickson will hear us."

"You mean she doesn't know?"

Callis shook his head.

"Mrs. Erickson has been with you since she was born— you're her family. Unless you somehow had something to do with the death of her parents, I don't think there's anything you could say—anything at all—that would turn her against you."

"Not against us," Katie whispered. "But we don't want her to be disappointed."

Kaylin knew they'd existed for longer than either she or Mrs. Erickson—but they were children to her eyes, just as most of the foundlings were. She couldn't imagine what they could do that could disappoint an old woman with Mrs. Erickson's life and experience. She would have said as much, but Mrs. Erickson was already shaking her head; she lifted a hand and cupped Katie's cheek, although there was no physical contact.

"Kaylin is right," she told them, lowering that hand, her eyes crinkled in a fond smile. "You were my older brothers and sisters for years. And then my younger brothers and sisters. I was angry the first time Jamal broke something, do you remember?"

"It was the magic crystal—the picture of your mom and dad," Esme said.

"Yes. I was very, very upset."

Jamal was studying his feet.

"But Jamal was still my brother, still my family; I accepted his apology. I forgave him."

"But it still makes you sad," Jamal said.

"Sometimes. I don't remember what my parents looked like anymore." She shook her head. "I love you all. I will always love you all, even if I'm angry or disappointed. But I think it would help me if you would answer Kaylin's questions."

"How?"

Mrs. Erickson winced. "I met some new friends today."

"Outdoor friends?"

"Not like Amaldi and Darreno, no. Not like you either, although closer. They were trapped in a large, dark cavern, and when I entered the cavern and they realized I could see them, it seemed to...cause problems."

"Are they here? Or are they like us? Could they leave the cavern?"

"Yes—with both my help and Kaylin's."

Kaylin saw a hint of excitement, of hope, in two of the children, and none whatsoever in Jamal and Esme.

"How?"

"I'm not quite sure. Kaylin...could carry them somehow.

She couldn't see them as I saw them, but…once I did, she could help me."

"Could she carry us out of here the same way?"

Kaylin shook her head. "I can't even touch you." She demonstrated this by swatting Jamal's head; her hand passed through him.

"But how could you touch them?" Katie demanded.

"I don't know. But to me, they didn't look like people. They looked like written words."

"And we don't?"

"No—you definitely look like people to me. Short, young people, but people."

Jamal made a face.

"We—being Mrs. Erickson and I—are trying to figure out a way to let you all out of the house, but to be honest, neither of us really know a lot about ghosts, and we definitely don't understand why they get trapped."

Mrs. Erickson cleared her throat.

"Okay, *I* definitely don't understand it." She glanced at Mrs. Erickson and made a mental note to ask her more about trapped ghosts when the kids weren't all ears. Like, say, tomorrow at the office. "Teela—who is not Azoria—is going to come in if it's all right with you."

"And if it's not?" Jamal asked, arms folded, expression mutinous.

"I'll remind you that it's Mrs. Erickson's house."

"We live here, too."

"Are you paying rent? I mean as far as I can tell you're breaking windows, which is what thugs on the outside do."

"What's rent?" Katie asked.

"It's when you pay money to keep a solid roof over your head."

"Oh. To whom?"

"We call them landlords when they're good. We call them—"

"Corporal," Mrs. Erickson said sharply.

"—villains? Never mind."

"I want to know," Katie told Kaylin.

"Yes, but rule number two: the person who owns the house gets to make the rules, and Mrs. Erickson doesn't want to know. It's rude," she added.

"My dad used to say—"

"Katie, please," Mrs. Erickson said, turning as disapproving a look on Kaylin as the Hawk had ever seen from her.

Katie smiled like an urchin.

"*Anyway*, Teela would like to come in and examine the house. She won't be able to see you. She can't touch you, either. But please don't throw anything else at her, okay? She's done nothing wrong to any of you, and she likes Mrs. Erickson."

Teela left the neighbor on the lawn, but at least he was now standing on two feet. His shoulders were still shuddering, which strongly implied he couldn't stop weeping, but that was all Kaylin saw when she opened the door to allow Teela to enter. This time Severn followed her in.

"I apologize," Teela said to Mrs. Erickson, her eyes blue, her expression one of studied, deliberate neutrality. "While I admit it's not the first time I've seen a grown man weep, I usually understand—and even anticipate—the reason."

"I was very surprised as well," Mrs. Erickson said. "The last time I saw him cry was after his wife died."

"I am *not* his wife."

"No. But he hasn't been himself since then. Did he...tell you I'd stolen something?"

"Yes. He was groveling apologetically because he'd lost it, and he promised he would do something to get it back. He would not, however, tell me what it was; he assumed I was testing him, and that made him weep even more." The disgust she kept off her face was evident in her voice.

All four of the children were staring at her; Katie and Callis were huddled together, notably behind Jamal and Esme.

"I did not expect this reception when I offered to escort you home; had I, I might have sent my partner instead."

"That's Tain?"

Teela nodded.

"But this isn't Hawk business, is it?"

"I would be far more delighted if it were, but no. Not yet. It is, however, Imperial Palace business, as you suspect."

Jamal's eyes narrowed. "Ask her what she means," he demanded of Kaylin.

"I know what she means," Kaylin replied.

Teela frowned and turned to Kaylin. "You are speaking to the children?"

"To one of them, yes."

"Then tell us what she means."

Kaylin couldn't see how it could hurt. Everyone in the hall knew what had happened, Severn because of her name. "Mrs. Erickson can see ghosts, as you all know. She saw ghosts in a large room in the palace, and the ghosts saw her. They panicked because we happened to have a Dragon with us, and then they...possessed the Dragon."

Jamal's eyes widened.

"The Dragon wasn't particularly happy about it, but Mrs. Erickson explained that they were frightened, and she coaxed them out. They then agreed to let me escort them to my house, and that's where they are now. We weren't sure what would happen if they were brought here—although possessing the neighbor would be a distinct improvement."

Mrs. Erickson cleared her throat again.

"The Dragon is part of the Dragon Court, and in case you

don't know, the Emperor is called the Eternal Emperor for a reason: he's a Dragon. They can live forever if they want. So...the palace is going to be concerned. I don't think any Dragons have been possessed before, and Dragons can cause a lot of damage if they're not in control of themselves."

"Or if they are?" It was Callis who asked.

"Or if they are, but that's illegal and the Emperor would be angry. Teela?"

"With Mrs. Erickson's permission, I'd like to examine the house."

"Of course, dear."

Teela looked down the hall. "Kaylin, help out."

"What's she going to do?" Jamal demanded.

"If I had to guess, she's going to look for magic."

"What, here?"

"Here."

"And what are you going to do?"

"Help her. Look, if you're suspicious, you can just follow us; she can't see you anyway."

Teela was, indeed, looking for magic, or rather, for the sigils that the casting of magic left behind. Every mage left a trace of self, a trace of their magic, in the wake of the casting of spells. The stronger the spell, the longer that trace lasted. Only those with magical ability could see those traces, and they saw different things when they looked; it was why it was useful to have multiple mages investigate the scene of spell use.

Or that's how she explained it to the kids, all of whom did follow her. Although they should be used to the idea that they were both invisible and therefore safe, they crowded behind Kaylin wherever it was possible.

Teela's use of magic was the normal use, and Kaylin grimaced as the Barrani Hawk spoke. Kaylin's arms started up with the goose bumps and the hair on the back of her neck stood on end.

"Sorry," Teela said, without a trace of apology in the two syllables.

"It's fine. I'm used to it. At least it's not a portal."

"Wait, what's a portal?" Jamal asked.

"A portal is…like a door, but made of magic. If you walk into a portal, you walk between one place and another. Sometimes the second place isn't part of the first one. So if there were a portal in front of your house—at the door—it could lead to the very back of the house. Or outside of it."

"Or somewhere else?"

"Or somewhere else entirely, yes."

"You should mention that portals that cross dimensions require a different kind of anchoring magic; they are difficult to create, and can be difficult to maintain."

"They can hear you fine—you can't hear them." She turned to Jamal and paused. She knew he was a ghost, and therefore dead, but he seemed to be turning a familiar green—the color Kaylin was assured she resembled when she exited a portal.

"I think I know what a portal is," Jamal whispered.

Callis added to Jamal's shaky words. He screamed.

15

If Teela couldn't hear the ghosts, Mrs. Erickson could, and she moved fast for a woman her age, appearing around the door, dark eyes wide. She stumbled to her knees in front of Callis; she'd clearly recognized the voice.

"Callis, Callis, I'm here. You're in my house. You're safe." She had to repeat this a dozen times before the words reached the child. "Jamal, what happened? What's wrong?" Her gaze went to Teela, who was looking at Mrs. Erickson and Kaylin with a trace of annoyance.

"Teela did nothing wrong. I was trying to explain what we were doing here, what we were looking for, and I started to talk about portals."

"Portals?" Mrs. Erickson predictably asked.

"I think we're done with that topic," Kaylin said quickly. "Because whatever it was Jamal remembered, Callis remembered, and…he just started to scream." She turned to look at Esme and Katie; they were paler than usual, and silent, their eyes a bit too wide, as if they were seeing something Kaylin couldn't. As she didn't know how the dead could see, or even what they saw when they looked, she couldn't pin it on simple memory.

"I'm sorry. I'm sorry, Callis. Why don't you all come with me to the kitchen? I can tell you about my day—it was very busy but highly unusual, and I think you might enjoy it. I met a Dragon." She smiled brightly, the expression half-coaxing.

Katie said, "I want to watch her." She pointed at Teela. Clearly Mrs. Erickson had never bothered to correct their manners, because no one who might be offended could see them.

"I'm sure she means no harm. She's a Hawk."

"She's a Barrani. And she's a Sorcerer."

"She's not a Sorcerer," Kaylin told Katie. "Sorcerer has a specific meaning. She's a mage, yes—but a lot of Barrani are. The bad ones are Arcanists."

"Kitling, please."

"Katie, you're distracting them," Mrs. Erickson said, a bit more steel in her tone. "They're here to find out why you are trapped—or to find clues. I didn't have the aptitude so I don't have the necessary knowledge."

"If I'm quiet?"

"I think you'll distract Kaylin."

"But she's not a mage. You aren't, are you?"

Kaylin said, "I'm a very, very, very junior mage, but sometimes I'm useful."

"Oh. We're not."

Kaylin couldn't think of anything helpful or comforting to say to that, but she rallied. "You keep Mrs. Erickson company. She'd be lonely living here all alone."

Katie didn't brighten up at the words, but she did nod, and when Mrs. Erickson left, she trailed after her.

"Are you quite finished?"

"Sorry. They're—"

"Children. I know." Teela frowned. "There's nothing here that catches my eye—and I've been examining things very carefully. Can you see anything?"

Kaylin shook her head. "Mrs. Erickson isn't a mage."

"No, apparently she's something more dangerous. I find it surprisingly hard to keep that in mind—it must be your influence."

"She'd never purposefully harm anyone."

"That doesn't usually make a difference to my people. If she weren't mortal, it wouldn't make a difference to the Dragon Court, either. I'm frankly shocked that Sanabalis was willing to let her leave."

"She hasn't done anything wrong, and it would be against the Emperor's Law to have her detained."

"The Emperor *is* the law." Teela exhaled. "Next room."

The next room in the small house was clear, if one didn't count the dust and the cobwebs.

"She doesn't appear to use this room much. The house is small enough—I wonder why."

If Kaylin had to guess, she'd say the children avoided the room. "I can ask."

"Can you ask and return in reasonable time?"

"Guilty as charged. I'm afraid it has something to do with the kids—and if it does, there's probably going to be a bit of a ruckus."

Teela considered this with care.

"Why don't we scan the room and if something comes up, we can ask. If the room is clean, I don't see the point."

"You do, you're just being a coward."

Kaylin grimaced. "I've never seen the kids like that. They thought you were Azoria, the dead Barrani Lord we're not supposed to be investigating or mentioning. But if they thought you were Azoria, she wasn't dead when she was supposed to be; she couldn't be and have kidnapped those children."

"I am capable of rudimentary math, yes." Teela gestured and Kaylin's skin felt a wave of pain. "I understand why the Barrani believe she is best left to the dust of history—but given the events of today, I am no longer sure I'm in agreement." Teela frowned. "I think you'll want to talk to the children. I can't hear them; I'll wait."

"What have you found?"

"If you can separate Mrs. Erickson from the children, you might get more cogent answers from her."

"Teela?"

"Something is vaguely off in this room. There is no sigil that I can detect, no obvious magic. But Azoria was considered a genius. She could be enormously subtle, although that wasn't considered her strength."

"Did you know her?"

"I knew of her. I didn't pay much attention, given my position at the time, and by the time I had come into my own, Berranin as a line was long dead. Clearly, I should have been more watchful."

"She wasn't your enemy. You had enough of those."

Teela nodded. "What do you see here?"

"A really dusty room with spiderwebs on the ceiling. But it's darker. We could maybe open the curtains?"

Teela shook her head, and another surge of magic rubbed Kaylin's skin raw. She was annoyed to see that it had been used to call forth a light.

"It's not a normal light, so don't start whining."

Kaylin frowned. "It can't be a weaker light than you normally call up."

"No. It's much stronger; it illuminates corners that our natural vision can't always see clearly."

"That's not what it's doing, for me."

"What is it doing?"

"It's…it's kind of making everything look darker."

"Everything?"

"No—I can see the light reflected on the floor here and there, but the rest of the room seems to be in darker shadow."

"How much darker?"

"Darker. It was better without the light." Kaylin started to move toward the curtains.

"Don't touch them. Do not touch anything."

"Standing on the floor okay?"

"Where you're standing now, yes, and before you ask, I'm fine. But there *is* something off about this room. You can't sense magic? Your skin isn't reacting?"

"If someone hadn't used two spells, I might be able to answer that question helpfully." At Teela's raised brow, Kaylin relented. "No, when I entered the room my magic allergy didn't alert me the way it does with door wards and the spells you generally cast."

"That's less good. Fine, I'll be patient. Ask Mrs. Erickson about this room."

The children were not in the kitchen; Mrs. Erickson was. She was baking.

"I'm sorry to bother you," Kaylin began.

"No, it's fine. The children are upset and they're in the parlor."

"What are you baking?"

"Cookies. I know they can't eat them, but I find baking very calming. I like to make things that people can enjoy. It isn't world-changing, I know." She said the last apologetically. "Is the corporal concerned about something?"

"There's a small room behind the kitchen that's covered in dust and cobwebs." It reminded Kaylin of Evanton's storefront. "It looks sort of like I'd imagine an attic would when no one's been in it for decades."

Mrs. Erickson returned to her mixing in silence.

"Do you have an attic?"

"No. We have a half attic, and it was occasionally used for storage, but it's difficult to access without ladders, and it's hard to store things that weigh very much there now. I have trouble with ladders."

"And the room I mentioned?"

"It's not used anymore. It hasn't been used for a very long time. It was once a family room, admittedly a small one."

"The children don't like it." It was a guess, but it was also a statement.

"When my parents were alive, they didn't seem to mind it. I'm not sure why, but it became a place they began to avoid. Maybe because it reminds them of the loss of my parents. Maybe twenty years ago, they started to shout or cry anytime I went into that room—and you saw them today. It's a bit upsetting when there's very little I can do to comfort them or calm them down."

"Do you know why they started to hate it?"

"No. And after the first few times I asked, I didn't ask anymore. They became very much like you saw them just a few minutes ago. But in the beginning, they wouldn't enter the room; by the end, they did everything they could to stop me entering it. Why are you asking?" She didn't look at Kaylin as she asked the question, absorbed in the act of turning disparate bits of sugar and flour into something that would, with heat, become edible.

"Teela thinks there's something off about the room."

"Magical?" This time she did turn, her hands messy.

"She's not certain—but I think she's right. There's something about the room that doesn't feel right." As Mrs. Erickson began what looked to be an apology, Kaylin shook her head.

"If you ever get out of the house and head to Elani, there's a store there run by an ancient man whose storefront looks *far* worse than your room. It's not the dust. It's not the cobwebs. Teela would barely notice those. It's...something else. I didn't notice it until she invoked light—but the light somehow makes portions of the room look even darker. I'd like to borrow a lamp, if you have one," Kaylin added.

"You think the darkness is somehow caused by magical light? Give me a second; my hands are a right mess."

Aproned but with markedly cleaner hands, Mrs. Erickson lit a lamp with a glass hood. As she walked by what she referred to as a parlor, the children came out. Jamal glared at Kaylin.

"Mrs. Erickson doesn't have to go into the room," Kaylin told the truculent child. "We want a light that isn't magical in nature, and she's carrying it. I don't disagree with you; I don't think she should enter the room."

"But you can?"

"I'm the Hawk, not Mrs. Erickson. So is Teela. I think you all did a good job of keeping her away from it." She wanted to ask the kids why, but didn't want to see them melt down or cry in terror, so she refrained. She did, however, tap Mrs. Erickson on the shoulder and retrieve the lamp from her hands.

"I think you should go back to the kitchen—I'm sorry to have interrupted you."

"My mother used to love that room," Mrs. Erickson said,

as she handed the lamp to Kaylin. "My father loved it because she did. She was happy there."

The children said nothing.

"We didn't have a lot of money, but we had enough to get by. She had a painting done, of the three of us. I'd like to see it again; I haven't looked at it for the better part of two decades."

"I'll try to find it—do you want me to bring it out of the room?"

She smiled. "I'm sure you have better things to worry about."

Katie, however, whispered, "Don't find it. Lose it forever."

Kaylin made a mental note of that as she carried the light down the hall and into the room.

Teela stood in the exact same position she'd occupied when Kaylin had left. She raised a brow at the lamp, but said nothing.

"If magical light makes things darker, I thought normal light would let us see what the room looks like otherwise."

"It's not a bad thought, unless you intend to traipse all over the room because you can no longer see the darker parts."

"The kids didn't always dislike the room, for what it's worth. Mrs. Erickson said it started maybe twenty years ago. Before you ask, she didn't give specific dates. At first, the kids just started to avoid the room, but after a while, they started to demand she avoid it as well. They didn't react well to her entering it."

Teela nodded. "Two decades, give or take a few years?"

"That's what she said. The room was in use while her parents were alive; apparently her mother really liked it. She had a painting done of the family when they were younger, and Mrs. Erickson wants us to find it."

"It's on the wall."

Kaylin lifted her lamp. "Which wall?"

"The wall to the left of the door—it's behind you."

Kaylin nodded. "She said I can carry it out."

"I assume she meant without causing any damage to it."

"So do I. It's a painting, how hard can it be to move?" As the words left her mouth, Hope—who had been so silent she'd once again forgotten he occupied her shoulder, pushed himself to his feet. Kaylin stopped moving and lifted the lamp. "You have something you want to add? Do *not* slap me in the face with the wing."

Hope squawked without syllables and pushed himself off her shoulder, circled her face before he swatted her forehead with his tail.

"Technically he did obey you," Teela said, amused.

Hope squawked again, but this time it was more than angry bird vocalization, because Teela's amusement guttered. "He feels it very important that one of us avoid that painting," she told Kaylin.

"Does he think it would be harmful to Mrs. Erickson?"

Hope squawked.

"Is there a reason you're talking to Teela and not me when I asked the question?"

Squawk.

"He says it's too much like work to squeeze meaning into your pathetic language."

Hope hovered in air, squawking up a storm.

"I guess he doesn't like it when you take liberties with his words."

"Then he can use them himself." Teela looked thoughtful. "When you asked about the painting and possible effects on Mrs. Erickson, his response was: 'Too late.' And to be fair, he's telling me to keep as much distance as possible."

"It's a painting, Teela."

"Indeed."

"Her parents were normal, mortal parents."

"I have no doubt of that. But he feels that the painting itself is something I, in specific, should avoid. I don't believe you should take it outside of this room. I do believe that you're the one who is going to have to examine it for magical signatures, unless you believe your familiar is being overly neurotic."

"I'd like to."

"But you don't. Exactly my position, which will be right here."

"It's okay if I approach it?"

"You have Hope," she replied. "And the marks of the Chosen. His words, not mine. The amount of trouble you can trip over when you have both has lost bets in the office."

"Yours?"

"Don't be ridiculous."

Kaylin walked toward the wall that contained the door; the open door had partly obscured the picture. She considered shutting the door but decided against. If they found whatever it was that was off and it proved to be dangerous, closed doors didn't make speedy exit any easier.

She frowned.

"Teela, can you move the magical light toward the painting's surface?"

The bobbing light moved—swiftly—toward the framed painting. As it did, the image in the painting grew increasingly dark, increasingly murky. Kaylin could make out the shapes of three people and the height of one chair, but they had no color and no other features; it was as if she was seeing them in silhouette.

"Move it away now?"

The light retreated. Kaylin lifted the lamp—the normal lamp—and held it out, her arm at full extension. The cloudiness, the inkiness, was gone. Beneath the glow of natural—or at least mortal—light, she could see three people clearly. A man sat in the center of a large chair, a woman sat on the upholstered chair's right arm, and in the man's lap, a young girl, her hair done in braids and wrapped around her forehead.

A sprig of flowers was caught in the weave of the braids, its leaves an odd, luminescent green. Although the effect should have been cute or charming, Kaylin found it disturbing.

"Well?" Teela prodded her.

"You can't see it?"

"I can see the painting."

"When your light came close, it became dark and cloudy; I could barely make out the figures. Under this lamp's light, it looks like a portrait of a happy family. Mrs. Erickson wanted me to move it out of the study."

"And?"

"I don't even want to look at it, let alone touch it. There's something wrong with it."

"Be more precise."

"For one, there's a flower in the child's hair—I assume that's Mrs. Erickson—that's an opalescent green. The opalescence could be paint—but it's not reacting properly when I move the lamp."

Teela was silent for a long beat. When she spoke, her voice was all edge. "Describe the flower."

"It's a flower, Teela."

"This is not the time to fall back on ignorance or laziness. I did not ask you to *name* it. Describe the flower. Now."

"It's in her hair. It's small. You don't want me to get any closer to the painting and I have garden-variety mortal eyes—no pun intended."

"Then move out of the door and clear the space you're standing in. Leave the lamp on the floor where I can use it."

MICHELLE SAGARA

"Teela—what exactly is it you're afraid of?"

The Barrani Hawk appeared to be holding her breath; she released it in a long—and loud—exhale. "Let me describe the flower. Tell me if I'm wrong or right. Touch *nothing*."

Kaylin nodded.

"It's small, triangular in overall shape."

It was. Kaylin said, "Continue."

"The blossom, such as it is, is green—it should be a pale green with ivory and gold highlights."

She shook her head. "It's not. It's a vivid, opalescent green. It has three leaves, and at the heart of those three is...I don't know—purple, maybe? Generally speaking, I like purple—but this one reminds me a bit of..."

"Shadow?"

"Yeah, a bit."

Teela said something in Barrani that Kaylin couldn't understand. "We're leaving," she snapped.

"Teela—what's wrong? Is it not just a painting?"

Listen to her, Severn said. It always came as a surprise when he chose to speak to her this way, but his tone mirrored Teela's.

What isn't she telling me?

She doesn't want you to touch that flower, he replied.

But...it isn't just a painting?

Oh, it's a painting. But if she's right, it's a...seed-bed. That flower should grow nowhere but the green. And when it does, it doesn't look like that; it shares the same shape, but not the color.

How do you know that?

Severn didn't reply.

Kaylin bent and settled the lamp gently on the floor. She then stepped out of the room as Teela had suggested. Or demanded, which was probably the more accurate word.

Severn was in the hall; Kaylin saw that he'd unwound his weapon chain, which made no sense in a space this small—

the chain couldn't spin without embedding the blades in the wall. "I've been following your investigation," he said, as he looked through the doorframe. "This is going to lead to some very, very unhappy Barrani."

"Why?"

"Because, as Teela is beginning to realize, we can't abandon the Azoria part of your investigation."

"No," a familiar—and disembodied voice—said. "You can't. Teela is being careful, but it's in her best interests to leave that room immediately."

"Hello, Terrano. I'm surprised Jamal isn't throwing half the house at your head."

"He'd have to see it," Terrano replied smugly.

"I can see him," Jamal said, from down the hall. "You can't?"

"No. He's greatly improved by invisibility." Kaylin waited for Teela to leave the room; the Barrani Hawk shut the door firmly behind her. She turned to Kaylin, or so Kaylin thought. When she spoke, however, she spoke to the familiar.

"Can you protect her if the flower truly blossoms?" The words were formal, almost stilted, the cadence slightly off.

Hope squawked, but the sound was muted, almost devoid of the usual irritation that made him sound like an angry bird.

"I can take care of myself."

The next series of squawks were the usual ones.

"She's got me," Terrano said, his face absent the usual smug grin.

Kaylin wanted to shriek. "Tell me what's going on, someone?"

"We will—but not here."

"Is Mrs. Erickson going to be safe here?"

"Demonstrably. She's lived here for the entirety of her life. I will, however, emphasize that she should not attempt to enter this room; her children are right."

"But she used to use that room all the time while her parents lived."

"We'll talk about that later." Teela was pale, her eyes midnight blue, her hands slightly curved in fists. She turned to Severn and said, "It is not a room you should enter while you bear those weapons."

He nodded.

"I'm sorry—we couldn't carry the painting out of the room," Kaylin told Mrs. Erickson. The older woman had finished baking a tray of cookies, although by the look of it, more trays would follow. The baking that had been the only good part of a long day at the front desk made Kaylin's mouth water.

"At this point, we'd like to ask you to follow the children's lead. Don't enter the room. Unless one of us is here, don't open the door."

Mrs. Erickson looked concerned, but nodded resolutely.

"When was the portrait painted, do you remember?"

"I must have been eleven. Perhaps a bit older—it was a long time ago."

"Do you remember who the painter was?"

"Yes. Well, no. I don't remember her name—but I do remember her. She was tall and slender, had hair that reached all the way down her back. Her eyes were an odd shade of green and she had perfect skin. But it was her voice that I liked best; it was almost musical, although she never sang.

"We met her in the market—she was sketching people for donations, having just arrived in Elantra. My mother was friendly; she struck up a conversation with the young woman, and in the end, the woman offered to do a family portrait. She came to our house with her paints and easels; Father helped her, and Mother teased him about it. The painter was a very beautiful woman.

"Then we sat for her. She did my hair. I remember that—it was such a strange hairstyle, but she said it was common where she grew up."

Teela said nothing.

"And then she had us sit."

"The flower in your hair," Teela began.

"I'd almost forgotten about that," Mrs. Erickson said, with instant and genuine delight. "It was a flower from her home; she had it in a very strangely shaped pot. I told her not to pick it, but she said that it was meant for a very special occasion—and what could be more special than this? She said she had seldom seen such a content, happy family—that she envied us and she wanted to capture the mood of our family perfectly, because time touches all things, but moments can be captured and preserved.

"She picked the flower carefully, and she braided it into my hair. Then she asked us to sit in the chair—my grandfather's chair. I was a child, so I fidgeted a bit. The children disappeared during the painting."

"Disappeared?"

"Well, they went to play somewhere else."

Kaylin turned to Jamal, behind whom the other children had gathered. For the first time, they looked like the ghosts that occupied some of the more terrifying children's stories; there was something about their eyes, unblinking and slightly too large, that threatened to overwhelm the proportions of the rest of their faces.

"Jamal, do you remember this?"

He didn't answer. He didn't appear to hear her. Kaylin frowned and took a step toward him; she could see her marks begin to glow because the light was reflected in all of the children's unblinking eyes. "Jamal?"

Unsettled, Kaylin crouched to bring her face closer to his. He continued to stare through her—they all did.

"They didn't see her," Mrs. Erickson said, coming around the table, the brief delight of reminiscence broken. "But they won't talk about that room or anything in it. Oh, dear." Her expression became one of pure concern. "It's very hard to reach them when they become like this."

"Do they do it often?"

"Not often, no. Perhaps a dozen times in my entire life."

"What does it mean?"

"They're afraid, I think. But I could be wrong; sometimes they see things that I can't."

"But you can see the dead!"

"Yes. And the dead can see each other, or at least they can in my experience. The first time they reacted this way, it frightened me—I was young. But they returned to normal. I asked them what had happened, and they were surprised by the question. They don't seem to retain or remember whatever it was that put them in that state.

"And I didn't press it, even then. I think I was afraid they would leave." She shook her head. "I was younger then, and far more selfish. I didn't want to be alone, either. Now I worry about deserting them." She shook herself. "Nothing bad has ever happened to them when they're like this—they'll be fine tomorrow."

"They've never been like this for longer than a day?"

"No." Mrs. Erickson closed her eyes, squared her shoulders, and said, "I'll come by the Halls of Law tomorrow with the rest of the baking."

Teela said muted goodbyes. Terrano said nothing, being invisible. Kaylin thought it interesting that Jamal could see

Terrano when she couldn't, but any questions about what he saw when he looked at invisible Terrano would have to wait.

The neighbor was no longer groveling on the lawn, which was the only point of cheer in the otherwise tense and gloomy walk home. Severn rewound the weapon's chain as they reached the perimeter of Helen, who opened the door as if she'd been anxiously watching the streets for Kaylin's return.

Kaylin hugged her house's Avatar as she reached the front door. "How are the guests?"

"Surprisingly active, but they've made no attempt to leave their room. They are not, I think, afraid of the space itself, and I do not think they feel trapped. I can sense some of their emotions, but if there is thought, it is not structured in a way I was built to understand." She glanced at Teela, and after a pause, nodded. "An'Teela wishes to avail herself of the parlor."

"We can talk in the dining room."

"I don't believe she intends for all of the cohort currently under this roof to be in attendance."

"Good luck with that," Terrano said, snorting as he materialized.

Kaylin frowned. "We're missing someone. Where's Mandoran?"

"He's not in Mrs. Erickson's house if that's what you're worried about."

"Only Terrano would be that reckless," Teela added. She was paler than usual, or perhaps her eyes were darker; the effect was like a storm warning in the harbor.

"Come to the parlor," Helen said to Kaylin and her partner. "I'll have food there, so you can eat while you have what looks to be a difficult discussion."

Teela closed her eyes briefly. "Parlor. And, Helen? I might avail myself of something to drink if it were offered."

"Corporal Handred?"

264   MICHELLE SAGARA

Severn shook his head. "I don't drink unless I'm working."

"You don't drink when you're working, either," Kaylin pointed out as she followed Helen.

"Some of my work involves fraternizing with people who consider themselves highly important; if they offer a drink, there are times when I can't afford to refuse it." He walked beside Kaylin until they reached the parlor door, and then followed her in.

16

There were always enough chairs in the parlor; it didn't matter how many guests Helen—or Kaylin, in theory—was entertaining; she was aware of the needs of her guests, and she met them. The chairs that appeared were different from the usual chairs; they seemed more formal to Kaylin, and therefore less likely to be comfortable. Teela, on the other hand, didn't seem inclined to sit. She was pacing.

"Helen, how much of an exotic botanist are you?"

"I'm not really a botanist at all, dear. What I know of plants, I learned from my various tenants: some were avid, even ferocious, gardeners. You are asking about the flower Kaylin saw in the painting."

"I am. You can see it clearly?"

"I can see it as clearly as Kaylin did. Kaylin, do you mind if I show the others?"

Kaylin shook her head. Had she thought to do it, she might have requisitioned one of the Halls' portable mirrors, or one of the palace's memory crystals. The latter request was less likely to be rejected, given events involving Sanabalis, and the man who served as quartermaster to the Hawks had never quite forgiven Kaylin for the destruction of nonstandard but very expensive kit.

Helen, however, served the function either of the two devices would have served. "Do you want to take a seat?" Kaylin's home asked Teela. "The chairs are arranged in a messy circle, and I would like to create the projection in its center."

Teela took a seat. She hadn't personally seen the painting. Kaylin had. The younger Hawk wondered if this projection, this illusion, was the sole reason Teela had practically marched Kaylin home.

"It is," Helen replied. "This will be larger than it was in the painting for better visibility," she added to the cohort at large, none of whom were yet in the room. That changed as Helen worked. Mandoran and Terrano joined them. The others chose to watch from a distance.

A green ball of light appeared in the center of the chairs, at chest height. It was larger than Kaylin's head, and it started to spin. Filaments darkened and solidified as it did; Kaylin recognized the color those filaments adopted. It was just as unattractive in midair in the safety of her home as it had been in the painting.

Severn watched; if human eyes could change color to suit mood, his would have been as dark as Teela's.

The flower unfurled, the three petals falling slowly open; at their heart, pulsing in a way that was uncomfortably reminiscent of beating hearts, was something purple.

"Do you have other images of flowers similar in shape and size?" Teela asked Helen, without once moving her gaze from Helen's projection.

"I do, but I believe you are looking for a specific flower." She frowned then and turned to Severn. "You are certain?"

Severn nodded. To the group at large, he added, "Helen

is asking my permission to search my memories of the West March. I've told her to take anything of use that she can find."

"I can see why she wanted confirmation," Teela said. "It's not an offer I could make."

"No, and I wouldn't ask it of you. I didn't intend to ask it of anyone." Helen could be anywhere in her house at the same time; she could do two things at once with ease. A second ball of light—green, and the same size as the first— appeared. It began to spin, and filaments of light formed in the same fashion, but the color the light shed was markedly different. When the shape itself had come to rest, it was—in size, in texture—identical to the first flower.

But colors, however, were different. If Kaylin saw this flower with its white-green leaves, she might have assumed it one of the prettier weeds; most flowers had more color.

"Do you want to tell them?" Helen asked Severn.

"I think Teela already knows. Terrano?"

Terrano nodded, frowning. His eyes weren't the color that Teela's had adopted, but they almost never were; when something went badly, badly wrong he was just as likely to let curiosity rule his actions as caution. The only time she'd seen him exercise any was when they had fled through the outlands to the fiefs, or the place that the fiefs overlapped. He had avoided *Ravellon* entirely; even approaching it in the outlands had caused flickers of unease in his usual ready-to-go expression.

"Sorry—I think you'll want Serralyn for this," he finally said.

"I thought Barrani had perfect memory?"

"For anything we happened to be paying attention to, yes. This one looks like a weed to me—how much attention do you normally pay to those?"

"The green doesn't have weeds," Severn told Terrano. "Not the way the carriage roads here develop them."

Kaylin didn't generally come to Terrano's defense, but felt he had a point. "Pretty sure I saw weeds when I had to enter the green."

Teela lifted her fingers to massage her temples, which was Teela code for *Stop being stupid or I will strangle you.* While it had been an expression directed at Kaylin in her early years in the Hawks, it was most often used when she dealt with Terrano these days. "When we go to see the Consort, you will *not* talk about *weeds* in the green."

"Do I look stupid?"

"At the moment, it would be better if I refrained from answering that question." Teela's eyes lightened very slightly from the indigo shade they'd adopted. "This is going to get ugly."

"Sedarias thinks so as well. She wants to know what Severn knows."

Kaylin looked to Severn.

"She says he called it a seed-bed."

Kaylin was aware, then, that he had said the phrase because he was with Kaylin, and he felt he needed to impress upon her the seriousness of the situation. But they weren't words she'd heard from him before. Although it wasn't reasonable in any way—and she knew it—she disliked the fact that he knew things of import that he had never shared.

"Do you want Serralyn in person, or will you trust me to convey what she says?"

"In person," Kaylin told Teela, her answer overlapping with Helen's.

Serralyn immediately appeared in the room, without having to bother with something as trivial as the door.

"No, she did not, as you put it, pull a Terrano; I created a portal for her use," Helen explained. She gestured another chair into being, and nodded to Serralyn, indicating she should be seated. Serralyn, however, was staring at the two flowers Helen had visually created as show-and-tell in the center of the parlor.

She turned instantly to Kaylin. "You saw the viridescent flower?"

"Not in real life. In a painting." Kaylin then offered the group Mrs. Erickson's childhood remembrance.

"She didn't say the painter was Barrani?"

"No. Beautiful. Graceful. But she didn't mention Barrani."

"Would she have known?"

"She might not have known then—but she'd know in retrospect if her parents never explained the difference."

"She said the painter had this in a flowerpot?"

"Yes—I think she thought the pot itself was interesting and different. The painter told her that it was a special flower—Mrs. Erickson didn't want her to pick it because that would kill it."

"Did she add anything else?"

"Only that the painter said it was meant for a special occasion, and painting such a happy family was special enough. I'm paraphrasing," she added.

"I'd guessed." Serralyn frowned. "That's all?"

"Well, the painter arranged Mrs. Erickson's hair. It's a really odd style—nothing like you'd normally see in Elantra, or at least not the parts of it we grew up in."

"Odd how?"

Kaylin frowned. "Lots of small braids but bound up?" She turned to Helen's Avatar. "Could you show them?"

Helen nodded. The flowers moved, although they remained in the center of the circle; between them, the image of Mrs. Erickson as a child formed. Kaylin couldn't remember it clearly enough to describe it well, but whatever remained in her memory could be accessed by Helen. Helen really was a miracle.

"No, dear, a construct, although I do take your meaning." Her smile implied a hint of joy in an otherwise grave situation.

"This is…not good," Serralyn said. Of the cohort, she was often the one with the greenest of eyes; whatever she had sought in the confines of the Academia, she had found, and it sustained a wellspring of happiness that made her seem very unlike most Barrani. Her eyes now, however, contained no visible trace of green.

"Do you recognize the hairstyle?"

"Maybe. The historical books I've read have drawings, not paintings; the drawings are line drawings or woodcuts, where they exist at all." She hesitated, and then said, "Some of the drawings were meant to be instructional."

"This is a book in the Academia's library?"

"No, it's a book from the Arbiter's library."

"The place where Azoria was once a student."

Serralyn nodded.

"What does it mean?"

"It's— In theory it's ceremonial. Severn has correctly pointed out there are no weeds in the green."

"Is this a flower that grows outside of the green?"

"Not usually, no. And if it did—if this flower was some-how taken from the green and preserved—something was done to it while growing. It's mutated while retaining form and shape." She hesitated. "I would be very interested in the composition of that soil and the make of the pot in which the flower was transported—but I doubt we'll have access to that."

Kaylin felt she'd stretched her limited ability to be patient to the breaking point. "What's the significance of the hair?"

"In this case, only that it's ceremonial. What ceremony, we don't know."

"But you have suspicions."

"I honestly don't. I remember that it was a ceremony that was sometimes conducted in the green prior to a significant marriage—a ceremony of blessing that was intended to invoke peace and harmony." She hesitated. "The blossom braided into the child's hair was entwined there, or would have been, because of her age: too young for marriage except as a ceremonial joining of families of significance.

"Were the groom to be likewise underage, his hair would be similarly bound."

"And the flower?"

"It's a symbol of fertility—an important element of marriage for my people. But the blossoms are given by the green; if they grow, they are used. If a single blossom grows, it is given first—and always—to the bride; if more than one, both wear the flower."

"This wasn't done as a symbol of marriage."

"No, apparently not. Nor was the blossom given by the green, although it is possible it grew there."

"And she took it?"

"It isn't a flower that grows outside of the green, or outside of similar environs the Hallionne of the West March create. No Hallionne would create this."

"You think Azoria had something to do with it."

Serralyn was silent.

Kaylin exhaled. "Does anyone in this room not believe that Azoria was the painter? Show of hands?"

No hands rose, although Teela gave her the stink eye.

"We know that in form, the preparation was in theory for a Barrani marital ceremony. Mrs. Erickson was unaware of the significance of any of it, so clearly that wasn't its purpose."

"Awareness or permission are not actually required," Teela said softly. "The head of family makes the decision. There are historical examples of marriages enacted in this fashion that went spectacularly wrong when the child was made aware of the purpose of the ceremony itself—and ran off into the green."

"I doubt her parents intended to affiance her to anyone at that age, either."

Teela nodded, grim now. "And the painter was not in any way a legal guardian, at least by Elantran standards. She was a stranger."

"A stranger who owned a house that's mysteriously disappeared, but that would've encompassed the lot on which the Ericksons' much smaller, mundane house now exists," Kaylin said, voice even, temper beginning to fray.

"In case it is not clear," Teela replied, lifting a hand in Kaylin's direction, "I no longer believe we have any hope of abandoning any part of this investigation." To Serralyn, she said, "Tell Sedarias there's likely to be further trouble."

"She's intent on causing some herself," Serralyn replied. "She was not pleased to find that the opening salvo in communication was the death of her agents; it's poor manners. If it's all right with you, I'm going to head to the library. I want to speak with the Arbiters."

"Should I go with you?"

Serralyn grimaced. "It's not necessary. The Arbiters won't hurt me, and the chancellor has made clear what a very dim view he has about inter-student violence."

Terrano said, "Sedarias wants them to return here for the duration. Serralyn said no. How much do you trust the chancellor?" He asked the question of Kaylin.

"I'd trust him with Serralyn's and Valliant's lives, if it came to that."

"Theirs? Not yours?"

"Well, I'm not a student, and my survival won't increase

the general health of the Academia going forward. Look, he makes no claim of ownership. But they're necessary if the Academia isn't to crumble—and the Academia *is* the former Arkon's genuine hoard. Serralyn will be safe there."

"Not safer than here."

"Given our current guests and our utter ignorance of who or what they are? I'd bet on the Academia." She also bet that Sedarias was still feeling a tiny bit abandoned, and having a reason to have all the cohort under one roof again was a huge incentive for her.

Terrano nodded. "I'll go with her."

"Don't break anything. I have work in the morning and the Consort in the evening, and I am *not* looking forward to that."

"Neither is Teela," he replied.

"Teela is present and is fully capable of speaking for herself," Teela snapped. "Honestly, I cannot recall how it is that I have not strangled you yet."

"You'd regret it."

"I'm almost willing to take that risk."

Serralyn laughed. "I'm heading back to the Academia, and taking Mr. Not-Yet-Dead with me before he really makes you angry."

Sedarias came down to the parlor after Serralyn and Terrano had left it. Helen put away the fully dimensional images of the flowers and the young Mrs. Erickson. Kaylin was brooding.

"She's lived in that house for the entirety of her life, and she's been safe," Helen said gently, knowing exactly what worried her tenant. "A few more days are unlikely to harm her."

"What if she's never been entirely safe?" Kaylin demanded. "The children—I've never seen them like they were today. She has. What if they're somehow connected to that room, that painting? Look, I can't imagine a Barrani Lord of power being interested in cozy, happy families. I can't imagine them being so touched by sentiment that they would do all this work for free, as a gesture of kindness.

"Whoever painted that picture wanted something, and given the recipient of that flower, it was something *from* Mrs. Erickson."

"And do you believe that the painter received what she desired?"

"I don't know. Maybe she hasn't received it yet." Kaylin frowned. "Maybe the reason Mrs. Erickson can do whatever it is she does is somehow the result of what was attempted. Until we understand the intention behind the ceremony, we don't know. The new Arkon seemed to feel that Mrs. Erickson shouldn't have the power she does possess—it's why he was caught off guard."

"Did he believe that this was because she's mortal?" Sedarias asked.

"I think so. To be honest, things were chaotic enough I don't remember everything that happened."

"Teela does," Sedarias said, although Teela could in theory speak for herself. "I would have assumed the same, but Helen's reaction changes things." She then turned to Helen. "Could our guests shed light on this if you could communicate with them efficiently?"

"It is possible, but I have doubts that the light they could shed would be visible. The lack of ability to communicate heavily implies that there's almost no overlap between us and their current predicament. What we can say with certainty is that Mrs. Erickson has strong shamanistic powers, powers that have never been trained. My memories were somewhat damaged, so my recall is incomplete and cannot be the final word, but I have no memory at all of a successful attempt to imbue someone with a power to which they were not born."

Kaylin cleared her throat and lifted an arm.

"The marks of the Chosen are a different matter."

"Why? The power was granted to me when I was a kid; I wasn't born with it."

Helen's eyes darkened considerably as she considered Kaylin's words. Teela's couldn't get any darker, and Sedarias had adopted indigo prior to her arrival. Severn's eyes were brown and almost unblinking as he, too, considered what Kaylin had said.

"There may be conditions that must be met for the marks of the Chosen to be granted," Helen said. "No comprehensive experimentation has been done, and some research went into finding a definitive answer before it was finally abandoned." At Kaylin's expression, Helen said, "You are correct. The marks are external to the person who wields them, and there are many who would have killed—and did—to attempt to receive the power of those marks for their own use."

Silence then.

Kaylin's only hope was that Serralyn would find out more information that might prove useful now that she knew exactly what she was looking for.

Kaylin's last day on the front desk was the usual blend of annoyance and confusion; she had two missing persons reports, which she treated seriously and handed off to the correct people instantly. For these, she had no difficulty being almost perfect as a Hawk; she considered the possible consequences serious.

It was the vampire reports, the arguments about dogs, the *he stole my cat*, and the general attitude of people who expected that Kaylin, as an officer of the law, was somehow a gofer, that tended to wear her—or any other person who sat at this desk for too long—down.

Mrs. Erickson was late, which didn't help the background anxiety much; it cleared when the old woman entered the office, familiar basket over her arm. She smiled brightly at Kaylin, and Kaylin was reminded of just how much she loved the older woman's face because the lines etched there had clearly been etched there by time and that gentle smile.

She rose and retrieved the basket; it was heavier than usual.

"I bake when I'm worried," Mrs. Erickson said.

"That's…a lot of baking."

"I've been a bit more worried than usual." The smile with which she framed the words was apologetic.

"It's not your fault," Kaylin replied, with some heat.

"As I've gotten older," Mrs. Erickson said, "I've come to realize that *fault* doesn't really matter."

Kaylin exhaled, wondering if she'd ever reach that frame of mind. She was a Hawk because she believed in justice, in the laws—and fault featured very much in her job. "What are these?"

"Brownies. I haven't made them in a long time because cocoa is mostly too far out of my price range—but I had some I'd been saving for a special occasion." She smiled. "I'm not getting any younger, and I know from personal experience that I can't eat it when I'm dead. You should share it with the rest of the Hawks."

Kaylin nodded, but took a seat behind the desk and the basket she'd placed on it. "How are the kids?"

"They're perfectly fine this morning."

"They don't remember anything?"

Mrs. Erickson shook her head. "They never do. But it's better that way, for them—I think they'd live in terror for eternity if they couldn't forget." She hesitated. "You were concerned about the painting."

"Teela was concerned about the painting, but…when Teela's worried, it's never a good sign."

"Can you tell me what you fear?"

"Not yet—we're looking into it. Serralyn is a student at the Academia, and she headed out last night to begin research in earnest."

"About what?"

"About magic, painting, ceremony, plant life—anything that might give us answers, or at least better questions. I'll walk you home after work. Or Teela and I will walk you home. I have a meeting Teela considers important after that, so I won't be able to stay. Was the neighbor out this morning?"

"No. I'm a bit worried about him."

"He won't do anything—" At Mrs. Erickson's expression, Kaylin said, "You're worried *for* him?"

"A little."

Kaylin wanted to hit the desk with her head a couple of times to clear it.

Mrs. Erickson smiled. "Very good, dear. You should have heard Jamal when I let that slip."

"I'm afraid I'm in agreement with Jamal. If you'd like, you can pull up a chair and join me."

"I don't think Bridget would care for that."

"She certainly wouldn't." Sergeant Keele was looking into the room from the door behind the desk. "Our job at the desk is to take down reports and get yelled at by people who are panicking or upset. I do not want any of them to shout at a civilian when a perfectly respectable officer is here." To Kaylin she said, "Don't get up, I'll take that basket."

★ ★ ★

Teela joined Kaylin, as Kaylin had expected she would. Kaylin had removed her tabard before leaving the office, but Teela bypassed the lockers, and still wore hers.

"We will change when we reach the High Halls; I have appropriate clothing in my quarters there for *both of us*."

Kaylin failed to argue because Teela had used that tone.

Hope sat up on Kaylin's shoulder and smacked her face with his wing, covering her eyes as he often did when he thought there was something she should see.

In this case, it was Amaldi and Darreno. They were watching Mrs. Erickson from a distance, which was unusual for them. Kaylin immediately realized why. Teela.

"She can't hurt you," she told them, as she made her way to where they were standing. "She can't see you."

"Do you know who she is?" they asked.

"Yes. She's Corporal Teela. I'm Corporal Neya. We work together in the Halls of Law, which I'm assuming you haven't visited."

"We visited the palace," Amaldi said, "and the place you call the fiefs. And we've gone to the harbor and to see the ocean. Everything's different. We don't remember the city ever looking like this. And..." She lowered her voice. "There's a *Dragon* Emperor."

To people who had probably been Barrani slaves when they had first been put "somewhere safe," the idea of a Dragon as Emperor was probably shocking. Kaylin had told them about the race of the Emperor, but clearly they hadn't fully believed it.

"He's my boss," Kaylin told them.

"Kitling? We are going to be late if you keep this up."

Kaylin grimaced. "The woman who is about to start a lecture is an officer of the Halls of Law—the place Mrs. Erickson goes to every day, rain or shine. You probably don't recognize her. She wasn't a power when you were last allowed to walk the city. I have questions for you about the real reason you don't visit Mrs. Erickson's house."

They nodded. Amaldi's gaze slid off Kaylin's face, which wasn't generally a good sign.

"Kitling, you *know* what the Consort is like when she's angry."

Kaylin held up a hand, palm facing Teela. "Tell me why you've avoided Mrs. Erickson's house."

They both glanced at Mrs. Erickson, who was now looking worried, although it was clear the worry was not for herself.

They glanced at each other again, and then looked at their feet as if their feet were the only compelling thing on the crowded street. People did pass through them as they attempted to avoid answering Kaylin's questions. It made them seem very much the age they appeared.

"It's not safe," Amaldi finally said. "For us. It's safe for Mrs. Erickson because she can see. And you," she added, voice shaking slightly. "You can see."

"What do you see, when you approach her house?"

"Shadows," Amaldi whispered. Darreno reached for her hand and held it, his knuckles whitening; Kaylin wasn't certain whether he'd meant to offer comfort or receive it. "We see shadows—long shadows, and familiar ones. And when we approach that house we...cast shadows ourselves." She hesitated, and then as if steeling herself, lifted her chin and met Kaylin's gaze directly. "We each cast two shadows when we come close to that building. When we're anywhere else in your Empire, we cast none."

Kaylin cursed. The word seemed to mean little to Amaldi or Darreno, which was good; Mrs. Erickson heard it, which was less good.

"One more question before Teela comes and drags me off."

Amaldi nodded.

"Do you recognize the name Azoria?"

Amaldi and Darreno froze, wide-eyed.

"I'll take that as a yes. Was she the woman who, to protect you from the consequences of war, hid you away?"

Darreno nodded. He glanced at Amaldi and exhaled, or appeared to exhale. "Yes. She was our owner, our master. She treated us well. But she said she had plans for us, that we were special. She hid us away in order to preserve us—and we remained where she hid us, waiting."

"To be found?"

"To be freed. To discover to what ends our 'special' nature was meant to be put." He spoke with bitterness. "We didn't expect to survive it."

"You don't know that," Amaldi said.

Darreno did not argue.

Kaylin turned to Mrs. Erickson. "I'm sorry—I want to continue this conversation but I'm expected at the High Halls, and for some reason, normal Hawk wear is forbidden."

"You are not there as a representative of the Imperial Law, for reasons I'm sure even you know. I apologize for my own impatience; the last time Kaylin crossed the Consort's will she was depressed and unhappy for far too long."

Kaylin reddened.

"You're going to the High Halls?" Darreno demanded.

Kaylin nodded. "We're going to escort Mrs. Erickson home, first."

"Can we go with you to the High Halls?"

"Probably not to where we're going, but yes, no one can see you so it's probably safe for you to follow."

The only thing for which Kaylin felt grateful was that Teela hadn't chosen to drive. The High Halls grew as they approached it, and she thought she'd be happier to see Castle Nightshade right at this very moment. Teela didn't give her a chance to say as much. She ushered Kaylin into the High Halls in a hurry.

"You shouldn't have said yes," Teela told Kaylin while Kaylin was attempting to dress herself in the clothing Teela had deemed suitable. It wasn't that Kaylin disliked dresses, but they always seemed so fragile, and, given Kaylin, likely to suffer for it. The quartermaster wouldn't forgive her for damaging an expensive dress for at least the rest of this decade—if ever.

She also didn't like the way the garments revealed skin; the marks would be visible, and she'd hidden them as much as possible ever since they'd appeared on her skin.

"Stop slouching; you look like you expect to be hit at any moment."

"I'm not slouching—"

"Remember what you've learned. If you wear the equivalent of a sign saying, *Please don't hit me*, half of the people you meet will pity you, and the other half will assume you've done something to deserve punishment."

"Can I at least get a fancy jacket? My back is exposed."

"A jacket is unnecessary; it will ruin the line of the dress."

"Can I get a shorter dress? This one drags on the floor."

"We do not have time. Inasmuch as it is possible to do so, you wish to blend in with the fashions and customs of the court. You will not be met in the greater gathering space; the Consort will no doubt send servants to guide you. I will be beside you; if someone wishes to mislead or attack you, they will be attacking An'Teela." The Barrani Hawk smiled. "I am first of my line, but my line was born of a desire for vengeance that never once faltered.

"There is no family, no matter their import, that could

forget that; they will attack me only in desperation—and the desperate are often foolish and incompetent. Come. You are ready. Put on the boots—and be grateful I chose boots instead of lighter footwear."

"You did that because you didn't want to listen to me complain."

"And my reward is…to listen to you complain. Why haven't I strangled you?"

"You're too busy trying your best not to strangle me?" a familiar voice said.

Terrano.

17

"Why are you here?"

"Actually, I'm not here to follow the two of you—Sedarias trusts Teela to keep both herself and you safe. I wanted to speak to the heart of the building, and the Shadow that's currently keeping it company."

"Why?"

"They like me?" She heard him chuckle at her expression. "I learned a bit of chess while I was wandering the streets of your city, and it seemed like an interesting game. So I'm teaching them both to play it."

Hope, artfully arranged on her shoulder, lifted his head and opened one eye in invisible Terrano's direction. He squawked.

"Yes," Terrano said, more seriously. "That, too. You'll keep an eye out on the two of them? Because I'm kind of lying when I say Sedarias trusts them to stay safe."

Squawk.

"Don't let me make you any later," the cheerful, invisible joker of the cohort deck said.

"Is he gone?" Kaylin asked Teela.

"Yes." The Barrani Hawk's eyes were martial blue, an

improvement over the indigo they'd adopted yesterday. She turned and headed toward the large gallery that marked the public entry—for a value of public that seldom included people like Kaylin—into the High Halls.

Two people, however, were waiting in the gallery; they wore shades of ivory and green, flowing robes that were not designed to impress, but did anyway.

"Do you know why she wanted to meet with you?" Kaylin whispered.

"Yes. You as an addition has probably altered all of her plans and intentions." Teela's expression didn't change. "I am not looking forward to this."

As expected, at least by Teela, the two robed Barrani were not simply loitering; as Teela approached them, they moved to greet her. The grace and fluidity of their bows—and the length those bows were held—denoted actual respect, which implied that these were servants to the Consort, rather than minor lords allied with her.

They are, Ynpharion said. *But they are also Lords of the High Court, having passed the test set them. They come from minor families— and before you deride me as hopelessly judgmental, understand that I came from a family of similar stature.*

I haven't heard from you in a while. It was pleasant.

She could practically feel Ynpharion rolling his eyes. *Your house has been far, far more secure in the past few days than usual. But you leave your house enough to give me some sense of what's happening.*

Are you going to be at the meeting?

What do you think? He snapped in obvious frustration. Ynpharion was a bundle of frustration with a heavy side of judgment thrown in.

I take it that's a no.

It is my privilege to serve—to truly serve—the Consort, but I am Barrani, and of the court. She cannot be seen to favor me in the fashion she favors you; you are considered a possibly useful pet. She can show favor to An'Teela for reasons I hope are obvious.

Teela's powerful.

Yes. She also holds one of The Three. I have nothing to set me apart from the two who have come to greet you. The Lady can be certain of me, can trust me, only because she has my name.

Does she know about Azoria?

Yes. The name has caused ripples through the High Court; I would almost say the name is feared. I am not old enough to have been privy to rumors when they were current, and not stupid enough to search for them now. You will not listen—I do not believe you are capable of it—but tread with caution. If it is permissible to the Consort, allow An'Teela to do the speaking.

The Consort won't allow it, Kaylin replied, although she absolutely agreed with the advice.

No, likely not. She knows that you open your mouth and let words fall out—something Teela is far too cautious to do. I am astonished just how much trouble you can stumble into while blindly flailing.

And envious of it, which surprised Kaylin.

The High Halls were never what could be called crowded; although they were the absolute seat of Barrani power, they weren't like the Imperial Palace, with its many, many dignitaries, visitors, and bureaucrats. The halls seemed almost empty to Kaylin; they didn't seem empty to Teela, given how alert she now was. Hope was standing on Kaylin's shoulder, although both of his wings remained folded across his back. He was as alert as Teela.

As alert, Kaylin realized, as Kaylin herself. If the shape and the layout of the High Halls had changed when the Shadow trapped at their heart had been freed from both his cage here and the fetters that had enslaved him, she was uncertain that the High Halls had ever valued the safety of its guests.

"We value the safety of our guests."

Kaylin turned instantly in the direction of this new voice.

"Welcome to the High Halls, Lord Kaylin." A Barrani man had joined them, his feet moving without touching the marbled floors. This must be the Avatar of the High Halls.

"Indeed, as you suspect. It has been long since I have felt such freedom, and my gaze has turned outward, as well as in. I am not Hallionne," he added. "My purpose is not the purpose laid into the Hallionne upon their creation. The Hallionne were created as sanctuary fortresses in times of war. I was created to house those who ruled—and rulers are ever subject to the detritus of war, both obvious and subtle.

"I owe you a debt. I am not Barrani, to consider such debt a shame."

"Maybe you can answer a question for me as payment."

Teela stiffened. "Do not ask that question in the open halls."

The Avatar of the High Halls surprised Kaylin; he laughed. "There is no question Lord Kaylin might ask that would cause either offense or danger—to her. I am aware that your visit is considered sensitive, and many are the ears that desire to hear of it. They will not hear what she says while I accompany you. Nor will the people who are now bound to her. Ask in peace."

"Do you know of Azoria An'Berranin?"

"That is not entirely the correct name," the Avatar—who looked very much like a Barrani man to Kaylin's eye—said. "She was not An'Berranin when last I was aware of her presence."

"It's the name I was given—or the name that was used for legal documentation in the mortal areas of our city."

"It is the belief of most of the court that she perished after the first war. It is not your belief."

"I don't know, but if I had to bet, no."

"Then you must interrogate those who are certain she is dead."

"That's been tried. It didn't go well; it just caused more death. Whatever information there is, whatever is feared, people will kill to keep hidden."

"What do you wish to know?"

"Let's start with a couple of questions that might seem unrelated."

"Very well. An'Teela, with all due respect, it is safe for her to ask these questions of me, which is clearly not the case in general. I was not Hallionne, no—but like any living building, I am aware of those who dwell within my confines. I was fully awake at the time Azoria and her line were of significance.

"I was fond of An'Berranin—her father. Her brother was heir to Berranin, in the event of her father's passing, but I had no sense that he wished to rush toward his inheritance. If she adopted the title, both father and brother were dead." There was no question in his voice.

"The excision of Berranin occurred after the first war, when the building had significantly changed," was Teela's quiet rejoinder.

Kaylin nodded. "I've spoken to scholars at the Academia. They felt that she had a voracious hunger for knowledge, but murky ambitions."

"Even if my opinion was, like your scholars, entirely superficial in nature, she styled herself An'Berranin. Facts strongly imply that she had at least that much ambition."

"Or that she was the last of her line left standing," Teela added, voice soft.

The Avatar nodded. "Much of my thought was turned inward, after the first war; knowledge of what passed outside of the Tower in which I had imprisoned our foe was no longer within my purview. That has changed, although many of the lords of the current court are...uncomfortable with these changes."

"How much say do they get?"

"Your language is oddly colloquial; perhaps that is why young Terrano prefers to speak it." The Avatar smiled. "The Lord of the High Court is not uncomfortable with my reach; he has, indeed, encouraged it, much to the chagrin of those who nominally serve him. He is the final authority, where such authority governs me at all.

"But the imperative is the protection of the Lake, the succor of our race. And that was not the question you intended to ask."

Kaylin shook her head. "I've met two mortals who I believe are...trapped in the same way the occupants of the Academia were trapped when the Towers rose. But I think part of that entrapment was centered in the High Halls itself."

"Why?"

"Because they recognize the High Halls as they are now. I don't think they've ever seen the High Halls that took shape after the disastrous battle in the first war. It's only recently that they've been...awake, in a fashion. That's suspiciously the same period in which you've been awake, or at least more aware of things that occur outside of the Tower of Test."

He frowned.

Hope squawked loudly, and the Avatar stopped moving, arrested. He replied in a language Kaylin didn't understand. Hope continued his squawk while Kaylin attempted to cover the ear closest to the noises he was making.

"You feel that the power used was somehow mine?"

"Or that it was attached to you in some subtle way, yes. I'm not certain. I'd hoped that you'd remember if you were somehow asked to house a couple of mortals."

"I have housed rare animals that required very specific care; mortals would not be difficult."

Kaylin's knee-jerk reaction—which the Avatar was no doubt aware of—was instant annoyance at the comparison. She kept it to herself not because she hoped the Avatar wouldn't be aware of it—she had no illusions on that front—but because Teela would probably be annoyed.

"And An'Teela is indeed more terrifying," the Avatar said, smiling. The smile faded. "These mortals would have belonged to Azoria?"

Kaylin hated the use of the word *belonged*, but nodded. She knew that before the Empire rose, Barrani owned slaves, and most of those slaves were human. "Yes."

"I will retreat to examine my history. It is not as simple a task as you believe it to be. Ah, but first, I have a lesson with Terrano. He is teaching us—"

"Chess, yes. I know. I'm certain Terrano would be forgiving if the lesson was put off."

"Perhaps, but others would not be."

Kaylin wondered if those others included the Shadow in the High Halls.

"I will lead you to where the Consort now waits. I was reminded that you have not been to the High Halls of late, and the changed geography might cause both confusion and delay."

Geography, as the Avatar called it, had indeed changed. Although the High Halls remained composed of towering stone walls, arches, and ceilings, natural light—for a value of natural that involved a sentient building—was far more prominent. Where arches opened to the right as they walked, they opened into forest—aged forest that reminded Kaylin very much of her uncomfortable journey to the West March.

"At least there don't seem to be insects," she murmured.

"I offer apologies in advance," Teela told the Avatar. "Kaylin is second to none when it comes to whining. It's a small wonder she's survived it."

The Avatar chuckled. "She is not so adept at whining as some who make their home in the High Halls; her whining is merely more publicly accessible. It is almost charming in comparison."

"You have a building's view of *charming*," Teela replied, but she was distracted. "This is new." She'd clearly visited the High Halls since its transformation.

"Indeed; it was requested by the Consort. And Lord Kaylin, it is the Consort's will that moves us; the High Lord is subject to the rules and the games played by politicians. The Consort has historically played some part in the politics of her time—but her duties are duties that affect all of the Barrani.

"It is to safeguard the race that I was created, and to safeguard the race that I withdrew almost the entirety of my power to the Tower in which I had imprisoned the slave of our ancient enemy. I have spent much time in conversation with the Consort, the High Lord, and a handful of Barrani Lords of his court; I have spent some time in similar discussions with those who seek—as they always did—a change of ruler, a shift in power.

"But I confess that I find Terrano fascinating, and he is one of the few who has come to offer us information that seems to have no political use whatsoever."

"It's a game," Terrano said, losing all invisibility as the syllables finished. "There's no political use in a game—you play them for fun."

"I see. I will leave you here," he said to Kaylin. "You have your...familiar, and he will preserve you should unfortunate political games go awry. An'Teela. Lord Kaylin. I will take Terrano with me. I will return to guide you out when your meeting is done."

Here, as the Avatar had called it, was yet another entrance into a forest. A path, however, had been laid between trees that were taller and more impressive. It was odd to pass through the arch, and to see, as Kaylin turned to look over her shoulder, that the wall that arch was cut into on one side had vanished from view. It wasn't shocking; she'd expected it; she was in the hands of, if not Hallionne, a sentient building, and that building meant her no harm.

"You're thinking the High Halls will be far safer than they were before," Teela observed as she began to follow the path. "You're not?"

"This was the heart of Barrani power, and the Barrani—as you have constantly pointed out—made games of both war and assassination. If the High Halls were created to protect the cradle of our race, they were created with an awareness of the games Barrani play. For the most part, the Consort is considered apolitical because lack of a Consort is lack of progeny, lack of continuity. But do not believe that apolitical, for the Barrani, means what it means for humans."

"Do you feel less safe?"

"Me? Of course not. But I feel no safer. My safety is not in the hands of the Halls; it is in my own hands. Sedarias is the same. And were the High Halls to be safe—as you use the word—Sedarias's agents would not now be dead, and Sedarias not girding herself for ugly war."

"She was girding herself for ugly war before they died," Kaylin pointed out.

"She was girding herself, as you put it, for ugly war because she expected that she would not be the only claimant for the title. She *is* An'Mellarionne—but only while she lives, and she expects there are cousins and distant relatives who desire to change that state.

"This, however, is different." Teela lifted her head to look up at the height of the trees between which they walked. "You like the cohort."

Kaylin nodded. "I mean, I want to strangle Terrano half the time, I've bruised Mandoran's shins, and when Sedarias is in a mood, I want to huddle under the table with the quieter, sensible members—but...I do."

"Sedarias would have garnered instant respect at any point in the past. She has it now because the Barrani equate fear with respect, or respect with fear. But she has a flaw that is not entirely obvious to those who consider her either impediment or enemy. What is it?"

"It can't be her temper."

Teela chuckled. "As you say, it can't be her temper."

Kaylin considered Sedarias and her relationship—or the parts of it Kaylin had seen—with the rest of the cohort. She considered her relationship with her immediate family—brothers and sisters bent on killing her, both in the distant past and in the present. "She doesn't take it personally if people are trying to kill her," she finally said. "She expects it. She'll kill them first because that's what it takes to survive—but...she expects it.

"She takes it very personally when people attack the people who serve her, or the people she considers hers. And she's pretty possessive."

"You are becoming far more perceptive," Teela replied, nodding. "Most will not notice the difference—ah, no, most

Barrani will not mark the difference. You could cause Sedarias great harm should you choose to work against her."

"She'd kill me."

"I did not say you could harm her in a full-on assault, no. But that is not generally what *work against* means among my kin. Inasmuch as she trusts at all, she trusts you."

"Because I can't actually harm her."

"Is that what you truly believe? Perhaps that is what Sedarias would have you believe. What of Mandoran?"

"He trusts me."

"Because you're harmless?"

"He doesn't actually think I'm harmless," Kaylin countered.

"He thinks you are chaos incarnate—a title previously reserved for Terrano, who has the advantage of deliberately choosing chaos as an outcome. He trusts your intent, but given the difficulties that have occurred in the wake of an intent that is trustworthy, he feels pragmatically that you might as well be Terrano."

Kaylin wasn't certain how to take that. "Mandoran likes Bellusdeo."

"Yes. I like her, as you know. Serralyn likes her, but considers her tragic. Sedarias tolerates her because, in the end, the cohort owes her a debt. I have wandered off my point. The cohort can stand as more traditional Lords of the High Court because of Sedarias, but they are not well versed in the games of the court. I am, and Sedarias was raised on them.

"You will think Sedarias cold-blooded. Understand that the motivation for that appearance in the end is the safety of those she values. If she is considered to have sentiment for any of them, they will be the weapons wielded against her for the greatest amount of damage."

"Will her enemies believe she actually cares?"

"That is the question, isn't it? It is not unknown among

my kind; some of our greatest lays involve such doomed love, such costly devotion. Sedarias wanted the Tower because she knew in the Tower, the rest of the cohort could be safe. She does not have the Tower. She has Helen, while you live— but this will be a long war, and you are likely only to see the very edges of its beginning before age takes you.

"The cohort is Barrani only inasmuch as Sedarias has traditional ambitions. If she did not, I doubt most would care. Some of the cohort are willing to politick in order to build— or rebuild—their familial lines; some are willing to risk their lives reclaiming the lines that survived. But they do it in concert—they do it, in part, for Sedarias and her survival.

"In all of this, the Consort plays no part. She may have preferences, but as I'm certain you are aware, she is likewise singular in her ambitions. But the whole of the High Halls will bend toward her should it become necessary. There are very few who would dare to harm or usurp the Consort; there are many who desire their own progeny to be Consort."

Kaylin knew why that would fail.

"I think that the High Halls and the interaction with the cohort now and in the future might cause subtle, but very real, changes." Teela's voice held firm.

"You want those changes."

"Is that what you think?"

Kaylin nodded. "You were the only member of the cohort who wasn't trapped inside Alsanis. You had to walk forward on your own. But you never forgot them."

"I have Barrani memory."

"That's not why."

Teela exhaled. "No, kitling, that's not why. But understand that if that information is known, it will have the same effect upon me as it would upon Sedarias. None of us is invulnerable; all of us project invulnerability to discourage those who might otherwise think it safe to attack. It is safe for the Consort to mimic affection, or to openly display it, because of her import to the Barrani people as a whole.

"It will become far less safe if a replacement suitable to the duties she undertakes is found. So far, there has been no likely candidate."

"You check?"

"Frequently, but I am not the only one. Should a suitable replacement be found, should that replacement be credible, all of that will change or the Consort will perish. I know I have said this before, but it would be best for both of you if you refrained from public displays of affection that involve the Consort."

Kaylin nodded, remembering how little she liked Barrani society. If people could just care about the things they cared about, Barrani society would be a very different place. Why did so much devolve, in the end, to power?

Survival, Hope said.

The path through the forest continued when the trees fell away; they ringed a large clearing that was every bit as impressive as the space the high thrones occupied. There was, however, no throne here. There was a fountain in what seemed to be the center of the clearing, and sculptures that stood where trees otherwise might have grown, their lines clean and precise, draping cloth of stone replacing more martial, obvious armor.

The Consort sat on the lip of the fountain, gazing into the ripples of water as if she sought to read meaning from them. She looked up as they approached, and rose.

Her eyes were indigo, her expression remote. Kaylin regretted getting out of bed in the morning.

Teela offered the Consort a low bow—it was formal, elegant, and, as Barrani manners so often were, distancing, as if they were meant to be a wall. Kaylin internalized a grimace and bowed as well, secure in the knowledge that no matter how perfectly she executed her bow, it would always be inferior to Teela's.

The Consort made no move to stop her or interrupt her. Sometimes she hugged Kaylin in greeting, but that wouldn't happen today. Kaylin prayed this had nothing to do with Azoria.

"This garden," the Consort said, "is a reminder to me. You will note the statues; I asked the High Halls to create statuary—with a fountain—and a representation of all of the Consorts within his memory. Their presence is a comfort to me—a comfort and a command. I have heard, Lord Kaylin, that you are investigating an old criminal. It involves mortals, and their murders, and such investigations have nothing to do with the Barrani—or so we claim.

"But in the course of that investigation," the Consort continued, turning to face Kaylin, "you came upon a name that is not spoken at court." She didn't speak it now, either.

Kaylin nodded slowly, wondering if the Consort was familiar with this because of Ynpharion. If he was the source of the information, he didn't confirm.

"It is a name known to me, not because I had cause to interact with the person in question—I did not. She was executed before my time."

"You did not know her personally?"

"I did not. And I would not see her name raised in any place where Barrani might hear it spoken. Yet it has been raised."

Kaylin wondered, then, if the Consort was behind the death of Sedarias's agents; she froze at the thought, and kept it—with effort—from her expression.

"In some quarters," the Consort continued, "it has caused suspicion and death."

"Were you responsible for those deaths?" So much for effort.

"And you were doing so well," Teela said.

"Do you suspect my hand in this?" the Consort asked. "And if the answer is yes, as I fear it must be, does it make clear how much of an emergency I consider this? I would ask—I cannot entirely command, given your position in the Hawks—that you abandon all investigation as it pertains to that lone Barrani woman."

"And if I can't?"

"I will not threaten you, Lord Kaylin; I am well aware that threats would be of little use. I ask of Teela that she keep her former comrades in check, if it is at all possible."

"Terrano is playing chess with the Avatar," Kaylin quite reasonably pointed out. "And he's not exactly the most subtle of players."

"No." The Consort exhaled. "No, it was not at my command that those agents perished. I am not the only lord of this court who considers the history surrounding this one woman to be a great and terrible secret that must not be shared. But had they not died, I would have considered giving that command."

Kaylin glanced at Teela; her eyes were now as dark as the Consort's. Neither woman spoke. Kaylin, uncomfortable with the indigo silence, chose to fill it. "Her name is known in the Academia. One of the librarians and at least one of the scholars were involved with her when she was a student there. She's old," Kaylin added, as if it needed to be said. "I did attempt to ignore her name when investigating what is definitely a cold kidnapping case and a...questionable series of murders. Of children.

"But she used to own a house that no longer stands on the lot; it's vanished, almost as if it never existed. She owned that house less than one of our centuries ago. If you believe she was executed, you believe she's dead. But we have reason to think that she was not, in fact, dead when she signed the deed for a house that mostly doesn't exist.

"It's possible that someone signed her name with appropriate identification—forgeries exist and some are quite good."

"There is a reason," the Consort said, her words stretched and thin, "that you do not believe that to be the case."

"There's more than one." Kaylin glanced at Teela, who didn't give her the stink eye which meant, *Stop speaking right now*. "The first: I can see the ghost of a house when my familiar places his wing over my eyes. It seems to fade in and out, but the outlines are clear and they're nothing like the small house that currently stands on that property.

"I've had some experience with buildings that are not-quite-there, the most recent being the Academia. I've also had experience with the students and teachers who'd been trapped there since the Towers rose to ring the fiefs.

"The house I can see only with Hope's aid isn't a normal building. The events that have occurred in the small house that seems to have replaced it are...not normal events. Teela didn't care," she added, sliding more firmly into Elantran, which did earn the stink eye, "until we were investigating the small house."

"You were searching for signs, then."

"That's not why we escorted the current owner home, no. She's had some trouble with a bullying neighbor, and while she's generally considered dotty, she's harmless and she bakes for the Hawks.

"But the neighbor was stricken at the sight of Teela—a reaction many Hawks would sympathize with. It's just...he thought she was someone else, and he fell to his knees groveling and weeping. He was apologizing for losing something precious, which he believed his elderly neighbor must have stolen.

"His behavior was so...wrong." Kaylin grimaced. "There's more, but technically we're not supposed to talk about ongoing investigations."

"You refer to the elderly woman's stated ability to see ghosts?"

I did not inform her of the petty interactions of mortals, Ynpharion said before Kaylin could ask.

"I said technically," Kaylin said, wondering who among the Hawks—if it was a Hawk problem at all—would have passed the information on. It wasn't the first time she'd wondered either, given the effect the name Azoria had on the Barrani. "Clearly we have an informant in the Halls of Law. Do they report to you?"

18

The Consort, the only Barrani Kaylin had ever met with white hair, raised a pale brow at the question. As her eyes were already almost black, they couldn't get any darker; Kaylin imagined poor manners would take a back seat to everything else. Or hoped they would.

The Consort surprised Kaylin. "No. They do not report to me; nor are they beholden to me in any but the general way."

"The general way?"

"I am the Lady; I am the mother of our race unless and until someone suitable for the duties I have undertaken is found. The Barrani in general believe that I would fight—as our kind does—to retain my position, because they believe that position comes with power. I will not argue; it does. But it comes with a burden of responsibility and duty, the shouldering of which can break us; we can never set it aside. Were someone suitable found, I would gratefully pass on the weight of that burden."

That was unlikely to happen. If Kaylin grew to hate being a Hawk, she could quit. There would be consequences, of course—she had no idea what she would do without that job to define her. The Consort didn't have that option. And it was the Lake that somehow chose the successor.

"My mother did not want me to become the Consort," she continued, eyes dark. "Did you know? She did not want that for her daughter."

No, of course not. She knew, better than any, how costly the burden could be; she, too, had borne it. And because she had and could, she had no desire to see those she loved suffer for the sake of a title, a position. It probably made her very unlike most of her kin—just as the Consort was.

"But if given a choice between me and someone the Lake did not accept, it was me. Come, I am restless. Walk with me. I would leave An'Teela behind, but she is already entangled in this; I could ask my brother—" she obviously meant the High Lord "—to forbid all investigation, but I can see the color of An'Teela's eyes; she will not obey."

"But he's the High Lord!"

"Yes. And if obedience was owed to power, we would have no assassins, and you would have no need of the Halls of Law among your own kind. She will continue, now, until she has answers—or until she understands how damning, how damaging, those answers could be to us as a people."

The Consort began her walk at a slow, measured pace, but her hands, twined behind her back, were white-knuckled; they almost appeared to be shaking. Any annoyance at a spy in the Halls of Law bled away, as if those shaking hands cut deeply. Teela shot Kaylin a look, which more or less promised a dire lecture at a later point; Kaylin grimaced and hurried to catch up with the Consort.

"You are aware that my position is, in theory, apolitical. You are also aware that I am sister and Consort to the High Lord—and the High Lord's position is the very opposite of apolitical. Only in times of external war do the various attempts to unseat a High Lord grind to a halt; it was ever thus.

"My brother is not my father; my father was a man of stone. The High Lord speaks to me, and to our brother, Lirienne, when he is concerned. Perhaps I should not have come across the information that was given to him—he is given so many reports, I might be forgiven for missing one.

"But I could not ignore this one. Do you know why?"

Kaylin shook her head.

"I can speak of it to you because, although you are mortal and not kin, you have seen the Lake. You understand its composition, and you understand why, in the end, it is the source of all Barrani life. Were I to perish unexpectedly, you—as lord of the court—would be called upon to fulfill the duties I could no longer fulfill. This is not broadly or widely known, but An'Teela does know it.

"You are therefore slightly safer than you once were. And because of this, I am slightly less safe—but I do not begrudge it. It has been a solace and comfort to me to know that in the event of an emergency, you, who bear the marks of the Chosen, will shepherd the children who cannot wake without the blessing of the Lake.

"You were not raised as a possible Consort. You were not educated as a possible Consort. Our history, such as it is, is barely known to you—but you know the broad strokes. When you entered our Tower you saw and touched things that almost none of my kin could see or touch—and you survived.

"You and I have been at cross purposes before. I was angry at the risks you were willing to take, and that anger has not fully abated—but that risk pales in comparison to this one, where my duties are concerned. No, it will not end the world. But it could harm or empty the Lake from which our life flows."

Teela lowered her chin; she had joined the Consort and Kaylin, but walked behind, as if she were a simple guard or escort.

"So, I will speak, here, in a place that no others can reach, of a history of the Lake and the struggle to earn the position of Consort by those families who cannot understand, given their nature and beliefs, that the position cannot and will not be given to those who desire it purely for political purposes. Were there a council which made the decision, were it an election, perhaps they would hold sway.

"It is the Lake that decides, not the High Lord or his many allies or rivals. There was a time when belief in that was at an ebb—people who have power believe, in the end, that the power they have must prevail. It was a disaster—worse than a disaster. It has shadowed all of those who guard and guide the Lake. If children's stories loom large in your life, imagine that your bedtime stories are actual history. It is a history that is very seldom discussed—but you've stumbled across a name that features in it.

"And to speak of that history, I must speak a name that is cursed; beyond the import of the historical lesson it teaches, it is *never* spoken."

"Azoria," Kaylin said.

"Kitling, what does *never spoken* actually mean to you?" Teela said, in obvious frustration. She spoke in Elantran.

"It's easier for me to say it; it clearly has more weight for the Consort. I was *trying* to be helpful, Teela."

"And if this is a result of *helpful*, it better explains the chaos you continually cause."

"This didn't start with me!"

The Consort cleared her throat, and both of the Hawks turned toward her. To Kaylin's surprise, the indigo had paled enough the Consort's eyes looked almost normal—for any other Barrani. Besides Serralyn, the Consort was the only Barrani whose eyes were frequently green. "I am grateful that you chose to accept my invitation, both of you. An'Teela, she is correct. I find it difficult to speak the name. But she speaks the name because nothing I say will make sense if it is not spoken at least once; she confirms her suspicions."

"I believe context makes it clear, but subtlety has never been Kaylin's strength."

Kaylin shrugged.

"You have heard that her entire clan was excised."

"And that she's dead, yes."

"That happened centuries ago. Before I was born, but not before my mother's time. We do not speak of her. We want no word of her to exist in the polity at large. Even the Arcanum does not mention her name. And yet, somehow, a woman dead centuries ago, buried, all traces that could be easily found obliterated, has led you here. I asked An'Teela to bring you to the meeting we had planned—which was partially social in nature—because I hoped to plead my case in the most private of the spaces the High Halls could provide: please, stop investigating."

It was Teela who said, "I am sorry. It is not possible now. I understood your plea, if not the reason for it, your eyes so seldom adopt that color. But the rumors of her death may have been exaggerated or greatly exaggerated."

The indigo once again overwhelmed normal blue as the Consort paled. "Come," she said. "It is not far now."

The Consort led them both to a small round table, better suited to Helen's version of a garden than the High Halls. There were no chairs; in their place was a circular bench that circumscribed the table itself—which appeared to be made of wood, although it seemed to Kaylin that the wood was rooted in the ground beneath it.

"Please, be seated," she said, seating herself first as if to prove that the bench was safe.

Kaylin glanced at her familiar, but he seemed focused on the Consort; he had no squawks to give. She sat at the same time as Teela did; they formed the points of a triangle as they took their places.

"I will not offer refreshments unless you desire them," she said—to Kaylin. Teela's eyes matched the Consort's in color, which clearly indicated neither had any desire for food. Kaylin shook her head.

"Did you know?" Teela asked.

The Consort shook her head. "If we had known, a greater portion of the resources offered us would have been spent in pursuit and execution. Were it not An'Teela who presented this news, I am not certain I would have believed it. Or that I believe it now. But there must be a reason you believe this.

"And if she is, as you suspect, alive, that changes the complexion of our immediate future. I am grateful for your intervention with the High Halls; the threat she posed in ancient times she posed after the loss of its oversight. I believe the change in the High Halls will make the Lake far safer. But safer is not safe." She exhaled.

Spoke a name.

To the center of the table came what looked like a miniature mirror—a small pond that seemed, from this height, to have no bottom, no end. In it, Kaylin could see the swirl of lines, tiny filaments of moving gold. The Lake.

"You are aware that the Lake is the containment and home to all of the True Words that give life to the Barrani," she said. "You have touched it; you have carried those words, returning some to the Lake and some to those they can inhabit.

"You are aware that I, like my mother, will seek the solace of an end to pain and duty in the...waters. I hope it will be far in the future."

Kaylin was unsettled. The Barrani could live forever. They were Immortal. What would make them throw away eternity? But even thinking that, she knew. Had she not come to the Hawks expecting to die—and grateful, in the end, for that opportunity?

"She was put forward as a candidate for Consort by her family. Her father was powerful, as were his allies, and as many powerful men before him, he desired a daughter who was equal to the High Lord. He desired the power that would accrue to the family should she be chosen.

"We have been unconcerned—we who occupy the Consort's throne—because we know what the Lake seeks. She did not have the softness, the empathy, the hidden reverence for life, for birth, the hope for the future—and she would never develop it."

"Killianas was under the impression that she was indulged by her father. He's the Avatar of the Academia. I wanted to know what he knew, but he would not discuss it."

"Was her father considered affectionate?"

"An'Berranin came to visit her during her time at the Academia; Killian seemed to feel there was affection there."

"Killian is an Avatar," the Consort said, voice almost remote. "But the rules that govern his existence—and the Academia— are not the rules that govern the High Halls." She placed both palms on the table's edge as if bracing herself.

She then opened her mouth and began to sing.

It was music that was unadorned by instrument, by harmony— but harmonies could be heard, regardless. Kaylin had seen the Consort sing before—in the West March, in a desperate bid to wake the Hallionne—and she was reminded of that now. Reminded and alarmed. She started to rise, and Teela clamped a hand on her shoulder. Teela's hand was trembling ever so slightly.

To the clearing came a figure Kaylin recognized, given he'd escorted them both to the Consort's small pocket forest. But the Avatar who had offered guidance and the Avatar who now stood to one side of the Consort were somehow different; Kaylin wasn't certain why. It wasn't the clothing; the robes were very simple Barrani robes; it wasn't the hair, which was the usual sleek drape of Barrani black. The color the skin had adopted was fair. Nothing was different.

But somehow, everything was.

The Avatar looked at both Teela and Kaylin as if he recognized neither. His eyes were dark—as dark as the Consort's, as dark as Teela's. The Consort's voice fell on a tremulous, high note, and then she lowered her chin, breathing heavily, as if recovering from great exertion.

"They are not a threat," she said. "They mean no harm."

"You are troubled, daughter. You are afraid. Should I remove them?"

"No! No, please. They carry news, and perhaps one day I will be glad of it because I will have had advance warning. I did not plead for your presence in order to cause them harm; I believe they will be necessary in the near future, and they will go where we cannot."

This familiar yet strange Avatar then turned to Kaylin and Teela as the Consort continued to speak. "I wish you to examine the Records you have about the Berranin line."

"Time period?"

"Perhaps a century prior to its excision."

"Do you wish to know how they ended?"

"If you possess that information—I believe they ended after you had been forced, by circumstance and the need to protect us, to withdraw."

"If that is the case, the information I have may be of little value."

She shook her head. "I wish to know about the relationship between An'Berranin of that time and his daughter."

"He had two daughters; he mourned the death of the one who died."

The Consort's pale brows rose, as did Teela's. "We were not aware that she had a sister. How did the sister die?"

"She failed a challenge set her by her sister. Her death was not kind."

"Was her sister Azoria?" It was Kaylin who asked.

"Yes. But the two were close, she and her sister. You did not know of the sister."

The Consort shook her head.

"She was barely adult when she perished; she made no mark upon history. But she made a mark upon her father and the sister that remained. He was certain that Azoria was responsible for her death."

"Was she?"

"Yes, in a fashion—but she did not intend to kill her sister; I believe she wanted to frighten her in the way some siblings and friends do. That is not what happened. Her father showed great favoritism for the younger daughter—it was the youngest he intended to offer as possible Consort. I believe, however, that in spite of his political intent, she might well have succeeded; she was gentle. She was considered weak; she was not. But she was not easily influenced."

"And her sister?" the Consort asked.

"Azoria intended to become the guardian of the Lake in her sister's stead. She could not. It was not in her, but she was determined to try."

The Consort nodded.

"She failed the first test. She failed the second. I believe there were other attempts. But you are Consort, so I will tell you this: it was her hope that she might find the word at the heart of her sister's life, and that she might, in so doing, absorb it or carry it."

"She wanted to resurrect the dead."

"Yes. That was the start of it. She knew what the Barrani know: that the words come from—and return to—the Lake. She reasoned that her sister could therefore somehow be found, that amends could be made. But she would not have access to the Lake unless she passed the many tests.

"Her father wished for her to pass those tests; if she was not the favored daughter, she was nonetheless his daughter, and in this fashion she could prove to be of use. But he did not forgive the death of the sister."

"No one told her that she could not pass the test if that was her sole ambition? The words that grant life are not the lives themselves; she might find the word, but that would return none of her sister to her or her family."

"She did not speak of that ambition; she was not a fool. If that was her goal, she knew that she would be disqualified before she could even begin. She desired her father's forgiveness at that time. This would be her atonement. And it would prove to him that he had *two* special daughters."

The Consort looked down at her hands. "It is better," she said softly, "to accept what is given—or what is not given— no matter how bitter the lack might seem."

"You are Consort," the Avatar said. "She is not."

"This happened before the war, before the fall of the Halls?"

"Yes. I believe at some point she understood that the test was not political; that the adjudication could not be bypassed by either personal power or wealth. She had nothing the Lake desired—in that, I believe she felt the Lake and her father were similar. It was bitter."

"She spoke to you?"

"She spoke to me then. She desired entry into the Lake."

The Consort's brows gathered together, as if in thought. "You told her that you could not grant that."

"I told her I could not—my core functions would prevent such intrusion, regardless of my desire. The Lake is both strong and the balance delicate; the risk was far too high. She accepted that."

"She did not," the Consort said, voice much softer.

"She did. While I was whole, she did not make the attempt. She traveled beyond the High Halls in search of knowledge."

"Did you not think she intended that knowledge to be used against you?"

"Against me? No. It was not personal. But she wished to understand many things; she was always inquisitive, and her ability to piece together disparate strands of information was second to none while she lived in the High Halls. She traveled to the Academia, and remained there for some time. I thought she had perhaps found a calling that was larger in all ways than the desire to resurrect her sister."

"She did not come here," the Consort said softly, "to resurrect her sister, so perhaps in that regard you are correct." Her hands bunched in fists. "Or if she did, that was not the story we were told—it is not the story the Lake tells in its mourning."

Kaylin waited.

"She may have accepted that you could prevent her from reaching the Lake—but the war happened, and the Shadows infiltrated, and you were forced to cage both the Shadow and yourself in the smallest part of the Halls. The protection you afforded the Lake was severely weakened." She turned to Kaylin. "I believe you could find the Lake. I am always aware of its presence. But at the moment, only those invited into the heart of my personal responsibility can reach it.

"What you found the first time, and what she found when she intruded, are similar. The High Halls could not fully offer the protection it had offered before it imprisoned the great Shadow in the depths of the Tower." She closed her eyes. "We know that she spent time in the Academia. But we did not have access to those who might have given us information about her studies—the Academia was lost to the rise of the Towers.

"Your discussions with the various denizens of the Academia is far more complete than the brief investigations that were done—and those brief investigations were shut down, and word of the damage done forbidden. Do you understand why?"

Kaylin nodded. "You were afraid that someone with similar ambitions might follow the same paths Azoria had walked, and do the same damage."

"Yes. She entered the Lake—we know not how, although some acquaintance with the friends you shelter within your home suggests possible answers. Your friends were changed by their experience in the green, and they changed themselves while imprisoned in the Hallionne Alsanis. She was not likewise imprisoned, and she was not likewise exposed to the *regalia* at too early an age—but perhaps you have suggestions or suspicions of your own.

"Regardless, she appeared at the edge of the Lake; she injured the Consort of the time. The defenses inherent in the Lake rose to protect the Consort, her blood mingling with the words, as if that was always the intruder's intent.

"And then she…began to devour the words she could reach. She…ate them, internalized them. The words dimmed in her hands and as they did she discarded them. They crumbled, becoming ash. They were lost to us. They would never again enliven those newborns who slept, waiting their call.

"Even now, there is a scar in the bowl of the Lake where she but stood." The Consort bowed her head.

"How was she defeated? If she drew power from the Lake, if she could absorb the power inherent in words that might sustain you for eternity, how did you save the Lake?"

"The mistake made was the mistake you make; it is inherent in your question. You are Chosen, and the marks you bear have power—but they are not the words granted us by the Ancients. There is no power in them beyond the power to quicken life; there is no power that can be taken by any who are not newborn."

Kaylin wanted to argue, but didn't. She understood that this wasn't an intellectual discussion for the Consort; it touched upon her deepest fear and invoked a lasting horror. And perhaps it should.

But Kaylin was thinking of Starrante and the birthing place of his kind: a place where the tiny, ravenous spiders traversed webs devouring each other until only one remained. The implication: that in the devouring, the remaining Wevaran contained all of the small words or small elements that emerge to become a word, a True Name. Bakkon had been horrified that Starrante had talked about these birthing mysteries of their race.

Kaylin understood that horror now. She wondered if the assault on the Lake had been an attempt to somehow grow strong in the same way, if Azoria meant to become something new, something greater than the sum of the parts—the words themselves.

It hadn't worked out that way.

"There was a battle by the Lake. We are not warriors," the

Consort said, "but Consorts are Barrani, and we are trained for just such an intrusion, just such an attack. She was driven out; she was injured and believed close to death."

"She did not attack the Lake with the aid of Berranin." Teela sought confirmation.

"That was not conclusively proved—and the Lady was near death. The attacker was of Berranin, and Berranin paid the price."

Kaylin did not argue against what was obviously the harsh application of Barrani law. But if the father and the rest of the clan had had no hand in the attack—and possibly no knowledge of it—they would not meet death in the Emperor's Empire.

"An'Teela?" the Consort then said, after the silence had lengthened.

"I better understand your fear. But if, in that attack, she did not derive the power she believed she sought, I think it unlikely that she would make the attempt again. She, or any Barrani."

"Would that I had your belief. If she continued to study forbidden arts, or arts unknown to us, we believe had she survived—she would have made the same attempt." The Consort lowered her chin. "And now you tell me that you believe she has survived."

Kaylin hesitated. "It might be better to say she's survived in some fashion. If you could identify names, if you could look at the words in the Lake and recognize some part of the life they lived, you'd know if she'd returned to the Lake in any form." She had, as she so often did with the Consort, abandoned High Barrani for language that was more natural for her.

"Consorts carry a weight of responsibility, but they are people, Lord Kaylin. They are people with emotions and experiences. Were such a thing possible, Consorts might have been tempted, throughout our history, to strike out or strike back when the balance of power is in their hands; they might consign the word to an eternity of isolation.

"Perhaps for that reason, we were not granted that ability. Historical records are quite clear: she is dead. Her line is dead. I have no reason to believe that the historical records were built on a foundation of lies."

"No reason except the hints of her, the traces of her, that we stumbled across."

The Consort nodded. Her indigo eyes turned to Teela, and remained there. "Tell me."

"Our investigation led us to a modest house—for mortals. You would not consider it suitable for any purpose, but to the mortals it is a reasonable, if small, home. Were it not for the fact that it is much smaller than the houses to either side, it would not be notable at all.

"The old woman who is its sole occupant would likewise garner little attention in most normal circumstances; she is considered a bit fanciful."

"Fanciful?"

"She believes she can see the ghosts of the dead."

"How did you come to meet her?"

"She makes a daily trek to the Halls of Law, where she offers those Hawks at the public desk baked goods and gossip. The gossip, however, involves the ghosts she sees and their remarkably mundane concerns. She has been a fixture of the office for all of the years I've occupied it," Teela added.

This was almost a lie. Barrani were never scheduled for desk duty.

"Kaylin was on desk duty a few days ago, and the old woman came with gossip that involved Kaylin's duty partner. Kaylin also has a weakness for food which an older woman could easily exploit, but this particular visitor is not one of them. She likes to bake. She likes the Hawks. She's lonely.

"But you are aware that Kaylin is Chosen; you are aware that she has a familiar. On occasion, the familiar will allow his master—" Hope squawked at the word, which Teela ignored "—to look through his wing. If he notices something out of place, he will raise the wing and place it across her eyes.

"When she looked through the wing at the foot of the mortal's modest dwelling, she could see the…ghostly outline of a much larger building above the old woman's residence. It was research into that that allowed Kaylin to stumble across the forbidden name. If, as we have believed, she is dead, someone thought to play a joke on the government: her name was listed as owner a century ago, in mortal time. No other records list that name, but these were found in the taxation Records.

"Kaylin recognized the styling as a Barrani name—and in the experience of the Halls of Law, Barrani ownership of buildings in certain areas has generally led to the discovery of many, *many* broken Imperial Laws. It was natural that she attempt to find information about the owner, given the lack of the building the mortal theoretically owned, the lack of a legal lot partition, and the presence of a modest, small house in roughly the same geographic location."

The Consort nodded.

"But the name has history, and the history is dark; it drew attention Kaylin had not considered possible from tax Records. Understanding the sensitivity of the investigation, I chose to accompany her when she returned to examine the interior of that house.

"The first unusual thing occurred before I managed to reach the house itself. The neighbor—about whom Kaylin will say nothing or she will rant about bullies for far longer than either of us have the patience to endure—threw himself at my feet, weeping and groveling. He felt he recognized me. In fact, he was certain that I was…someone else. Barrani, to humans who do not interact with them with any frequency, look very similar. He assumed that I was a different Barrani woman—one with whom he had some sort of relationship."

The Consort looked mildly disgusted, but nodded.

"In and of itself, this would not give rise to suspicions that a historical criminal somehow escaped death; it is a small shadow, a strand.

"It is the interior of the house—or rather, one room—and the story of the old woman who lives there, that provides the stronger concern. The woman was born in the house; it was owned by mortal parents. They had one child that we know of, and they grew old and died in the house, leaving it to their daughter.

"When the current occupant was perhaps eleven years of age, they met a young woman who was painting in the common for coin. It is not unusual for mortals. She was striking, graceful, and very talented according to the woman who was a child at the time." Teela exhaled. "With your permission?"

The Consort nodded. Kaylin, who was about to ask, *Permission for what?* felt a wave of magic crawl across her arms, up her neck, and down her spine.

"This painter was so taken with the child and her parents that she offered to come to their house and do a private sitting. She arranged the family in a chair they owned, but took special care with the girl." Teela gestured. In the center of this small table, the painting that Helen had brought to life appeared.

The Consort froze.

"The hair was arranged by the artist. The flower, brought in a planter, was placed in the braided hair by the artist. The child was then asked to sit with her parents. Do you recognize the styling?"

The Consort, however, didn't seem to notice the complicated braiding; her eyes reflected the flower, as if it were the only thing she could see. "Is this accurate?" she asked, voice soft. "Lord Kaylin?"

"Yes. Although I'm not sure Teela's magic captures the livid quality of the green." She hesitated, and received a warning glare from Teela. "My familiar did not like the painting."

"I wish to speak with the mortal. You will bring her here. Now."

19

"I'm afraid that won't be possible," Teela said, reverting to Elantran.

Kaylin now understood exactly why Teela had been so scrupulously careful to mention neither name nor address. Technically, neither she nor Teela were allowed—by oath and by law—to discuss ongoing investigations with anyone but Hawks or Swords. Teela skirted that edge here, for obvious reasons, but she did so with attention to detail. She had failed to mention many of the significant facts.

Kaylin hoped that the Avatar could not, or would not, remove those facts and lay them across the figurative table, but knew the Consort would find out; Ynpharion could no doubt listen in, and probably was.

There was silence in the wake of that thought. Perhaps he couldn't at the moment; Helen could also prevent the name-bound from reaching out or listening in on any conversation that occurred within her confines, unless she deemed it an emergency.

"She is mortal. This investigation has already caused a handful of deaths—but those deaths fall under the auspices of the Barrani caste court. Any harm done to the mortal will most assuredly not. She is known to the Hawks, and she is held in affection by them; they will not let it go should the worst happen. Kaylin will be chief among them.

"I speak of these things only to offer you tangible reasons for my refusal to set the investigation aside. I will be pursuing all possible traces until solid answers are unearthed. There is too much at risk, given what you have revealed here; I am certain that the criminal continued to pursue other avenues of study—but those avenues were not Barrani in nature. Barrani, as you are well aware, are not the only Immortals.

"Kaylin's early investigation produced some answers and raised questions. She went to the Academia. The chancellor and the living heart of the Academia owe Kaylin a great debt. What questions they felt they could answer, they answered, although in the chancellor's case, that amounted to nothing. The Arbiters who govern the library space and the scholars who taught when the Academia was not what it has become also answered questions." She turned to Kaylin.

Kaylin, mindful now of the consequences of too much information, forced herself to adopt High Barrani. "Killianas believes that the student in question was not interested in knowledge for power's sake; he also believed that her father was fond of her, from their interactions on campus. This implies that the Academia—or part of it—came before she attempted to destroy the Lake.

"Killianas's drive is scholarship; his responsibility is the health of, the well-being of, the Academia. There is dependence on a student body—but I believe that dependence requires the right kind of student. Were I to study there, I would not be what he requires. His requirements seem independent of race; they may well be independent of frivolous things like personality."

"Yet he was aware of her ambitions?"

"Only inasmuch as they devolved to knowledge and study."
She frowned. "I might be misinterpreting; I haven't spent
much time in the confines of the Academia, and much of what
I've said is inferred. One of her masters was Larrantin. One was
Arbiter Androsse—an Ancestor. One was Arbiter Starrante.
I believe each considered her an excellent student—someone
who worked hard to untangle each lesson she was given.

"It's possible that in her studies there, she chanced upon
ancient ceremonies, or information that concerned them; it's
possible that in her studies there, she came upon information
about the plant."

"The plant in its healthy form grows only in the green,"
the Consort said. "I have seen it there. Teela has seen it there.
It is quite possible you stepped over it, considering it a weed.
It is a flower that represents the heart of the green; it is not
rare there. But those flowers do not leave the green."

Clearly, one of them had. "Is that by law or custom?"

"It is by the will of the green."

"The will of the green is not exactly spelled out," Kaylin
said. She had some experience with the will of the green—
most of it life-threatening, all of it infuriating in its opacity.

"The Warden and his many servants interpret for those
of us to whom the green does not speak," was the Consort's
more stilted reply.

"The Lady is beloved of the green," the Avatar of the High
Halls said quietly. "Beloved, as well, of the Hallionne. She
does not require outside interpretation. I believe she is falli-
ble in many of the ways the living are—but in this, I would
trust the information she offers."

Kaylin nodded. "I'm sorry," she said, in her native Elantran. "I think it was the flower that most alarmed Teela."

"Teela," Teela said, "can speak for herself. Yes. The flower alarmed me. The flower, the style of hair—I could not quite put my finger on why it looked familiar; it is not a styling given to our kin. Or perhaps it is no longer used; I confess I did not study ceremony. I knew what was demanded of me by the green on the occasion I was chosen—by the green—to perform the *regalia*. No part of that involved this flower, although in the area where the telling was done, these flowers were present.

"None of the flowers were so visually deformed; in none was the green so livid."

The Consort nodded. "There is a reason the flowers are not to be taken from the green. On the rare occasions it has been tried, the green has been displeased with the scholars who made the attempt. But in all of those cases, the flowers wilted. The soil could not be found that would allow them to thrive."

"I'm not sure I would consider this thriving," Kaylin replied, frowning. "Is it possible that she removed the soil from the green when she took the plant?"

"No. When removed from the green, the soil retains the characteristics of the West March; whatever properties it possesses within the green are inherent to the green. It is possible that she experimented with the soil while in the green—but I consider that unlikely." It was the Consort's turn to frown. She looked to Teela. "It is possible that such experiments might be conducted in one place, and only one that I can readily think of."

Teela was silent for a beat. "Hallionne Alsanis."

"The Hallionne Alsanis, yes. Although Alsanis is not of the green, he is connected to it; if she was adept at hiding her thoughts, she might have asked permission of Alsanis."

"Alsanis wouldn't require the permission of the green?"

"I would think that he would, but it is not a subject much discussed between us; of the Hallionne, Alsanis was closed to me—to all of us—for centuries." Because of the cohort. "But I believe some of your cohort grew close to Alsanis, and they may be able to ask him. The loss of Alsanis did not occur in the criminal's time."

Teela nodded. "Understand that if I broach this subject with my former confederates, I cannot entirely control the direction the inquiries will take. Would that be an acceptable risk to you? You are well aware of the difficulties they can cause, having been subject to them in the recent past."

"I am. I have weighed the risk, and I do not believe the threat they pose could rival the threat that she once posed. In the worst case, they would have killed me. That would not harm the Lake."

Kaylin stared at her for some time before remembering she had to blink. She had always understood how seriously the Consort took her responsibilities, but…to consider her own life of lesser value was unexpected.

"Yes," the Avatar said, almost fondly. "There is a reason most fail the tests. There are those who do not value their lives—but they, too, fail; life must have value to them if they are to husband and guard the Lake. The Consort does not wish to throw away her life; she values it, and finds joy in it. But better that than to lose the eternity of possibility inherent in the names."

"She can't hear you, can she?"

"No. I, too, owe you a great debt. My responsibility and devotion must be given to the Consort—and indeed, there is joy in that. But were it not for your intervention, I would not now be here to protect the Lake and the woman who tends it. Your thoughts are clear, even to me, but none of them are turned toward harm. The Lake accepts you; in an emergency, you could be called upon to deliver the breath of wakefulness to the young. In her fashion, the Consort trusts you—but she thinks you are naive and idealistic, in a world where that is not an advantage.

"I will not reveal that which you do not wish revealed unless and until it becomes critically relevant. But I agree—the cohort, and your Terrano, are possibly the best source of information. I am uneasy; An'Teela's concern is almost fear—and that is very, very rare."

"Do you know anything about this flower?"

"No. I am not of the green, nor have I ever been. We do not move around very much," he added, almost apologetically. "But I have captured too much of your attention; attend the Consort now."

"I hoped, when I first asked you to join An'Teela, that I could convince you to halt your investigation. An'Teela's words and demeanor have convinced me that this would be unwise. I will bespeak the High Halls to make certain they are aware of the possible danger. I believe Terrano regularly attends the Avatar; perhaps Terrano might be willing to talk about his own highly unusual research, undertaken during his long stay in Alsanis."

"We call it *captivity* in Elantra," Kaylin said, before she could stop the words from leaving her mouth.

"Perhaps. But Alsanis is fond of the cohort, as you call them, and it is my belief that the cohort, if they sought escape, sought to do so without damaging their caretaker; the fondness was reciprocated."

Kaylin saw no reason not to agree; she nodded. "Toward the end, he couldn't completely contain them."

"Yes. Terrano has spoken, with an almost childish glee, of his successes. To the Avatar," she added, with a fond smile. "Sometimes he recounts Terrano's tales." The smile slipped away. "But there is no similar fondness for the woman we assumed was long dead.

"Chosen. An'Teela. Find her if she exists. Give us as much

warning as you can. She would be older than Terrano, and if she was likewise entrapped, may have learned similar tricks or skills."

"She was nothing like Terrano," the Avatar said. This time, given the direction the Consort looked, other people could hear him. "I was very angry with Terrano when I heard of what he had attempted, but his regret was genuine, and as with you, I owe him a great debt. He is…not what she was. Perhaps his time with the Hallionne preserved some innate youthfulness; I cannot say.

"But I would trust him with the Consort and the Lake."

"And not her."

"No, Chosen. You have asked how my powers may have been used; I will, if you desire it, allow you to enter what would have been her chambers, had she survived."

"But—they'll be in use."

"Ah, you misunderstand. Your Helen could re-create any room that any tenant who has accepted her hospitality has occupied. When I was forced to withdraw the greater measure of my power and functionality to prevent the Shadow from destroying the heart of the Barrani, changes to the building did not occur. But she lived within my walls for the better part of what we assume was her life. As did An'Berranin.

"When you are finished, I will return for you, and I will lead you to that suite."

"No," the Consort said, standing so swiftly she would have knocked a chair over had they been seated in individual chairs. "I would examine these chambers myself. Kaylin is Chosen, and An'Teela is perceptive, but this now encompasses those responsibilities that are mine in their entirety."

Ynpharion did not interrupt their somber passage through the forest.

"I do not think it wise if the Chosen is to examine anything," the Avatar said. Kaylin glanced at him, and then at the Consort.

It was Teela who said, "The Avatar can create portals that move us from one section of the Halls to their destination; he is explaining the reason we are walking. Your inability to walk through a portal is well-known."

"I can walk through a portal," Kaylin said. It was true. But it was also true that she was wretchedly nauseous when she emerged. She frowned. To the Avatar, she said, "The painting of the mortals that Azoria created remains in the mortal's home."

"Ah, yes. I have taken the liberty of once again enclosing our conversation; the name that you mention should not be heard by anyone else."

"It was dark in the room—and the darkness grew stronger when exposed to light."

The Avatar nodded, eyes the color of obsidian.

"But...there was something about the atmosphere there that felt almost like a portal path, to me."

The Avatar turned to the Consort. "With your permission, Lady, I would like to involve Terrano in this investigation and the discussions it spawns."

Teela's *No* was instant, but it wasn't Teela's permission the Avatar sought.

The Consort frowned, glanced at Teela, and then nodded. "An'Teela, *any* information, any conjecture, that might somehow solve this mystery, is necessary."

"Terrano is almost—but not quite—as disaster prone as Lord Kaylin," Teela replied. "I trust his intent. I am not at all certain I trust the consequences that might emerge from it."

"If the High Halls feel it would be of aid, I am inclined to trust them," the Consort replied. No hint of the frostiness of the powerful at having their decisions questioned was conveyed in her voice. "And if Lord Kaylin is considered the greater unintentional danger and she is necessary, I believe we are not increasing the risk." As she spoke, she smiled, and the color of her eyes shifted to a regular, dark blue.

"It must be nice to be so optimistic," Teela replied, in Elantran. But her eyes also lost the uncomfortable indigo that had characterized so much of the previous discussion.

"Serralyn wants to know if she can come, too." It was Terrano, emerging from thin air, who asked the question. "She's at the Academia now, but I think she thinks she has information we might want."

"Far be it from me," the Consort replied, "to deny her; An'Teela seems to feel that she will pose less of a danger than you might."

Terrano's smile was breezy, his eyes nearly green. "The quiet ones are always the ones you have to watch out for."

If the group had left the confines of the Consort's inviolable space, the rest of the High Halls had not been informed; there were no other people in the halls through which the Avatar now led them. No guards. No oathsworn. No one.

Terrano was chatting with someone in the silence, his expressive face shifting in such a way that Kaylin could almost hear the words he didn't speak aloud.

"I do not recognize these halls," the Consort said softly.

To Kaylin, they looked like any other part of the High Halls: towering ceilings with their impressive stained glass at heights that would make them impossible to clean. There were the usual stone alcoves, and each contained either a statue or a small tree of some kind; one contained flowers that seemed to have spilled out of their now-invisible planter to trail across the floors. Oh, no, they were vines of some kind that had flowers attached.

Since the flowers were not a livid green that hurt the eyes, Kaylin assumed they were safe, but as this was Barrani space she took care to avoid touching anything but the floor.

"Serralyn can travel quickly," the Avatar remarked.

"She can—but she hates to do it; she says it makes her nauseous," Terrano replied. "She's worried enough that nausea seems a reasonable risk."

"She does not have Lord Kaylin's sensitivity to portals."

"No—only Kaylin's that lucky."

"Good. It will save us time."

Serralyn did look a little green to Kaylin's eye when she appeared in the middle of the hall. Terrano immediately ran to her, although Kaylin noted he couldn't be bothered to even mimic walking; his feet didn't touch the floor. He slid an arm around her shoulder, and she leaned into his chest, head bowed for three long breaths.

"I don't know how you can stand this," she murmured, the acoustics of this magnificent hall magnifying her softly spoken words. "It really makes me feel Kaylin's portal pain."

"It doesn't make *me* feel sick." His tone conveyed worry, but also comfort.

She nodded and looked up, pulling away from Terrano to offer the Consort a perfect bow. The Consort bid her rise when it became apparent that she intended to hold that bow until that permission was given.

"I am sorry that we must meet again under such difficult circumstances. But I am very curious about your experience with the Academia, and I would enjoy your company if you chose to visit when things were less dire."

Serralyn's eyes were a warring mix of blue and green; the Consort's immediate words brightened them, but the situation dampened any surprise or joy.

"Terrano said you would travel from the Academia."

Serralyn glanced at Terrano. "Yes. I did. He really isn't supposed to do that."

That referred to the public acknowledgment of the fact that Serralyn and he were in communication, which strongly implied that they were namebound. At home, within Helen's perimeter, it didn't matter; everyone living there already knew. But in the High Halls, it would—especially as Sedarias grew more active.

"We are aware that the circumstances of your captivity forced you all to become closer than is the norm for our kin," the Consort replied. "And yes, I agree. He should be far, far more careful."

"Careful isn't in his nature," Serralyn replied. "Not even Sedarias can force him to behave for more than ten minutes at a time. It's a good thing he's pretty hard to kill." She said the last with a sunny smile.

"Sedarias might lose her temper?" the Consort asked, returning that smile. "When young, my older brother had a foul temper; it drove both my parents to despair."

Serralyn's brows rose. Teela's did as well. The expressions were separated by laughter—Serralyn's. Teela didn't feel that speaking of the current High Lord in this familiar and familial fashion was in any way appropriate.

But if the Consort hoped to put Serralyn—and Terrano—at ease, it worked. Teela was stone-faced throughout, but made no attempt to argue against that ease; Kaylin wasn't even certain she made the private attempt. On some level, and inasmuch as Barrani were capable of it, Teela trusted the Consort.

Kaylin trusted her as well, but had forced herself to accept that trust or no, the Consort was still a powerful Barrani woman. It was not wise to cross her, and if crossed, there were consequences. The Consort had attempted to cage and entrap the cohort.

Then again, the cohort, through Terrano, had tried to kill her, so…maybe they were even? Ugh, Barrani. Sometimes trying to untangle their interactions gave her a headache. Today, however, that wasn't her concern. She hoped. She'd expected the Consort to ask that the investigation be shelved, and had braced herself for the anger that would follow the refusal. But Teela had taken the refusal in hand, and Teela had a weight and power in court that made the refusal make sense to the Consort.

And now they were following the Avatar of the High Halls down a hall that the Consort had never seen, to a room that maybe didn't exist anymore, except in the building's memory. Or a room that could be pulled out of the nebulous nothingness from which buildings worked.

"That is not quite the way it works," the Avatar said. He then frowned. "You did not mention your Helen's newest guests."

"I had other things on my mind. Are they important?"

"Yes. Very."

"Could you tell me why? Or how? Or…what they even are? They're not like the words in the Lake."

"No. They are not of and for the race known as Barrani."

Maybe something good would come out of this visit. Kaylin was still not used to the idea that the High Halls was now a sentient building. "Do you know what they are?"

"Unless you wish to take the risk of transporting them here, I cannot be certain. I would not harm them, but I am uncertain that you could make that clear. I do not believe you would be in danger, but it is not yourself for whom you are concerned. And I consider it a risk.

"You left someone here, and he chose to remain; he is comfortable with us, and there are no misunderstandings. But he is, as you are aware, mobile in a fashion I am not. I can, however, ask…Spike to examine them; if you are willing, he can follow you home." The Avatar's expression was one of distaste.

"Has Spike done anything wrong?"

"Far from it. But I dislike the…name…you assigned him. It is entirely inappropriate."

Kaylin shrugged. "So come up with an appropriate name. I don't know anything about Spike's people; I only know he was enslaved and I got tired of saying 'it.'"

This seemed to scandalize the Avatar, who was silent for a long beat.

"I'm not sure I could pronounce his name. Starrante chose a name that could be pronounced by the majority of the student body, but I get the impression that that's not his actual name," Kaylin said.

"Let us go to the chambers; they are at the end of the hall. They are not re-created," he added quietly. "They are the rooms. You are familiar with Records, in their oddly limited form—Terrano has explained them. I am like, and unlike, your Records. I know that while I was collapsed inward, no new rooms were created, and there was some…hierarchical demand for the rooms that remained, unchanging.

"That was not always the case."

"So you're going to make more rooms?"

"The High Lord has requested that I do not for the time being; I may alter halls and create spaces—such as the Consort's—but he believes the political fractures such instant access would cause would be problematic. I have created no new rooms, at his request; he believes that the changes to the Test of Name, and the changes to the Halls themselves, require some time to fully absorb.

"I am not a Hallionne," he added. "That was not my function. The Barrani are not children to be coddled or kept apart or protected. Barrani have murdered each other within my walls since I first rose. They will no doubt continue."

"Couldn't you stop them?"

"To what end? They would merely kill each other in different places, where sentience such as mine is absent. They are what they are. Ah, my apologies, Lady. Kaylin's thoughts are very loud and very chaotic. The room that I will show you, the room that you will examine, are the Berranin rooms as they were when they were last used. The contents are the same; they have not been altered. Nothing has been taken from them, at the command of the High Lord of the time. My preservation functions were at the forefront of my will; I preserved them, although I could not replace them.

"I could bury them, but could not entirely destroy them. I can find the rooms used by various lords throughout my existence."

Serralyn's eyes nearly fell out of her head. "*Any* room? Any room with authentic contents?"

"Any room with the contents that were left in them when the rooms were retired. The Berranin case was special; the line was eradicated. No one wished to step up to claim any of the contents for fear that they would be considered part of the line. There were therefore no claimants. You will not find that to be true of most of the retired quarters."

"But...some?"

"Some, yes. I see you are happy. Why?"

"It's history," she replied. "It's like...living history. There are professors and students in the Academia that would be so excited to be here right now—it's like we're walking into the past, we're stepping back in time." She spoke Elantran, not the stilted High Barrani that dampened excitement.

"You really should learn to speak with Spike. You would find his experiences very interesting."

The Avatar stopped in front of two ornate doors; they were closed.

Kaylin stopped for a different reason. "What are the markings on those doors?" she asked. "Are they door wards?"

"No. They were Berranin symbols; Helen marks the doors that lead to the quarters your friends occupy. Here, the Barrani who have the significance to be granted permanent quarters choose the marks that define their line. Why do you ask?"

"Serralyn?"

Serralyn stepped forward. She didn't touch the doors, but did lean into them. To Kaylin's eyes, they were carved of wood in a stylized representation of a vine, or vines, twined out from a central flower, as if they were leaves. "I am not familiar with the Berranin heraldry," she finally said. "This was theirs?"

"This was the one that was chosen," he replied. "Do you recognize it?"

"Did you carve it—I mean, did you cause it to be created as it was?"

"That is an odd question."

"Why?"

"I was asked to use this pattern in the creation of the doors, yes."

"So you did this, not someone from the Berranin clan?"

"I did."

Serralyn was silent for a long beat. "I would ask that you carefully—*carefully*—unwind it."

"Pardon?"

"If what you've said is true—if this is the actual room, the actual doors, preserved for eternity, I would ask that you very carefully unwind or unmake only the symbols on the door itself. I don't think it's safe for us to touch."

"It is safe. I will not allow it to cause harm to any of you—you are with the Lady." The Avatar's eyes were black now, all whites lost to concentration and assessment, just as Helen's eye color often was. "What is it that you fear?"

Serralyn frowned. "You're like the Hallionne, aren't you?"

The Avatar nodded.

"I'm *trying* to think at you. I'm trying to give you the information I think I have. Can't you hear it?"

"No."

Terrano cleared his throat.

"I can hear you clearly; your thoughts are the equivalent of shouting at great volume in an empty, stone room. They echo. But your companion's thoughts are very murky."

Serralyn's eyes lost green. "How did she ask you to create these symbols? Did she simply visualize? Did she sketch? Did she show you the image by magic?"

"I fail to understand your questions, but there is an urgency to them. She had a very specific order in which the vines were to be laid—but the flowers at the center of the symbol were to be created both first and last. I can show you, if you are concerned."

Serralyn nodded. "But not on the doors, and images only." She frowned and then shook her head. "My apologies; I have been informed that my manners are appalling when I'm studying something too intently. I have no right of command—anything I say is a request, and if you are unable to accommodate it I apologize for asking for something difficult."

"It is not difficult," the Avatar replied, his eyes obsidian as he studied her face, her eyes, her expression. "But I am now concerned for other reasons. The Barrani—especially the elder Barrani—are careful to guard their thoughts or to hide them by emphasizing elements that would otherwise be considered gentle noise.

"You are not one of them. Terrano's thoughts, as I said, could be heard clearly from any corner of my territory, but he is now as confused as you are."

Serralyn's eyes lost all green then. "Just what did she build here?" she whispered.

"That is a very relevant question. I would have answered: she did not build. I did. But there is an interference here that appears to be centered around the doors. And it is the doors that are your concern. You will, I think, become an important scholar in future."

Serralyn should have been pleased by the compliment, but if she was, her eye color didn't shift. "Please," she said softly.

The Avatar nodded. Barrani buildings clearly had Barrani memory. Although the Avatar didn't move, the space a yard in front of the doors began to shimmer in place. Absent the wood in which the pattern had been laid, the pattern began to form. As he'd said, he'd started with the flower at the center of the design. It was a flower Kaylin recognized.

"Was the flower that color when you began the making?" Kaylin asked, because the flower had color on the doors—it was the color of what she now considered a healthy plant.

"Yes."

"But…it was going to be part of a door, and the flower on the door is…wood."

"Yes. But I was asked to start with the flower in the center—and end with it as well." As he spoke, the flower began to grow vines, slender vines with budding leaves; they curled outward, spreading in a circular pattern, one clockwise, one counterclockwise. The movement slowed as Serralyn held up a hand; she approached the illusion and walked around it, examining the leaves and the vines as if they were words she could read with great effort. She then nodded, and he continued.

She watched as the vines grew up, and up again, until they curved, as if to close a circle; they grew down in the same way. "This is exact?" she asked.

"It is."

"Kaylin." Kaylin joined Serralyn, leaving the Consort and Teela behind. "Do you recognize this? Look at the way the vines are being laid in circles against each other. Look at the way they entwine."

Kaylin didn't have Barrani memory, but she didn't need it. She understood exactly what Serralyn was now looking at: this pattern, this odd braiding, had been done with Mrs. Erickson's hair when she had been a child. Into that hair, the blossom had been placed—but Kaylin was almost certain that the flower placed there hadn't been the livid, disturbing green that the painting had captured.

20

"Where did you see this?" she asked Serralyn, as the pattern continued to form.

"Arbiter Kavallac met me when I entered the library; she said she'd noted the area of study, and had found books in the library that had last been studied before the fall."

"She didn't happen to say by who?"

"Not in so many words, no. The librarians believe in the privacy of their students, just as the Academia does. The Academia has rules—or laws, if you prefer—but given the nature of the Academia itself, the rules are enforced by Killianas, and at his discretion. Within the library, the Arbiters are the law. Arbiters Kavallac and Androsse have continued, according to Starrante, their argument; it's recommended that students avoid the library, as the arguments are intense.

"Starrante, however, believed that the intensity of the argument wouldn't be a problem for some students."

"So, you."

"And Valliant, yes. Robin hasn't been allowed to enter. I'm not sure what you did or said when you visited—but Kavallac's eyes were almost blood red the entire time she offered to guide me."

"Androsse?"

"Wasn't present. I'm not sure if this was their compromise or not, but it doesn't matter. I thought I'd be in the library for weeks—around classes—but it was less than a day. Kavallac was following Azoria's trail, and it seemed to end here."

"Did she tell you what the book contained?"

Serralyn shook her head. "She gave me the book; she expected me to draw my own conclusions, based on my field of study and my experience."

"What was the book about?"

"A ceremony," Serralyn replied. "An old ceremony." She hesitated and then said, "An Ancestral ceremony."

Silence eddied out, as if it were a large stone dropped into a pool of conversation.

It was Kaylin who broke it. "What, exactly, was the ceremony meant to achieve?"

"It was, in form and function, a type of joining."

"A wedding ceremony?"

Serralyn shook her head. "Marriage in modern terms was not a concept held in much favor by the Ancestors."

"Then joining *what*?"

"The green," she replied. "Although that is not what it was called by the Ancestors—it took me a bit to understand that. I don't know that Dragons had Ancestors the way the Barrani do, but Kavallac understood the difference. She attempted to explain it, but only when I asked. It's thought that the green extended much farther, in the time of the Ancestors, than it does now; I believe the Ancestors may have somehow destroyed or despoiled it. What remains in the West March is the heart of what it once was."

Kaylin turned to the Avatar.

"If you mean to confirm whether or not the green existed when the Ancestors ruled much of the continent, yes it did. It is older than the Hallionne. It is older than the High Halls. In the distant past, the Ancestors could speak to the green, and the green would answer—but not in a language that the Barrani can understand. Some can intuit meaning; the green hears them in ways that do not entirely involve simple linguistics."

Serralyn listened as if the Avatar's words were now the only relevant words in the room.

Kaylin, however, had the answer to her question and wanted to move on. "So this was a ceremony developed by the Ancestors—Androsse's people."

"By some of his people, yes. Understand that while the Barrani and their Ancestors share an appearance, they are fundamentally different peoples. The Ancestors were frequently unstable in a way the Barrani are not." He then turned to Serralyn. "I believe similar rites exist among the Barrani.

"These rites were tied to the *regalia*, and you are far more aware of the dangers inherent in that ceremony; it is one of the few that survived the twilight of the Ancestors."

"Azoria was Barrani," Kaylin pointed out.

"So, at one point, was Terrano," the Avatar countered.

"You do not consider him Barrani now?" the Consort asked.

"No, Lady. He considers himself Terrano; the race and circumstance of his birth, given the utter callousness with which his forebears approached the *regalia*, are of less value to him. Regardless of external designations, it is possible that Azoria exposed herself to environments, rituals, or races that could subtly undermine the cage of her creation. If she spent much time in the company of Arbiter Androsse, she may have first attempted to re-create herself in his image.

"Thus her disastrous attempt to take over the Lake."

"That is not what the Lake remembers."

"Lady, no person is only one thing, nor are their desires entirely singular. I know the stories you have been told; I believe them to be true. But there are other truths. Although I did not experience all of her life, or her theoretical ending, I was aware of her. She was like, and unlike, Terrano; it is the reason Terrano is welcome here, and she would not be were she to have survived in some form.

"Perhaps the desire to atone, the desire to resurrect, started her on the path she eventually walked—but when the Lake rejected her, she was unwilling to surrender to rejection. She began to search for better answers."

The Consort did not care for the use of the word *better*. Fair enough; Kaylin personally hated it.

"But if she died—if her words returned to the Lake somehow—and yet she persists, I would not recognize her." He returned to the image he had been slowly building. "This was the end of it," he told Serralyn. They all watched as the second flower was placed almost exactly across the first, as if they were halves of a whole. The second portion was wood, and as they watched, the color and texture of woodgrain expanded from the flower, just as the vines first had, until the whole seemed a carving.

"I'm not certain," Serralyn said, "that we should open those doors."

"Do you think we'll find her in the room?"

"I don't know what we'll find—but I'm not sure it will be safe for most of you."

Terrano, however, was grinning. "I don't count in that most," he told Kaylin. He studiously avoided Teela's growing glare.

"You're willing to let Terrano open the doors?" Kaylin asked Serralyn.

"It's Terrano," she replied, with a very familiar shrug. "He's difficult to stop."

"And me?"

"I'd let you open them."

The familiar squawked.

"She has the marks of the Chosen, and she has you. She's not Terrano, no. But she survives things Terrano survives in entirely different ways. I'm perfectly willing to let them scout ahead."

"Sounds like a go to me," Terrano said. He turned to the Consort, but continued in Elantran. "I think we need your permission."

She turned to Kaylin, as if Terrano had not spoken. Forgiveness clearly had a different meaning for the Consort than it did for Kaylin. "If you are willing to take the risk, and the High Halls believes it can contain whatever remains in the room, you have my permission."

Terrano returned the favor; he ignored the Consort and headed to the doors.

"If it's a ceremonial joining," Kaylin said, "why is it on a door?"

"It's a ceremony of containment and joining. Or at least that's what I managed to glean; the book was written in Old Barrani, not the Ancestral tongue. I think it might have been their version of the *regalia*; without it, the power of the green…" She shrugged. "There's a reason children aren't exposed to the *regalia*. My guess is that this was a substitute for adulthood in the Ancestors."

"Then why did she make those braids and put that flower in—in her hair?" She stumbled over not saying Mrs. Erickson's name, and almost blew it.

"Braiding was done, for both men and women. The flower was part of the braiding. If the old woman had been an Ancestor, it would be considered normal." Serralyn exhaled. "I think the flower is the connection to the green or the power that lies at the heart of it. But...the flower in the painting was not that flower; it was distorted, twisted.

"I'm not sure if that was the intent, or if it was the outcome. Those flowers don't thrive outside of the green." Serralyn hesitated.

"You might as well go all in," Terrano told Kaylin. "Never mind. Serralyn's concerned."

"She is concerned," Teela cut in, "for your continued well-being." Teela spoke Barrani.

Terrano shrugged. "She's never really liked conflict much. I'm not worried. Where was I? Oh, right. The flower. Serralyn theorizes that the flower itself isn't so much planted in the green—no, that's not right. Are you *sure* you don't want to explain it?"

"It depends on how badly you butcher the explanation," Serralyn said. She was annoyed. "What he meant to say is: the green, as we're all aware, is not normal space. It's not a Hallionne, and it isn't like the Academia or the High Halls. All of those ancient buildings came later.

"Living with Helen, and living with Alsanis, made clear that much of the space that makes them like gods within their own boundaries is...like the outlands. It's a miasma of possibility that the buildings themselves control and transform at need. The outlands are all of that, but without the driving intellect or will behind them.

"So, if we think of the outlands as a kind of geography, the buildings with sentience claim ownership of part of that space. They can extend that ownership beyond their boundaries, as long as no other will or intent interferes with theirs.

"I think the green is like the sentient buildings—but older. It wasn't designed or created the way the sentient buildings were; we weren't meant to interact with it in the same way. The will of the green implies sentience—and I believe the green is sentient—but it's not a sentience that we can easily access or understand.

"And I think the green was also planted in the outlands, but boundaries were less transcribed, less exact. The forests of the West March seem like normal forests—but they're not. They aren't part of the green, but they're not like the trees you see in the streets of Elantra, either. The rivers that wend through the forests are likewise closer to the elemental water than the rivers within your city.

"This leads me to suspect—and this is *entirely* conjecture and I could be wrong—that the green's roots, if you will, extend for a greater distance than what we think of as the green. Alsanis and the green overlapped—that much we know—but it's my belief that the green's influence over the outlands was, at one time, far stronger than it became. For us, the green is contained.

"But for her? I'm far less certain. The Ancestors were not a concern by the time the first war with the Dragons started. She was not a known concern when that war, and its disastrous consequences, changed the High Halls.

"I think she may have been able to carry that flower from the green because she had figured out how the flowers were rooted—and in what—and could mimic that space in some fashion. I don't think the green or its influence reached Elantra; I don't think the green could, at this point in its history. The flower was brought here less than a mortal century ago. At the time it was plucked, it wasn't the color it is in the painting." She hesitated again. Terrano, near the doors, rolled eyes.

"My turn?" he asked.

"Only if you have something useful to add."

"Serralyn isn't sure how, but she feels that Azoria could replicate the conditions that allowed the flower to blossom."

"How?"

"That's why she's hesitant. Serralyn can't answer that question. She's been thinking about it, and doing tangential research in the hope the sparks from that secondary research might start a fire, metaphorically speaking. If the flower only grows in the green, and the flower was clearly growing in a pot, she could replicate those conditions. That part's clear.

"What's less clear is what happened after. Azoria braided Mrs. Erickson's hair. She plucked the blossom. She entwined it in the braid. She then painted a portrait. She had a good eye," he added. "For portraiture. In my opinion. I wonder what she would have painted had she different subjects."

"That," the Avatar unexpectedly said, "you might see. In these rooms, while Azoria occupied them, she asked that I create a studio, a room in which she might paint. It was meant to be a private space; only those she condescended to paint were allowed to enter them at all—and only one of the rooms, admittedly the most conducive to visitors."

"She painted other subjects?"

"Yes. As most will who are interested in portraiture."

"How many of them were Barrani?"

"That is a very odd question," the Avatar replied.

"It's the High Halls," Kaylin said. "And Barrani aren't generally interested in other races."

"Azoria was unusual, as you are now aware. Is the portraiture relevant?"

Serralyn frowned. "This room, this door—it's interfering with your ability to easily read thoughts. I am making no effort to hide or obscure mine because I'm not as good with words as many of my friends, and I'd rather you just read them; it would make things a lot easier."

The Avatar's expression shifted as he studied the door. "I apologize, Lord Serralyn. It is seldom that the Barrani invite such inspection. I initially assumed you were like much of the rest of your kin; I have been attempting to listen to what you are not masking and…were you not attempting clarity of thought and communication, I would, again, assume you were like An'Teela. It is disturbing. I would ask you all—including Terrano—to stand far back from this door. Lady," he added, with more gravity, "especially you."

"Why?" Terrano predictably demanded.

"Because the reach of those vines is long. Do not," he added more severely, "worry for *me*. My Avatar is present, and if it is destroyed, it is equivalent to the loss you might suffer breaking a fingernail. At most."

Terrano was clearly put out—enough so that Serralyn and Teela had to physically grab him by the arms and escort him down the hall in the wake of the Consort, who made no argument at all. Kaylin followed behind, and when they reached a wall, they stopped and turned.

The Avatar was standing in front of the doors of this unearthed room, unmoving. He might have been made of stone. Kaylin felt her arms begin to tingle, and grimaced.

"Magic allergies?" Serralyn asked.

She nodded.

"You don't normally have that reaction to older magic."

"Older?"

"Well, words and the bindings of words and the things the Ancients created."

"She may have been old for a Barrani, but she wasn't an Ancient. I think I'll be fine."

"It's getting worse, though."

"It was. But I don't think this is in response to the Avatar's work. I think it's something she did after the design of the doors was set."

Teela cursed softly, which surprised everyone, including the Consort. Hope, sitting up on Kaylin's shoulder, plastered a wing against her face. Through it, she could see the doors—or what appeared to be doors when seen through normal eyes.

They were not doors when seen through her familiar's wings. The flowers, carved or created to retain a semblance of wood, weren't wooden, and the vines, against which a patina of woodgrain had been laid—and remained—weren't, either. They moved. Kaylin reached out, wordless, for the Consort's nearest arm and pulled her in close, looping an arm around her shoulder. "Hope," she snapped.

I know. Do not let the Consort leave this sphere.

"This what?"

Squawk. It was the frustrated, shut-up-now squawk.

"Hope wants you to stay right where you are," Kaylin told the Consort.

"And the rest of us?" Teela demanded.

"He didn't say anything about you three. You can stand closer to me if you want to be safe."

Serralyn immediately joined Kaylin, taking up position on the side the Consort didn't occupy. When the familiar had first protected Kaylin from magic, she could see a shield rise, like a bubble around both her and Bellusdeo. She could see nothing now, not even through the wing. But she understood that whatever protection he thought to provide was centered around her.

Beyond holding tight to the Consort, who might have preferred more personal dignity, she focused on other concerns. The emblems carved into the door—the emblems that strongly resembled the braiding Azoria had so meticulously done with Mrs. Erickson's hair—unwound, unspooling. They didn't magically vanish; they shot out, some to the doorframe, as if it served as an anchor, and the rest directly toward the building's Avatar.

They passed through the Avatar, extending and thinning as they traveled—at speed—down the empty hall. Terrano chose to stand his ground; Kaylin could see his back. Teela chose to step away, hand on the hilt of a sword that Kaylin hadn't seen when they'd arrived.

Kaylin exhaled only when the strands, now thin and almost invisible to the winged eye, failed to grab or pierce Terrano.

You are not safe yet, Hope said.

The tendrils passed Terrano, disappearing as they dissipated.

"Do not move," the Avatar said. "I am almost finished, but things are more complicated—more layered—than anticipated. This was not my intent, when I first created the doors and the rooms that lay beyond them."

"Do you think they were meant to be a trap?"

"No, Chosen. I believe they were meant to contain something."

"Not the room?"

"Elements of the room. Had these rooms been available for use, I believe they would, in the end, have caused damage to their occupants."

"Did they cause damage to her?"

"No, but she was the primary architect of the spell. She would have made exceptions for herself, and for whatever it is she hoped to become."

The word *become* echoed in the hall.

"You think she wanted to be like me?" Terrano asked, drifting toward the Avatar. The Avatar didn't warn him off or send him away.

"I do not think she could have conceived of being like you," was the more severe reply. "I am frankly constantly surprised—and confounded—by you. She was Barrani, at heart, and you...are Terrano."

"Do you think unraveling the doors will destroy the contents of the room?"

"I think that was part of the intent, yes. Serralyn's intervention, however, alerted me to the possibility, and I believe I have preserved the contents." He did not sound pleased.

"If you were unaware, could the doors have damaged you?" Kaylin now viscerally understood why the Avatar wanted the Consort well away from these rooms.

The Avatar didn't answer.

It was Terrano who spoke. "Define *damage*. If the High Halls was unaware of the minute perturbations contained in the creation of the doors, those spells were nonetheless laid against elements of the Halls themselves. I think, were he not prepared, it would have been bad."

"And you?"

Terrano shrugged, a cheeky grin tugging his lips up. "I'm always prepared."

Serralyn snorted. "Is it safe now?" she asked the Avatar.

"It is safe to enter," the Avatar replied. "But I now see odd strands that are rooted far too deeply. I intended to leave you to your investigation—but I will not do so if the Consort is to remain with you."

"Meaning we can't investigate?"

"Meaning," Terrano said, "that he's not leaving if she isn't."

That seemed perfectly fair to Kaylin. One glance at the Consort's profile made clear that the investigation would proceed with two extra people. Given that one of them was the High Halls equivalent of Helen, this was fine. She started to walk down the hall as the doors—untouched by any obvious hands—rolled open.

Whatever Azoria An'Berranin had been in life, or in the life she'd lived in the High Halls, she wasn't given to ostentation. Perhaps her father had been. "Did he also occupy these rooms?" she asked.

The Avatar could follow her thoughts well enough not to

demand more context. "Yes. But he was an austere man; ostentation of the kind you imagine requires expenditures of power, and he was not a man given to sharing power."

"He was Barrani," Kaylin said, shrugging.

"Power means many things to many people; only those who are concerned with status spend that power in an attempt to imply wealth and influence. He was less concerned with appearance than security, but he did have a hall in which he entertained guests of relevance or value. They were not, however, her rooms; her mother saw to them, when she lived. Her younger sister continued that work; Azoria had very little interest in either hospitality or the comfort of visitors. Where it was necessary she could attend to those things, but she seldom felt it necessary."

"And her younger sister saw the need for it."

"Not exactly. The younger sister enjoyed offering hospitality. She enjoyed making choices that pleased her father's guests. It is for this reason she was better loved, if not better trusted; most believed that she was simply the more socially adept of the two. This was true," he added. "But she enjoyed the duties she undertook.

"As oldest, Azoria should have stepped into that role; she did not. She considered it irrelevant, and left it to her sister. Her younger sister felt Azoria was an unappreciated genius, and that she herself had little of value to the family. She supported and adored Azoria."

"Yet Azoria killed her."

"It was an accident; it was not intended. But as you've surmised, there was some resentment, some misunderstanding. Azoria felt she was doing everything in her power to strengthen Berranin. Everything. Her younger sister—"

"What was her name?" Kaylin asked.

"Leyalyn. Is it important?"

"I just wanted to know. Sorry for interrupting you."

"Very well. Leyalyn, to Azoria's mind, was worth far less, could offer far less, to advance the power of Berranin—and yet, in the end, it was Leyalyn who was adored. Azoria did not hate her sister, but could not untangle the envy. It is not uncommon. Leyalyn herself believed it would be Azoria who raised her family's profile, Azoria who shone the most brightly. She never questioned it. She was not maneuvering for affection—it was simply given her because of her interests and her generosity.

"Leyalyn's father wished for a daughter to become Consort. He thought Leyalyn could—but if she could, that would mean that no genius, no work, would ever allow Azoria to claim what she felt was rightfully hers. Azoria understood the needs of Berranin as a whole; she did not understand what the Lake required, but very, very few did.

"You could tell Barrani what the Lake requires; most would not believe it, regardless. Follow me."

Barrani rooms often lacked interior doors, but an exception had clearly been made; there were sturdy doors here. "These are Azoria's personal chambers." He gestured at the doors; they were not heavily engraved, as the first doors had been.

"No. The magics here are very simple, and much more easily disentangled. The changes to the entry doors were done quite late."

The doors rolled open in silence.

Kaylin stepped through them into a short hall. Straight ahead was an arch, but it was at the center point of a T-junction. The arch revealed a room of light and air; beyond it an arch opened—without doors—onto a balcony beyond which was a garden beneath a cloudless sky. Kaylin shook her head. "Not here."

"No." The Avatar then pointed to the left.

★ ★ ★

To the left, a single door was partially open as if someone had forgotten to close it when they left the room. Kaylin approached this unwarded door and pushed it wide open.

Inside this room was an easel, a chair in front of it, and a chair behind. The walls in this room were bare, but huddled against each of them, even the wall which was mostly window, were shapeless tarpaulins. Kaylin approached those beneath the window's light and very carefully pulled the rough cloth back.

There were paintings here. Kaylin didn't know much about painting, but she knew what she liked. Azoria's work was, to Kaylin's eye, good. She'd clearly been interested in portraiture; all of the visible canvases were of people, but the canvases, still stretched, were stacked in a lean against the wall that supported them. Kaylin began to separate them, looking at the people she'd painted in various poses. Some were unfinished; they stood, in very fine and detailed clothing, in a cloud of white, as if background were irrelevant. All were Barrani.

Teela, after a moment's pause, joined Kaylin, choosing to examine the canvases to the left of the door as they entered. Terrano and Serralyn took the right side. Kaylin would have warned Terrano to handle the paintings with care, but Serralyn was clearly in charge there.

Kaylin recognized none of the subjects. That made sense: most of these had probably been painted before the High Halls had collapsed in on itself to contain deadly Shadow.

"Yes," the Avatar said. "Her later work is elsewhere."

Kaylin rose. "Where are the rest?"

"In her gallery. I do not believe she allowed a single person to enter it in my time. Here, she did entertain subjects. Some, she gifted the paintings she had done; some she abandoned, unsatisfied. And some, she retained for her own personal reasons."

"Does it break any rules if we see them?"

"No—it is unusual, but were I reluctant to breach her privacy, I would not have retrieved these rooms. They are not rooms which will ever see use again; she cannot return to them. And if, as you fear, she is still a danger, it is information we require. The privacy of a person long dead is of far less import than the safety of the Consort and the Lake." To Kaylin, he added, "I am not Hallionne. That was never my function."

Given the deaths that occurred regularly within the High Halls, he was definitely not a Hallionne.

"The gallery," the Avatar said. "Lady, please remain here."

"You said it was safe," Kaylin—who had not been asked to stand back—pointed out.

"Where the Lady is concerned, we practice an abundance of caution."

Of course, Kaylin felt the same impulse, but felt minor resentment regardless.

"It is why people are complicated," the Avatar said.

"Yes, but in this case I resent you, not her."

"That is true." The Avatar smiled. Lifting a hand, he opened the door.

Kaylin knew that the light—the sunlight, the open space—wasn't real. Whatever lay beyond open windows and arches was like a painting; it looked genuine but it couldn't be touched, couldn't be entered. She expected that this gallery—it was *called* a gallery—would be full of artificial light, something that mimicked sun.

"She believed that sunlight would damage paintings."

"Artificial sunlight?"

"It was not always artificial," the Avatar replied. "And she was not wrong."

Kaylin could see a hall in dim light. A window of a kind existed at the far end of the hall, not the normal Barrani open arch. The light from that spread out to touch walls; the walls were farther apart than the gloom and dim light suggested. Not a hall, then. A long, narrow room.

"Can you add light to the room so we can examine it?"

"I can," the Avatar said, but after a longer pause.

"Don't," Teela told him. "Don't add anything that she herself did not add when she entered this gallery." Something about her tone was pure Hawk.

Hope's wing remained over Kaylin's eyes.

Only when he lifted it—briefly, as if to make a point—did she see that the gallery was well lit.

"Teela."

Teela nodded.

"It's a much darker room when seen through Hope's wing." It reminded Kaylin of Mrs. Erickson's unused parlor.

"Hope?" Kaylin said.

No.

"I need to be able to see what's in the room."

The Avatar fell silent for two long breaths. "Lady," he said, although he didn't look at the Consort, "I must ask you to leave."

The Consort stiffened; Kaylin thought she would argue.

"She is arguing," the Avatar then said. "Lady—there is something very strange, very off, about this enclosed space. It *should not* be possible, and it implies that I am not in full control, not fully aware, of what has been done."

Teela turned to the Consort, her eyes indigo. "He requires your permission to remove you. Give it." It wasn't a request;

the Consort might have been Kaylin for all the respect she was now offered.

"And will you leave Lord Kaylin at risk?"

"Kaylin is a Hawk. This is her investigation. I'll be here to partner her because Hawks do not operate on their own unless their partner is incapacitated or dead, and her partner is not on the premises. She is not the mother of our people— you are. And you have already seen the cost of Azoria's attempt to take the Lake. If the Avatar is uncertain, you cannot responsibly take the risk." When the Consort failed to nod, she continued. "You are aware of the difficulties and injuries caused to Hallionne Orbaranne in the West. They were not predictable; she did not understand the avenue of attack. This may well be similar—and you are the largest target; it is your control of the Lake, the Lake's gift to you, that she lacked. Or lacks."

"It wasn't hard," Terrano said. "I'm aware of what we did, of how we worked our way through Alsanis and Orbaranne. I can't see the same cracks here—but the High Halls are aware of what we did, and they're looking. Look, I'm sorry that I almost caused your death, and I'm doing what I can here— with the Avatar—to make sure it doesn't happen again. I mean, from anyone else."

"You wish to hold the record, do you?" the Consort asked, one brow lifting—as did the corners of her lips. She was genuinely amused. "Very well. My preference, given the nature of the possible difficulty, is to remain—but I will concede."

Almost before the last syllable was uttered, she vanished.

Kaylin poked her familiar. "Okay now?"

Hope smacked her face with his wing, and then adjusted it so it sat only across one eye. Wingless, the room was bright. Winged, it was dark. The darkness seemed to gather nearest the walls, but it looked far more natural than it had in Mrs. Erickson's home.

"The room there was fixed and very small," the Avatar said. Clearly whatever had prevented him from easily hearing thoughts was no longer interfering. "It would therefore be less obvious. Terrano, *do not touch the paintings*."

Serralyn had a death grip on his left shoulder the moment the Avatar spoke.

There were paintings—or frames—on either side of the long hall. In the light, they appeared to be very similar in composition to the paintings in the studio portion of Azoria's chambers. Through the wing of the familiar, Kaylin could see dim outlines. There were no ugly, livid flowers; none of the subjects had braided hair.

But she recognized two of them the moment her eyes touched them.

Amaldi and Darreno.

21

Do not touch the painting, Hope told her.

"They're Amaldi and Darreno. Two of the so-called ghosts."

Hope nodded.

"These are the ones you could see only with the aid of the familiar's wing?" Teela asked.

Kaylin nodded.

"Should we attempt to unravel or destroy the painting?"

Her instinctive answer was no. Thoughts followed instinct as she shook her head. "Not yet. I think we have to lead the two of them here before we make the attempt."

"Why?"

She hesitated then. "Because I'm not sure that what will come out of the paintings will be what got trapped inside them. The ghosts in Mrs. Erickson's house—the children—died at different times, but always at the same age. I found one report in historical missing persons for one of them—but it was marked resolved. She was found.

"And thirteen years later, she was arrested for mass murder, and she was executed. But the ghost remained trapped in Mrs.

Erickson's house. I don't think that's where they died—if *died* is even the right word for it. I think the ghost of 14 Orbonne, the building Azoria owned, is where they met their end."

"But Amaldi and Darreno weren't ghosts."

"Not in the same way. I think they must have escaped their confinement—a confinement of which they were unaware—when the High Halls became whole again. There might have been fractures, small cracks in continuity, when the change happened."

"That is entirely possible," the Avatar said, voice soft.

"Can you discern what was done here?"

"Not yet, but I will. Is it important to you that the two mortals survive?"

"Yes."

"Very well. I must ask: Why?"

"Don't ask that," Teela told the Avatar. "You'll be here all day. Kitling?"

Kaylin, who had opened her mouth to offer a heated reply, snapped her jaw shut.

"The rest of the paintings, please? If, as you suspect, the shadows imply entrapment, it is possible that disentangling those who did not—as Amaldi and Darreno did—escape will give us answers if we wish to fully free them."

Serralyn remained in the center of the hall, closest to Kaylin. From what she assumed was safety—or as much safety as unknown arcane arts could allow—her gaze swept the gallery. Terrano, however, locked his hands behind him and drifted toward the paintings.

"Can you see the shadow?" Kaylin asked.

He nodded. "I don't see it quite the way you see it."

"How is it different?" She aimed this question at Serralyn, not Terrano; Serralyn could see what Terrano saw, but had a better chance of explaining it.

"The paintings that you and Teela see as flat paintings with the usual brush strokes aren't what Terrano is seeing. No, *don't look this way*," she snapped at her fellow cohort member. "I *hate it* when your eyes look like that, and I think Kaylin has suffered enough portal trauma."

Kaylin was curious what Terrano's eyes looked like, but chose not to ask, given Serralyn's vehemence. The word *portal*, however, caught her attention. She had felt that the parlor's floor was similar in atmosphere to portal space. If magic caused her arms and skin to ache—or worse—she preferred pain to the nausea portals caused.

"You're right," she said quietly. "This space—it's like a kind of warped portal space. Not all of it—but closer to where the shadows you can't see are."

"I can see them," Terrano said. "I can see the threads of something that looks a bit like a spell—but not like the ones our people generally use. There are places near the paintings that you don't want to stand."

The Avatar's attention was either on Terrano or on what Terrano could see.

"You probably see them as shadows or darkness," he continued, "because the threads of them aren't visible to you, but the marks of the Chosen offer a glimpse of what they look like to someone who doesn't have the right eyes."

"I can see them through Hope's wing."

"Or that."

"This is some pretty seriously twisted work." Coming from Terrano, that couldn't be good. "You said she was Barrani, right?"

"Yes," the Avatar replied. "She was not like you."

"Maybe she didn't start that way," Terrano replied. "I'm not sure even I could accomplish what she accomplished here."

"You were not concerned with caging others; you were concerned entirely with your own freedom."

"And revenge."

"I do not believe that."

Terrano shrugged. "Believe what you like."

"I can hear your thoughts. You make even less attempt to mask them than Lord Kaylin."

"You better not be listening in when we play chess, Abel."

Everyone in the hall froze—except the Avatar.

"It is, I am told, a diminutive. A sign of friendship or affection," the Avatar then said—the Avatar who had not introduced himself by anything remotely resembling a convenient social name.

"It is, from Terrano. Most Barrani consider it rude, with all the fallout that entails."

"Ah. Mortals do not?"

"Teela calls me *kitling* all the time, and I've yet to be offended."

Both of Teela's brows rose. She didn't humiliate Kaylin by recounting every time Kaylin had, as a teenager, complained about being treated like a child.

The Avatar shocked them all. He laughed out loud. "I am grateful to all of you," he said. "It has been so long." The laughter faded. "Have you chosen a painting?"

Terrano nodded. "They all have these…vines, for want of a better word. Can you see how they're connected to you?"

The Avatar said, "No. I can see what you see. Please continue."

"You're a sentient building, and in theory *all of this is yours.* How can you not see it?" Kaylin demanded.

"That's the part you're not supposed to say out loud," Serralyn told her, eyes once again close to their normal green.

"It's why she isn't seconded to any investigation of the

various caste courts," Teela said. "She tends to speak before thinking. I will say, however, that her exposure to the Barrani High Court—and Sedarias—has made the incidences of that far less frequent."

Because Sedarias, within Helen, said whatever *she* was thinking. Most of it angry.

"I can see what Terrano sees," the Avatar replied. "There *is* a reason Terrano was able to escape Hallionne Alsanis. His attenuated connection to his name allowed a flexibility that most Barrani do not possess, and he utilized it."

"He has a name, though."

"Indeed—but what he became did not change. His vision is flexible in ways that even I find astonishing. What he sees— what was done here—would evade my notice. But Azoria was not, when I was at the peak of my power, like Terrano."

"She was probably more subtle about it," Kaylin offered.

"She was indeed. Yes," he added, although no one had asked him a question. "I am prepared. I can see the shape of the containment—I cannot see what it contains."

Terrano said, "Neither can I."

Serralyn inhaled breath on a hiss, and stepped forward instantly; she placed both hands, palm flat, against his shoulder blades, as if to shore him up. The effect was disturbing; her hands passed through his shirt, vanishing beneath its folds as a wave of...transparency flowed up her arms.

Kaylin started forward and ran into Teela's outstretched arm. "Just watch with Hope's aid. Touch nothing."

"But Serralyn—"

"This is not the first time they've done something like this," Teela replied. "I would help but I am not nearly as adept or flexible as they; I lack experience. I do not want to develop that experience, either."

★ ★ ★

"Can you even see what he's doing?" Kaylin asked her familiar. *Don't talk. I am concentrating.*

Kaylin took that as a *no*. Or as a *maybe*—Hope didn't really care for uncertainty, or at least not his own. Through his wing, however, she could see the shadows…billow. She could see them both darken and brighten, and realized that Terrano was somehow unwinding things, and as he did, the dark filaments had become more solid, more visible.

Those filaments were centered around the paintings that hung on the wall; he had chosen one at random, ignoring the two she had forbidden him to mess with. This painting was of a well-heeled Barrani woman. Her hair wasn't braided, her eyes were a martial blue, and the corners of her lips were turned up in what would, on a different face, be a smile.

"Do you recognize her?" she asked the Avatar.

"Yes. But I do not see what you see; I see it only because you do." His tone was odd; the words seemed to crackle.

Terrano stood facing this Barrani woman of long ago. "I'm going to start," he told them, without turning to look at them. To the Avatar, he said, "Don't let any of these touch *anything*," his words a biting bark of sound.

Kaylin didn't argue. There was something about the ebon vines that screamed hunger and death; she felt the air drop in temperature as he worked. She would have thought this fanciful had her breath not become visible, just as it was on winter patrols when the day was cold.

"I have them," the Avatar said. "They will not touch your friends."

"You didn't even see them!" Terrano snapped.

"Kaylin has her familiar, and Teela is standing with her," Serralyn said, in her most reasonable tone.

"You're not."

"No. But you need me here."

Terrano didn't argue. They were physically almost one thing, which was disturbing in a different way—and why, given she'd seen them as literal splashes of angry color in Helen's training room, she couldn't say.

"I apologize for the temperature," the Avatar said. "But it is necessary. Ah, please do not be alarmed."

Kaylin meant to tell him that cold didn't alarm her, but she had no time to utter the words; the ground cracked in front of her feet. Hope squawked.

"Yes, but I have asked him for his aid."

Something dark and distinctly shadowy rose through the fissures created by that cracking.

"Please don't tell me that he called the Adversary here."

"That is not what we now call him, and yes, I did."

Shadow filled the hall.

The cold no longer bothered Kaylin; the Shadow did. She knew that the Shadow was no longer under the control of whatever lived in *Ravellon*—if *lived* was even the right word— but everything in her tensed at the sight of it. It had killed so many of the Barrani who had come to face it during the Test of Name. Killed them and yet kept them locked in torment as ghosts—ghosts who wept and pleaded, continuously, for freedom, for an end to pain and torment.

She understood that he had been enslaved, that he had had no will—but even so, he carried out the orders he was given with anger, with malice.

He is not what he was.

But he'd done those things; she'd witnessed them briefly but they remained with her, as did the unsettling pain of the damned.

They are not damned now, Hope continued. *They have returned to their source. He contains or entraps nothing. But…containment and entrapment was his sole activity for a long time; the Avatar has asked for his aid for a reason.*

She wished she had gone with the Consort.

But no, no—that was simple cowardice. Had she gone, Terrano might have attempted to untangle one of the paintings of the two mortals, to possible disastrous results for those mortals. She needed to bring them here, as much "in person" as out-of-phase, trapped souls could be.

And to do that, she needed this room to remain in one piece. She had a feeling that the Avatar couldn't just re-create it at whim, as Helen could; something would be lost.

"Yes," the Avatar said. "He will not harm you, Lord Kaylin; he avoids the Barrani because of their mutual past. Those who are fully Lords of the High Court—as you are—find him alarming."

With good reason. She said nothing as it approached Terrano—who did not seem at all surprised. Or alarmed. Kaylin almost shrieked when a Shadow tendril reached out from the mass of the Adversary—as she privately called him—and planted itself in the nape of Terrano's neck. Taking shallow breaths, she forced herself to remain still; Serralyn didn't seem alarmed, and she realized belatedly that the Shadow was doing what Serralyn herself was doing.

"They provide an anchor for him," the Avatar said. "But he is…in too many places at once, and some of those, Serralyn cannot safely reach. My friend can."

Friend. "You really have been spending a lot of time with Terrano lately, haven't you?"

"Yes. It is enlightening. To my friend as well; what Terrano now does is clearer to him."

"Was this Shadow magic?"

"He does not entirely understand that question, but Azoria did, indeed, reach a source of magic that is not normally accessible to those born Barrani. He recognizes the taste of it."

Taste. Kaylin didn't ask.

She could hear the whisper of the Shadow's voice; it was a chorus of sound, forced into syllables, as water, scooped out of the ocean, might fill a glass.

Terrano cursed in Elantran. The Avatar stiffened; it was not Terrano's lack of good manners that alarmed him. As Terrano unwound the nimbus of darkness that surrounded the painting he had chosen, as the strands took on color—some a gray and some a deep black—the painting itself began to bulge, the canvas contorting the careful brush strokes that had formed the image of a woman.

"Don't let them touch anyone!" he shouted.

It was late; the filaments, unbound, were far more like slender tentacles than they had been, and they reached out, as if grasping at air, looking for something to twine around. They passed through Terrano—just as the vines on the doors to these chambers had passed through the Avatar; they passed through Serralyn because she was, in a very disturbing way, part of Terrano at the moment.

They did not pass through the Shadow.

Terrano shouted a word Kaylin didn't recognize and couldn't pronounce if she tried.

It is their name, Hope said. *Do not move. Teela can avoid what is to come; I must protect you. It is not you personally they seek,* he added.

No, she thought, as her arms began to glow. It was the words they sought. The marks of the Chosen.

Yes.

"Why?"

They will not find what they seek in the Shadow.

The Shadow, the Adversary of old, lifted a limb—not a hand, it was too shapeless for that. The darkest vines, the ebon vines, stopped their grasping search then; they came to the Shadow, whose limb was the same color, almost as if they were part of the Adversary himself.

He spoke. Kaylin lifted her hands to her ears—or would have, if Hope weren't in the way of one of them. This was not a language she recognized; it was an echo of, a distortion of, something familiar. A wave of nausea struck, as if she had, without warning, entered portal space.

Hope bit her ear.

The shock of pain swamped nausea as he smacked her face—hard—with his wing. What Terrano had attempted, the Shadow finished. The darkest of the vines, the ebon ones, were...absorbed. Or devoured.

"Yes," the Avatar of the High Halls said. "It causes some discomfort. But I can now absorb the rest of the mass."

"What did you need Terrano for?"

"To see it, Chosen. To see it, to begin the disentangling of it. Neither my friend nor I would have noted what was done, for Azoria entwined perfectly the elements of two things that otherwise could not coexist. It was masterful."

Kaylin had an entirely different word for it.

"Yes, it would have been considered an abomination. But the Ancients understood that if they created, if they gave their creations some freedom of will and thought, they might grow in directions of which the Ancients themselves could not conceive. Almost, I am in awe."

It was a dark awe—the other side of horror.

"What was the...spell meant to achieve?"

"You will now see for yourself," the Avatar replied. He gestured at the bulging, distorted canvas, and it continued to stretch, the image now pulling away from the canvas on which it had been painted, the flat dimensionality of the figure stretching and shifting in place to become an actual person.

No, not a person. A perfectly preserved corpse.

"I am grateful that we sent the Consort away," the Avatar said.

Kaylin was certain that the Consort had seen her share of corpses. A long dead Barrani woman—one whose death had probably occurred before the Consort's birth—would be unlikely to upset her.

"You do not see as she does. If you can fulfill her function in an emergency, what you see are the words, as if they were the marks that adorn your body."

"What would she see?"

"A vessel," he replied, voice soft. "A vessel emptied of that light, that life."

"But...that's what a Barrani corpse *is*."

"No, Lord Kaylin, it is not. You have encountered those who have attempted to divest themselves entirely of the dependency of True Names; they are closer to this, but they are not the same; the attenuated connection exists."

"The words flee the body when the Barrani dies."

"That is what should have happened, yes. It is not what happened here. You cannot see it—or perhaps you could, if you knew how to look. Perhaps your familiar can aid you in this, perhaps not. The words did not leave the body; they were entrapped, and they were slowly destroyed. Devoured.

"They were devoured while I maintained this suite of rooms, these hidden cages." She heard cold anger in his voice.

It is not anger, Hope said. *It is beyond something so simple, so superficial.*

She looked down the long hall. "Don't destroy this place," she told the Avatar. "Destroy the paintings if you must—you know how, now, and Terrano can help the two of you. But don't destroy the paintings of the two humans—preserve them, if you can. I'm not sure what she intended—we don't have True Names, and she must have known that—but she told them that she was sending them somewhere, hiding them somewhere, to save their lives.

"That's clearly not what she intended, but…it's possible we can free them. I think, if you destroy those paintings now, they might never return to their bodies."

"I will do as you ask, Chosen. But I will, as you've suggested, destroy the rest of the containments."

The Shadow spoke in a rumble.

"My friend believes that this was meant to create a space where those words could be siphoned for power; you are in danger if the marks of the Chosen can be likewise consumed."

They could. Hope had eaten one.

"My words aren't names." Kaylin's tone was quieter. "They don't quicken life. They don't sustain it or they wouldn't be on my arms. Whatever purpose they're meant to serve, it's not that. The Barrani names—the True Names—*can* be used to sustain life, even if that life was not originally Barrani in nature."

"The words have power, regardless. Perhaps Azoria did not understand the difference. Or perhaps she found a way to drain the source of her life of that power. She might still exist, but she would not be what she once was. Perhaps," he added softly, "she required the power essential to Barrani life, and did not realize her own could be so consumed: the Barrani are eternal."

"The Barrani can die," Kaylin countered.

"You do not believe she is dead."

"No," Kaylin said. "I believe she was alive—and mobile—at least eighty years ago. I think she created a home for herself in amongst the mortals somehow. That home is visible but… out of phase. And I think we need to reach it if we're to end the threat she poses. Or posed." Kaylin grew more thoughtful. "I think she continued her experiments. A painting such as this—but far darker—exists in a purely mortal home."

"I do not see the point. Mortals are not born the same way, and they do not require—do not possess—the names from which power was apparently leeched."

"No—but who would have seen the point of this when it was done?" She gestured to the walls in general, where the paintings, in their frames of death, still hung. "It's possible she had no other choice; she could not randomly kidnap Barrani without alerting them to her presence, her existence. But she had clearly begun to experiment with mortals centuries ago; Amaldi and Darreno are here.

"And the children are trapped in Mrs. Erickson's house."

Teela cleared her throat.

"But those children are dead. We know that their ghosts remain—and those ghosts aren't like Amaldi and Darreno. We know that their bodies became vessels for...something. Something murderous. Something that looked like them, that grew as the bodies grew, and that eventually went on a killing spree for which they were duly executed."

"All of them?"

Kaylin nodded. "All four. Whatever she had learned to do creating these paintings must have been refined or changed somehow. I don't know if these paintings ever contained flowers—but the flowers in the green, or one of them, was brought to a mortal woman's house, and it is part of the painting she created there.

"I don't see any hint of those flowers in any of these paintings—even the ones that contain the two humans."

The Avatar was silent for one long beat. He then turned to Serralyn. "That is a possibility," he said.

"Serralyn, share."

Serralyn said, "I'm beginning to agree with Mandoran. Everyone else heard what I was thinking—if you had our names, you'd hear it as well." She winced, no doubt at Sedarias's reprimand. "It's clear from what was done here—or from what was undone—that the power for these cages, the…soil in which these vines were rooted, was the potential of the outlands, of the miasma from which the High Halls forms all things within his boundaries.

"She doesn't have that now. She didn't have that when she did whatever she did almost a century ago. But if she didn't have power and needed it, if she studied the green and the areas in the world that were older than the High Halls, she might have found some way to root things…in the green."

"She was pretty far from the green," Kaylin pointed out.

Serralyn nodded. "But the flower grew, regardless—and it grows nowhere else. There must be a reason she brought it, a reason she made those braids, a reason she planted the flower in Mrs. Erickson's hair. I think whatever power she needed to create the enchantments she created she intended to draw from a very tenuous connection to the green.

"And…from Shadow. Shadow seems—given what little we personally know of it—to be more elemental in nature. Fire, earth, water, wind—they're called, and they answer, but the location of the summoner doesn't seem to matter."

Kaylin said, "I think it's mostly rooted in Shadow; the nimbus of darkness is stronger around the painting."

"But Mrs. Erickson isn't dead and she isn't trapped," Serralyn pointed out.

"Because Azoria was very unlucky, in my opinion." Kaylin hesitated. "She may have been attempting to do…something with the children, but it ended up killing them."

"Legally, they weren't dead."

"They're dead. They were dead the moment she did…

whatever it is she did." Kaylin exhaled. "We need to get into that damn house."

"The one no one can see?"

"Teela could sort of see it—I think it's dependent on time of day and magical aptitude. But I'm certain it's there. We need to get into it."

"Have you considered that getting into it, as you put it, will bring you face-to-face with possibly the greatest criminal the Barrani have ever known?" Teela snapped.

"Yes—isn't that the point?"

Terrano laughed. Serralyn didn't. Teela rolled her eyes.

But the Shadow that had come, at the Avatar's request, approached Kaylin, two limbs lifted. She stood her ground, although her first instinct was to dodge; Hope was with her, and Hope didn't seem alarmed. He was alert, but he wasn't quivering with tension the way he often did when danger was present.

She watched as the Shadow began to cohere, to condense; limbs formed, and if they didn't quite conform to Kaylin's version of normal, they were definitely arms and legs. A head formed with an unfortunate number of eyes, but those eyes receded until there were only three. Kaylin realized that the Shadow was attempting to adopt a form with which she might feel more comfortable.

"He is no longer imprisoned here, but he is very wary of the world beyond my borders," the Avatar said. "Like Spike, he is free now, to make his own decisions, to pursue his own path. He has chosen to remain within my borders for the moment because he is certain that here, he will remain free.

"But the people to whom he once spoke, the people to whom he once listened, are either dead or enslaved as he was enslaved. He is not what I am; he is not what the Barrani are. But he believes that Azoria did, indeed, utilize Shadow to create these cages; she balanced them with the material from which I create.

"She is not here; he believes she attempted to create similar cages, but without access to the materials that comprise a building such as I. Shadow, however, she could more easily access."

"Could she draw power from Shadow?"

"She did not draw power directly from me—that, I would have noticed. But it is possible she did not choose to do so because she did not wish to attract attention. The power that she might wield is not power in the sense the Arcanists use the word; she might *make* or *create* with it, but she could not make or create life; she might sustain it in a minor way—we can create food, and that is consumed.

"My friend believes it possible—but transformative, should too much power be drawn; subtle alterations might occur. Azoria was not stupid; she was demonstrably capable of caution, of hiding intent and work. Shadow is more subtle than fire; one can make a statement *of* power by summoning fire, but one cannot innately consume that power."

"So…he thinks she used too much Shadow?"

"He thinks it likely."

"But…he's Shadow. Like—that's most of what he is."

The Avatar's brows rose. "Are the fish that swim in the ocean the ocean?"

"No, they're fish."

"Exactly. They breathe water. They thrive in it. But they are not water. The analogy fails when we consider my friend, as fish probably do not understand water in any absolute way. He is considering the wisdom of leaving the High Halls."

"I think it's a terrible idea," Kaylin said immediately. "We know he was powerful, and we don't know that he'll remain safe—and free—if he leaves. He's not certain, either; if he were, I'd give you a different answer."

"Is your permission required?"

"Yes," was the flat—and possibly inaccurate—reply.

The Avatar was silent for some time; the Shadow—still trying to compress itself into mortal form—rumbled. Kaylin was confused. The Shadow had very clearly taken on Barrani form when it had been trapped in the High Halls.

"That was illusory," the Avatar said quietly. "And it was not a form taken; it was a form evoked. What you saw was born of your own experience, manipulated; it was not what the Shadow was. The attempt is being made to…be themselves in your presence, but I agree it lacks a certain visual acuity. We are not the same, and my attempts to teach what I instinctively know have not been as successful as one could hope. But they have a suggestion: take Spike with you. Spike is capable of recording and storing information gained, and Spike has clearly been entirely free of compulsion since first gaining freedom.

"Spike is also accustomed to you, and to your Helen; I feel that this suggestion is the most flexible and the most reasonable. Spike will not have the ready answers my friend might have, but Spike will certainly have more information than Terrano, his friends, or you.

"Spike also has the same immunity to Shadow—to unaspected, unenslaved Shadow—that my friend has. Listen to Spike if a warning is offered."

Kaylin nodded. Spike then emerged from the Shadow that was not quite the Adversary but definitely not person-shaped. He was, as he had been before, a ball with protrusions—he looked like the head of a mace, removed from any useful way of wielding it.

Kaylin held out a hand, and Spike flew to her palm; she

could feel the protuberances as he sank, quite literally, into her flesh. This was not the first time it had happened. Hope squawked at him; Spike clicked in response, but adjusted his spikes so they didn't dig further into her palm.

"I think we should confer with Helen before we make our way to fourteen and a half," Serralyn said, voice subdued.

"What she means is Sedarias wants us to come home first."

"I'm against it," Teela said, joining the verbal part of the discussion. "If we return home first, we're likely to approach Orbonne Street in the company of the entire cohort."

Plus one, Severn said.

Kaylin winced. It was, no doubt, dark now—but darkness seemed to be the time to attempt to approach the absent number fourteen. It was also the time when Ferals came to hunt; it was the time when Shadow was the strongest.

She lifted a hand—the one that didn't contain Spike. "I think," she said, "that we should find Amaldi and Darreno and bring them here, first. We don't know what the enchantments Azoria laid are—but when we free them, we'll have a better idea."

"And if, in attempting to free them, you instead cause their death?"

22

"You did not want those paintings touched because you were afraid of the effect interference might have on the two people you characterize as out of phase."

She nodded.

"You cannot be certain that they *are* out of phase in the same way the Academia's occupants were—you reached for that explanation because you've experienced it. I am willing to allow your friends to enter the High Halls—if I am aware of them at all. But I would ask that you take Terrano with you if you intend to make the attempt.

"It is clear that what was done to the children in Mrs. Erickson's home was not what was done with Amaldi and Darreno. Perhaps it is what would have occurred, had she retained access to the Berranin suite; perhaps later iterations were forced on her because she did not have the same access to...material and power."

"So Amaldi and Darreno would have been the intended and perfect execution of...whatever it was she was attempting. When she lost this gallery, this studio, she had to attempt to repeat that spell?"

"That would make sense—but the living often make very little sense. And you have not answered the question."

"I know." Kaylin turned to Teela. "We need to find Amaldi and Darreno. They won't enter Mrs. Erickson's house—I'm not sure why. But...I only got involved in all of this because they recognized Severn's weapon, and they told Mrs. Erickson about it."

Silence.

"They weren't trying to take the weapon; they were afraid of it—but they were very aware that Severn was not Barrani, and it was a Barrani-only weapon." More silence, and not the comfortable kind.

"Wow. When you stick your foot in things, you *really* choose the worst possible place to try to stand, you know?"

Kaylin glared at Terrano, but otherwise held her peace. "Come on, Spike, let's go. Could you manage not to be seen?"

Spike whirred and clicked.

The familiar snorted a small cloud of silvery steam, and Spike returned to Kaylin's hand. This time, when the spikes for which she'd haphazardly named him—or her, or them— bit flesh and drew blood, the familiar made no noise.

Kaylin turned to Terrano. "Let's head home."

Teela took a day off work on Kaylin's behalf, which is to say, she appeared at Helen's front door just as breakfast was starting. Helen let her in—of course she did—and Teela marched into the dining room, glancing at breakfast, and at the people who were, and were not, eating it.

Mandoran, Terrano, and Serralyn were at the breakfast table, alongside Kaylin, who felt slightly hungover, which was annoying because she'd reached that state without any drinking whatsoever. Spike sat somewhere above her shoulder, on the opposite side Hope occupied.

"We're off the normal duty roster today," Teela announced, without bothering to take the chair that Helen helpfully materialized for her use. "Tain is not pleased."

"He's not joining us?"

"No."

Terrano said, "Good." When both Teela and Kaylin glared at him, he shrugged. "He's a stick-in-the-mud." He paused, and then added, "Why exactly do you people use that phrase?"

"It means—"

"I know what it means—I just don't understand why. Never mind. We're going to Mrs. Erickson's?" he asked Kaylin.

"I guess so. Normally we don't start things until after her visit to the Halls; she's been visiting later in the day and staying until I leave. I'm not even certain she'll be awake."

"We won't be there immediately. If we're fast enough, we can find your two not-dead ghosts, take them to the High Halls, and return to the Halls of Law to escort Mrs. Erickson home." Teela looked up. "We may be late to return."

Helen's eyes were obsidian. "Serralyn, Mandoran, and Terrano have been discussing things; Valliant has joined in, but not in a way that Kaylin can hear."

"Do you have any input?" Kaylin asked.

"Not useful input, no. I understand what Serralyn believes was done—but the High Halls and I are not driven by the same mandate. I belonged to what you would call an Arcanist before my emancipation; my imperatives at the time would not have allowed the search the High Halls allowed—but I, too, would have kept the research rooms."

Terrano's eyes lit up.

"No," she said, before he could ask. "You have seen the rooms I created for our new guests. So has Kaylin. Were Azoria to be resident here, she could make far more use of me, I think, than she was able to make of the High Halls."

Not a comforting thought.

Less comforting, however, was the thought that followed Kaylin's sudden question. "Do you think there was a sentient building at Orbonne Street? I mean, you have an actual, legal address."

Helen's reply took a long time. "To my knowledge, no. But my knowledge, as you know, is imperfect now. I knew of the Academia—we all did—and of the High Halls. I know of one other building, but the geography seems wrong for it, and I am not at all certain the building itself is awake. We are not invulnerable, as you are fully aware."

Kaylin deflated. "It would explain how a building could be mostly invisible while still occupying the same space. And it would explain how fourteen and a half can exist in the space fourteen theoretically once occupied."

Helen nodded. "As I said, I have imperfect memory, a consequence of my emancipation. Perhaps if you asked Killianas, you might receive a different reply."

"I don't want to ask Killian, because we'll no doubt get at least one tagalong."

"Larrantin?"

"Yes, but he's not the one I'm afraid of having to explain."

"Bakkon?"

Kaylin nodded. "The Swords will be screaming for my head if I happen to escort a giant talking spider through the city streets. And they'll have some cause."

"I think Larrantin might have knowledge I lack," Serralyn said. "And he was one of her teachers."

"Yes. But the teachers who would be the most useful to interrogate are actually Arbiters who mostly can't leave the library." She thought of Androsse and made a face. "We might be able to get Bakkon—but I *really* don't want the Swords

to come after me when he causes screaming panic and fleeing crowds."

Serralyn frowned. "I think I *might* be able to help with that.
But I'll have to meet you at Mrs. Erickson's—I won't be able
to join you in your hunt for the two mortals."

"Sedarias thinks that's a good idea," Terrano told Kaylin.
"But Serralyn thinks it should be relatively easy for Bakkon
to…kind of attach a nascent web strand to her, and use it to
portal himself to where we are." Before Kaylin could speak—
and she'd opened her mouth to point out flaws in this possible plan—he lifted a hand. "Returning to the rooms he now
occupies shouldn't pose any difficulty."

"He's staying at the Academia?"

"Liatt has offered him residence, and he's accepted the offer
in theory—but I think he hopes to spend at least a decade
chatting with Starrante, and doesn't wish to waste time and
energy by going back and forth.

"Are we ready to go?"

"Almost," Kaylin replied, around a mouthful of breakfast.

"If you're not ready in five minutes, you'll have way more
company than you want."

She ate quickly.

Amaldi and Darreno were easy to find; they were in the
first place Kaylin chose to look: by the well, where she'd first
met them. Darreno was standing; Amaldi was crouched over
a huddle of children who seemed—at this distance—to be
playing with dice. They were a bit too young to be betting,
and were gleeful in their triumphs and angry in their losses—
normal children, in other words.

Amaldi seemed to be trying to intuit the rules of play, but
she looked up as Kaylin's shadow crossed the children's game.

The children also looked up, one with a guilty start; she could guess who'd brought the dice.

Not wanting to immediately appear unhinged to a group of children by talking to the air above their heads, she asked if they had seen a woman who exactly matched Amaldi's description; given she was a strange adult, the children were both relieved and willing to answer, the answer being no.

"If you do see her, can you tell her I'll be waiting to the west of the fountain?"

The kids nodded.

Amaldi, hearing all of this, moved to follow Kaylin toward that west-of-fountain spot; Kaylin had chosen it because it was mostly deserted, and the presence of two Hawks—one Barrani—would make sure that mostly became completely in short order. Darreno followed Amaldi as she moved.

Hope's wing remained firmly attached to Kaylin's face as she turned toward the two people Teela couldn't see. Terrano and Mandoran were waiting with Teela, and they watched as Kaylin approached. Mandoran shrugged and shook his head: no. He was willing to believe that the two existed—he did trust Kaylin, in spite of Sedarias's best efforts—but he couldn't pierce the veil that separated them from the rest of the world.

Terrano, however, was frowning.

"Can you make yourself invisible?" Kaylin's voice was a quiet hiss, sort of like a whisper but with more urgency.

"Why?"

Because his face—especially his eyes—were starting to transform. Serralyn had been right. It made Kaylin more than queasy, in part because she couldn't be certain it wasn't visual artifacts that came with portal vertigo.

"But I can see them now," Terrano said, with a note of smug mixed in with triumph. "It's going to give me a bit of a headache."

"Fair—you're giving me a worse one."

Amaldi took a step back—a large one—when she saw Terrano—but he was facing her, so the elongation of eyes and the shifting color were front and center. Darreno placed a steadying arm around her shoulders, but he was now grim.

"Terrano has that effect on people," Kaylin said, keeping her voice low.

It was Darreno who said, "We've seen that before. The eyes. The...color."

Kaylin stiffened before she exhaled. "We have a few questions for you, if you're willing to answer them. We'd obviously like to ask them when we're not in the middle of the street and we won't look like we're talking to ourselves— I'm a Hawk, and no one wants Hawks to be less than perfectly sane."

Amaldi nodded; she had stepped toward Kaylin and away from Terrano.

"We've been offered the use of the High Halls, if you're willing to have the discussion there."

"We?"

"The person beside me, who can't see you, is An'Teela, a Lord of the High Court."

"But she's a Hawk!"

"Yes. It isn't really complicated; she was bored and thought it might be fun for a few decades."

Darreno rolled his eyes. Clearly he was familiar with the concept of Barrani boredom, and An'Teela, while in possession of a significant title, couldn't see him or otherwise use him to alleviate said boredom.

"Would you be willing to come with us to the High Halls?"

Amaldi hesitated. Darreno, however, said, "They can't see us. They have no way of hurting us. Kaylin's Mrs. Erickson's friend."

It was the last comment that decided Amaldi. "Is this about Mrs. Erickson?"

"Not directly, no. Maybe a bit." Kaylin moved her foot before Teela could step on it. "We need to ask you questions about how you ended up being Mrs. Erickson's ghosts. We could also have this discussion at Mrs. Erickson's."

"No," Darreno said, before Amaldi could answer. "We will risk the High Halls, if we are with you."

The moment Kaylin set foot on the wide stairs that led into the towering building, the Avatar of the High Halls was there, waiting. Spike wobbled his way off Kaylin's shoulder, chattering—or so she assumed, given the noises he was making. She had a suspicion that Spike and Starrante would communicate with ease.

We would, Spike said. *I would like to meet the Arbiter.*

Amaldi and Darreno stared at the height of the ceilings in comfort, not awe; these were the Halls they had known when they'd lived as Berranin slaves. The Avatar greeted them, which surprised Kaylin; he could see them. It surprised the two phased mortals as well, but their surprise was tinged with desperate delight: they had spent far too long being invisible.

"Terrano's attempts," the Avatar said, "were useful in this regard; I understand what he did, and can mimic it without the adverse visual and physical effects." He offered the two mortals a nod. "Has Kaylin discussed the relevant difficulties with you?"

Darreno shook his head. "She said that there were things she needed to discuss, which might impact Mrs. Erickson. She wanted to discuss them here."

The Avatar nodded. "Come, then. Let me offer you the hospitality of the High Halls. You will not be in danger while you are here. Follow me."

★ ★ ★

He did not lead the two—and their companions—to the Berranin chambers. Instead, he led them down the halls with the highest of ceilings; his feet, and theirs, made no noise. Terrano's were likewise silent. Mandoran couldn't be bothered, and Kaylin and Teela were walking in boots on marble floors.

No one spoke, as if by silent consensus, until the Avatar turned to the left, through arches that were almost as tall as the ceilings. The arch opened up into an outdoor space; trees surrounded a clearing, and in it, to the far side, was a pond that almost reminded Kaylin of the pond in Evanton's elemental garden.

"It is like, and unlike, that," the Avatar said. He gestured and chairs rose from the stone tiles that emphasized the nature of this man-made clearing. "Please, make yourselves comfortable. There will be no interruptions."

"The Consort?"

"She is aware that you have arrived, but for the moment, she will refrain from joining you. Yes," he added, "at my request."

Darreno and Amaldi stared at the offered chairs; it was Amaldi who chose to attempt to sit in one. Her brows rose into her hairline as she swiveled in that chair, looking at her only companion. His brows rose as well, but he immediately chose to take the chair beside hers.

"I didn't fall through," he whispered.

"No," the Avatar said quietly. "As I said, I have made some adjustments based on Terrano's attempts. I cannot make you entirely visible to other people while you visit, but I will see you."

"Can we visit whenever we want?" Amaldi asked.

"Yes, for now. And no, Mrs. Erickson would not feel at

home or welcome here. If you are visible to me, you will not be visible to the Barrani; she would."

Both Amaldi and Darreno nodded emphatically; it made Kaylin smile. Yes, they were attached to the old woman for pragmatic reasons—they were lonely, she could see and talk with them. But Mrs. Erickson was a gentle person; she was kind. She understood the pain of the invisible and she reached out in all the ways she could. And they responded, just as the Hawks did, frustration and disbelief giving way to affection.

"Lord Kaylin?"

Amaldi and Darreno exchanged a confused glance before they both turned to look at Kaylin, who reddened. She really hated that title; in the office it was used to mock her. Technically it was accurate, and this was perhaps the only place it could be considered necessary. Ugh.

Kaylin exhaled. Inhaled. "You won't enter Mrs. Erickson's house. Why?"

The two exchanged another glance. It was longer, and it wasn't followed by words.

"Okay, let's move on. Did Azoria Berranin ever paint portraits of you?"

Amaldi said, "Yes. I think half a dozen, at least of me."

Darreno said, "I only sat for two. Why are you asking?"

"Because we found two paintings, one of each of you. No, actually, we found dozens of paintings of various Barrani. Some, however, were hung in the walls of her gallery—it's those that are the biggest concern. Your paintings—one each—were in that gallery as well."

Darreno frowned, but nodded. Amaldi began to stiffen. The reactions were different.

"Why is this important?" It was Darreno who asked.

"We think that she created powerful enchantments around

the paintings she made: they're a type of magical cage. The cages made of Barrani portraits were, we think, perfected."

"What did they do?"

"They trapped the Barrani within the painting itself, and then slowly leeched them of life force. All of the Barrani portraits contained dead Barrani."

Amaldi looked down at the surface of the table; Darreno looked at Kaylin. "You think she was attempting to do that with...us?"

"It honestly doesn't make sense to me, either—whatever it was she hoped to do with the two of you—"

"She said it was to protect us," Amaldi whispered.

It's what they'd said the first time, but Kaylin understood now. "You didn't believe that."

She shook her head. It was Darreno who said, "What choice did we have? Death immediately or death later. That was it. And death later offered hope that we might survive. We pretended to believe her because it made no difference to our choices. Yes, she painted us. She wasn't happy with her first attempt—of me—but seemed satisfied with the second attempt. She patted me on the head and praised me for my patience.

"She was less happy with Amaldi's sittings." His expression darkened. "Show her," he told his sole friend. He looked at her arm, covered as Kaylin's were covered.

Amaldi shook her head. "It doesn't matter. She eventually got the painting she wanted." She exhaled. "Why is it important?"

"We think you were...put into the space she created, as if the paintings themselves were a pocket space in which the subjects could be entrapped."

Darreno said, "This isn't about our freedom, is it?" The question was bitter. Of course it was.

Kaylin shook her head. "Not just yours, no."

The two exchanged another look; it was longer. Amaldi broke the ensuing silence. "What do you want us to do?"

"We don't know what the paintings were meant to achieve when they weren't of Barrani. But there's a painting hanging in Mrs. Erickson's house. She's not—she's not trapped the way you are, and she's mortal. The painting itself might be irrelevant in a decade or less."

"You're worried about Mrs. Erickson," Amaldi said, voice soft.

Kaylin spoke. "I'm worried about Mrs. Erickson, but I'm also worried about the children who are trapped in the house— they're actual ghosts, unlike the two of you. They've been there since the house was built. They can't leave. Mrs. Erickson keeps them company; she looks out for them as she can.

"But Jamal knows—they all know—that she won't live forever. She's worried about them. I think the house is becoming too much to handle on her own, but she won't leave until she's carried out, because those children are still trapped there. I would like her to leave—I want to remove that damn painting and burn it—but I understand why she won't."

Amaldi tensed. Darreno, Kaylin realized, had been tense since they'd entered the High Halls.

"Why have you never entered her house?"

It was Amaldi who said, "Because it was hers. It was Azoria's."

I want to ask them a different question, Severn said.

Go ahead. What do you want me to ask?

Ask them about my weapon. They recognized it—that was the start of this.

What, now?

The weapon is tied to the green, he said. *I intend—I intended— to meet you at Mrs. Erickson's, to find some way into the building*

*you can see. But if the power she sought in the green was the weapon
I carry, it might be smarter to leave it at home.*

What, where it can be stolen?

I can leave it with Helen, if that makes you feel better.

Kaylin exhaled. "I have a related question."

Amaldi nodded.

"Well, two. The first: How do you know it's Azoria's
house? The entire house that Mrs. Erickson occupies was
built by her parents on what was probably a small, empty lot."

Amaldi's brows gathered toward the bridge of her nose, as
did Darreno's. "Is that what you see?"

"Yes. On the inside *and* the outside. But...at night, I can
see the ghost of a larger building—a building that wouldn't
really pass for a house in that neighborhood; most lack the
tower. And the scope. The two buildings don't seem connected at all."

The two once again exchanged an uncertain glance.

It was Amaldi who said, "It doesn't look that way to us."
She hesitated, but before she could speak, the Avatar did.

"Ask your second question." His eyes were a curious color,
almost gray, but oddly shining.

"The first question is relevant, and it's not quite answered
yet," Kaylin replied.

"The second question is, as you put it, extremely relevant."

When Kaylin failed to ask it immediately, the Avatar took
matters into his own hands.

"Amaldi, Darreno, according to Lord Kaylin, she started
her investigation because the two of you recognized the
weapon Lord Severn carries, and spoke to Mrs. Erickson
about it. How did you recognize the weapon?

"Understand," he added, when they failed to answer immediately, "that your former master is considered one of our
greatest criminals. It had been assumed that she was dead,

and therefore irrelevant. Even now, we have no proof that this is not the case, but the circumstantial evidence is now against that assumption.

"It's possible that she *is* dead; in any Barrani sense of the word that might be accurate. But if so, the spells she cast and the machinations she began seem to linger in echoes. You are part of those echoes. And possibly part of the solution. But we do not entirely understand the whole of her plans, the goals she might have had. In truth, were it not for Lord Kaylin's familiar and young Terrano, I doubt I would have been aware of your existence at all. It is not to my liking.

"But you should not recognize the weapon in question. You did. How?"

The question made almost no sense to the two out-of-phase mortals; that much was clear to Kaylin. She lifted a hand. "Can I handle this?"

The Avatar frowned. "You did not ask the question."

"I was trying to deal with the first question—which for our purposes is the more practical one. Look—you're Immortal. You *have* time."

"We do not have time to waste if Azoria remains a problem."

"Teela, can you give me a hand here?"

Teela chuckled. "Allow the mortal to deal with the mortals," she suggested, her tone making it less of a command than the words themselves implied.

Kaylin then turned to Amaldi again, as the Avatar fell—reluctantly—silent. "You can see Mrs. Erickson's home as part of the building that stood there before it was built?"

"It's still there. The building is still there. We weren't sure—when Mrs. Erickson first approached us—that she couldn't see it, didn't live in it. We weren't certain she wasn't another mortal slave."

"It didn't take long to figure it out," Darreno added. "But we spent a lot of time walking through the streets of this city—it was new to us. We slept, but...obviously, this time, it was a long slumber. There were so many people—so many people like us—and so very few Barrani. We avoided the High Halls."

"You slept before now?"

"Yes, we told you that—but before, when we slept, she would wake us."

"She could see you."

Darreno nodded.

"Could anyone else?"

The two once again exchanged a glance. "No. Not usually. She wanted to know which of the Barrani could see us."

"Only Barrani?"

"She was Barrani; I don't think she considered mortals relevant."

"And those that could see you?"

"She befriended them. She painted them." He was silent for a longer beat, because he already knew the results of that for the Barrani.

"Did you enter the green?"

"Yes."

"Was she with you?"

Amaldi shook her head. "The Warden of the time refused her entry—at the behest of the green, or so she was told."

"And that kept her out?"

"No, not permanently. *No*, for our master, was simply a more complicated version of *yes*. But it took time, and we were some part of that; we could enter the green. The green was aware of us in a way the Warden and his various guards and novices weren't. She told us how and where to attempt entry; we would go in, and return."

"Return?"

"Azoria could travel very quickly. She could reach the West March without the overland march. She could call us to the High Halls because...we didn't have normal bodies. We would go in, and she would call us back. She had us attempt to take things from the green—"

"That is a terrible idea," Teela said.

"Normally, yes. But she had changed us. Hidden us. We couldn't be killed."

"By anyone but her," Darreno added.

"The green sometimes talked to us. We couldn't understand it. The first time, when we failed to respond, it...kicked us out. But we were allowed to enter again, and we did *try* to answer when it spoke. I don't think we ever succeeded in making ourselves clear. But once—twice—when the green spoke, it showed us many things.

"One of those things was the weapon your partner carries."

"It looked like that?"

"Yes?" Darreno frowned. "I'm not certain what they look like to you."

"Long weapon chain, blade at either end."

"That's not what it looks like to us. What we knew was that the weapons were highly, highly desirable. They were created by the green, or at least protected by the green, and if the green judged a Barrani worthy, they were offered to that Barrani. If one who wasn't worthy—in the green's view— touched the weapons or attempted to wield them, they died. Many, many Barrani wanted them."

"Of course they did. They're powerful."

"We were shocked to see the weapon in the hands of a mortal. We wondered if...if the mortal was like us, maybe. If she'd finally managed to perfect whatever she'd intended to perfect, and had finally found someone she could send into the green to retrieve them. Had she been present, we would have been rendered irrelevant. Useless.

"He shouldn't have the weapon. He does have it. The green must have decided he was worthy of it. She would have been *so* angry. So many Barrani wanted that weapon.

"She was no different. But as she was not allowed entry to the green, it was clear that the green—or the weapon itself—would never consider her worthy. We spent some time visiting the green; she was frustrated, in the end. But our entries into the green eventually yielded enough information that she could enter without the Warden's permission. It was easiest to enter through the Hallionne, but the Hallionne was prepared for that; she had never liked the Hallionne, and seldom chose to stay within their borders.

"The Hallionne, in turn, mistrusted her for reasons I do not believe they would ever share. But if she could enter the green, she could not find the weapon. She searched for some time. We attempted to avoid her when she returned empty-handed; she was always angry. Her father knew that she made the attempt; they argued. He did not believe she would ever be found worthy."

Kaylin winced.

"They often argued; we avoided her—when we could—after her father visited. But the last time we woke, she wasn't there. We have been awake since then, but we have had more freedom, and far less visibility. It wasn't until Mrs. Erickson that we found anyone who could see us at all. We liked her. We like her now." Darreno rose from the table. "You wish us to visit the paintings in the gallery because you want to know what the paintings might mean to mortals."

Kaylin nodded. "But it's not without risk. We know that the Barrani were dead in any way that mattered. We don't know what will happen to you and Amaldi if we break the enchantments—I didn't want to risk it without your permission."

"Could you have broken those enchantments without our presence?"

Kaylin hesitated. "You know Mrs. Erickson lives with ghosts—with actual ghosts—right?"

They nodded.

"I think they may have started the way you started—but Azoria didn't have the power of the sleeping High Halls to draw on. I think she may have attempted to draw on the power of the distant green—but whatever she used, it wasn't enough. She kidnapped four children. They died. They died, but their bodies didn't.

"Those bodies went on to search for something—they each got caught for breaking and entering—and eventually, to slaughter their immediate families, or at least the families they were living with at the time. I don't want that to happen again—and if we broke the enchantment and you weren't there to occupy your own bodies, I'm not sure what would.

"But we really don't know what she did. We don't know if, somehow, when your bodies are released they immediately experience all of the time they haven't until now. You might return to your bodies and die instantly by aging."

23

Darrono nodded, as if this was not a surprise. To Amaldi he said, "They can't tell with the Barrani. One century or ten, the Barrani trapped wouldn't age. We're the only mortals they have."

Kaylin nodded. "If we knew what would happen, we'd tell you. But right now, you're alive."

"Is that what you'd call it?" Amaldi surprised Kaylin; her voice was soft, low, a hint of anger beneath the surface of the words. Amaldi had always been the more social of the two. "Do you know what I miss?" It was clearly a rhetorical question. "I miss being able to hug people. I miss being able to help Mrs. Erickson with her buckets, to offer her an arm before she stumbles.

"I miss being able to *eat*. I miss being able to smell the baking she carries to the Halls of Law. I miss being able to sing so that other people can hear me—that was what I was known for in Berranin, before Azoria. I miss being *visible*. I miss what little relevance I had as a person in the world.

"Have you ever been so tired death seems like the better option?"

"Yes," Kaylin replied, without hesitation.

"I'm almost that tired." She didn't ask Kaylin for any explanation of her own circumstances. "Being visible had disadvantages. I remember wishing I could be invisible when the Berranin halls were noisy. But I wanted that because in my daydreams I imagined invisibility would be under my control. I miss people. Even Barrani people."

"I think she thought, initially, that she could preserve us for longer," was Darreno's quiet addition. "Had she given us immortality, or effective immortality, she would have been respected and sought-after by the Barrani who valued their aging slaves."

"Not only the Barrani," Kaylin said quietly, aware that during their time as slaves in the High Halls, Barrani were the only visible, the only important, people. That had changed; they knew it. But watching it wasn't experiencing it. Watching it, when shelter and food weren't necessary, was very different.

She wondered how they would manage were they to be introduced to Elantra as living, breathing people, and filed that away for future poking. It would only be a concern if they survived what the Avatar would attempt.

Amaldi joined Darreno, who remained standing. "Yes," she said. "We're willing to take the risk. If it helps Mrs. Erickson— if it saves Mrs. Erickson—I feel we owe her that. She's the only person to whom we've mattered since we woke this time. And if it somehow helps Mrs. Erickson's children, that would probably help her, too."

"It would," Kaylin said, rising as well. She understood that the concern of the Avatar was not a concern Amaldi or Darreno shared; if the Barrani perished, they probably wouldn't care.

The Berranin suite remained as they had first encountered it, except the doors were now plain and unmarked. Amaldi and Darreno could follow the halls the Avatar laid out; there was only one point at which they shimmered in place. The Avatar frowned, apologized, and adjusted something entirely invisible to Kaylin's eyes, and they resumed their walk down the halls.

"They're different," Amaldi said.

"Yes," the Avatar replied. "These rooms no longer occupy the physical location they once occupied, and I have strengthened the...privacy defenses that make them impassible for all but the few I choose. I believe you will find the interior almost unchanged, but if you do not, I would be very interested to hear how it differs."

Hope, somewhat indolent until that moment, sat up, complaining. He lifted a wing and placed it across Kaylin's eyes as the doors rolled open.

The rooms were the same as Kaylin remembered, as was the hall, the T-junction, and the placement of both studio and gallery.

"Terrano has investigated the studio and its various tools; he believes that there is some enduring enchantment on some of the brushes, but it's minor; one could easily pass them off as preservation magic."

"Are they preservation magics?"

Terrano shrugged. "There are differences between this enchantment and Sedarias's similar attempts. They're subtle. I wouldn't have noticed it had I not been looking. Serralyn agrees. The enchantment on the palettes, however, is different. It feels the same. If I weren't paranoid, I'd consider it harmless. The paint itself isn't enchanted.

"But...it's not normal paint, either. Serralyn spoke with the Arbiters; Kavallac feels there might be a combination of paint and enchantment that creates a larger enchantment; it might bypass the cautious. Not all of the paint is augmented,

MICHELLE SAGARA

but all has been preserved by the High Halls. Can you ask your friends—"

"Terrano wishes to know," the Avatar said to those friends, "if you know how these paints were made. Serralyn—and through her one of the Arbiters—believes that some of the pigments, some of the base sediments, may be found in the green."

Amaldi nodded. "We could, with effort, retrieve some of the plants in the green. They did not last long—not as they were. But she continued to make the attempt."

"I think she managed," Kaylin said quietly. "I'm sorry, are you both ready?"

Amaldi reached out; Darreno took her hand. To Kaylin's eye, they looked more like children than they ever had. "Yes."

The paintings were no longer shadowed by strange fog; they remained on the wall, where they had first been placed— but they were paintings now. Nothing remained within them. Only two were different when viewed through Hope's wing: Amaldi's and Darreno's.

"We should have had Serralyn meet us here," Terrano said. "She's waiting at Mrs. Erickson's, because she needs to be there if Bakkon is going to join us."

"Why did we want a *giant spider* to join us again?"

Terrano rolled eyes. "Bakkon is worried, and he wants to examine the space; he thinks that Azoria may have learned things Starrante didn't intend to teach her."

That shut down any possible argument; an image of Azoria as a spider, eating the weaker to grow strong enough to leave the darkness was enough to destroy her appetite.

Hope bit her ear, but not hard enough to draw blood. Kaylin glanced at him; he pointed his snout in the direction of the two mortals. The command was clear; she walked toward them, moving behind where they had chosen to stand, which happened to be directly in front of, and slightly between, the two paintings that represented them.

Terrano approached the paintings, standing between them. He stopped, as he had the first time he'd attempted this de construction, just out of reach of the twin nimbuses of gray, and lifted his arms to hover to the left and right. This was fine. The third arm which protruded from the center of his chest was less mundane. Neither Amaldi nor Darreno could apparently see this.

"Is your friend going to join you?" Kaylin asked the Avatar, who stood to one side of the cohort member.

"It is not necessary. What he achieved the first time, I could clearly see; unless this is very different, I believe we should be fine. Serralyn, however, did what I could not easily do."

Teela cursed—a Leontine word. Turning to Kaylin she said, "You'd better protect her." Ah, no. It wasn't to Kaylin she was speaking, but Hope. She then stepped behind Terrano, drew a deep breath, and placed her palm against the fabric of his shirt.

For some reason, watching Serralyn literally become an extension of Terrano hadn't been disturbing. Watching Teela do it felt *wrong*. Teela was part of the cohort. Kaylin knew this. But on a visceral level, Teela was Teela.

Wrong or not, she did. She grimaced, wincing as if she'd picked up a piece of hot metal with bare hands. Kaylin took a step toward them.

No. You are where you need to be, and she is where she needs to be.

Kaylin swallowed words, nodding.

You cannot be what she is; you cannot be what they are. Accept that. You can be where they are, but what Terrano now does is...

*highly unusual. Necessary. I wish I had met Azoria while she still
lived. I almost wish I had answered her call.*

"Her what?"

Hope shook his head. *Pay attention.*

Kaylin nodded. She reached out with both hands and placed
them on the shoulders of the two mortals who waited.

Terrano unraveled the binding that surrounded the canvas, just as he had the first time. He worked deliberately but
slowly; any speed gained was due to familiarity. He had a
much clearer idea of how to unravel the spell Azoria had cast.
As before, the fog was separated into distinct colors; as before,
some of those strands were obsidian. As before, once separate,
they seemed to spread: shadow vines with shadow thorns.

But there was a third thread in this mix, one absent from
the enchantments built around the Barrani portraits Kaylin
had seen.

"Yes," the Avatar said. "Yes, and no. Watch. Touch nothing."

The third strand was a pale ivory surrounded by a patina
of gold; it reminded Kaylin of her marks. She had never understood how they chose the color that they adopted when
they started to glow. She stiffened when those strands began
to struggle as Terrano worked. They then reached—slowly—
for Amaldi and Darreno.

No, Hope said, as Kaylin's hands tightened.

Amaldi and Darreno couldn't see what Kaylin could see.
They didn't apparently notice when those strands began to
twine around them. At first it was a single thread, but more
threads followed. All of the threads that Terrano teased apart,
all of the gray and the black that he slowly stripped away,
were at heart pale ivory and gold. She could see that light
only as the darker colors thinned; in some cases, they shat-

tered, shards floating into nothingness, no doubt at the intervention of the Avatar.

Only pale gold remained, and all of those strands, all of the components of that cocoon, now reached for the two mortals. Kaylin's hands were white-knuckled; they were now the only thing she could clearly see. The golden strands didn't touch her.

Kaylin.

She inhaled, bracing herself; exhaled and forced her fingers to relax. This was the decision Amaldi and Darreno had made, forced on them in the end by Azoria, by the Barrani, by their existence as slaves in the very distance past. She lifted her hands, stepped away, and lowered her arms, her hands becoming empty fists.

"Terrano," the Avatar said. "Step back."

"I'm not sure I'm finished—"

"You are finished. Step back now."

"I'm really not certain it's done—"

"An'Teela, please."

Teela grimaced, pulled her hand out of his back—literally—and then grabbed him by the arms and carried him away from the paintings before he had time to struggle or escape.

"Thank you," the Avatar said. He then turned toward the two.

Hope lifted the wing that had been plastered to her face for so much of the day. Even without the wing, Kaylin could see the golden lights that stood in the hall as if they were two glowing cocoons. As she watched, the light tightened, molding into the shape of limbs, body, neck, head—all familiar.

"Breathe," Teela said.

Kaylin exhaled the breath she hadn't even been aware she was holding. The strands that had been drawn tight by an unseen hand slowly became transparent. She could see Amaldi and Darreno appear as they faded entirely. Amaldi blinked. Her hand remained locked in Darreno's; for the first time, she tried to disentangle them. Darreno's hand tightened.

Kaylin approached them as they both blinked. Hope's wing was no longer plastered across her face, but she could see them clearly. "Amaldi?"

Amaldi turned toward Kaylin, her eyes bright and wide. She spoke. Kaylin couldn't understand a word that came out of her mouth.

"No," the Avatar said. "You would not; the language has not been spoken among your kind for a very long time." He turned to them and said, "You will find it helpful if you speak High Barrani instead."

"But she always understood us before," Amaldi then said—to the Avatar, and in the requested High Barrani.

"Yes, and that is a question for scholars. You will need to become proficient in her tongue the more traditional way. I believe it will be necessary; An'Teela believes understanding of High Barrani is not common among your kind."

Teela spoke two words; Kaylin immediately felt the sting of the Barrani Hawk's magic as a full-body slap. "Apologies if this is uncomfortable," she told Amaldi.

Amaldi blinked and took a step back, into Darreno, who had not moved. "You—you can see me?"

"I can see you now, yes." Teela turned to the Avatar.

He shook his head. "They are mortal, to me. Entirely, utterly mortal, in a way Lord Kaylin is not. We can assume, then, that the enchantment was harmless to mortals."

Kaylin's nod was slower. "We can assume that it was harmless to these two. I've got four dead children as a counterargument. Maybe she was attempting to re-create this spell; maybe she had an entirely different motivation."

"They are unharmed, and unaged; physically, their bodies

appear to have been perfectly preserved. I believe, however, that their presence—in spirit—was essential."

"Why?" It was Teela who asked.

"You could not see the enchantment as it unraveled. The power of the Halls and the power of Shadow were entwined around the...lives of the two mortals. It was not the same enchantment that entrapped the Barrani in their portraits; there, the two powers were not binding a third power. If life itself can be considered a power."

"It has been considered power historically. The Emperor frowns *very* heavily upon research related to live sacrifices." Teela glanced at paintings that no longer contained people. "Do you believe that she somehow gained power from the two mortals?"

"No more than she might have gained from her servants, although the invisibility might allow for undetected surveillance and the gathering of information."

"Do you think the bodies would have been released when the enchantment was broken?"

"I do."

"Would they have remained empty?"

"Yes." He paused, and added, "Here. Is that now your concern? Do you believe that enchantments were broken in such a way that the bodies were then occupied by something else?"

"I think that's the only possible explanation for what occurred. But...I can't see how that would have been of value to Azoria. If power couldn't be gained by human sacrifice— and I wouldn't put that beneath her—I don't understand what she was even attempting."

The Avatar nodded.

"But if we don't understand what she was attempting, we won't understand where it went wrong."

"I think you must visit this phantom house," the Avatar replied.

Kaylin frowned. "You think there are paintings in it?"

"No, that is what you suspect. I am, however, uncertain that you will be able to do what Terrano and I have done here. If it is true that your children cannot leave your Mrs. Erickson's small home, it is unlikely that you will be able to take them to the location in which they were once trapped."

Kaylin shook her head. "They're not like Amaldi and Darreno. They're dead. They're trapped. Humans aren't like Barrani or Dragons—they don't live forever. I don't know where the dead are supposed to go, but we don't return to the Lake or whatever the human analogy might be. We don't have words at our core. And most of us don't get trapped the way they've been trapped."

"Interesting. Do you not believe mortals require bodies?"

"Of course we do."

"But these ones don't?"

"I told you—they're dead."

"But present."

"Demonstrably."

"It is always a conundrum," the Avatar then said. "So much of the horror visited upon us happens because we do not accept what we are; to live peacefully, that acceptance is necessary. But if we accept limitations without question, we never excel." The Avatar gestured. "I will keep these rooms as they are; Serralyn wishes to visit when things are, as she puts it, back to normal.

"I do not believe that same decision should be reached with regards to the phantom house." He turned to fully face Kaylin. "Spike will continue to accompany you, and I will see that Amaldi and Darreno are offered rooms here." He frowned. "Spike, please assume a less visible form."

Spike seemed to notice that Hope was allowed visibility, and clearly felt this unfair; there was an exchange of clicking—speedy clicking—before Spike trembled indignantly and...vanished. She knew where Spike was because the noise continued.

Kaylin shook her head as the clicking diminished. "While they try to get their bearings, they can stay with me."

"Kitling, maybe you should ask before making decisions on their behalf—they are not children, and they may have preferences."

Darreno said, "We are not children, no. But we would prefer—if possible—to avoid residence in the High Halls at this time."

The walk home made clear that neither Amaldi nor Darreno were accustomed to actual, physical presence. Darreno didn't tend to move out of the way when people approached; he expected that they would pass through him, which was awkward. Amaldi seemed to adapt more easily; her excitement was stronger than her fear.

Helen was waiting at the door when Kaylin returned home with her two guests. She was standing in the doorway, her eyes their usual brown, her lips turned up in a welcoming smile.

"You must be Amaldi and Darreno," she said to the two visitors. "I've heard so much about you both." Her smile deepened. "Kaylin has asked me to prepare rooms for you, if you wish to accept her hospitality; you are also free to refuse. I am Helen, Kaylin's home."

Darreno frowned but said nothing.

Amaldi, however, stepped forward, extending a hand; Helen clasped it in both of hers. "Yes," she said gently, although Amaldi hadn't spoken. "I am a bit unusual. Speak in any language you like while you are here." She then lifted her head. "Dinner is waiting, if you are hungry."

It was a revelation to watch Amaldi eat. Even Darreno seemed moved by food—or rather, by his ability to actually eat it. Kaylin joined the two, but the rest of the cohort didn't; the dining room was therefore less crowded. Helen had the ability to make it smaller, but didn't; Kaylin wasn't always comfortable with shifting, unpredictable architecture.

When Terrano, impatient as always, appeared in the dining room doorway, she rose. "I'm sorry," she told her two newest guests. "I have to leave now, unless you want to listen to Terrano complain."

"I don't mind." Amaldi's voice was bright.

"I do." Darreno's was less so.

"They're exhausted," Helen said. "I will see them to their rooms when they've finished eating." To Amaldi, she added, "You will need sleep and food going forward. Normal sleep."

Mrs. Erickson was chatting with Serralyn and Severn on the front porch of her home when Kaylin and her companions arrived. Mandoran and Terrano were present, as was Teela, and Terrano had chattered so much on the walk from Helen's that Teela was audibly grinding her teeth. Mandoran didn't help. By the time they reached Mrs. Erickson's house, the sun had fully set; the moons were high.

Kaylin poked Hope, who sighed and lifted a wing to place it across her eyes.

"Do you see it?" Teela asked softly.

Kaylin nodded. In the darkness, the moons could be seen shining through the transparent outline of a much larger building.

Mrs. Erickson rose. "The children weren't comfortable

with guests tonight, and the weather was nice. I've just been chatting with Serralyn."

Terrano headed for the door, which was ajar; Teela attempted to grab him by the shoulder, but her hand passed through him; he turned and stuck his tongue out. Kaylin would have been impressed by this sterling display of maturity had she not had her own behavior in the past to compare it to.

"Terrano," she said. "It's not your home."

Terrano shrugged. To Mrs. Erickson, he said, "Is it okay if I go inside?"

"Of course!" the old woman said.

Serralyn rose as well—there were only two rickety chairs on the porch—and said, "I've been explaining what we hope to do to Mrs. Erickson."

Teela's eyes darkened, although in the evening light the difference wasn't as marked.

"Bakkon is going to join us, and most people have never seen a giant spider."

"He is not a spider," the Barrani Hawk said.

"Well, no, of course not—but he looks a *lot* like one, and I don't want his presence to cause such a huge shock that..." She trailed off, but Kaylin understood: she didn't want Mrs. Erickson to have a panic attack—or worse. "He really is a gentle person, and he wanted to come because he has some suspicions about what was done here—or what was tried." To Kaylin, she said, "Mrs. Erickson has been telling me about her friends."

"Have you seen them?"

Serralyn shook her head. "I might be able to do it if I follow Terrano—but it gives me a terrible headache, and I'm not sure that will be helpful."

"Why doesn't Terrano get headaches?"

"He *is* a headache; he doesn't get them," Teela said.

Mandoran laughed. He approached Mrs. Erickson and offered her a very correct bow, or correct if she had been Barrani. "Kaylin has said a lot about you."

"Oh, dear."

"No, it was all good. She also said you bake?"

Mrs. Erickson's smile deepened. "It happens I do, and I
didn't manage to get to the High Halls today. Come, I made
cookies. I hope you'll all eat them—they really don't age
well."

"Please wait a moment," Serralyn told the old woman. "I'll
let Bakkon know that we're all here."

"I don't have a mirror," Mrs. Erickson began.

"I don't need a mirror—Bakkon's attached a bit of web
to me, and all I have to do is pull it. He'll follow the strand
here, without walking through the streets." She glanced at
Kaylin, and added, "The Halls of Law get really busy when
people are afraid, and a lot of people are afraid of garden-
variety spiders that are utterly harmless. A Wevaran is going
to generate a lot of panicked reports."

"That makes sense. I admit I'm curious," Mrs. Erickson
replied.

She was also nervous, to Kaylin's eye. To Kaylin's surprise,
she could see the thread Serralyn mentioned; it was bound
around her wrist, so slender she'd missed it on first glance.
Serralyn tapped it gently, as if afraid it would break.

Bakkon emerged from thin air, two legs at a time, as if
he was carefully cutting a hole in reality through which he
could step. She couldn't see what lay behind him, and wondered if he could just…spit web that could portal him back
to the Academia.

Kaylin, being petty, hoped the neighbor was spying
through one of his windows.

Mrs. Erickson watched with interest as Bakkon emerged.

He lifted his foremost legs, and traced a pattern in the air. If Kaylin remembered correctly, that was the Wevaran version of a bow.

Mrs. Erickson returned a human version of a bow in response. Clearly Serralyn had explained enough about Wevaran to the old woman. Serralyn might have been impatient, but Kaylin was now grateful that the excursion to the High Halls had taken so long.

"I am pleased to meet you. I am called Bakkon by your kind."

"I am called Mrs. Erickson," she replied. "Although before I was married, I was Imelda."

"Interesting. We do not have your social customs. Which name would you prefer?"

"Serralyn tells me you are quite, quite old."

"Yes, I would be considered ancient by your kind. Or imaginary." He clicked a bit, which Kaylin interpreted as a chuckle.

"Mrs. Erickson is a name given to elders—it's a sign of respect. I wouldn't feel right, asking you to do that."

"Respect is not independent of age?"

"It's complicated. Please just call me Imelda."

"Very well. Imelda."

"Do you eat?" she asked. "I don't have a full meal, but...I have snacks, if you'd care to join the boys."

"Boys?"

"She means my friends—Terrano and Mandoran."

"Is Severn not a boy?"

"No, he is."

"Is he not your friend?"

"He is. Mrs. Erickson thinks of Severn as an adult."

"I find this very confusing," Bakkon replied. "Severn is

younger than either of your friends. Or is 'boy' not a term for an immature male?"

Teela coughed into her hand. "It is, and in this case, it is appropriate." Looking up, she said, "They take no offense, Mrs. Erickson; they are determined to remain immature, regardless of actual age."

The door to Mrs. Erickson's home had not been designed for Wevaran. It was wide enough that enterprising carpenters could maneuver their wares into the house, but Bakkon wasn't furniture. He frowned; he could retract his side legs to a certain extent, but the doorframe was too narrow.

"If you could move away from the door," he finally said, "I will enter the house in a slightly different way."

"Bad idea," Terrano said, coming out of the kitchen. His eyes were red and black; from a distance it looked like they were bleeding. These weren't normal Barrani colors, but that was fair; Terrano wasn't normal Barrani, either. "Very, *very* bad idea."

Bakkon froze. "Let me test something. It will cause no damage to your home, Imelda."

Bakkon stepped away from the doorframe, allowing Kaylin, Severn, and Teela to enter; Terrano, Mandoran, and Serralyn had already followed Mrs. Erickson in.

"Please move away from the door." A series of clicks enveloped Bakkon's syllables.

"What do you think he meant to do?" Kaylin asked Terrano.

"Portal past the door," Terrano replied. He glanced at Kaylin. "Do you feel comfortable in this house?"

"It's a house," she replied.

"You don't feel nauseous? You don't feel dizzy?"

"No. Except for in that one room."

Bakkon began the particularly disturbing sounds that meant

he was about to spit web, which was how the Wevaran formed portals.

"This house isn't normal."

"What precisely do you mean, not normal? We can all see it, and I walk into it the normal way. Mrs. Erickson lives here, and she can leave and return. And bake."

Bakkon spit webbing through the doorway, aiming for the floor some two yards away from where Kaylin now stood. The web didn't land. Between leaving the Wevaran's mandibles and hitting the floor, it vanished.

"Can you do that again?" Kaylin's words exactly overlapped Terrano's.

"I can," Bakkon replied, "but I think it risky. Terrano is correct. There is something very unusual about this 'normal' home if my understanding of mortal dwellings is not lacking."

"Do you know where your web actually landed?" Kaylin asked.

"I am attempting to follow the strand—but I do not believe I will be able to answer that question; the strand is... entrapped, I believe."

"Can someone follow it back to you?"

"A very good question. I will investigate the building from the outside. Serralyn?"

She nodded instantly and headed toward the door to join him.

The door slammed shut in her face.

24

Mrs. Erickson looked at the closed door. She then turned to her guests. "I'm sure it must have been wind," she said, in the least convincing version of certainty Kaylin had ever heard. She turned toward the door, but Teela stepped in front of her, joined by Serralyn.

"I don't believe the door should be touched," Teela said, in official Hawk voice.

"Do you think it's dangerous?"

"I think it could be."

Mrs. Erickson looked doubtful. "Cookies?" she asked Terrano and Mandoran.

Mandoran smiled. "I'd love some."

Terrano, however, was now staring at the door. His eyes continued red; his hands became transparent. "I *really* wish he hadn't done that," he said.

Serralyn was pale; her hands were in fists. "I brought him here," she whispered.

"I think he's trapped on the outside."

Kaylin turned to Mrs. Erickson. "I need to open a window." She hesitated, and then said, "No, Terrano needs to open a window."

"You want me to tell Bakkon to go home?"

"Immediately, yes."

"If he asks why?"

"Tell him it's Starrante's fault."

Serralyn's eyes rounded, which was fine; they reddened instantly, as if all of the small blood vessels had burst at once, which was way more disturbing. But of course they did. She was the student at the Academia, and she was the one who had discussed Azoria's phantom home with the Wevaran. He had come because of her. And she was part of the cohort; what Terrano knew, they all knew; what he could do, they could— with greater or lesser difficulty—learn.

As if she could hear the thought, Serralyn said, "Don't worry; my eyes are fine. This is easy. Some of the other stuff Terrano does is…not. He's always been the most flexible of us—but he can often overfocus. There's a saying about trees mortals have?"

"He can't see the forest for the trees?" It was Mrs. Erickson who answered.

"Very much like that, yes. What he sees, he does see—he has a pretty garbage imagination."

"Hey!"

"But sometimes he doesn't pick up the nuances of what he sees; he can't build a bigger picture. Don't look at me like that, I wasn't the one who said it first. So I've been asked to observe as well. I'm not certain about sending Bakkon home, though."

"He might be in danger there?"

"It depends. Webs aren't meant to be spit out and retracted— if they were, we'd call them tongues. But the way a Wevaran moves, the comfort a Wevaran takes in geography, is rooted in the webbing. If he spit something into this space and he can't immediately sever it, something might be able to crawl along the webbing he's built, and if they can, they're going to find both Bakkon and anyone else in his immediate vicinity."

"You're worried that Azoria somehow took those long-ago discussions with Starrante and Androsse to heart."

"Yes."

Bakkon had been quite upset with Starrante when he heard what Starrante had discussed; Kaylin remembered that much.

"Which means you're worried that she's here, somehow."

"You're not?"

"I've passed beyond worried to terrified."

Serralyn nodded. "Mrs. Erickson doesn't seem to be affected by Azoria."

Mrs. Erickson was listening to the conversation, although she did pay attention to Mandoran's chipped plate, filling it almost as if gentle hospitality was a habit. "I'm fine," she said. "I've lived here all my life."

"So have the children," Kaylin replied. "Where are they?"

"Jamal is probably in the back room. He wasn't best pleased that I had guests."

No, of course not.

"He wasn't terrified of Serralyn, though—not the way he was of the corporal."

"And Terrano?"

"I don't think male Barrani invoke the same fear. And Serralyn seems almost human in comportment. Why are you asking about the children?"

"I think it's important that we keep an eye on them now," Kaylin replied. She looked at her arms; the marks had begun to glow a steady gold. "I'll go find them if you want to head into the dining room with everyone else. I think Terrano has opened the window there."

Terrano had not only opened the window, but was leaning out of the frame. He was conversing with Bakkon. In clicks and gestures. Kaylin blinked. He had sprouted an extra pair of arms in the interim, and was waving them gracefully and somewhat precisely.

Mrs. Erickson blinked and rubbed her eyes as she looked at Terrano's back. "Well," she said, voice shaky, "Serralyn *did* warn me that Terrano was highly unusual. Does he do this all the time?"

"Only when it's necessary." Kaylin glanced at Serralyn's eyes; they were very disturbing. Mrs. Erickson, however, hadn't noticed them.

Serralyn nodded. She joined Terrano by the window, but didn't sprout arms or otherwise attempt to speak to the Wevaran in his native tongue. Nor did she speak Barrani; it was as if she was now afraid of what might be listening. The natural Wevaran tongue was less easily translated—although Azoria might have learned it, if anyone else could. Barrani memory was perfect, but recall required a level of concentration; if Azoria listened from somewhere, her attention would be on their discussion.

"Don't worry," Serralyn said. "The giant spider won't hurt anyone."

Kaylin blinked in surprise, but nodded. She then turned and said, "I'm sorry, I got distracted. I'll go get the kids." She turned on her heel.

Severn said, "I'll go with you."

She started to answer but forced her mouth to close. *You can't see them.*

No. But something changed when Bakkon attempted to test the waters. I'm not sure what Terrano saw or sensed, but the house has changed.

The marks on Kaylin's arms had ratcheted up in brilliance, but they remained gold. *I'm worried about the children*, she told him. *They wouldn't enter the room that contains the painting—but it wasn't just opposition; they became almost catatonic with terror.*

Severn nodded as Kaylin reached the room in which Jamal—according to Mrs. Erickson—went to sulk and vent his displeasure.

If something has changed in this house—if the door suddenly slammed shut at someone else's will—it might affect the children.

How? The question was asked in Severn's usual pragmatic tone; it held no ridicule or disbelief.

I don't know. But they were trapped in this house—the figurative door has always existed for them. I don't think they were killed in this house—but I could be totally wrong. They were lucky, in a fashion: Mrs. Erickson could always see them.

Severn nodded. *According to the Arkon—the new Arkon*, he added to lessen possible misinterpretation, *that is her power.*

Do you think Azoria knew? Do you think that's why she chose Mrs. Erickson?

The house was transferred to her family before she was born. There was nothing that would indicate magical ability to anyone. Azoria may have been able to detect something that we couldn't detect.

How? Sanabalis strongly implied that there were different tests—and those required the most protected room hidden in the palace. There's no test she could have made that wouldn't be seen or remembered—certainly by Mrs. Erickson. Although I hate to admit it, I don't think the Imperial Mage responsible for dismissing her magical aptitude or potential failed to perform the usual tests.

Good, Severn said, and meant it; she could feel the relief.

Good?

I think there's a reason that Mrs. Erickson never fell to the possible enchantments Azoria placed in this "normal" home. I was curious about one thing, and I did a full audit of tax and property Records. With permission, he added, as he caught wind of her surprise. *The home was transferred to the Swindons—to Mrs. Erickson's mother—when she was pregnant. Care to guess who sealed the transfer?*

Azoria?

Yes. According to the paperwork, she gave a parcel of the lot she owned to the Swindons—and she allowed them to build a house suitable to the lot itself. A small house. Before you ask, no, we have no Records about how the house was constructed, but we do know who owned it. Legally, it now belongs to Mrs. Erickson. In the past, however, it belonged to Azoria.

You think she…approached Mrs. Erickson's parents?

When they were expecting, yes.

You think she tried to do something to Mrs. Erickson before she was even born?

Severn didn't answer, which was answer enough.

How did she even meet the Ericksons?

There's no information in regard to that, and no further legal Records of any kind surrounding them. It's likely—but not impossible—that Azoria did occupy the house that once stood here, and that she hired human servants to tend to daily tasks. If Mrs. Erickson's mother was one of those people, she might have offered the land and the small house—in keeping with servant houses historically—as a gift, perhaps a wedding gift. This is entirely conjecture. I haven't had the chance to ask Mrs. Erickson herself.

No—things have already gone pear-shaped. We can ask her later.

"Jamal? Esme?" No answer. "Callis? Katie?" She looked

over her shoulder at her partner. "Either they're not here or I can no longer see them."

"Should we ask Mrs. Erickson?"

Kaylin shook her head. "I want Mrs. Erickson to stay by Terrano and Serralyn if at all possible. We should really move her to somewhere safe—but I don't want to risk opening that door."

Severn nodded. He, too, thought there was a chance the door would no longer open into Elantra.

It was Mandoran who joined them; Kaylin half expected Terrano. "You haven't found the kids?"

She shook her head.

"Mrs. Erickson is starting to worry."

"She can stand in line," Kaylin snapped, and then instantly felt guilty. "Sorry."

"You want to feel guilty, you're going to have to work harder," was Mandoran's cheerful reply. "You've got *nothing* on Sedarias." His wince made clear Sedarias didn't appreciate the comparison. "She thinks the children were trapped here for a reason. They were afraid of the painting; they couldn't leave the house. I think any attempt to leave the house might land us someplace we don't want to be—but Sedarias thinks otherwise."

"What does she think?"

"She thinks this house is still attached to, still part of, the phantom house you can see with the aid of your familiar. If it's the house we want to examine, she thinks our only option is to open that door."

"The windows still opened to the street, though."

"Yes. Bakkon has decided to remain where he is, which gives us a window: we probably don't want him standing outside of Mrs. Erickson's house when the sun rises. Whatever Serralyn was afraid of, he's considered, and he's decided that there's a risk. He also had choice words—according to Terrano—to say about Starrante, so I imagine the Arbiter is going to get what passes for an earful if we manage to escape things unscathed.

"I'm sorry I can't help you look for the children. I've never gotten the hang of the eye shifts. I can shift my entire body in certain ways, but I can't just shift random parts of it."

"But you're…"

"Yes. I can do *most* of what Terrano can do, and if anything had happened to Terrano, I'd've been next in line to carry out our plans. I don't have to warp my eyes for most things, though."

"Why does it involve a change of eyes?"

"He could explain it better. Or at all. But it's a recent addition to his metamorphic stable. I think he picked up the idea from Serralyn's contacts with the Wevaran. He can see the ghosts here if his eyes go strange. Serralyn can as well but she sees other things when she does it; she finds it really, really uncomfortable. She's doing it because she actually likes Mrs. Erickson. And Bakkon. She's really worried."

As he spoke, Kaylin headed to the living room—the other room possessed of a window. If a giant spider was present, she would have expected Jamal to be here, staring out through the windows he kept promising not to break again. None of the children were here, either.

Kaylin understood why Serralyn was worried; she was worried herself. Mrs. Erickson *had* power, but absolutely no knowledge, no way of using that power. Her ability seemed to affect the dead—or the ghosts—but it was entirely without effort on her part.

She could see Severn's blades in a fashion that even Kaylin couldn't. She could see Amaldi and Darreno, something Kaylin couldn't do without the direct intervention of her familiar; even Terrano required intense concentration and physical modifications to do so.

The two had been affected by Azoria's magic. Azoria had taken a flower—possibly multiple flowers—from the green itself. And the weapon that Severn carried was tied to the green.

Mrs. Erickson hadn't even been born when Azoria first came into contact with her, through her mother. What had Azoria done? Kaylin couldn't believe that there was no intent in the gifting of this house to the newly married, newly pregnant mortal. But what? What had her intent been?

If we understand the criminal's motivations, and we know what their capabilities are, we are far more likely to find the evidence the law requires. Who had said that? Marcus, she thought. Marcus, in the very early days.

But she didn't understand the motivations. She didn't understand the capabilities. She didn't even know if Azoria was truly alive.

Focus on the power, Severn said quietly. *It's like following the money, to the Barrani. If you believe the Consort, Azoria attempted to either absorb or destroy the Lake. There are two possible reasons for that—but the most likely...*

She wanted the power. She thought she could somehow absorb the words in the Lake and become more powerful. Kaylin considered Androsse. *She could have wanted the power of the Ancestors. Androsse's ancient kin.*

Androsse's unstable ancient kin, yes.

Her experiments with the Barrani in the portraits appear to have been successful on one front: they were drained of life. I don't know if that was done before she broke through the protective barriers that sur-

round the Lake, but I think it had to be. There's no way she would
have had the freedom to experiment after she was caught.

Severn nodded.

*So she must have had some reason to believe she could do it, that
it would work. If she could make it work with individual Barrani,
she had no reason to believe it wouldn't work with the Lake. But
there's something we're missing. I think she could absorb power from
the Barrani—but maybe she couldn't absorb the actual words. If what
she wanted wasn't simply power via sacrifice...* Kaylin headed up
the stairs.

*If she wanted to be as powerful as Androsse...maybe what she
wanted was to take the words and to somehow combine them in her
core? She wanted the complicated and intricate True Names of the
Ancestors, and believed she understood True Words well enough to
somehow build a new name for herself?*

"Mandoran, can you run something by Serralyn?"

"Sure. What?"

Kaylin explained the one possible theory that had begun
to cohere from all of the disparate bits and pieces of information she'd been given over the last several days.

Mandoran's normal Barrani eyes darkened. "She's cursing
up a storm—on the inside—and smacking herself in the face."

"That means she agrees?"

"That means she agrees. She reminds you that the Wevaran
develop their name by eating their siblings; the words that become their True Name exist in disparate pieces; they come
together to form a whole only when one of the siblings has
devoured literally all of the others. I used to think the Lake of
Life was a terrible idea, but the more I find out about other racial birthing customs, the more grateful I feel that we have it."

"You can say that again. Ask Serralyn one other thing.
What do mortals—wordless humans—have to do with all

of this? How can they fit in? Why did their bodies not die when they...died?"

"She thinks there's one possible answer. If we consider Azoria's attempts to capture the actual words at the core of the Barrani a failure, she nonetheless drained them of life, of life force. Power, but not innate power, not intrinsic power; it did nothing to change her base nature. She thinks that if Azoria could have absorbed the Lake and made out of it a new name for herself, she would have been like unto a god."

"Which god?"

"What?"

"Well, *a* god. The Barrani don't really talk about gods much."

"She asks you not to be 'so bloody literal' at a time like this. But...she thinks that if Azoria somehow managed to damage her own name, and she was adept enough not to die, she might be like the ones we call vampires now. If her name cannot sustain her, it is possible the lives of even mortals can, for a time."

"But this was a century ago. Or more."

"She has no other guesses, and she hasn't studied forbidden magics; she can't tell you what the value of a human life is worth when it comes to Barrani years." It was a grim thought. If the children had been murdered a century ago, each of their potential lives could cover that time period—but the *bodies* hadn't died; the bodies had been executed.

"Serralyn says: being alive is complicated."

The upstairs yielded no children's ghosts; the only room Kaylin didn't thoroughly check was the room in which the painting hung. She did stand in the open doorway, but she didn't enter. Mandoran cursed, and drifted slightly farther in; his curse wasn't aimed at the two Hawks he'd been shadowing.

"This place is…really messed up," he said. "Even looking at it is giving me a headache."

"Why?"

"It's like she's taken a room and sliced it into layers and moved those layers into different planes, while insisting they visually overlap. It is really, really ugly."

The room didn't look like that to Kaylin—or Severn. "I've stood in that room before."

"I don't see how."

"So did Teela."

"Then we can assume the room has changed somehow. This would not be a safe place to enter at the moment—at least not for any of us. You might manage; Severn might manage. The scientist in me wants to tell you to give it a try and see what happens." He winced again. Clearly one of the cohort didn't find any humor in the suggestion, which strongly implied Sedarias.

"Fine." Kaylin exhaled. She was worried about the children, which was ridiculous—they were already dead. But the worry had grown much, much stronger as they'd searched. It wasn't like Jamal—who defined possessive—to be so absent when Mrs. Erickson invited visitors into the house. Esme was usually visible as well, but Katie and Callis were far more timid; had it only been the two missing, she wouldn't have worried so much.

But Jamal? No.

"The children were terrified of this room; they wouldn't enter it, but they wouldn't talk about it, either. They'd just go almost catatonic for a while—according to Mrs. Erickson. She hasn't said they've shown up, has she?"

"No."

"Can you check?"

"Serralyn can." Pause. "No. She's worried. I mean, Mrs. Erickson is worried."

"Can you ask Serralyn to ask Bakkon how he feels about the front door?"

"He considers it very unwise to touch it."

She spit out a bit of Leontine. Why was life like this? "Ask him how he feels about *us* opening the door and leaving through it. I don't think it's going to take us outside the house—but I think further in might be our only option."

"He asks why you consider this wise."

"We don't have a lot of choices. I suppose we could try to leave through the window—but Mrs. Erickson isn't young, and she's going to find it a lot more difficult than a door. I'm also really worried about the kids. There has to be some reason they've never been able to leave."

The pause was longer. "Bakkon feels that there is a high probability that the front door—for those contained within the building—will not open to the porch; he urges caution. His attempt to portal through the window was a failure, and he is unwilling to try again—he feels that part of the space itself is slightly familiar—but it's off, it's tainted."

Kaylin turned to Hope. "Well?"

The door. His next words surprised her. *Bring Mrs. Erickson, if she is willing to take the risk.*

Kaylin was *not* willing to take the risk. "She's too old to be fighting."

Not all fights require the vigor of youth, was the acid reply. *But I will not argue if you feel her home is somehow safer.*

"I hate it when you make a good point."

Mrs. Erickson's small front hall wasn't meant to hold as many people as it now did. Terrano had drawn away from the window. "Bakkon says he can hide himself from the eyes of those who have no magical ability—but he feels it necessary to remain here until more information is forthcoming. The idea that something might traverse his personal webs has given him hives, not that you'd be able to see them given chitin and hair. I think we might be able to see how the Wevaran fought, though."

"Why?"

"Why do you think? If we all get out of this safely, he's going to murder Starrante."

"Can we sic him on Androsse instead?"

Serralyn snorted. "The Arbiters can't leave the library, and anyone who is stupid enough to attack them *in* the library deserves whatever they get."

"You should remain on the Erickson side," Teela said. "You can speak with Bakkon, and we can—hopefully—maintain that connection."

"If we can't, I'll be on this side. Any research I've done won't be accessible."

"No. But Terrano is our best scout, for obvious reasons."

The rest of the discussion was conducted in the cohort group mind.

Mrs. Erickson stepped into the silence. She looked at Kaylin, and held out both of her hands. "I can't find the children," she whispered.

Kaylin nodded. "I couldn't, either. They're not upstairs. They're not in the bad room. They don't seem to be anywhere."

The old woman's eyes went to the closed door. "Do you think they're there?"

Kaylin hesitated. She did, but she didn't want Mrs. Erickson to panic. "It's possible—but they couldn't leave the house, remember?"

"Dear, I'm old, not deaf. Serralyn believes these buildings are connected—the door no longer leads outside."

"They didn't open it."

"They don't have to open internal doors, either. If they left, I don't think they left by their own choice—they would have said goodbye."

Kaylin wanted to argue. She couldn't. Hope had said she should bring Mrs. Erickson. She hadn't won that argument, and she knew, given Mrs. Erickson's expression, that she had even less chance of winning this one.

"Listen to Terrano or Teela. If they shout an order, obey it."

Mrs. Erickson nodded. "You know that I can see them. You know that I can calm them down if it's necessary."

Kaylin nodded, glancing at Teela. She expected Teela to argue in her stead, but Teela nodded. She, too, felt that Mrs. Erickson's presence would be helpful. Somehow.

No. She doesn't believe that—but Teela has never been good with children. She's concerned that if Mrs. Erickson remains she's in danger. Mrs. Erickson was clearly a target—but we don't know what Azoria hoped to gain. And no one wanted Azoria—or what was left of Azoria—to gain anything.

She turned to Mrs. Erickson. "We'll find the children."

"I hope so," was the soft reply.

Mrs. Erickson had never lived in a house without ghosts. They were part of the childhood she remembered, part of the childhood no mortal could remember, and part of all the rest of the various events of her life. She'd been worried about leaving them behind when she eventually passed away—but she hadn't considered that somehow, these stalwart and often annoying companions would leave first, without warning.

There was more nervous bickering, which almost all of the cohort seemed comfortable with, the exception being Teela. It was decided—grudgingly—that Serralyn would remain behind for at least as long as it took to determine whether or not the name bond would hold across the two spaces now separated by one closed door.

Teela glanced at Severn; he nodded. She then gestured. Kaylin's hair stood on end, but she accepted it without complaint; Teela had chosen to open the door at a relatively safe distance using magic. Kaylin would have done the same had she been skilled enough.

The door opened, and as Bakkon had predicted, it didn't open onto the porch.

"Why Androsse?" Teela asked, as she approached the door, her movements slow and deliberate. Another wave of magic slapped Kaylin's skin, and again, she made no complaints; she knew what Teela was now looking for.

"The Ancestors—yours, and couldn't you guys come up with a better name?—had multiple words at their core. Whole sentences, maybe more. It's the reason they could fight the way they fought: they can exist in multiple spaces at once," Kaylin said.

"So can the cohort, and they're not possessed of multiple words."

"No, but…"

"But?"

"They were altered by the *regalia*, as you well know. Look, I'm not certain that what she's built here has much to do with having sentences instead of single words. But I think she felt Androsse and his people had vastly more power because of the genesis of their life force. I think you guys prove that's not the case—you practically existed without your names; there was a very, *very* tenuous link to them.

"Still, I think Androsse imparted the usual arrogant better-than-you-pathetic-descendants garbage, and she bought it. I'm not saying it's about power, exactly—but the Ancestors were definitely more flexible. They could do things Barrani can't normally do.

"I think Starrante's stories of the birth and coming-of-age of his own kin—and the Wevaran do have words, but to be honest, I have no idea how many—possibly suggested a different avenue to gaining them. Her first attempt on the Lake may have been her attempt to turn the *Lake* into the hunting ground of the immature Wevaran."

"And all of this is just guesswork."

"It's good guesswork," Teela replied, meaning she agreed with it.

"Let me scout ahead," Terrano said, as Teela reached the doorframe. When Teela glanced over her shoulder, he added, "You know how hard it is to trap or cage me. I'm not sure what we're going to find—it may be a boring, normal house."

"Definitely not normal," Kaylin told him. "And I could use a bit of boring."

Terrano passed through the frame. Kaylin was half expecting the door to slam shut on his back, but it didn't. Teela was in the way.

The door didn't hit her—she was prepared for that; it bounced off an invisible barrier. The doorknob left a small indent in the wall.

Hope squawked. Teela gestured. Light formed in a ball in the Barrani Hawk's hand; she tightened her fingers around it and then pitched it through the door's frame. Light instantly flooded the hall.

"Give us a little warning!" Terrano shouted.

The lower lighting in Mrs. Erickson's hall gave way to much harsher, brighter light. In it, Kaylin could see very

Barrani architecture, which confirmed her opinion that Mrs. Erickson's family home had always been a servant's home.

Azoria's front foyer was built of stone and marble; the ceilings couldn't be seen from the doorway, although a staircase, winding its way toward the heights, was visible. It reminded Kaylin a bit of the West March; the stairs twined around a central pillar. The pillar was of stone, but it was a darker shade than the pale stone used in the High Halls.

If Kaylin had reached this foyer in either the very wealthy parts of town or the High Halls, she wouldn't have blinked twice—but this building occupied no physical space in what she generally called reality.

"Terrano?"

"I'm here. I'm almost blind, but I'm here. Give me a couple of minutes. Also: don't touch the door."

"What do you see?"

"It's trapped. There are strands woven into the surface on this side in a pattern. So far, only the door seems to be problematic."

"Yes. It almost slammed shut behind you."

"I think it's safe to enter—I can't promise we can get out the same way. I think the door opens and closes a portal."

"It's not a portal," Kaylin said. "Or not a normal one. I don't feel anything like portal space. Teela?"

Teela walked into the foyer. "You're right. There's no portal."

That would explain a few things—chief of which was the portrait room that no one, until Kaylin and Teela, had entered for decades. Somehow the buildings remained connected, even when the front door exited onto the porch.

"I've got a painting further in," Terrano said.

"Enchanted?"

"Not in any way I can see. It should be safe to look at. Serralyn can hear me; so can Sedarias, which means I can hear her. Bakkon doesn't want her to follow, though."

"Why?"

"He's afraid the door will close, trapping us all in what he now calls Azoria's web."

25

"He wants her to stay behind to open it if it slams shut?"

Terrano nodded. "While it's true the door is likely to open to the porch and the street now, he believes he can interfere in a way that would allow Serralyn to open the door to this place. Or reopen it, if we're stuck here."

Kaylin glanced at Teela. The Barrani Hawk shook her head. "If I were willing to remain here, I could keep the door wedged open. I can maintain the spell from a distance, but not indefinitely, and it would take some concentration." Given her expression, it was a long way of saying she wasn't willing to be a living door wedge.

"Can we, I don't know, pull up one of those stairs or something and physically wedge it open instead?"

Severn coughed into his hand.

"We could try. It's a remarkably mundane solution."

"I'm a remarkably mundane person."

Mandoran laughed.

"It's not like Azoria can storm into the Halls of Law and accuse us of property damage."

"True. It might be easier to find something in Mrs. Erickson's living room than it would be to disassemble parts of the stairs on this side."

"Mrs. Erickson?"

Mrs. Erickson nodded.

"Severn will go with you; he can carry whatever furniture you choose to risk."

She chose to risk a dining room hutch which was a lot heavier than a chair. Mandoran went out to help Severn move it, which involved removing its contents first. Even empty, it was heavy. Between the two of them, they dragged the hutch into the doorframe, which left very little space to maneuver around. Mrs. Erickson returned to the foyer before they placed the hutch in the doorway; Severn carried the foyer end, and Mandoran slid between frame and hutch, elongating himself to do so.

Serralyn didn't follow. She saw them through and then returned to the dining room window. Bakkon had, according to Severn and Mandoran, moved his bulk to the porch, so Serralyn didn't have to lean out the window and shout; they were conversing. Neither were certain the mundane solution would be a solution, which is the only reason Serralyn chose to stay.

Terrano hadn't taken the stairs; he'd decided to investigate the first floor. There were side doors in the main foyer area, but he avoided those, choosing instead to head past the staircase into the hall beyond it. It was a very, very Barrani hall; it would have been perfectly at home in the High Halls.

Kaylin didn't understand why the Barrani were so enamored of high ceilings. Probably because they never had to worry about cleaning them. Regardless, these were tall enough she could only see the ceiling in the distance; if she wanted to see the ceiling above her head, she'd be better off lying flat on the ground and looking up.

"I've checked the ceilings," Terrano told them. "The light is magical in nature, but it's normal magic. There doesn't seem to be much in the way of interactive enchantments beyond the door itself—at least not on this level. But this hall is interesting. Look at the walls."

Kaylin nodded. Ahead, at what appeared to be the halfway mark, she could see alcoves in the wall; they were well lit, probably by the same magic Terrano had detected in the ceiling. Or so she assumed.

But as she approached them, she could see that they contained framed paintings.

Hope's wing tightened against her upper face. The alcoves weren't symmetrical across the two sides of the halls; they were staggered. She came to the first one and realized she was holding her breath only when she exhaled. The painting was of a Barrani woman.

The painting looked like a painting when viewed without Hope's wing. It looked the same when viewed through the wing, but the little monster insisted that she examine it with his wing—by smacking her face with it. "Can you give me a hint that doesn't involve smacking my face?" she snapped.

"You can't see a difference?" Teela asked.

"No. It's a well-lit alcove. A portrait of a Barrani woman hangs on the wall beneath the light."

"I believe I understand the problem," the Barrani Hawk said. "Terrano. Light?"

"I can see the light without the wing, Teela."

"There's no light," Terrano said. "The ambient light of the hall, yes. The light above the painting, no. But you can see it with or without the wing?"

She nodded, looking at the marks on her arms; they had

continued a steady glow, and she realized as she looked that they were the color of the light she could see, winged or unwinged.

Terrano, however, had returned to the alcove and was now examining the lighting slowly. He shook his head. "I don't want to mutate my actual eyes, but whatever it is you're seeing, I can't see."

It was Mrs. Erickson who said, voice soft, "It's a ghost. There's a ghost trapped there."

Kaylin turned to Mrs. Erickson, remembering clearly what had happened the last time unexpected ghosts had responded to her presence. She then turned to the painting. "It's a Barrani woman."

Mrs. Erickson nodded. "It isn't a Barrani ghost." She stepped toward the painting and lifted a trembling arm. The children who lived trapped in 14 1/2 Orbonne had always been visible to Kaylin; she couldn't see the ghosts Mrs. Erickson saw now. She could see the light detach itself from the height of the alcove at Mrs. Erickson's approach; it traveled to the old woman's palm.

Since all present knew about her ability to see ghosts—and even believed in it—Mrs. Erickson wasn't worried about appearing to be delusional. "I'm Imelda," she said. "What's your name?"

As she spoke, the marks on Kaylin's arms brightened. Kaylin, who could see Jamal and the children, could now see a dim, transparent woman who had placed her hand in Mrs. Erickson's, adjusting the position when their palms failed to connect. She was older than Kaylin, but younger than Mrs. Erickson. All color had been leeched from her, but her hair was long, her cheeks delicate, her chin pointed; her arms were slender as were her fingers.

Kaylin could see her lips move, but couldn't hear the words; Mrs. Erickson could.

"I'm not trapped, dear, and I'm not sure if you can see the others, but if you can, these are my friends. We're trying to free the people trapped here."

The ghost could see her friends, and she froze at the sight of the Barrani, her hand obviously tightening.

"I don't know when you came here," Mrs. Erickson said quietly. "I imagine it was a long time ago. Corporal Teela is a Hawk. She works for the Halls of Law. But she's here because she understands magic in a way most of us don't. This is Terrano, and this is Mandoran. The young man is Corporal Handred.

"And this is my friend, Kaylin Neya. She's also a Hawk. You can come with us; you don't have to stay here."

The ghost nodded; to Kaylin's eyes, she seemed close to tears. As if she were much younger than the age she appeared to be, she followed Mrs. Erickson.

All of the paintings that were surrounded by this soft nimbus of light lost that light as the party slowly progressed down the hall. The ghosts remained invisible to everyone but Mrs. Erickson and Kaylin, but they couldn't speak to Kaylin; she couldn't hear them. Nor could she touch them, as she had touched—had carried—the ghostly words.

Only once did Mrs. Erickson react with shock. "Kaylin," she whispered. "Kaylin, can you see her?"

Kaylin nodded.

"That's—that's the woman. That's the woman who painted our family portrait." Her voice was a whisper of sound; she knew it was rude to speak about other people when they were actually present, something all of the Barrani in Kaylin's life could stand to learn.

Kaylin had believed that Azoria had approached the Erickson family under an illusory guise. Looking at Mrs. Erickson, she could no longer believe that. But she couldn't believe that the woman whose ghost occupied this hall had been responsible for the painting, either. Azoria had occupied the woman's empty body, wearing it as if it were clothing.

Mrs. Erickson attempted to speak with the painter, but the woman remembered neither Mrs. Erickson—as a child—or the painting in question. To her, Mrs. Erickson was a stranger. Or possibly a savior.

In the end, Mrs. Erickson had gathered a dozen ghosts. None of them were children. Something had gone wrong with the children. Something had gone wrong with Mrs. Erickson, whose painting remained unoccupied, if one didn't count a warped and distorted flower.

This woman's physical body had entered Mrs. Erickson's life after the children. Were the children the experiments? Were they chosen because of their youth, because their bodies could, in theory and without mass murder, exist for decades before they would have to be discarded due to age?

Kaylin considered this as she patiently waited for Mrs. Erickson to speak to each ghost. None of these ghosts were children. One was Kaylin's age, but most were a handful of years older.

The cohort had been exposed to the *regalia* as children. The results of that exposure were behind the creation of laws that expressly and permanently forbade such exposure going forward.

Maybe human children were similar, somehow, to the cohort: too young to be fully formed—if that was even a possibility for mortals, given how much age and experience changed them. She couldn't hear these ghosts; she couldn't ask

Mrs. Erickson their names and rush off to the Halls of Law Records to see if these people appeared in Missing Persons— or worse, in legal files about their executions for mass murder.

But...they were here. They weren't in Mrs. Erickson's house. They served a purpose; Kaylin couldn't imagine that it was a purpose they themselves had any say in choosing.

She glanced at Mrs. Erickson and her huddle of moving ghosts. Mrs. Erickson's quiet voice was a constant stream of gentle words, first to one, and then to another. Interestingly enough, the ghosts could, apparently, see and hear each other.

The hall came to an abrupt end at a T-junction, but aside from a cursory glance to the left and right, the halls that continued were of far less interest than the last of the paintings hung in this hall. All of the other paintings had been portraits; the hall seemed to have been designed to house them. This, too, was a portrait—but it was much larger than life; it was of a Barrani woman.

The background was not landscape as Kaylin understood it; it was almost, but not quite, formless—the fog of the outlands; the fog that existed as material from which sentient buildings created everything. She could almost swear that fog was moving. In its center, as if she were the heart of a building herself, stood a Barrani woman. Her eyes were not Barrani eyes, but everything else about her was: her raven hair, her perfect skin, her relative height.

All of the ghosts huddled around Mrs. Erickson froze in place, but Kaylin didn't require their reactions to know what she was facing: this was Azoria Berranin. She had painted herself.

Through Hope's wing, Kaylin saw no hint of the enchantments with which Azoria bound the Barrani in the High Halls; she saw no hint of the darker enchantment that hovered around the painting she had made of the Erickson family. This was a painting on a very, very strange canvas.

"Oh, dear," Mrs. Erickson said, in the softest of voices. She turned to Kaylin. "I think we should go upstairs before we make any hasty decisions."

Hasty decisions? Kaylin frowned. "What do you see when you look at the painting?"

"I see a door in the center of the painting, encompassed by Azoria. You don't see it?"

"None of us see it."

"I can," Terrano said.

"Fine. None of us with the eyes we were born with can see it." She exhaled. "Terrano, scout upstairs?"

"Probably a waste of time," he said; he clearly wanted to go through the door almost no one else could see. The fact that he hadn't done so meant Sedarias did *not* want him to go through said door.

He dragged his feet away from the painting, complaining bitterly.

Mandoran grimaced. "I'll go with him. I'm not certain he won't get himself into trouble if he's left on his own." He grinned at Kaylin. "Serralyn's suggestion."

Kaylin then turned her full attention to the painting. Hope, rigid on her shoulder, was staring at it as well. He squawked. Kaylin reflexively covered the ear closest to his mouth.

"Don't worry about Terrano," Teela told her. "He knows this entire building could be trapped, and he knows how to recognize and evade traps most of us will never see."

"I wasn't. I don't have a sense that Azoria is in this picture— but I have a very strong sense that this is not a door we should open. Not yet."

Hope crooned.

"When?"

Kaylin shrugged, uneasy now. "Let's go upstairs. I want to find Jamal."

"You expect him to be here?"

"I think he must be. The house opened up before we opened the door—it's possible the kids were drawn here. Or worse." She hesitated. "The ghosts that are trapped here serve a designated purpose."

"And the children didn't?"

Kaylin glanced uneasily at Mrs. Erickson. She didn't reply.

The stairs were solid; if the building had been unoccupied for a century, age hadn't troubled any of it. It was the silence that made it feel creepy. Yes, she had once lived alone—but she'd lived in an apartment building, and the sounds of other tenants were always present, sometimes annoyingly so. Even when the neighbors fell asleep, the sounds of the street beneath her shutters reminded her that there were other people in the world. And angry dogs.

Here, only the sounds they made as they climbed were present; when they reached the top of the stairs, which then opened up into a wide platform, the only thing that broke the silence was the sound of breathing.

Beyond the landing an open gallery followed the shape of the foyer, hemmed in by delicate railing. On the left part of the oval gallery was a hall with less impressive ceilings than the great hall on the first floor.

Perhaps because she was listening so uncomfortably, when she heard sounds in the distance, she turned instantly. Severn was already on the move.

"Teela?"

Teela nodded. "Mrs. Erickson?"

"That sounds like Jamal," the older woman said. Kaylin heard nothing that sounded like Jamal, but didn't doubt that

Mrs. Erickson could. She let Mrs. Erickson take the lead, in part because she didn't think the older woman could be stopped, short of physical restraint.

The sounds that no one else could hear came from the hall, bypassing the second-floor gallery entirely. This was fine; there appeared to be no paintings hung in it, although Kaylin had time to give the statues on display a suspicious glance as she passed them.

The hall was very similar to Helen's hall of tenant—or guest—rooms, although the doors weren't adorned by simple silhouettes to indicate who those guests might be. Down the hall was a set of double doors. Kaylin assumed that those doors were the destination to which Mrs. Erickson marched. She was wrong.

Mrs. Erickson veered to the left, to one of the closed doors. She opened it without hesitation, as if all possible risk was negligible in comparison to her desire to find Jamal.

Kaylin didn't have to call in Terrano or Mandoran—they were both in the room, although Terrano's physicality was pretty sketchy. She couldn't see Jamal, and wasn't certain if Mrs. Erickson could, but the older woman ran into the room, heading toward a door in the far wall.

The room was Barrani in style; the furniture was sparse, but the decor made the emptiness seem a deliberate choice, an evocation of elegance. These looked like guest rooms; they were shorn of any evidence that they had ever been occupied.

Mrs. Erickson paused in front of the closed door; she'd reached for the handle to open it, but pulled back at the last second. Kaylin caught up with her quickly.

"Jamal is behind this door," she said, voice low. Kaylin glanced at her; there was a ferocity in the older woman's expression Kaylin had never seen before. "You can't hear him."

"No—but I believe you can. Let Terrano open the door."

Mrs. Erickson hesitated. "I think it may be dangerous," she finally said. "There's something off about the doorknob. That wouldn't have affected Jamal—he can walk through doors and walls—but I'm not sure it will help anyone else."

"Is Jamal alone, or are the others with him?"

Mrs. Erickson raised her voice and asked exactly that question. Kaylin couldn't hear the answer. "The others are with him—he held on to them, and he won't let go. When the door opened into this place, the children were called here. He thinks he might have been able to remain in our house, but they couldn't."

Tell her to call him out, Hope said, his voice far deeper than it should have been at his size.

"Jamal doesn't exactly *listen.*"

You do not understand her power. She has used it passively because she does not understand it, either. Tell her to command *him to come to her.* When Kaylin failed to heed Hope's advice, he snorted; a small stream of silver smoke hung in the air. *Do you not trust Mrs. Erickson?*

"Intent isn't everything."

It will be of great help to the children who have watched over her for the entirety of her life. There are only two wills here. Let her exert hers.

"What about what the children want?"

Silence.

Kaylin knew the answer. Parents grabbed children by the arm—or ears—all the time; they could enforce their will on the children who were their responsibility. How was this different?

"Mrs. Erickson," she said softly, "my familiar—the squawking thing on my shoulder—feels that if you command Jamal and the children to come to you, they won't have any choice. They'll come."

"I don't think he's spent much time with the children."

"As much as I have." She exhaled. "He thinks that you have the ability to command complete obedience."

"How?"

Because they are dead, and she is a Necromancer.

Kaylin looked at the door. "Ask Jamal," she finally said, "whether he'd choose you as a master over Azoria."

Mrs. Erickson's hesitation was marked. She asked the question, gentling it until it had no meaning.

Kaylin's arms were now almost blinding, the marks were so bright. "Jamal, can you hear me?"

"He can hear you. I've told him you can't hear him. He wants to know why."

"Tell him it's the door."

"He...doesn't see a door," she finally said.

"What does he see?"

"A wall. Four walls, actually. A low ceiling. No windows. No doors."

Kaylin glanced around the rest of the room. Terrano joined Mrs. Erickson and then shouldered her out of the way.

"Not a good idea," Mandoran said out loud, although the words were clearly meant for Terrano. "It's not a door."

"Why would she have a *trapped door* when she can't have visitors?" In spite of his snappish reply, Kaylin noted that Terrano didn't attempt to touch the door. He studied it, instead. "I think it only works in one direction."

"Then don't touch it," Kaylin snapped. "We don't need to fish you out of a stone block with a hole in it."

"You don't need to help me escape at all."

"If Jamal and the children—who can easily walk through closed doors and solid walls—are trapped there, it might take you longer than we'd like to get out. It might get even messier if the space collapses entirely; the children won't be injured—they're already dead. It's probably not going to do great things for you."

Mandoran broke out laughing. Terrano glared at him.

"Sedarias implied that it might be better for the rest of us," Teela said; she stood in the doorway from the hall, her back to that hall, arms folded. "The doors in this hall are enchanted; the enchantments seem consistent with door wards. The enchantment on that door, on the other hand, is different, and it is much stronger. I would concur with your familiar. It is in the best interests of the children that Mrs. Erickson utilize her power."

To Mrs. Erickson, she said, "They would obey your request if they were capable of it on their own; they are not. But if our legends are true, they will have no choice but to obey."

Mrs. Erickson clearly had the same doubts Kaylin had.

No, Kaylin thought, frowning; that wasn't true. There was something in the old woman's expression that was far, far too troubled.

"It would be best for them." Teela's voice remained gentle. "Ask Jamal, if you do not believe me."

"I promised," she whispered. "I promised them I would never use that power again."

Oh.

"Jamal!" Kaylin said, raising her voice. "Mrs. Erickson made a promise to you—I'm going to assume it was when she was a child. She needs to break that promise now. It's the only way she can be certain she can save you all."

"He isn't answering," Mrs. Erickson whispered.

"Just—let her make this one exception? Give her permission? Please? She's not leaving this room without you, and I don't think we have a lot of time; we've gathered the rest of the ghosts trapped here, and I think we need to get them out of this building."

"Jamal—Jamal says that's what she wanted. That's what she wants. She wants me to...do what you've asked me to do."

Kaylin turned to Hope. Hope was silent for one long beat. He then sighed. "How does Jamal know that?" she asked.

"I don't know, dear."

"Ask him. It's important."

She did as asked. "He isn't answering."

"But he's still there?"

"Yes—they're all still there."

Kaylin nodded. "Jamal, I can't hear you—only Mrs. Erickson can. But we need to know how you know that. Nothing you can say will hurt Mrs. Erickson. Nothing you can say will change how she feels about you. You've been by her side for her entire life. You're family. If you know because you were sent to watch over her, that's fine. You were children. You didn't ask to serve Azoria; you didn't ask to be kidnapped. Or killed. Mrs. Erickson is never going to blame you.

"But we're here. We're in the...other side of the house. And we need to do something here that will release Mrs. Erickson from whatever danger, whatever plan, Azoria made before she was born."

"He says you can't," Mrs. Erickson said.

"We don't want to endanger her," Kaylin continued. "But if we don't understand what she wanted of Mrs. Erickson, we might do exactly that in our ignorance. If you know, we need to know—especially now."

Mrs. Erickson's expression changed. "He's crying," she said. "Jamal doesn't cry."

Kaylin softened her voice, but continued to put volume into it. "Tell us why. Mrs. Erickson won't break her promise to you and the rest of the children unless you give her permission. You know that."

"He—he thinks they can't be with me now. He thinks I'm in danger. Because of them."

Kaylin was beginning to get frustrated.

"You are," Terrano said. "Maybe it's time to retreat."

Kaylin looked around the room. Nothing had changed. "What do you see?"

Terrano shook his head. "Not see—hear. You won't hear it unless you listen carefully. But I hear it, and because I can, Mandoran hears it as well. Teela doesn't—but that's deliberate on her part. Something is speaking, but it's phased; it's both here and not here."

Kaylin hated the whole stacking space concept. It was very difficult to get her head around it. She understood the theory—many things could exist in what was theoretically the same space, but they existed in a different layer, on top of or beneath the layer which contained her.

Yes, Severn said.

Why isn't this a problem for you?

It is a problem, but I don't use the same analogy you're using. Layer is the wrong word, it's the wrong conceptualization; it implies something flat. It doesn't matter right now. If Terrano can hear someone speaking, someone is speaking. He can exist in multiple spaces simultaneously. I'm guessing Azoria learned how to do the same thing

Kaylin poked Hope. "I don't suppose you have a version of wing that works on cars?"

He nipped at her finger, squawking loudly. He did smack her face with his wing, but held it there, baring his tiny teeth.

"He is telling you that the wing is not a literal mask, which you might have noted when you could both *hear* and interact with Amaldi and Darreno. He assumed that you understood this."

Kaylin grimaced in the direction of the Barrani Hawk.

"Here," Mandoran said, holding out a hand. "I've got it now."

She looked at his empty hand, and realized after a few seconds that he intended her to take it in her own. She did. It wouldn't be the first time that Mandoran had drawn her into a slightly different space.

The moment their palms connected, Kaylin could hear a voice. She couldn't hear words, or something that sounded like syllables; she heard sibilance and moaning. As she listened, it grew louder. To her ears, it wasn't a Barrani voice. Nor was it human.

"Before you ask, I'm not the academic here. I can't tell you what's speaking."

"Is it getting louder because I'm actively trying to listen?"

"You wish."

She really did. She turned to the door. "Jamal—something is coming. You don't need to come out—but you need to tell us why you think Azoria did what she did. What did she order you to do?"

There was a longer pause, and when it was broken, it was broken by Mrs. Erickson. "He says…he says they were ordered to watch me. From before I was born. They didn't expect that I would be able to see them because no one else could. But something changed for the children—either here or in my home. Azoria couldn't see them when they were in my home. She might not have been able to see them at all once they'd left this place.

"They didn't know that at the time. They discovered it later, when she came to our house—before I was born." Mrs. Erickson frowned. "My parents considered her their benefactor; they were happy to see her, if a bit embarrassed; she was a grand lady and they were servants. But she came to visit from time to time. That stopped before I would have seen her, but the point Jamal is making, or trying to make, is this: she couldn't see them.

"He thinks she did look. They could hide from her—they can hide from *me*—but Jamal became bolder in those years. He'd take more risks. He eventually just stood in front of her and let her know exactly what he thought of her. She didn't react. He says the only time she did is when he walked right through her; she stopped then, looking around. She whispered because she didn't want to alarm my parents.

"But her words then weren't commands. There's something about *this* place that seems to give her power.

"The children weren't drawn to this building until tonight; they just couldn't leave my house. But they did talk to me, they did interact inasmuch as they could. They were still children then." They were still children now. They were the age they had been when they died. "When they realized that she couldn't see them and couldn't…force them to obey, they chose to continue to watch. They meant to protect me or offer warning if it became necessary.

"They didn't know what they had been ordered to look for. I don't think she intended that I see them at all. But they saw her, and she was aware of their presence, when she came to paint the portrait of my family." Mrs. Erickson's brows rose.

"Jamal knew that any painting she made of anyone was bad. It wasn't safe. But my parents loved the painting; it was a great comfort to my mother in the years after my father died. Nothing terrible happened to my parents, although they were part of the painting. The children didn't like the painting, of course. They were deeply worried and deeply suspicious. But my parents spent time in that room, near that painting, and it didn't affect them. It didn't affect *me*. I played in that room as a young child; it was where my mother liked to sit when she was knitting.

"I do remember the children telling me that it was a bad painting," she added, an odd smile adorning her face. "The artist was bad. My parents looked terrible. My hair looked stupid. I asked about the flower. They couldn't see it. I assumed that was deliberate, at the beginning. I'm not so sure now.

"After my parents passed, the children began to avoid the room. And as the years passed, avoidance became apprehension, anxiety, and eventually terror. I avoided the room because whenever I drew close to it, the children started to panic. Jamal sometimes breaks things when he panics, and it grew harder and harder to reach them through their fear. But you saw what they were like."

Kaylin nodded.

"Seeing the painting—seeing images of my parents—became less important than the children; I closed the door to the room, and I acted as if it didn't exist. The first time the room had been entered in decades was when you visited." She frowned. "Jamal says the house began to change when the two of you entered the room.

"They began to hear Azoria through the closed front door; they could sense that she was somehow searching for them in an attempt to find them. But, dear," she added, obviously to Jamal, "that doesn't explain why you said what she wants is for me to—to break my promise."

Silence.

"He's not answering."

"Jamal—"

"He says she thought I would be special. She did something, made something—I'm not sure which. A necklace or a ring. She gave whatever it was as a gift to my mother, an heirloom that might be given to the child she would bear. Jamal just called it jewelry, and I don't think he's being deliberately difficult."

"Well, that's a change."

"He heard that." She winced, but a hint of smile was preserved; it melted away as she continued to speak. "I've told you my parents didn't have a lot of money. They felt so lucky to be given the land for this house, but they had to build it, and that was costly. My mother ended up selling what little jewelry she had—she had a baby on the way, and they needed to have a roof over that child's head. I think she must have sold whatever it was she was given; it would have been the most valuable piece she owned.

"Jamal thinks my mother was meant to wear whatever she'd been given during the pregnancy, and possibly beyond it. But...my parents were practical people, and not given to sentiment. If the gift received was too rich, too impressive, too ornate, my mother would have set it aside regardless—she wouldn't have wanted to tempt thieves."

Kaylin knew exactly what that was like. Wealth spoke of power if you were careless enough to flaunt it; it meant you weren't concerned about thieves—or worse. She also knew that in Elantra, not the fiefs of her childhood, there was less fear of theft—but regardless, Kaylin didn't wear valuables. She thought she would have liked Mrs. Erickson's parents, had they ever been able to meet.

But she considered one thing as Jamal continued to speak—inaudibly—to Mrs. Erickson. Every single one of the children had not, according to the law, died. Their ghosts gave lie to that, but their bodies had been found, and their bodies had returned to their homes. Every one of them had been arrested for breaking and entering.

She wondered, as she considered, whether or not they had been searching for whatever it was Mrs. Erickson's mother had sold. All had died, executed for murdering their own families or the people they were living with. What had possessed them? Azoria herself? But she'd inhabited the body of the painter without becoming psychotically insane.

But there had been no further ghosts, or at least no ghosts sent to watch and report on Mrs. Erickson. Had the last child finally found what Azoria had been seeking?

She shook her head. The neighbor.

The neighbor had accused Mrs. Erickson of theft; he wanted to push his way into her house to find…something. Jamal kept him out, and there was enough of his own thoughts, his own beliefs, in him that he was frightened of ghosts. He had never managed to enter.

But upon sighting Teela that one time, he had remained in his own house; he didn't come out to the lawn to watch for Mrs. Erickson's arrival. His reaction to Teela implied— heavily—that he had been in contact with a different Barrani woman. To mortals with very little experience with Barrani, all Barrani looked the same.

The neighbor had been broken. His hostility to Mrs. Erickson had come, in the end, from Azoria, even if that hadn't been her intent. Whatever her intent had been, it had been garbled in the neighbor's head. He didn't know what he was looking for. He knew that it was in Mrs. Erickson's home.

Maybe he wasn't looking for the same thing the possessed bodies of the dead children had been looking for. Maybe Azoria thought it was somehow still in the house, unused, unseen. Maybe he'd intended to do something with the painting— take it off the wall, make Mrs. Erickson look at it—Kaylin didn't know.

"Jamal believes that when my mother passed away, I was to have whatever jewelry she'd been given. That I might wear it in memory of my mother, to whom I was quite close. But… he says she did sell it—he heard her talking about it with my father. So…I was meant to wear it. I was meant to sit in the room with the painting. I was meant to…" Her brows rose.

"Mrs. Erickson?"

"I was meant to become a vessel, he says. I was to become like the children—and Azoria would become me." She looked down at her wrinkled hands. "I don't understand. What would she want with *me*? She has forever. She has power. She clearly had wealth."

Kaylin and Teela exchanged a glance; neither answered the question. But in the room, the answer suggested itself: Mrs. Erickson was a Necromancer. She could control the dead.

Sanabalis had called her a shaman. Someone who could see the dead, communicate with them, possibly help them disentangle themselves from the land of the living.

Why would Azoria want a shaman—or even a Necromancer? What did she intend that she wanted that power?

It was Severn who answered. He said what Kaylin couldn't quite put into words, solidifying the threat: *If she destroys the Lake, the Barrani are essentially dead.*

And she would rule them.

26

"She probably never expected the High Halls to rise again," Kaylin said out loud. "And she probably wanted to see what Mrs. Erickson was capable of before she made her decision." She turned to Teela. "Do you think she could take over the body by forcing the soul out?"

"You don't think that's what she did with the children?" Teela asked.

Kaylin considered the one ghostly woman Mrs. Erickson had recognized. "I think she might have. But if she did, she wasn't entirely in control, given the way their actual bodies died. The ghosts here—the ones that emanated light—were clearly under her control; she possessed one of the bodies in order to create the painting we found in the sitting room.

"I don't know if that possession occurred while the woman was alive. But her ghost is here. And the painting was done after the children were killed. I don't understand, though. If she could possess a living body, as she clearly did the painter's, couldn't she have commandeered someone Barrani instead? She'd have the advantage of familiarity and brute strength."

Teela raised a brow at the word *brute*. "We don't have ghosts the way you have ghosts. You've met the Barrani version of the undead before; the attempt to delink life from True Name produces them. But the source of life, even separated, still exists; if the name cannot be used to control those who attempted to divest themselves of that weakness, it is nonetheless the source of their half-life. If you destroy the body, the name once again returns to the Lake to await rebirth; if you do not, the name maintains an attenuated connection to that body.

"I do not know what might happen to our infants in the absence of those words; the words *are* ours; they are part of who we are. Their bodies do not wake; they do not decay. They are almost inert. It is possible she could become the animating force behind an infant—but the parents would know. If the child woke without the blessing of the Lady, it might be considered an abomination or a mutation; I am uncertain the body would survive.

"Nor am I certain that stripped of the animation of the True Name, the adults would survive. To test this, to test what Necromantic control might make of such emptied bodies, we would have to have bodies, and we would have to experiment."

Kaylin's mouth flew open, but Teela lifted a hand to stem the obvious outrage that was certain to follow.

"I speak merely of the gaining of precise knowledge, and yes, the Emperor would reduce anyone who attempted to draw conclusions in that fashion to ash.

"This is beyond my areas of expertise and study. Serralyn, however, says—with some urgency—she thinks the hair binding, the flower, the painting—they were made entirely to prepare Mrs. Erickson for possession. Azoria clearly had some success in her possession of mortal bodies before, but that possession was obviously less than perfect. If Mrs. Erickson had the potential power Azoria wished to use or claim, she couldn't afford that mistake."

"But how did she *know* what Mrs. Erickson might be capable of?"

"It's possible," Teela said, "that she created it. And if you somehow question the power of it, you have only to consider Lord Sanabalis. Had Mrs. Erickson wanted to, she could have been in control of a Dragon. I admit I am surprised—but not displeased—that she survived that unintended disaster."

Mrs. Erickson had dealt with the ghosts of children for all of her life; she could easily listen in on multiple simultaneous conversations.

Jamal could clearly hear what was being said; he couldn't join in the conversation. But he could still speak to Mrs. Erickson. She turned to the door when—Kaylin assumed—Jamal started to speak again.

"I have a question for you," she then said, turning to face Teela and Kaylin.

Kaylin nodded.

"Is Azoria dead?" Mrs. Erickson's voice was completely steady. None of the usual softness, the tone that implied her constant, unchanging kindness, adorned the words.

Teela answered. "We were told she was dead; her line was excised. Her family no longer exists. That is as much of an answer as I can give. Barrani died—recently—for investigating her history; I do not believe Azoria responsible for their deaths.

"I'm not sure, at this juncture, how to define *dead* or *alive* when it comes to your perceptions. The children are ghosts. Amaldi and Darreno were not. Kaylin only assumed that the latter two weren't actually dead because of how she could see them. She assumed Jamal and the other children were dead because she could see them without intervention. And because you called them ghosts.

"Amaldi and Darreno weren't dead. To your eyes, however, there was no difference between them and your children—if one ignores the fact that your children have always been trapped in your house. I believe the answer to your question is a very qualified yes: yes, she is dead. I do not doubt that her body, or perhaps a very, *very* clever simulacrum, was destroyed."

"But if it were destroyed, her name…" Kaylin paused. "You don't think her name returned to the Lake."

"No. Had it, none of us would be here, having this discussion. If she managed somehow to drain the life out of captive Barrani—and we have no idea how long that might have taken—it's not a stretch to believe that she did the same to her own name. It may have been inadvertent. From the few stories that have survived, she was very like Terrano when it came to choosing between experimentation and her own physical safety. If she began her experiments long ago—and we have evidence she did in the preserved Berranin suite—we might draw conclusions from what we found.

"Perhaps she understood that she would face execution if her attempt to interfere with the Lake failed; she no doubt hoped to move into a different, but eternal, body.

"She almost certainly attempted possession of Barrani first. Until and unless she removed the names, it was probably impossible. Given the existence of her gallery, I'm almost certain she tried." Teela's eyes were narrowed. "Perhaps the destruction of the names at their core wasn't about gaining power, but about hollowing out the force that made each Barrani victim unique.

"If they were possessed of a name, she might command or

control them should she discover that name—but she could not *be* them."

"How could she try? The gallery was in place when Berranin was wiped out. It's been tucked away in the folds of the High Halls. You can't think that she'd be able to return to it?"

"Before the High Halls rose again? I do. It would have to be subtle, and it would imply a knowledge of the High Halls—at least in its severely hobbled state—that no one would be comfortable with. It would be, if not easy, simpler: she was dead. She was no longer a concern."

"So...Jamal and the other children were test cases?"

"What do you think? They're the only ones who are trapped as they're trapped; the ghosts Mrs. Erickson freed in here are, to her eye, different."

"Do you think they were experiments and sometime between then and now she perfected the ability to...to kill people, leave their bodies intact, and take over?"

"Yes. Serralyn says yes."

"And Mrs. Erickson?"

"We don't know how she gathered the others, but it seems clear to me that Mrs. Erickson was special; the intention when it came to Mrs. Erickson was also special. My guess? Some of the ghosts on this side of the building were servants who 'quit'; they disappeared. Mrs. Erickson's mother wasn't one of them—but she was pregnant. It's possible that Azoria attempted to influence the...shape of the baby, the baby's mortality. To imbue it with something extra."

Kaylin glanced at Mrs. Erickson. "Sorry about this—we talk about people in the third person who are actually right beside us all the time. I think it's a Hawk thing. Or bad manners."

Mrs. Erickson shook her head. "The truth often sounds awful—but I did not have an awful life."

Kaylin doubted that her early life had been good. A child who had literal imaginary friends? A child who could see the echoes of the dead? How many friends wouldn't be totally creeped out by that? How many would believe her? How many would think it was just a cry for attention?

Your friends are not without intelligence, Hope said. *But they are, in my opinion, wrong. Azoria sensed something in the quickening. It was not a certainty. The introduction of the painter was proof, if it were needed, that she had mastered the art of taking human form, human body, well enough that she understood how to use her knowledge and her power in a different form.*

"Mrs. Erickson never displayed the power that Azoria was hoping for."

"Not until our interference, no. I believe Azoria would have been gratified had she accompanied us to the palace. I think her experiments turned toward the unnamed, the mortals who live and breathe without our dependency on True Names."

"Or eternity."

"Pardon?"

"You get forever unless you waste it in political Barrani games. There's no way someone who has eternity is going to surrender it for a few decades of constantly imperfect life."

"True—if she had a choice. I don't believe she intended to be accused of treason; I don't believe she intended to lose the entirety of her family and her line. The rooms in which she did the bulk of her work were sundered from her; if she could visit them again, she could not do it the traditional way—by walking through the doors." Teela frowned. "Convince Jamal."

Terrano, however, shook his head. "This is a containment. It's meant to somehow trap ghosts. I think it's possible to break it."

"Or we could just have Jamal give Mrs. Erickson permission."

"I don't think that's the smartest idea. Not if we have alternatives."

"And I don't think you should try to break things you don't understand. Look, to Azoria, the starting point of *dead* is the freeing of True Names. If you somehow walk into whatever this space is, how do you know you won't be trapped there as well? We already know that Azoria could somehow leech words of power. You still have your name—did you want to become fuel for whatever it is Azoria has become?"

"Not really, no. But I don't think it's that kind of trap." He moved forward. Teela attempted to grab him by the shoulder and failed; her hand passed through his body.

Kaylin turned to Hope. "Make him stop."

Hope squawked; Terrano shrugged. Hope then squawked up a storm of screeching syllables.

"Good point," Terrano replied, grimacing. His body, which looked pretty much the same as it always did, began to shimmer in place; it became a livid green. Terrano at least retained Barrani form. But the color he'd adopted—possibly at Hope's urging—was familiar for other reasons.

It was the color of the flower in the painting Azoria had created—the flower twined into the braided nest of Mrs. Erickson's hair.

"Why that color?" she demanded.

Terrano ignored her.

"He can't hear you in that form." Or not. Teela was annoyed. "He doesn't see color. Hope suggested that he 'stand' in a slightly different space, and he considered it. He moved. Sedarias is just one side of enraged—the wrong side. I know I wanted to somehow reach these people again—I wanted them to be with me. I cannot for the life of me remember why."

Mandoran snickered. He was behind Terrano, and Kaylin watched as he—more slowly—shifted into the same shade of green. She realized that Terrano had lost some visual definition by comparison. "Don't worry about him," Mandoran said—in words Kaylin could actually hear. "I'll anchor." He held out a hand to her.

Kaylin stepped forward and took it.

"Teela?"

Teela nodded. "With your permission, Mrs. Erickson?"

Mrs. Erickson was staring at a very closed door. She nodded, and Teela placed a hand firmly on her shoulder.

Terrano moved toward the door, passing through Mrs. Erickson as if she no longer existed. He lifted a palm. As he'd just walked through Mrs. Erickson, Kaylin had no doubt he'd pass through her in the same way if she was in his path. The door, however, met the flat of his palm and remained there.

"The door exists across most of the planes Terrano has any experience with," Mandoran explained. "But not all. He thinks he can open it by sliding between two planes and... pushing."

"Pushing?"

"More or less."

"Serralyn says less," Teela told her. "I am *almost* at the point of agreeing with Mandoran— this would be much easier if you knew our names."

"You're just trying to annoy Sedarias enough that she'll show up."

"Terrano listens to her more than any of the rest of us—at least when she's present." In a quieter voice, she said, "Terrano is reckless. He always has been. Sedarias can keep him anchored in a way that Mandoran can't." She made no mention of herself.

Terrano's livid green arm—Kaylin could swear the color

itself was pulsating, like a very bizarre heart—passed through the door.

"He asks us all to step back," Mandoran said. "Right now."

Teela pulled Mrs. Erickson away, practically lifting the old woman off her feet.

Hope, however, said, *Remain where you are standing.*

"What about everyone else?"

Squawk.

Kaylin watched the door through Hope's wing, her hands becoming fists. She understood why Sedarias was angry. She'd accept anger if it meant that Terrano could free the children. Jamal's fear was infectious.

The door didn't open.

Instead, the center of it melted, something that might once have resembled wood dribbling onto the floor, where it pooled just beyond everyone's feet. Everyone's but Kaylin's. Mandoran, green, didn't seem to be standing on the floor; the melted door passed through the base of his feet without touching them.

"Jamal!" Mrs. Erickson shouted. She tried to pull free of Teela, which was impossible. Kaylin, with better training and far more muscle, couldn't have managed it.

But Kaylin turned toward what was now a jagged, oval hole in what had appeared to be a door. Jamal was standing on the other side of it, looking out, his eyes wide. He seemed to be afraid to cross the threshold, but when he saw Mrs. Erickson struggling to free herself, he immediately sprang into action.

Teela said, "Don't. Come over here and bring your friends."

Kaylin frowned and turned to her fellow Hawk. "You can see him."

"I can see him now."

"That can't be a good sign."

"No, probably not—but if you consider any of the things

that have happened in the past week a good sign, you have deeper problems. Jamal, bring your friends. We need to let that space collapse as soon as possible. If we can leave this place with Mrs. Erickson, we can guarantee her safety—but she won't leave without you."

Jamal hesitated, but when Mrs. Erickson nodded, he turned back and shouted an all clear to the other three. Esme came out first, but she was followed quickly by Callis and Katie.

"Terrano, let go."

"He's trying," Mandoran said. "Don't worry about him. I've got him. I'm not letting go."

Chosen. Kaylin turned to Hope. *Call your partner.*

Her partner was in the room. She blinked, and then said, "Severn I think Hope wants you to draw your weapons. Mandoran come back to where the rest of us are."

"I can't—I might lose the idiot."

"What is he *doing?*"

Kaylin turned to Teela, who was less likely to offer an explanation that made no sense to people who were safely ensconced in reality.

Teela didn't answer. Something flew past them all, leaving a strong wind in its wake. Had Hope panicked in any way, Kaylin would have been far more worried; as it was, the familiar rolled his eyes in resigned disgust.

"Was that Sedarias?"

"What do you think?" Teela muttered a Leontine imprecation under her breath—probably because she was too close to Mrs. Erickson and she didn't want to offend. She relaxed her hold on Mrs. Erickson's shoulder. "Mandoran is useful as an anchor, but Sedarias has always been best at pulling the idiot back to safety—probably because she's terrifying when she's worried. Her worry is far worse than her anger."

Kaylin could see that, almost literally; while Sedarias wasn't visible to her eyes—even with Hope's help—the detritus of her passing, or her presence, lifted anything not bolted down in the room except the people.

Teela moved suddenly, without warning; she gestured and the room's door—the room they'd first entered—slammed shut. Kaylin felt it as a slap of strong magic.

The windstorm that was Sedarias began to calm, the movement of small bits of furniture—and two chairs—slowing as she did. They fell to the floor in more or less the right orientation, although one teetered on two legs before righting itself.

The Barrani cohort leader then appeared out of the folds of moving air. Her eyes were indigo, and they were glaring murder at Terrano, who appeared at her side, his hand in the pincer grip of hers.

"What?" he said, meeting that glare head-on. "The kids are free and I'm not trapped, either." He winced as her hand tightened.

"If we had any hope of remaining undetected," the Barrani Hawk said, "it's gone."

Hope squawked.

"I said *hope*."

The familiar snorted as Kaylin walked—quickly—to Mrs. Erickson's side. She was now surrounded by children, only two of whom were crying. To her surprise, one of the two was Jamal.

"I'm sorry," he whispered, repeating the words as if they were a mantra from which he might derive some kind of peace.

Mrs. Erickson shook her head. "It's all right, Jamal. You've been my friend for my entire life. With the exception of broken windows and dishes, you've never caused me a moment of pain."

"You grew up."

"Yes. And you didn't. But I still think of you all as my best friends. And maybe the children we never had. I hoped, you know. I hoped that maybe my husband would stay, the way you had all stayed."

"Don't hope for that."

"No, I grew to understand that. People learn new things, even when they're adults. I've learned a lot of new things in the past week. It doesn't matter whether or not you stayed because you wanted to, or because you had no choice. You kept a very lonely girl company—and you never left me."

"It does matter," Katie said. "You've been trying to figure out how to get rid of us."

"No, Katie. I've been trying to figure out how to *set you free*. If I die—and old people do, eventually—I won't be able to stay with you."

Katie clearly wanted to say that they'd have each other; she even opened her mouth. But the words wouldn't come out. She opened her mouth to try again, and this time, her mouth stayed open because this time, the doors Teela had slammed shut shattered.

Sedarias caught the splinters of wood that flew into the room in a whirlwind very similar to the one she'd *been* moments before. Wood bits hung in air, held by Sedarias in her not-quite-normal form. Nothing followed the shattering of those doors; nothing attempted to enter the room.

But the sound was louder, now—the clicking and moaning very similar to the underpinning of the Wevaran speech with which Kaylin was familiar.

Sedarias allowed all of the debris to drop in one motion; pieces of wood clattered to the floor. She had one hand firmly around Terrano's; glaring at him, she dropped him as well. Teela had been right. Sedarias could reach Terrano far more efficiently than any of the rest of the cohort—strange, given that they were almost polar opposites when it came to personality.

Beside them both, between Sedarias and Kaylin, Severn finally fully unwound his weapon chain. Mrs. Erickson winced then, and looked away; what she had seen, what she could clearly still see, was too blinding to watch for long.

Mandoran remained green, although the color flickered across his skin as if reflecting very ugly flame. Terrano, green, looked normal, except for his eyes, which were disquietingly large in an otherwise properly proportioned Barrani face.

"It's nice of her to give us a warning," Kaylin said.

"Make certain you hold on to your children and your new friends," Sedarias told Mrs. Erickson, as she turned to face what remained of the door. Azoria Berranin might be dead, but if she was, she'd clearly managed to take some of her power with her.

The moaning, low shriek that had been looming background noise became focused and rougher, the voice almost grating in its texture. In it, Kaylin could hear words, but the words were harshly voiced, the syllables almost breaking in the wrong place.

Terrano's livid green dimmed into a more natural nausea-induced green as his feet once again touched the same floor as Kaylin's feet did. "Serralyn says: Bakkon is going to strangle Starrante."

"How does he think he's going to find a Wevaran neck?"

"With less difficulty than the rest of us would?"

"Bakkon thinks Azoria's been where Wevaran start. She's vocalizing the way Wevaran vocalize," Teela added.

"He doesn't think. He knows. He is absolutely certain." Terrano paused; Kaylin assumed Serralyn was feeding him urgent information. "He thinks she's been in the darkness for a very long time—she's not out of it yet. We have an advantage. There are no Wevaran young. No Wevaran clutches."

"If there had been, she'd be responsible for genocide."

Instead of mass murder.

"So...she wants to somehow eat us?"

"Anyone here who has a name, yes. Bakkon feels that the imperatives of the birthing place drive her now. He's uncertain that that's always been the case—but he's *very* unhappy at our inclusion."

"Inclusion?"

"We're now where she is."

Kaylin knew almost nothing about Wevaran beyond the superficial appearance. But she had thought that the birthing place, the place where the hatched little spiders ran around in almost mindless hunger, had been like a dark cave. A space empty of anything besides little proto-Wevaran.

"Serralyn says the Wevaran birthing places are extensible, individual to the parents. If you were expecting darkness and caves, you've failed to understand that. Bakkon is certain that the space we are now in is one such space. He wants Serralyn out of Mrs. Erickson's house."

And she wouldn't leave. But Kaylin was certain Bakkon—outside of the house—wouldn't leave, either. Not until he knew what the outcome would be.

"Ask Bakkon—"

"Eat or be eaten." Teela had clearly asked the first question on Kaylin's mind.

"How do we eat? And, ummm, are we supposed to consume each other if we want to leave?"

"The good news: no. We just have to make sure that we're not eaten."

"What, exactly, constitutes being eaten?"

"Looks like we're about to find out."

Hope squawked, his grating angry bird voice much louder than usual. It had to be. The sound that appeared to have shattered the doors became louder as the thing that emitted it finally came fully into view.

"Serralyn says that Azoria isn't giving us a warning—it's entirely a Wevaran instinct. The desire to be the best or the strongest, the desire to survive, is what produces the adult that eventually emerges. The clutchlings challenge each other. They do it automatically. They don't and can't sneak up on each other; it's one-on-one combat all the way down to the end."

Kaylin half nodded; she was staring at Azoria Berranin. An'Berranin. If she'd expected Azoria to look like a mishmash of Barrani and spider, she'd been wrong. Azoria looked like a slightly deranged Barrani woman; she had the same black hair, the same fair skin, the same pronounced cheekbones, jawline, and long, elegant limbs. She wore Barrani clothing— a robe that was both simple and yet reeked wealth.

The only difference Kaylin could see was the eyes: Azoria had a third eye in the center of her forehead, and it was definitely not standard Barrani issue. It was red, and as Azoria stepped foot across the ruined threshold, it rose on a slender stalk.

Ah, no. She had other eyes that Kaylin hadn't seen at first glance: they rose from the shadows of her hair.

"How dare you intrude upon my domicile?" she said, as the lids of the extra eyes opened, exposing a shining red.

"We're Imperial Hawks," Kaylin replied. "And we're investigating a series of kidnappings and murders. The Eternal

Emperor's Law encompasses all of Elantra—and this house is part of Elantra."

"Eternal Emperor?" she practically spat. "The *Dragon*?"

Kaylin nodded. Azoria's eye stalks were swiveling, but she now faced Kaylin.

"I am no citizen of his accursed Empire," Azoria hissed, eyes darkening in color. Kaylin looked at her mouth; it remained Barrani in shape and size. If *devour* was the correct word, it, like the darkness of the birthing place, was clearly metaphorical.

"There are special rules that govern the Barrani," Kaylin continued, speaking in her official Hawk voice. "If your crimes involve only other Barrani, the High Court in the High Halls has the right of adjudication. If you wish to claim that exemption, you will have to prove that your crimes are uni-racial.

"You must be aware that humans cannot officially be slaves. No sentient race can, by Imperial Law. What you do when it involves other races becomes a crime that the Imperial Hawks must investigate. If you have been judged to have broken the Emperor's Law, you are subject to the Imperial Court, where you will be tried. But again," she added, her voice lowering, "you must be well aware of that." Her hands became fists, and she didn't bother to force them to relax; she was thinking of the children—the ghosts trapped by Azoria in Mrs. Erickson's house—and the eventual fate of their bodies.

"I have committed no crimes," this Azoria said, walking slowly toward Kaylin. "This house is legally mine."

"This house barely exists in historical Imperial tax Records," Kaylin replied. "But let's assume it did. You owe probably eight to ten decades' worth of taxes on the property—taxes which no doubt have gone unpaid in the interim. Which, while it isn't as dramatic as kidnapping or murder, is still considered a crime.

"However, as the house doesn't exist, the deed to the building—and the surrounding property—belongs to the Ericksons, and I assure you they *have* paid their taxes, without fail, and on time. We're not standing in your domicile; we're standing in an extension of Mrs. Erickson's home. The intruder here is you, and we are empowered to remove you. To remove, in fact, anyone Mrs. Erickson does not consider a guest."

Azoria's natural Barrani eyes rounded; her lips thinned. Her normal hands became fists just as tight as Kaylin's, and just as white-knuckled.

"You will die here."

27

If air could tighten, the air did. It wasn't cold; it was almost viscous—like liquid one could breathe with effort.

Chosen.

Kaylin grimaced. The marks on her arms had been glowing a steady gold, but as Azoria approached, that color changed: they took on a gleaming green cast. Kaylin had asked what Azoria needed to devour. She'd killed humans; she'd taken over their bodies—imperfectly at first, if the children were anything to go by, and more perfectly thereafter, given the painter. None of those deaths had clearly served the purpose this...space was intended to serve.

But Kaylin's marks were ancient words, True Words, things given her—without choice on her part—for reasons she had *never* understood.

It was to those marks that Azoria's gaze fell, her brows rising, her eyes widening. "What is *this*?" she demanded, her voice slightly distorted. "Why do you bear the marks of the Chosen?" It was an aggrieved fury, studded with the usual Barrani judgment and arrogance.

Kaylin shrugged, a fief shrug; it was petty, but she knew that nonchalance infuriated people like Azoria. "I was Chosen."

"Impossible! You are mortal!"

"Then I'm lying and these aren't mine."

"They shouldn't be. They shouldn't be yours." The words were heated.

"You can take it up with the Ancients, then—if you can find them. I didn't ask for them."

"Give them to me. Give them to *me*, and I will allow you to leave unharmed."

Kaylin shook her head. "You know that's not the way it works. Or maybe you don't. But that's not the way it works." No. If she could have gotten rid of the marks at the age of twelve, she would have given them to anyone who asked. She might have—and she was far less proud of this—given them to some other poor sod, just to be free of them.

And she wouldn't have the life she had now, and she loved that life. Mostly.

Hope squawked. Kaylin wasn't certain who he was speaking to—she assumed it was Azoria. Azoria clearly heard the sound of his voice, and turned toward him, her eyes rounding before they narrowed in simmering resentment. Her body blurred in place, flickering as if the form she wore required concentration.

Hope squawked and spread his wings in one sudden snap of motion; the wings extended far beyond their normal size; they stretched across the whole of Kaylin's face as they continued to expand. She noticed the moment the texture of the wings—still transparent—shifted, from something that might have been a glass rendering of leather to something with actual feathers, and she knew that Hope was no longer sitting on her shoulder; when he spoke, she knew he wouldn't be squawking.

"No," he said. "But those who are not meant to hear will hear nothing intelligible. It is the nature of my communication. Do not waste time or breath arguing with Azoria; she understands reality only as it pertains to her. The world beyond her is part of her story; there is no independence in any of it.

"To Azoria, the world reflects her. Whether it bows to her needs or defies them defines whether or not it is 'good' or 'evil.' The lives she touches are, in some measure, there for her needs, her purposes, her examination. She can empathize only when those other lives map directly onto her own. She has moments of great generosity—which you will, of course, never experience. But the generosity is that of a noble ruler, a noble *owner*. She will be kind to those things that are hers, and the imperative to do so is entirely internal.

"You are, to her, evil. You attempt to take things which are rightfully hers. You have the marks of the Chosen, and she recognizes them. And Severn has the weapons the green hides from almost all of her kin. She is angry," he added, lifting a hand, palm toward her, as if rejecting her utterly.

A pale shield spread from that palm in all directions, becoming a sphere. Kaylin had seen it before.

"No, you have not. She is powerful, Kaylin—or she was, while she lived."

"I don't think she's dead."

"Neither does she. And I see that my assumption was not entirely correct. But she is not alive by Barrani standards."

Azoria hissed in rage. Clearly Hope had intended that she hear some of his words.

"What do you know?" she demanded.

"I know who you are," Hope replied. "And I know that you could never pay the price my use demanded."

If the marks of the Chosen had angered her, Hope's words enraged her. Her form flickered again, but this time it lost some of the cohesion of a Barrani body. Although the eyes in the hair—and on the perfect skin of her forehead—had been foreign and disturbing, she had nonetheless looked almost normal.

"Severn," Hope said. "Join us."

Kaylin couldn't take her eyes off what Azoria was becoming, but she spoke to Hope. "We can't—Mrs. Erickson and the children are *right there*."

"Yes, Kaylin. As are those who were trapped in this house in Azoria's webs. But you have failed to understand something important."

"Go ahead."

"They are dead. There is nothing you can do to protect them. That time—their time—has long passed. Any intervention you offer here will not bring them back. Perhaps, were they to be taken to Helen, she might create a space in which they could be contained safely, and they might know a fraction of a normal life—but you cannot."

"Mrs. Erickson isn't dead."

"No. No, she is not. Azoria does not appear to recognize her. She considered herself a scholar, a genius, but she was always vain—as are most of the living, the vanity being defined entirely by the lives that have shaped them."

"What do you mean?"

"She would not now choose Mrs. Erickson, even were her rituals and spells to activate; Mrs. Erickson is old."

"The Barrani don't care about that."

"Because there is no difference to the Barrani. Age implies power. There is no weakness that arises from it. Azoria has lived a mortal life. Several mortal lives. Look at the ghosts that Mrs. Erickson partially freed. Are any of them elderly?"

None were.

"It is not vanity alone, of course; it is power. But she cannot perceive the power in the age and wisdom of mortals; there is too much concomitant weakness. An'Teela will protect Mrs. Erickson." He raised his voice. "Severn."

Listen to him, Kaylin said, through the name bond.

I'm actually trying.

You're standing still.

Yes. Whatever Azoria is, the weapons of the green don't like. The only reason I'm standing still is because I do have some control.

Kaylin frowned. *You're sure it's the weapons? You're certain it's not Azoria somehow attempting to feed on them?*

I'm certain. He didn't elaborate. Nor did she ask for more information. She trusted Severn to know himself. *They want me to attack, but I'm uncertain what will happen to the power of the blades if they strike Azoria in this place. I think it's what she wants at the moment. There's something off about it.*

You think?

"He can't come. He's holding steady instead of charging ahead—the weapons of the green apparently want to dice her into small bits. She can't hear me, can she?"

"No. She is aware that you are speaking. And she is possibly aware of what I am to you."

Kaylin shrugged. "She can't get any angrier, can she?"

Hope didn't reply. Not to Kaylin. But he lifted his head, retracting the spread of his wings as he gazed at Azoria, or at what she had become.

Her skin had spread, the shape of her face changing, the smooth regularity of Barrani arms bending in the wrong way. From those arms, hands that had appeared to be Barrani began to shift in shape as well, fingers melding together to become pincers, although they retained the color of, the implied texture of, flesh, not chitin. Her body remained more or less as it had first appeared.

"It will change," Hope said.

"Will ours?"

"No. We are no part of this breeding ground. This was a space she entered as participant; she understood only half of its imperatives."

"How do you know this?"

"Because sometime in the not-too-distant past, she attempted to summon me. I listened; she was close enough that I could hear her voice. But she could not offer me the sustenance I require. She was—she is—brilliant, but she has never understood the way knowledge and self must fuse.

"It is the weakness of being as she is: she is at the center of the universe, and she sees herself as unchanging; as the one essential element, the only actual truth."

This didn't make sense to Kaylin. "She does what Terrano does."

"Yes, and no. Terrano's goal when he began his divergence from the laws that governed the body of his birth, was freedom. He did not wish to deprive others of theirs unless it accomplished that goal. He did not see the cohort as a tool; he did not see it as an impediment. He considered it a responsibility. Had they not been imprisoned, he would never have become what he is.

"His is a bright mind, a curious mind; he will always seek answers to the questions that arise. But he is focused only on that. It is why the Academia itself both accepts his presence and rejects his inclusion."

Kaylin flinched as Azoria's face began to lose the appearance of a Barrani face. Just as her hands had done, elements of that face warped and distended.

"Sedarias!"

Sedarias glanced at Kaylin.

"Don't let her touch any of you in any way."

The leader of the cohort looked annoyed by the words, but she did draw sword. So did Teela. Teela's sword, however, drew Azoria's immediate attention.

"Terrano could not have become Azoria because he has no desire to have power over others. Did he cause injury and possible death in his desire to escape captivity? Yes. Yes, he did. But if Alsanis had simply allowed the cohort to leave, he would have ignored his people—and yours—entirely. He made no attempt to justify his actions to either you or his victims. She believes that as she is the center of her own life, she is the center of all. I did not answer her call, but I heard it.

"I answered yours."

"I didn't call you! I had no idea that something like you could even be called. I'm not a Sorcerer—why would I even think of summoning a familiar?"

"Why, indeed? But look at you. You have bumbled your way, in ignorance, into becoming Chosen, and you have, at your side, a familiar that might once have served Sorcerers of old. Were it not for Severn and Teela, she would immediately attempt to devour you whole."

"Devouring me won't give her either of those things."

"No—but you do not *deserve* them, Kaylin. She does, as she worked so hard and so thanklessly. If she is not to have them for all of her effort, no one shall."

Teela's sword was glowing a very, very odd color.

"She's not a Dragon," Kaylin began.

"Did you believe that the Dragonslayers were only effective against Dragonkind? You have seen the swords in use to great effect, and they were not used against Dragons at that time. The weapons are empowered to fight many things, and they grant their users powers they would not otherwise possess."

Azoria's flesh lost the perfect, unblemished Barrani skin. A hint of color began to spread across her face, her arms— an opalescence that Kaylin had seen many times. Shadow.

"Things will become hectic very soon," Hope said, voice soft. "I can only slow time for a very narrow period."

"Slow time?"

"Hers. You didn't think she was standing in the doorway observing us for no reason, did you?"

Kaylin was certain that Severn had heard what Hope said; she shouted a warning to the cohort to let them know that whatever Azoria might unleash was incoming.

Mandoran cursed—in Leontine—and said, "When we get home, we're exchanging names! This is *stupid*!"

"Not a great time to get into a screaming match with Sedarias," Kaylin snapped.

He laughed. "You think we haven't already been enduring that?" And because of a lack of their names, Kaylin wasn't.

Kaylin then turned the whole of her attention to Mrs. Erickson and the children. Yes, they were dead. She knew that. And in theory death was the worst thing that could happen to someone; beyond death, the living had no real responsibility.

But that wasn't true of Mrs. Erickson, because she could see the dead.

And it probably wasn't entirely true of Kaylin, either.

"No," Hope said, voice soft, eyes so narrow they were almost closed. "She has discovered that she gains no sustenance from the dead. It is the living upon which she must feed."

"Is she dead?"

Hope said, "According to the Barrani, she is dead."

"I know that, but—"

"According to the Barrani, so were the cohort—they were barely attached to the names that had given them life. I do not think the separation the same; they did not use their names the way Azoria attempted to use her own. Alsanis protected their names, and protected the attachment—slender and attenuated—that their bodies retained to those words.

"They shifted and changed their forms because escape required it. But they had as much time to learn the extent of those changes as Azoria herself had. She was not exposed, as they were exposed, to the *regalia*; the *regalia* alters people in subtle fashion but children are not yet…fully themselves. Azoria was, when she began to walk this path."

"I want to know how you know all this, but it's going to have to wait." Kaylin pivoted on one foot. "Terrano, Mandoran—somewhere in this house, Hope thinks there's a name. A True Name. He thinks it'll be like yours was, except without Alsanis hiding it or preserving it."

"Did we not assume that her words were drained of power?" Mandoran asked.

"Hope clearly didn't," Terrano replied.

"What are you standing there for? Go!"

"Wait—why me? Terrano is the one who can leap through planes!"

Terrano folded his arms. "Did we find our names, or did you?"

Kaylin cursed in voluble, but brief, Leontine. "Hope— talk to them!"

"She will enter the room, and she will see you leave it. Or rather, she will see you vanish. I do not know what she will make of that. Come. You know where we have to go."

"I don't want to leave Mrs. Erickson!"

"If you hurry, Mrs. Erickson will be the safest person— living or dead—in that room. You must move quickly, Chosen. If I must keep this up for any longer, you will have to pay the price."

She knew what that meant.

She had asked him, a few times, to use the power for which familiars were legendary. He was willing to do so, if she was willing to accept the consequences. Had those consequences been hers to pay, she would have done it with fear, and likely future regret.

But no: he demanded that she sacrifice some of the things she wanted, desperately, to protect. She'd stopped asking, but she'd wondered—as she wondered now—what Sorcerers would sacrifice, or would have, in the past.

Anything, he replied, as she began to sprint toward the door in which Azoria was standing. *But it was seldom understood that in order to sacrifice something of value, one must value something other than oneself.*

She flinched, turned sideways, sliding as she did between Azoria and the destroyed door. She'd long since perfected the art of fleeing through a crowd.

"Then what did they sacrifice, if you did what they wanted?"

Their limbs, some portion of their personal power, whether that be monetary or magical. To sacrifice, one must highly value the thing one intends to exchange. Love is useful, in that regard.

Had she not been running, she would have been outraged.

Love is not necessary. One can value power without loving it; one can prize currency, without loving it. In time, the marks of the Chosen might serve as a sacrifice—but that time has not yet arrived, for you.

"You already ate one!"

Hope laughed. It was a sound more felt than seen; there was warmth and movement in its almost musical cadence. *Yes, that is true. But that was not a sacrifice on your part. Were you a different Chosen, it would have been.*

Kaylin leaped down the stairs, two and three at a time, her palm skirting the railing. "Why did you eat it, then?"

Power and sustenance. If you do not fully understand the marks you have received, you utilize them instinctively.

She considered that as she hit the foyer floor and turned toward the gallery from which Mrs. Erickson had so gently extracted the dead. Widening her stride, she sprinted down the hall, thinking about Mandoran's True Name, and wishing that she actually *had* it.

What she hadn't wished for was Terrano's name. She certainly hadn't wished for Terrano.

"You're going for the door in Azoria's self-portrait." He appeared at her side, keeping effortless pace with her all-out run.

Kaylin said, in slightly labored syllables, "I'm going for the door I couldn't see, yes."

"Sedarias sent me, before you try to get rid of me."

"I can talk to Severn. Stay upstairs where Azoria is!"

"In case you hadn't noticed, Severn isn't a big talker, and he has his hands full. Sedarias can't hear Severn the way she can hear me, and she wants me here." Terrano wasn't sprinting, so he had no trouble finding the breath for words. "You couldn't see the door. I'm here to help with that."

While Kaylin believed he *could* help, she was willing to bet that wasn't the primary reason he was here. He'd wanted to open that door the moment he saw it, and he now had an excuse.

The first thing Kaylin noticed as the painting came into view was the lack of its central figure. Azoria Berranin, framed and larger than life, was no longer *in* it. The painting's former background was now foreground. She had thought the outlands more vivid, more real, than the woman to whom they had served as background, and in her absence, that im-

476   MICHELLE SAGARA

pression solidified. The painting appeared to be a portal, or a window into the outlands.

But this wasn't a sentient building. She was certain of that. *No. No, it is not.*

Azoria had used the High Halls' connection to the outlands, and the High Halls were definitely sentient. Azoria had clearly learned how to reach that space without tapping into the roots of the High Halls or any other sentient building.

Terrano came to a stop to Kaylin's right; he offered her a hand. Kaylin grimaced and took it. She glanced at her shoulder, but Hope wasn't on it; he was at her back in what she thought of as his Aerian form.

Terrano cursed in Leontine. "I have no idea," he muttered, "how Mandoran manages to move you. You're like deadweight."

"What the hells does that mean?"

"Don't distract me—he's trying to explain it. Just…let me know when you see the damn door."

Kaylin muttered a Leontine imprecation and continued to stare at what remained of what had once been a portrait. Something flickered directly in front of her, and as she turned her head to look at Terrano, she caught a glimpse of something that might have been a door from the corner of her eye. She turned to the painting and lost it. "Almost there—I can see something out of the corner of my eye, but I can't see it when I look straight at it."

"Yeah. It's like faint starlight. I'm not standing in the right place yet, but closer. Do *not* let go of my hand until you have the door in sight. Sedarias says: or at all. Seriously, you don't *want* any of our names—you'd never get away from Sedarias."

Kaylin grinned in spite of the urgency of the situation. "That's it—I can see the door. It's very faint, more like the ghost image of a door than a door."

"Yeah, that's what it looks like to me as well. There might be a slice of space in which it looks totally normal, but if there is, it's not one I've experienced. Yet."

"But if it's a ghostly door, how are we supposed to open it?"

"Pardon?"

"How do we grab the doorknob?"

"Okay, we're definitely not seeing the same thing; there's no handle."

"No? Do you see an actual door?"

"Yes. It's a door, with a glowing ward in the center."

Kaylin couldn't see a ward. "Please don't tell me that the ward is bright green. No, let me amend that. I don't want the ward that you can see and I can't to be bright green."

"Sometimes we don't get what we want. What makes you think it's green?"

"Because you're green again, and...so are the marks."

"I don't look green to me."

"No? What do my marks look like to you?"

"Colorless."

"I *really* hate subjective reality. If you don't mind, I'm going to try to open the door the normal way."

"Door wards *are* the normal way."

"Fine. The poor person who can't afford door wards way. Better?"

"Slightly. Sedarias says she will chop off a hand if you let go of me."

"Yours or mine?"

"She wasn't specific. She always worries that I'll get lost."

Kaylin glared at him for a beat, and then reached out to touch the ghostly door. Because she was moving slowly she noticed that her hands, like the door, were pale and transparent, but that transparency was tinged green.

★ ★ ★

I'm not sure where this will take us, and I'm not sure we'll remain in contact, she told Severn.

Severn didn't answer. Using their bond, Kaylin risked a glimpse of the room she'd deserted; she could see that Azoria had learned the fine art of spitting, Wevaran style. Severn's chain was spinning; the webs didn't find purchase there. But they'd found purchase on random parts of the floors—and walls—and Mandoran's shouted warning made clear that they weren't just revolting blobs. No one was to stand in them, and no one was to be hit by them; he thought they'd teleport whatever body part they hit into a different place, while leaving the rest of the body behind.

Azoria, in the brief glimpse Kaylin took, had only sprouted two extra arms, but her face was no longer Barrani. It wasn't Wevaran, either; it was like a flesh mask of a bad artist's hastily crafted version of a Wevaran, if Wevaran had Barrani skin.

The eyes, on the other hand, were waving in the air at the height of their stalks.

Take the eyes out, Kaylin told her partner. *We'll hurry.* She took a deep breath, prayed that the handle worked and the doorway wasn't an actual portal, and reached out.

The handle of the door felt solid beneath her hand. She gripped it tightly, felt no magical blowback, and twisted the knob. The door, which should have swung open, dissolved instead; only the doorknob remained. That, and the oddly glowing frame.

"Yes," Terrano said, although she hadn't asked. "It's a portal. Don't let go of my hand."

Kaylin nodded as Terrano pulled ahead, almost jerking her off her feet. She closed her eyes, which sometimes helped, and entered portal space.

★ ★ ★

She suspected, as lunch attempted to escape her stomach, that portals from one place in a building to another didn't cause nausea because she remained in the same general space. She had very little hope that this portal would be like Hallionne portals, and indeed, it wasn't.

"Just keep your eyes closed," Terrano said.

She had tucked her chin, and her shoulders were curling toward what passed for ground. She didn't need to see, given Terrano's presence—and attempting to see what existed in portal space, as opposed to outlands space, never made things easier.

She felt the passage as if she were walking through molasses— or worse; the air felt heavy in her lungs, and her chest ached with the effort of drawing breath.

"We're almost through," Terrano said gently. He spoiled this act of kindness by adding, "I'd've been through to the other side ages ago if I didn't have to drag you along. You can open your eyes but if you're going to throw up, give me some warning."

Kaylin opened her eyes slowly.

If she'd hoped that somehow, beyond the door, there would be actual geography, she was bitterly disappointed; she was standing, by Terrano's side, in the outlands. Here and there light flickered sharply, as if it were lightning in distant, ground-level storm clouds.

She once again looked at Terrano; he was green, the green less vivid, less repulsive, than the green of the flower in the painting.

"Okay," she said. "We're here. We need to find a word."

"No problem. I'll follow you."

That, an oddly familiar voice said, *would be a waste of time— and I believe time is of the essence to you.*

She turned to look in the direction of the voice, and saw nothing.

Terrano sighed. "I forgot about you."

Apparently so did Lord Kaylin. As the words continued, they became deeper, the slight whir replaced by a rumble. Had she any doubt about whether or not this was the outlands, she lost it as Spike, invisible at the command of the High Halls, began to unfold.

In reality—which was increasingly becoming an extremely ill-defined word—Spike was a small ball with spikes that covered most of his spherical surface. In the outlands, Spike could become enormous, and clearly, he was doing so now.

The High Halls bid me follow you for a reason, Spike said. *You cannot perceive what you refer to as the outlands with any subtlety. I believe Terrano can, but it requires work on his part.*

"Did the Avatar tell you to tag along because he thought we'd end up here?"

You will have to ask. Spike towered above them. From a distance, he looked Draconic, but neither Kaylin nor Terrano had the advantage of distance. Long neck, long tail, six legs that could barely be seen above the constant, moving fog, only Spike's eyes retained color, and it was the familiar speckled black Kaylin had always associated with Shadow. No, that wasn't entirely true. When he opened Dragon-sized jaws, the interior of his mouth was blood red.

Perhaps you wish to ride, he told them both. *We will have to cover a great deal of ground, as you call it, and you may lose me otherwise.*

In any other circumstance, the possibility of losing something the size of a Dragon would be laughable. Not here. Also: Spike was considerate enough to create a riding space that wasn't hard, spiky, or scaly.

Look ahead, Chosen. You might be able to see what we are following; it is a very, very fine thread.

Kaylin nodded. She did try, but she couldn't see what Spike could see. Neither, apparently, could Terrano—but he was more annoyed at the inability. They both climbed up Spike's back.

"Hope?"

Don't be ridiculous, her familiar said. He glanced at Spike, shrugged, and transformed, from an almost Aerian-like being to a much more Draconic one. *I am perfectly capable of following Spike's trail without the need to encumber them.*

Kaylin nodded. "Hold on tight," she told Terrano.

Spike began to *move.*

28

Holding on to Spike was more work than ideal. If he'd offered to carry them, he clearly wasn't accustomed to passengers—or to keeping them neatly on his back while he was tearing up the fog that passed for ground in the outlands. Kaylin regretted not asking for Hope's help, because she was certain he wouldn't let her fall.

She was distracted by a distant building—an oddly shaped blur that seemed faintly familiar. It had no tower, and what appeared to be walls or roof were uneven in composition. It was the only feature in the otherwise gray, foggy landscape, and it appeared to be Spike's destination.

As they approached, she revised her opinion. It wasn't a building. It was a large—a giant—word, in shape and form similar to the marks on Kaylin's arms. Long before Spike slowed to a stop, she could see the curve of line, the placement of the dots and strokes that implied meaning. Something—besides its existence and its height—felt off about it.

She slid off Spike's back. Terrano did the same, but he hovered above the fog that obscured the ground. Kaylin, sadly, didn't. Beneath her feet she could feel something with the give and consistency of flesh. It didn't collapse beneath her weight, which was all she could really ask of ground—but she wished she could walk above it the way Terrano was.

Spike raised his head. His neck, extended, was longer than Hope's in his full Draconic form. *Here, Lord Kaylin.*

Kaylin nodded. She reached out to touch what she assumed was a terminating stroke; it was cold and hard beneath her palm, and it had the consistency of rough stone. "Hope, do you have any idea what the word means?"

It does not, as you suspect, have innate meaning. It is not a True Word. It is not a name.

"I'm pretty sure it's why Azoria isn't technically dead."

Terrano, never one to be unnecessarily cautious—or cautious at all—approached the area beyond this long stone line, where the mass of the characteristics that defined the marks Kaylin bore were gathered. "Hey—come here. Over here."

Kaylin nodded. "Over here," however, had to be reached the hard way: by climbing up onto the stone and walking across it until there wasn't enough room between the flat, slight curve of its shape and the elements that rested above it.

This wouldn't be the first time she had seen True Words as enormous, but again, this felt off. It felt wrong. Maybe because it was stone—and felt like stone—beneath her feet, and to her touch. "Does this look like stone to you?"

"Yes—badly quarried, badly finished stone," Terrano replied. "But I want you to come here. Look at this part."

"I'm *trying*," she snarled. "Can you still hear the rest of your cohort?"

"No. Not easily."

"I don't care if it's easy or not—is it possible?"

"Maybe? It's a bit jumbled, but I recognize Sedarias's voice; it just doesn't resolve into words."

Kaylin couldn't hear Severn at all. Nor could she reach

any of the Barrani whose names she held. She could—and did—manage to wedge herself between two levels of stone to finally reach a visibly impatient Terrano. "Is she worried?"

"She's always worried. Don't look at me like that—worry won't solve anything. But figuring this out might."

"I'm sorry I can't walk through stone," she snapped. "What are you looking at?"

Terrano muttered a brief word in mangled Leontine. He knew what Teela knew, but actual pronunciation took a bit more practice. "Here, can you see this?"

She shook her head. "It looks like stone, to me." The stone in question was a vertical line that rose far above their heads, possibly to support a horizontal line at the height. "But I couldn't see the door in the painting, either. Is it a door?"

"Not exactly."

"What exactly is it?"

"I'm not certain. From one angle it looks like a crack."

Kaylin couldn't see a crack, but given Terrano's color at the moment, that wasn't surprising. "Hope, do you think you could go back to normal size?"

I do not think it necessary. What Terrano perceives as a possible crack, you are capable of sensing on your own.

Spike, however, whirred and clicked; if Hope was reluctant, Spike wasn't. Kaylin held out a hand, and he came to her palm immediately, the protrusions for which she'd named him biting into her palm. He then proceeded to melt there, vanishing into a vaguely metallic puddle.

Kaylin joined Terrano. He lifted a hand, but she shook her head. "Hope says I should be able to sense it on my own, and I don't need any more complaints about my weight."

Terrano grinned, but lowered his hand as Kaylin reached out to touch the column.

Hope was right. If she couldn't see a crack, as Terrano, still tinged vivid green, could, she could feel a sudden difference in texture. It wasn't door width; it was only person width if the person was a starving four-year-old. But it was warmer than stone, and when she pushed against it, it had give.

It reminded her of the unseen ground that occupied most of the outlands.

"Spike, is this where the connecting thread is?"

He whirred and clicked in response, which was the largest disadvantage of small-Spike form. Hope, however distant he might have been, said, "He does not understand your question."

"We see a very, very large structure in the shape of a word."

Click. Whir.

Spike sees a word. The thread is attached to the word. I do not believe the stone structure both you and Terrano see is visible in the same way to Spike.

Which made no sense, but the outlands, combined with an almost dead Arcanist, was a place where sense was always going to be in short supply. And that was unfair. Spike could see clearly enough to bring them here at great speed. What he could see or sense was real.

"Is the word Spike sees as large as the one Terrano and I see?"

He does not understand the question, but says that it is like your marks.

Her marks were small enough to fit across her arms. But she knew enough now to know that how those marks were perceived varied by observer—one of them being Kaylin herself.

"Hope—does the building itself look like a word to you?"

What does it look like to you?

"Like...an attempt at a word, or an attempt at several words."

But not a True Word?

She shook her head slowly as the import of the question grew roots. "This isn't a word," she finally said. "It has the right components, the right…parts, but it's not a True Word. It's…an attempt at creating a True Word."

"With delusions of grandeur," Terrano added, his tone implying agreement.

"But there's a word here somewhere. A real one. It's that that we need to find."

Terrano nodded. "I think that's your job," he said. "I don't see words the way you see them."

Kaylin placed her hand flat against the part of the structure that felt disturbingly fleshlike. "I can't see the word; I can only see the larger structure. But…it has to be here."

Barrani—some Barrani—hated the existence of their own True Names, because the names that granted them immortality were a weakness that could be used against them, rendering them slaves to the will of another. Attempts to free themselves from those shackles had not historically gone well. Kaylin couldn't tell if this was another attempt to do the same, but doubted it.

This was different. Azoria had taken something from the Wevaran, something from the Ancestors; she had learned enough to place her home in a pocket space that was attached to Mrs. Erickson's home or land. She had learned enough to somehow capture the souls of living mortals and bind them, as if they were equivalent to Barrani names.

Kaylin wondered if some of the dead were here, in the outlands; if those she had devoured or those she had murdered had become the clay out of which this edifice of words had been built.

Where would Azoria's name reside? At the heart of the structure. At its center.

Kaylin withdrew her palm because she needed it. She unsheathed her dagger.

"Are you sure that's a good idea?" Terrano helpfully asked.

She wasn't. But she was angry and she knew it. "If you've got a better idea, I'm all ears. Short on time, though."

"I think I could fit in there, if it's passable." Passable to Terrano didn't mean the same thing for Kaylin.

"And I think that would be about the stupidest idea ever if you don't want to become part of a large, fake word."

"What?"

"This is what she's been building. I don't know how long it's taken, and I don't know if it's stable or if it gives her the power she hoped for when she first thought of it. I don't think adding your name—an actual True Word, a word imbued with eternity—is going to help us in any way. But it won't hurt her."

"So stabbing it is *better*?"

"I'd be willing to bet on it."

"You're willing to bet on anything. Fine. Go ahead."

Kaylin drove her dagger into the invisible fault line, praying that the structure didn't scream in response.

Praying never worked.

The screaming wasn't the worst thing—it sounded like the voice of a terrified crowd, one that anticipated pain and death. No, the worst thing was the blood. As if this small patch of the outlands was actually alive, Kaylin's dagger pierced skin; as she withdrew the blade, liquid followed.

It was a pale liquid, golden in color, and it reminded Kaylin of the pool in Tara's Tower, of the ancient mirror in the heart of the Imperial Palace. Of the blood of the Ancients, spilled so long ago, its true purpose lost to time. She almost dropped the knife, the impulse to reach—to treat—the wound she had caused was so visceral.

Her marks flared to life, gold as the blood that continued to spill from the wound.

What has she done? Hope said, his voice unnaturally soft, as if shock had robbed it of volume.

It was a rhetorical question; Kaylin made no attempt to answer it. Nor did she answer Terrano's sharp "What are you doing?" when she placed both hands against the cut.

"Can you see the blood?" she asked.

"Yes. It's golden," Terrano replied. Spike was silent. "But you made that cut for a reason."

It didn't seem like a good reason now. Kaylin couldn't explain and didn't try. As the marks of the Chosen continued to glow she used the only power they'd granted her that she could deliberately invoke: she attempted to heal the damage she'd done.

The wound wasn't wide; it was deep. She felt that as she began to push her awareness into the foreign body, seeking the damage, and seeking the damaged blood vessels that were shedding so much liquid. The wound, however, was far deeper than she'd realized. She knew better than to act in anger; the cause for that anger seemed petty now. If Azoria had built this place, it wasn't Azoria she'd stabbed.

I'm sorry, she said, as she continued to expand her awareness. *I'm sorry I hurt you. I didn't—I didn't know you were alive.* She knew now. Something lived here. She couldn't sense any of the usual features she expected from living bodies—lungs, heart, limbs—but she did find a head, a face, something that might have been the remnants of a person, trapped here and suspended somehow in a tangle of stone and steel. Had it been a corpse, she wouldn't have been surprised; there was only so much damage and shock a body could take.

It wasn't a corpse. She felt the truncated nerves and bones where limbs might have once been: four, all absent. The scalp had been scarred, the skin abraded so badly the flesh had rippled beneath it; she found a mouth, and the stub of a tongue, evidence of teeth, where teeth might have once been. Only the eyes—two eyes—were whole.

There was no word here, no True Name. Just what remained of a person of indeterminate race. Human, Barrani, Aerian, Tha'alani; the jaw was wrong for Leontine.

"Kaylin?"

"I've—I've found a person. But...their blood shouldn't be golden."

"You've found a person?"

She nodded. "I don't think I can heal them—they're really badly injured—but I'm not sure fixing those injuries when they're stuck in whatever this stonelike substance is will work."

Spike clicked.

"It is not stone, Spike says."

"What is it?"

"Carapace."

"But—it's not their shell. I'd swear it."

"Carapace can be removed."

She nodded, and reached for the external skin of the entrapped entity. "Oh."

"Oh?"

She shook her head. It was never wise to act in anger, but she was beyond anger now, and well beyond wisdom. Whatever was entrapped here wasn't human. The sides of this pillar weren't stone; they were calcified *scabs*. She couldn't tear them off—it would take days, equipment, and manpower, none of which she had. But she could heal the skin beneath them; could try to force the body into its ideal, healthy state.

That is not wise, Hope said. *You are expending far too much power.*

But the marks were now glowing, and as Hope's words trailed off into unanswered silence, they began to rise from her skin, flat forms becoming three dimensional forms that grew in size. They were all True Words—this much she recognized, in part because she could hear them, and the language felt familiar—a tongue she felt she should know, or could. She'd tried to speak True Words, but had never succeeded without aid; she did not try now. But she trusted the marks of the Chosen; she trusted their power to heal anyone who wasn't dead yet.

It had always been borrowed power.

She didn't hear the first crack. She did hear Terrano's shout, half alarm, half glee, words garbled and distant. She saw new skin grow, shimmering faintly as it dislodged what she'd wrongly assumed was rough stone. And she heard voices as she reformed the missing part of the tongue; felt the ground beneath her feet shift. She almost lost contact, but the land stabilized—as if what she healed was now aware of her presence. That wasn't unexpected—it's the way healing worked with normal people of all races. But she wasn't aware of them in the same way; she couldn't hear thoughts or brush against stray memories. She tried, but only once; she got swept away in a torrent of images and sounds that she couldn't process.

What had Azoria done? What had she found? What had she made?

The ground shook again; she could hear the loud thud of heavy objects striking softer ones. Also: Terrano cursing. Nothing hit her on the way down, which she attributed to Hope's interference. Or Spike's.

But her arms began to ache; her legs joined them. She felt sweat dribble down her eyelids.

Yes. I told you—you use far too much power.

"It's not my power!"

A sword is useless without a wielder. Wielding the finest of blades takes effort, will, practice—it is not trivial. But...I would have said this was beyond you; it would have been beyond the Chosen in the distant past. You have done enough; pull back.

"I'm not finished yet—"

You are finished, Kaylin, Hope said. She was grabbed by the arms and borne almost instantly aloft, but she was carried by hands, not Draconic claws.

"What is it? What was I healing?"

If you cannot answer that question, no one here can. But come, look. You will not see this sight again should you live another century.

They didn't have *time* to sightsee, and she opened her mouth to say as much, but forgot how to speak for a moment.

The building—the large word—was collapsing as Hope hovered, the slabs of...dead skin falling into the fog of the outlands as if they were thunder. It wasn't the collapse that caused the loss of speech; it was what lay beneath her feet, shaking itself loose. It was a giant, with skin of shining gold. The missing arms and legs weren't Kaylin's work, but she understood why Hope had pulled her out; the giant was free enough, whole enough, to do that work themselves.

Shoulders emerged, and when they did, Kaylin saw that the creature had been almost prone; it rose, twisting shoulders to either side to shake off the last of its captivity. It lifted its head last, and it had fire for eyes, fire for hair—but that hair waved in the air as if the fire were serpents. Or some progenitor of the Tha'alani, writ large.

When it spoke, Kaylin understood why it had sounded like

a crowd: multiple voices came from that single mouth. She really hoped that being stabbed hadn't angered it.

It continued to unfold, to grow in height, in width; she could see golden filaments streaming out from its shoulder blades, as if they wanted to be wings. A gauze of light clung to those filaments. As she watched, that light spread, and spread again, until wings had formed.

Hope was utterly silent; had he not been forced to hover, Kaylin was certain he wouldn't have been aware of her at all.

"Spike?"

Silence.

The only person who seemed willing to break the silence was Terrano. "I think the small lights might be the remnants of your people."

"My people?"

"Mortals. There's something about the quality of it that's different, if you look at it the right way."

"There are no words, though?"

"There must be," Terrano replied. "Azoria didn't build whatever that is. She might have found it, but she didn't build it. Given what she was attempting to do with Mrs. Erickson— assuming she could somehow see or sense Mrs. Erickson's gift at all—it may be that whatever we're looking at isn't actually alive. But Spike was certain that this was where the strand of Azoria's life led."

Kaylin nodded, frowning. "It felt alive to me. You can't heal the dead." As she spoke, she could see movement in the fog of the outlands, as if they had become clouds. Storm clouds. She could not see the creature's feet, but the storm was gathering around where legs implied they would be.

"We need the word," she said, voice even softer. "We need to separate it, somehow."

"You think it gives her some kind of power over a god?"

God. The word rippled. Hope and Spike didn't take issue with it.

"I don't know. I don't even know if what the word was is what it is now."

"What were ours, when you found them?"

She frowned.

"We weren't attached to our names when we first attempted to escape; we'd drifted from them, but we didn't intend to desert them. Our ability to speak to each other the way we do *is* the name bond. When I refused to have the name fully returned to me, I couldn't hear the others anymore. I liked the peace and quiet, but...I missed them. Their voices and their opinions had been part of me for so long it felt as if I'd lost something essential. What did my name look like?"

"Almost transparent; it was small and diminished—but it was still a True Name, a True Word. The thing that you were changing—the thing that changed—was you." Her frown deepened. "I think your name might have become different had you not relied on the name bond. And I know there are things you can't do because you accepted it. It defines some essential part of the physical you. Just...not as clearly as it does for people who weren't subjected to the green, the *regalia*, and centuries of captivity."

"You think I'm looking for something like that."

Terrano nodded.

"I wouldn't have found your names had Alsanis not preserved them. You were his captives, yes—but you were his guests. I think he grew very fond of all of you, like a foster parent. She doesn't have Alsanis—and frankly, I don't think he could have grown fond of her in the same way."

"Why?"

"Because she's not like the rest of you. You're all different people, and I really only know half of you at all—but you're all capable of loving."

Terrano grimaced, as if he were a teenager at that awkward age. Kaylin recognized the expression because she'd been one herself.

"What Azoria wanted wasn't that, in the end. Look, if I'd met Sedarias under any other circumstance, I would have assumed she was the usual cutthroat Barrani."

"She is."

"Yes, she is—but she's more than that. I think, if she had to choose between the cohort and being that typical Barrani, she'd choose the cohort."

"*Never* let her hear you say that."

Kaylin laughed. "Hope, I need to approach that being."

Hope failed to move.

"You heard what Terrano said, right? I think, if we don't get that word out of him, we're never going to be free of Azoria."

I think you have nothing to fear now. If that word is foreign, They will remove it themselves. There was a reason that you were forced to heal that being; Azoria simply took advantage of it.

"Will it make her stronger, if her name is somehow part of him?"

You have a very ghoulish imagination.

"I'm a Hawk. We tend to see a lot of the worst people can be. Will you let me take this risk?"

I don't want to.

"You're *my* familiar, right? In theory that means you don't have the choice."

I could drop you.

"Yes, but I'd like you to do it gently. Look—I think the wings *are* the gathering of the life force of mortals Azoria somehow stole. I kind of hoped they'd be released—but I don't know what that would mean in this place."

And Azoria's name might be likewise absorbed. You do not understand what you are seeing.

"I know we don't want that. Not if it's somehow still attached. She's a murderer several times over. If she's not stopped, that will continue forever." Probably literally forever. She lifted an arm; her marks circled it, like a moving, layered bracelet. "And I think I can get their attention."

And if you have Their attention, what will you do with it? Will you surrender the marks of the Chosen in their entirety?

"That wasn't my intent."

Your intent might matter very little.

"I'm used to that. Put me down."

I will, when the transformation is complete.

"Transformation?"

The outlands are responding to the will of this being, just as they would to the Hallionne. Watch, if you can, without talking.

Hope was right. He almost always was, which was the kind of extremely helpful that could also be annoying. Fog rose, and rose again, changing color and texture: pillars of something pale, by the dozen, reached for what passed for sky in the outlands. The sky itself shifted color as they rose, as if persistent gray was as much part of the outlands as the ground fog; gray gave way to a deep azure—the ideal of a cloudless, perfect day. In the distance, stars emerged in great numbers, as if they were accessories to the radiance of this single being.

No walls rose between pillars, but the ground became paneled wood beneath his feet, and the wood did not instantly become ash. There was a moon in the sky, low and bright, but no other light was necessary; the being shed it continuously, as if they meant to be living sun to the moon's light.

Trees grew last, but grew tallest. Kaylin, not a botanist, didn't recognize them. She thought it likely that Serralyn might, but Terrano couldn't bespeak her from whatever this place was becoming.

Only when the trees' branches began to bud and blossom did this being turn their attention to Kaylin. Hair rose in tendrils, as if they were fingers, but they fell short of the trees that had grown like forest. The only place the trees didn't touch was the space in which Kaylin and her companions hovered.

"Come. I would speak with you, Chosen." Even at this distance, his words were clear, and there was nothing that implied he'd raised it to cover the distance.

Hope flew Kaylin to the ground, where a path of stone formed beneath her feet.

He then dwindled in size and took up his perch on her shoulder, lifting a wing to smack it across her face. She noted that the wing, for the first time, trembled as it lay across her eyes. The wing didn't change anything she could see. The ground-side vantage, however, made the being who had emerged seem even larger than it had from the air. It—he?— was beautiful. Barrani beauty, so envied by the merely mortal, was a pale, pale shadow of the beauty of this creature, which was odd: fiery tendrils for hair, fire for eyes, wings that looked far more Draconic than Aerian, and skin that looked like gold lit from within, wouldn't normally have implied beauty to Kaylin.

"Did he just call you Chosen?" Terrano whispered.

Kaylin nodded. The marks on her arms still rotated at a distance from her skin; she imagined the other marks were also active, but less visibly so. Whatever power she'd used to heal what she could touch hadn't dimmed their radiance at all, but she was uneasily aware, as she began to walk down this path, that that radiance was the color of the person who'd summoned her.

He stood, arms by his side, eyes upon her progress; she began to walk more briskly.

By the time she reached him, he had dwindled in size, but not in presence; he towered over her, but she could actually meet his gaze without toppling over backward making the attempt.

"Chosen, welcome," he said, before she could speak. Which was good, because her mouth was dry and words had deserted her, probably for her own safety. "You may speak without fear of giving offense. I owe you a great, great debt, and the ability to cause offense is not in you; you might even stab me and be forgiven." As he spoke, his eyes kindled briefly; Kaylin didn't believe him.

"You have done so," he said. "And my blood has fallen— as it fell before—upon the words you bear. You are a very, very fragile vessel; were the choice mine, I would not have chosen you to contain them. But those who know life know change and error; I would have been wrong."

He didn't ask her why she'd come, why she'd stabbed him, or even why she remained.

"No, but it is not necessary, in this space. I know. And I understand what it is that you seek; I understand—far better than you know—why you do so. Come." He held out a hand. Kaylin found herself walking toward it, her own left hand raised as if to take it, before she could even consider movement.

She was uneasily certain that had he demanded that she kill herself, she'd be bleeding before she'd fully processed the command. Regardless, her palm was against his palm before she'd had time to form intention. Or anxiety. In a disturbing way, obedience felt as natural as breathing.

"You have questions."

She didn't, but the minute she heard the words, she did. "Why were you here? Why were you trapped? How could Azoria—how could *anyone*—imprison you?"

"We do not die as you die. We do not live as you live. You have seen my blood," he added, "before you injured me here. It was not the only blood I shed, not the only blood required to build what we desired to build. We are purpose, Kaylin."

She hadn't given him her name, but wasn't surprised to hear it. She had healed him, after all.

"My purpose was to die."

29

Kaylin examined him as a healer, looking for death. She couldn't see it. The connection between them—two palms—didn't imply death. She'd touched corpses before, while watching Red in the morgue. This was nothing like that.

"No. I told you, death for us, death for you, it is very different. You are so slight, all of you—even the one whose vestigial name you seek. I gave what I was meant to give."

She felt no resentment in this being. No anger. No sense that his life was a universal injustice. No *Why me?*

"Are you dead now?"

"No. No, Chosen. I am not, and I find it strange. I had purpose. I had meaning. I did what I was meant to do. Without purpose, what point life? I am one of the youngest of my kind," he added. "And more attuned to the living because of it. The eldest were not; they could barely see the living, and could not always countenance their import, except in an intellectual way.

"But the youngest could. We were born—and that is not the right word, but it will have to do for now—into a world, into the many worlds, where life dwelled. Those worlds were replete with the idle creations of the elders before us. And we marveled at the mutations of those creations, achieved without further interference. Always, always, the delight of the unexpected, the unpredicted. It was the unpredicted that quickened us; some sought it actively, seeing in change the reason for life at all.

"That was not my purpose. It was not the reason I was born, the reason I became."

He fell silent. That silence was broken by the warbling of birds.

Kaylin felt...outrage. Outrage that his parents—if they could be called that—had birthed him simply so he could *die.* She had seen neglected children, children who would have been better off as orphans, and children whose parents treated their entire existence as accessories. This was worse.

"No," he said softly. "It is not. We exist, we come into being, with purpose. It is not what defines you—but your kind often seek the echoes of greater purpose without fully understanding the cost. I do not rage. I do not feel that I was thrown away, that I was meant to die in the stead of others. Perhaps that is not something you can fully comprehend. You have seen my blood in the Lake of Life."

She stopped breathing for a long moment.

"Do you consider it unnecessary sacrifice? From the moment they were born, the entire Barrani race has lived, breathed, grown because of my blood. You have seen my blood in the chronicle—I believe you call it a mirror. There are places you have not touched, have not seen, but should you, there are traces of me in all of them."

"But—"

"How came I to be here?" He smiled as if in approval. She thought a promotion from corporal to something higher wouldn't have so instantly warmed her, and flushed at the thought.

"You think of this as...the *outlands*. As a place that exists beyond the borders of your plane. Your reality. But you have seen it in the heart of the being you call home; you have seen it in Hallionne, created to be shelter and peace for those who were weary."

"I've seen it around *Ravellon*," she said.

"Yes. Even there. It is not *a* place. It is *possibility*, except in one way: it cannot create sentience. Life? Yes. The trees you see here are alive. The insects, should I choose that detail, alive. But even the forest creatures of your world cannot be created entirely from the ether without will and some small part of ourselves as the price demanded.

"This is what all worlds were before they were touched and shaped; this is what all worlds came from, when words were invoked. The speaking was difficult; it drained the speakers, the words flowing from them to be lost forever, the lands whose tale they told immutable, fixed, the lives within them separate, the possibilities narrowed." His smile was odd. "To us, then, your worlds might seem almost dead."

"What?" She glanced at Hope.

Hope's head was bowed, his eyes closed, his tiny jaw shut. He had withdrawn the wing that revealed nothing more unusual than her own eyes could see, and had folded it across his shoulders. He stood, however; the indolent drape that implied boredom was nowhere in sight.

"They are not dead. To those of us who came after, they are teeming with possibility. It is a constrained possibility. It has its own boundaries, its own form—but within that form, so many variations. You are one of them."

He then raised his empty hand. Kaylin didn't understand the words he spoke.

Hope lifted his wings, pushed himself off Kaylin's shoulder, and came to stand on one of this being's fingers. It made him look both tiny and far more transparent; she could see the entirety of the being's hand through Hope's body. He seemed to flicker there, and almost without thinking, she reached out to grab him.

The being looked down at her. "I mean him no harm. But he is ancient, and if whimsical, he has the ability—defined as life is defined—to choose his own purpose. I wished merely to discuss what the consequences of those varied choices have been."

"I'm sorry," she said, retaining her hold on Hope, "but we don't have time. Azoria is out in *my* plane of existence, and she's trying to kill most of my friends."

"Most?"

"Some of my friends aren't in Azoria's strange mansion, or she'd be trying to murder them, too."

"I see. I wish to speak with him, but I understand at least the constraints of time. What I do not understand is the loss of purpose. I do not understand why I exist as I now exist at all. I understand only one thing: you woke me. I believe, given the extent of my injuries, this person you sought *tried*. But you have the words of my people; she did not; she was not Chosen." His eyes narrowed. "They are not your words, but they are yours to use. There is a telling there that I have not seen before. They are your purpose. And if they have spoken to me, if they have chosen to wake me, it means I am needed once again."

"For what?"

He looked genuinely confused, and when he answered, his words were syllables with no meaning to Kaylin's ears.

Hope, however, squawked. Loudly.

"It is not yet time," was the soft reply—but this time, Kaylin could understand it. "And I am not yet whole enough to face any duty. Come, Chosen, find what you must find, do what you must do. I must think now."

Kaylin nodded. Closing her eyes, she looked for Azoria's name.

She had never asked any of the cohort whether her knowledge of the name she had carried back to them would have given her the power of control over them when the names were almost unattached to their corporeal selves. She expected to find the remnants of a Barrani True Name, thin and almost devoid of light.

"No," the being said, "I cannot sense it. If it is to be found at all, you will have to find it. I am uncertain that a simple creation's breath could control or contain me. But your kind were oft surprising and confounding." She didn't tell him that Azoria was definitively *not* her kind, being Barrani. She understood that to this being, there was probably very little difference—even if his blood was the Lake in which the entirety of the Barrani race rested, awaiting birth or rebirth.

"Can you find Azoria? Are you aware of her?"

"No, Chosen. But I know what was given the Lake, and there is nothing of that in me now. I understand your fear. It is not irrelevant. I am too new, and too unaware. Waking is rebirth. Sleep is death. Neither of these words describe what I am, but you would perish long before the end of the tale of who I am, even diminished by sacrifice and purpose."

She could not see the words in him. Not by touch, not by healing. She could feel the weight of her marks, the light of them, the exhaustion in focusing the power inherent to them; she sensed no like words in the being whose hand she touched. It was these words, however, that she looked for now—or rather, words like them.

She felt, as she continued her search, a strange but familiar sensation. It took her a moment to place it: she had felt it when she had taken a new name from the Lake of Life—writ small and entirely unlike the actual Lake she would later see. This was...his blood, something entirely unlike hers, or Barrani blood, or Leontine blood.

No wonder she couldn't perceive thought, intent, memory: it was...words. It was True Words—things she could hear if she listened carefully. But she'd never understood them beyond a flash of insight, an instinctive touch. She would die of old age—or starvation—if she made the attempt to do that here: there was just *too much*.

She didn't try. But she thought she knew now where she had to look for Azoria's name—or what was left of it. It was here, in an environment that was almost natural to its unhoused form. She almost wanted to give up before she'd started; there was just *too much* here to examine. Too much from which to separate a single transformed word. Azoria had seen the Lake of Life. Given Azoria, she might have understood that housed in this sleeping remnant of an Ancient god was a lake, very like the Lake of Life.

Think, Kaylin, she told herself. *Think. What would you want, if you were Azoria? Would you be content to just embed the word?*

No. She wouldn't. Could she assume that Azoria understood what she had found? Yes. Better than Kaylin herself had. Azoria's life was not a Hawk's life. It wasn't the life of a child who had been born fief-side, where law was whim and subject to change without notice.

Kaylin couldn't have devoted the entirety of her life to study, to research, to ancient books and dead languages. She cared about living languages because they belonged to living people. The joy study gave Serralyn wasn't in Kaylin. Never would be. She had studied, with intense focus, the things that she was certain she could *use*.

If Azoria intended to somehow anchor her life in a god, she wouldn't randomly embed it. It wouldn't be *enough* to be one of so many, many words. It wouldn't give her control. It wouldn't be *her* power. No.

She had watched Red work in his morgue; she had seen injuries that were fatal. She considered where she herself might have lodged her True Name in such circumstances: the heart.

But she wasn't Azoria. That symbolism wouldn't be Azoria's. But the head, the mind: those were the things she prized, the things that she believed would yield power. The Ancient had been missing limbs, missing tongue. Flesh had been scraped and scarred so badly the scabs that had formed had become a prison.

And she remembered, then, the look of the gigantic word that they had approached in the distance. Not a True Word. Not a word that could ever return to the Lake. But it had been shaped as it had for a reason.

Entwining her fingers around fingers far larger than hers, she felt like a small child, but she took a figurative step back. Her sense of the giant, her sense of what he contained, she removed, layer by layer, until she was standing, in her mind's eye, at the edge of the Lake of Life writ large. The waters were clear—clear and golden; they promised peace, offered both hope and despair, joy and sorrow, purpose and oblivion. They promised life.

There was never total freedom in life. Kaylin knew that better than Azoria had. But she'd found joy and a kind of freedom in becoming herself. In allowing hope, not fear, to guide her path forward. No path was smooth. No path was perfect. She stumbled. She tripped. She made different choices as she got back on her feet and dusted herself off. But she'd come to understand Corporal Kaylin Neya; she almost liked what she was now.

Azoria had made a different choice. She wanted to become something greater than she was.

Once, Kaylin would have mistakenly believed that they had had the same goal, the same driving need: to become better than they were. To become more. But it wasn't the same. There were limitations that Kaylin had accepted as a child and as a fiefling that she should never have accepted—but there were limitations that could not be altered or changed: she was never going to be Immortal. She was never going to be beautiful. She was never going to be a hero. She was never going to see her mother again.

Azoria, in deciding to change her circumstances, accepted no limitations at all. The gift of immortality, the gift of life, was too scant, too stunted, too powerless. Azoria would have become a god, if she could.

She couldn't. No more could Kaylin, Chosen. Kaylin had killed in the midst of anger, fear, and bitter self-loathing. Azoria had killed for different reasons. Both were murderers. Kaylin couldn't judge her for that.

But Kaylin's atonement, if it was that, was to prevent others from being what she had almost fully become. To save the people who would be their victims, or their future victims. To add justice to a world that didn't innately possess it.

She let go of judgment, anger, hatred; she was entitled to none of them. Well, maybe hatred—but it didn't help. It had never helped. The Consort had made clear that one couldn't approach the Lake of Life that way. The moment the personal encroached, choices led to disaster, to mistakes.

Yes, she understood what she must do.

As she had once before, she plunged her hand into the Lake. Words scudded briefly against her palm. The surface of the Lake was illusion, an analogy she'd created. There was constant motion beneath the surface, and in that motion, she could feel the brief shape of passing words as they moved across her palm, across the back of her hand, and between her fingers.

She had come to the Lake once, and she had taken what she needed.

She came now to repay that favor. She couldn't speak words, couldn't pronounce them, couldn't even understand intellectually *what* was needed. Or why. So she asked the Lake, instead, for what the *Lake* needed.

In answer, something scudded against her palm, and the waters went still. She knew it wasn't water in any true sense; that she'd somehow made of this interior landscape a paradigm that she could understand, a way of approach that matched the only experience she had.

She carried that paradigm to its conclusion: she gripped this shape, this rough, almost spongelike texture, tightly, as she began to lift it from the waters. She had expected it to be difficult; had expected it to be almost too heavy to carry, too large to easily extract.

No. It was larger in size than the marks on her arms, spinning in their layered bracelets, but it was far, far lighter than any of the words or partial words Kaylin had carried from the Lake. It wasn't golden; it was almost ash gray—the huge word writ small and shakily exact.

She drew the word from the Lake and as she did, she lost sight of the water; her hand was no longer in contact with the hand of the Ancient. In the palm of her left hand she carried an ash gray word—a word that was not a True Word, a word that was, linguistically, a part of a language that did not have immutable meaning.

Just as Kaylin's spoken words didn't have immutable meaning.

"I see," the Ancient said. "It is a word from one of the many lesser languages." They smiled. "What do you call the language?"

"Azoria," Kaylin replied. "And it's not a language. It's a one-of-a-kind word."

"No language can consist of one word."

She nodded and then fell silent, thinking about what he had said. "No. This isn't a language. It's a single word. Language is... We use it to talk to people. To our friends. To our acquaintances. I mean, we avoid using words at all in the face of angry boss—"

"Boss?"

"It's like lord or emperor."

"Ah. Ruler."

"But we use language. It's the bridge between ourselves and other people."

"You said language."

Technically, the Ancient had said language and Kaylin hadn't argued. She considered the single word in her hand. "New words come into languages all the time. But this isn't meant to communicate. It's not used to...share."

It hit her, as she spoke, that the Barrani Lake, that the Barrani existences, were single words, part of an ancient language—possibly the first language—that the sum of those words was an entire race; that together, the Barrani formed a series of complex sentences, paragraphs, perhaps entire books or libraries of books.

That had never occurred to her before this moment.

Azoria Berranin had chosen to absent herself from that conversation. Kaylin looked up. "Can you fix this?"

"If by *fix* you mean return it to what it was before it was almost erased, no. It is not as simple as regrowth of a lost limb." Which wasn't simple at all.

"But I perceive that this is a dark, angry language, a language of isolation. Were it like your companion's oddly textured name, I could do as you ask."

"No, thank you," Terrano said, speaking for the first time, his voice uncharacteristically grave and respectful. "Lord Kaylin, we must leave. If you have found what we sought, we must return to our friends."

"Spike, can you take us back to the door?" Kaylin's voice was a whisper.

Spike emerged from the palm of her hand; she felt the tremor in the tips of his protrusions.

The Ancient's smile deepened, widened, as they looked at Spike. The recognition and delight in their expression cast a wave of envy—even jealousy—over the watching Hawk. When the Ancient spoke, she couldn't understand a word they said, but Spike's quivering increased. Kaylin knew it wasn't fear that caused it.

Spike whirred, clicked, shook in place.

He wishes to remain, Hope said. *The Ancient wishes to converse with Spike; Spike was, and is, a historian.*

"Can you take us home? Like, without having to devour the marks?"

Your marks were never worthy of being a sacrifice, Hope replied, voice soft. *They are your source of power, but it is not power that you prize.*

"Fine. Can you take us home without having to devour Terrano, or one of my limbs?"

Terrano glared at the familiar on Kaylin's shoulder. "I can take us back, thanks."

"You wish to leave?" the Ancient asked, looking away from Spike. "They say they have been tasked with your safety, and they should not abandon you."

"Tasked by who? No, never mind. Spike wants to stay

with you and I'm not his responsibility. I understand Spike's feelings. I'd stay if I could," she added, embarrassed to mean it so viscerally. "But I have what I came for, and if I don't get back, I might lose a lot of my friends. Their deaths won't be like yours. They won't wake again, no matter how much power we put into the attempt to revive them."

"And you wish to find an exit to your world from the planes of eternity."

Kaylin nodded.

"That, Chosen, I can do, if you will but relieve Spike of his duties. You will take that word with you?"

"That's the hope, yes. Is it possible?"

"That word is, in part, of this plane. I am uncertain that removing the subtle roots will not destabilize the structure of the whole."

"We're not concerned with the structural stability of this particular attempt at creating a word. It's bound to someone who was once Barrani; the heart of it came from the Lake of Life, and it will never return."

For the first time, furrows appeared across the immaculate gold of the Ancient's skin.

"First," they said, and gestured. Between two of the pillars to the left of Kaylin, an arch appeared. "Your exit. Second, the word you have retrieved. Understand that I was not born as destroyer. It is not my gift, not my strength. It was never my purpose.

"I will not help you destroy. I will not aid you in killing. But I owe you a debt, and when I discover what new purpose I have woken to, I will pay it as I am able. Hold tight to what you carry. You are Chosen, and I believe some part of your gift, as the Chosen of your generation, is being served by your decision. No other could have found what you sought, and no other could remove it from this place."

Kaylin offered the Ancient what she hoped was a perfect bow. Power expected both respect and reasonable manners, after all.

She then rose, turned to the left, and walked—swiftly—through the arch, followed by Terrano and Hope.

They found themselves in the hallway directly in front of the empty painting.

Noise returned, and not a little of it; the clank of steel against steel—or chitin—rang down the hall. Given that the fighting had been taking place on the second floor, in a different direction, the sounds caused Kaylin's anxiety to instantly peak.

"No one's died yet," Terrano said, his own eyes the indigo of Barrani worry. Or fear. Or rage. "Teela's injured; she's taken the brunt of the damage."

But Kaylin had reached out immediately for Severn; she knew Teela wasn't the only one injured.

You're back—hurry.

Mrs. Erickson? she asked, as she began to run. Severn wasn't looking at the old lady or her ghosts, the latter of which he couldn't see.

She's safe. With Sedarias's help, Teela's prevented any attempt Azoria has made to reach Mrs. Erickson.

Good. It's Mrs. Erickson's show, now—or it will be soon. She took the foyer stairs two at a time.

Had she not known where the room was, she would have had no difficulty finding it: the moment she reached the landing of the second story, she could hear the sounds of conflict. As she rounded a corner, she could see the flashes of light in different colors, and she could hear shouting and the sounds—like thunder—of magical combat. Closer, and she could see

where whole sections of interior wall had come down. No
one was fighting in the hall; when she'd left, Azoria had been
just one side of the frame.

She couldn't sprint and sneak a glimpse of the battlefield
through Severn's eyes, but she was close enough now it wasn't
necessary. Terrano kept pace with her; Sedarias might be
angry, but she wasn't terrified—not that she'd ever own it if
she were. Terrano, however, would know.

"I hope you know what you're doing," he said, raising his
voice to be heard.

She nodded. She hoped Mrs. Erickson would understand
what had to be done.

Three yards from what remained of the door, they slowed;
there was too much rubble. She thought she could see what
looked like a melted Wevaran limb, half-covered by debris;
she could certainly see blood.

The sharp intake of breath prompted Terrano to say, "Teela's,
minor wound. Not poisoned."

She stepped with more care; the last thing she needed was
to trip over stone and wood before she had reached her destination. But the destination loomed; from the hall she could
see Azoria's back. Were it not for the extra limbs and the eyes
that rose from the crown of her skull, Kaylin might have mistaken Azoria for a Barrani. But the limbs and the eyes were
present, and two of them swiveled toward the late arrivals.
Kaylin wouldn't have been surprised to see a mouth sprout
from Azoria's back.

But she had the attention she wanted now.

"Hope?"

Her familiar squawked. Quietly.

She lifted the hand in which she'd carried what remained
of Azoria's name—a word she had no hope of controlling be-

cause she would never be able to speak it. Not even the Ancient could. It was a word that had, over time, been eroded; all of the bright promise of its meaning forever lost.

Accepting your limitations might be bad, but accepting yourself, accepting your essential nature, was necessary. Kaylin now understood how easy it was to mistake one for the other.

"Azoria!" she said, raising her volume without shouting.

Azoria pivoted toward Kaylin then, all of the eyes on their flailing stalks almost lidless, they were so wide.

"You! What have you *done*?" Her voice was a shriek of sound that resonated in the hall—literally. It was like an earthquake made verbal. Kaylin, braced, retained her footing, her knees bent and moving. Had Azoria chosen to collapse the floor, she would have fallen.

"You didn't want the life you were given," Kaylin said. "You destroyed it with your own hands. But you destroyed many other people to do it." She focused on the new word she'd cupped in her palm as Azoria leaped from the room toward her.

Kaylin!

Azoria bounced off the barrier Hope erected. Hope squawked up a storm; his verbalization sounded scathing, even if she couldn't understand a word of it. Azoria didn't have that problem.

Get Mrs. Erickson in line of sight of the...door. Tell her: she can command the dead.

Severn didn't argue; he understood what Kaylin intended. Azoria, once Barrani, was impotent for the moment, and the moment was all Kaylin needed. The marks of the Chosen hadn't settled back into their home on her skin. She reached for their power, as she had in the outlands, and it came at her call.

Healing was the only power granted by the marks she instinctively understood. Sometimes she caused pain; sometimes she had to. But none of that was meant to destroy. None of it meant to kill.

Her fingers froze; she couldn't close them into fists.

She'd killed before. Once, in the distant past, she'd flayed the skin off slavers. She couldn't at this moment remember how; their deaths had been the product of her endless, driving rage. Azoria would kill all of them. She knew that. But the rage that she'd felt on that single, long-ago day had marked the end of childhood. She could not summon it back.

Power filled her palms regardless, and she understood only then what she was meant to do. She poured that power—healing power—into the remnants of what had once been a Barrani name.

Azoria screamed in rage—the rage Kaylin couldn't summon for herself. Beneath that rage was fear and pain, and perhaps that's all rage ever was: fear and pain writ large. Azoria renewed her frenzied attack on the barrier Hope had erected; she spoke broken Barrani—or Barrani interspersed with words that were never meant for Barrani use.

Kaylin, Hope said, *hurry. She is more powerful than she appears.*

Kaylin nodded; behind Azoria she could see the glint of a sword—no, two. Teela and Sedarias harried Azoria from behind—if *behind* was the right word. Azoria's extra limbs appeared to be omnidirectional.

They are, Severn said. *She's losing control. Whatever you're doing, keep doing it.*

Mrs. Erickson?

Holding up surprisingly well. She's distraught about the children, though—whatever Azoria did to them, it's upset her a lot.

Good. Keep close to her. I think we can end this immediately with her help.

Immediately.

As soon as I finish what I'm doing.

He didn't ask her what she was doing. But she knew now; the word, small and porous, was almost like a body to the touch; a miniature body. Unless and until transformed by Shadow, bodies knew their correct shape, their ideal health.

Azoria had done something to shift and alter the word at her core—but clearly she had done the work very carefully over the passage of centuries. It still supported her life. Had she tried—and failed—to repair it? Was that what she sought the power of the living for? Or was she a very broken form of Barrani vampire?

The creature thrashing and snarling in front of her could answer that question, but she clearly wasn't in a mood to converse. Kaylin closed her eyes. She couldn't see Azoria, but she could see the marks of the Chosen. As she watched, as she poured the power of those marks into the thing she held in her hand, she could see the faintest of golden light begin to grow. She couldn't see her hand, but could see what lay within it.

This wasn't justice. Azoria deserved to suffer.

She suffers, Kaylin, Hope said. *No happiness, no joy, would lead to what she has become.*

Kaylin bit back her visceral, knee-jerk reply, knowing that Hope was right. *But she destroyed so many lives.*

Yes. And those people did not deserve the ending she gave them. But you will free those who remain trapped when this is done. You have killed. Those deaths destroyed lives. Yet you are here, and you have grown to believe in yourself. She will die. Do not ask more of her ending than that.

But if I heal her name—

It is not her name anymore. She is not the cohort; you cannot simply offer to return it to her. There is no place in her that could house it.

But I gave the names back to the cohort. And they're not the Barrani they were born to be, either.

The cohort used—constantly—one element of their names. They
spoke to each other through the name bond. They offered each other
the knowledge of the names that give power; they knew *each other.*
That knowledge was predicated on the names themselves; some part
of what they could *become remained what they were when they*
made their covenant.

Look.

She did. A word, a True Word, now rested where her
hand would be. The marks that had encircled her arms retreated back to the base of her skin, but the light they shed
remained gold.

She opened her eyes; the word, she carried. Beyond it, the
woman who had once been blessed by the Consort at the
Lake of Life continued her frenzied attack; she couldn't see
the word, and even had she, Kaylin was certain she wouldn't
recognize it.

But Kaylin could now see the tenuous connection be-
tween Azoria and the name that she had all but destroyed.
She reached for it; it was as fine as spider silk, and as slender.
Without a second thought, she snapped the thread.

30

The name that had once been Azoria's life became weightless; it rose from Kaylin's hand, spinning slowly as if it were
sentient and needed to orient itself. It made no attempt to
return to Azoria. Azoria cried out a single word then, her
voice a Barrani voice.

Her name.

Kaylin didn't recognize it, but knew the utterance for what
it was. The word froze for one heartbeat, and then continued
its circling motion. It then froze again. Kaylin whispered the
name to no effect; it would never be used to control Azoria Berranin. The word leaped off her palm, flying away and
fading as it departed.

It would return to the Lake, as almost all Barrani names did
when the lives of the Barrani they had inhabited had ended.
The Consort would accept it, if she noticed the return at all—
Kaylin had never asked.

Azoria's physical form shed body parts—extra limbs first—
as if she were, absent that tenuous connection, slowly disin-
tegrating. But the form reasserted itself in Kaylin's eyes, the

eyes on the stalks that adorned her skull now an odd, pale
blue that was almost white.

Can you see her? she asked Severn.

*I can. In this place, we can see more of the dead than we could if
we were home.*

Here, the dead had substance. Kaylin wondered then if
Azoria had somehow built it that way, planning for the death
that would interrupt her ambitions, her studies, her research.
It didn't matter.

Tell Mrs. Erickson that the end of this show is hers.

As if she had heard, Mrs. Erickson could be seen in the
much enlarged doorway, Jamal by her side.

"Jamal," Kaylin said, raising her voice. "She needs your
permission. Because she promised."

Jamal looked at Azoria, and nodded. "Just once," he said.
"Just now."

Esme came to stand to Mrs. Erickson's other side, and behind her, Katie and Callis. All eyes were on Azoria.

"I am the lord of this tower," Azoria said, voice winter
cold. Her Barrani eyes were the same color as the eyes on the
stalks above her head. She gestured, and all four of the children froze in place as they were jerked off the ground. "The
living *and* the dead obey me here.

"You are no longer welcome guests—begone!"

The entirety of the floor began to shudder; Kaylin bent
her knees and concentrated on keeping her balance. Severn
caught Mrs. Erickson as she stumbled. The walls to front and
back began to fade in and out; the ground itself seemed to sag.

"Mrs. Erickson!"

Mrs. Erickson faced forward; Severn was behind her, and he
managed—somehow—to keep her steady. She faced Azoria—
or Azoria's ghost—and said, her voice clear and loud, *"Let those
children go."*

Mrs. Erickson had seldom seemed like a person given to fury, but all people could feel anger, and this was clearly her moment. The smile lines around her eyes and lips were re-purposed here, as was the timbre of her voice.

Azoria froze as Kaylin watched. "You—you do not know what you do here," she said, struggling to speak. "There are things here that we can accomplish that even the Ancients could not!" Even as she struggled, the children once again touched what remained of ground.

"Jamal, get behind me," Mrs. Erickson said. "And no, Azoria, this is *not* your home. It is *my* home. Your home no longer exists in our world. You are the intruder here, and you are not a person I would ever invite into my home as a guest.

"Stand down. You will not attempt to harm the friends I *did* invite, and you will release those poor souls you've murdered and trapped here."

The floors stopped moving; the walls reasserted solidity.

Mrs. Erickson then turned to the children. "You can go home, now. Wait for me there if you can. And if you can't, know that I love you all. You were the children we could never have. You made my life better, and I hope…" Her natural smile reasserted itself. "I have to speak with the rest of the people Azoria imprisoned, and…we have to figure out what to do with this place."

"Will you send her away?" Katie whispered.

"Yes, dear. But not immediately. We'll need to know who else is trapped here, and we'll need to free them as well."

Esme said, "We'll wait. Jamal?"

"I want to see her gone," he replied, voice so low it was barely audible.

Mrs. Erickson nodded. "I understand. But it won't be immediate." She paused, her shoulders relaxing; Jamal and the children were clearly unharmed—if that word had any meaning for the dead.

Jamal nodded. He looked up at the older woman, and said, "You won't do it again?"

"No. Thank you for giving me permission this time."

He nodded.

There were more trapped spirits within the halls Azoria had created—somehow—but the self-portrait that had hung on the wall was gone; the frame was empty, and the wall behind it visible. But there were other rooms and other paintings, some unframed and stacked in the dark. Azoria went through each one, Mrs. Erickson by her side. The dead Barrani woman had not yet accepted that she could not fight the compulsion; her answers were short and abrasive. They were also truthful.

Sedarias, Teela, and Terrano remained; Serralyn and Bakkon joined them.

Kaylin was exhausted. She wanted to go home, but she didn't trust Azoria. Mrs. Erickson might have command of the dead, but she'd had no training. Clearly Azoria believed this was a weakness as well—but the commands themselves appeared to be absolute.

Kaylin didn't understand enough about the dead to understand why this particular space could house and retain them. But the ghosts that had formed lamps and other household accessories could leave, now. They walked through the door that led to Mrs. Erickson's house. Mrs. Erickson didn't ask them to stay, either. She *did* ask them if they would be all right, because she wasn't certain they knew where they were going—but she had to confess, with some embarrassment, that she didn't know, either.

The dead did. Kaylin could hear their whispers of gratitude. She could see their tears of relief. And she could see them slowly fade from view—or at least hers—as they stepped across the threshold.

There were many, many questions that Sedarias wanted Azoria to answer. Serralyn wanted answers, too, but in a different way.

Mrs. Erickson, however, shook her head. "It's not right," she told them firmly. "We can't keep her here indefinitely."

"Why not?" Sedarias all but demanded.

"Because, dear, she's dead."

"She wants to stay."

"It's not that she wants to stay as she is now. She doesn't want to be dead. But she is. And it's time for her to leave. I don't know where she'll go," she added, a hint of worry in the words. "I don't know how she'll get there. She is one of a kind."

"For which we're extremely grateful," Kaylin snapped.

Mrs. Erickson looked at Kaylin and shook her head. Kaylin had seen that gesture before, but it had been aimed at Jamal. She reddened.

"I understand that there are many, many questions she might answer—but I don't believe that those answers serve a useful purpose."

"And your questions did," Teela said. It wasn't a question.

"Yes. The children have been trapped in my house for the entirety of my life. That shouldn't have happened. I'm grateful for it, which makes me feel guilty, but…it shouldn't have happened. By the time I understood that they couldn't leave, even if they wanted to, I had no idea how to free them.

"I've been worried about it for the past two decades. If you hadn't come to my house, they'd be trapped there for… as long as Azoria lived. She can't hold them now."

"But you could hold her here," Sedarias began. "And there's so much knowledge and research that we'd lose—"

"I think that's the point." Teela's voice was wry. "Mrs. Erickson doesn't think that research serves any good purpose."

"We don't know that."

"I think we do. Look at her now," the Barrani Hawk added, voice softer. "What do you see?"

To Kaylin's surprise, what she saw was a young Barrani woman. Hair a spill of black, the usual four limbs, the usual two eyes. The eyes were the wrong color, if they could be said to have color at all. All of the embellishments Azoria had made had faded. She looked young, to Kaylin's eye.

This wasn't justice. So many people had died because of this one woman. She struggled once again with her anger, her need to see Azoria punished.

Mrs. Erickson laid a hand on Kaylin's arm. "You're a Hawk, dear. Justice—imperfect as it is—is your duty. But there is no justice you can hand down when the criminal is dead. And I don't want to keep the children waiting any longer. There is also someplace they have to be, and I want to be able to say goodbye." She turned to Azoria. "Come with me," she said, her voice gentle. "It is time for you to go where you must."

"Where is that?"

"I don't know. I won't know until I'm dead. But I'm certain there's a place beyond this one." She offered Azoria a hand. There was no command in the gesture, but Azoria took that hand, and Mrs. Erickson turned toward her familiar front hall. "I don't know what will happen to this house," she said. "But I suggest that we leave it. I think, when Azoria crosses the threshold, things might collapse."

Terrano said, "I doubt it. But it won't be connected to our world in the same way." He had that *I'm really curious* look.

Sedarias grabbed him by the shoulder, her eyes a martial blue. "What? I could find my way back!"

"No."

Kaylin looked to Bakkon and Serralyn, the two late arrivals. Bakkon clicked a bit, and then found his Barrani. He seemed to be shuddering. "Let it collapse." His eyes were red. "It is an evil place; can you not feel it? It has the atmosphere of the birthing place, but no new life will come from it."

Serralyn nodded. There was genuine regret in her expression, but it blended with a quiet determination.

Sedarias wanted to argue, but Mrs. Erickson was a wall. A wall that Kaylin would defend with her life, if necessary. She acquiesced. Kaylin imagined the cohort would get a figurative earful about the wasted opportunities and possibilities later.

Oh, well. People were allowed to complain.

Bakkon returned to the Academia. Serralyn went with him. Terrano, Mandoran, Sedarias, and Teela left by the front door, because when they opened the front door it once again led to Orbonne Street. Hope, in his small form, was flattened across Kaylin's shoulder as if exhausted.

Severn said, "I'll wait on the porch," and left the house.

Kaylin turned to join him, and Jamal said, "We want you to stay."

When she raised her brows, Jamal added, "It's the last time you'll see us. You can't even say goodbye?"

"Jamal."

Kaylin knew he was doing it on purpose, but relented. She had some suspicions.

Callis was distracted; his gaze seemed to travel through Mrs. Erickson. And walls. Katie, Esme, and Jamal, however, were present, and at least one of them was tearful. No one pointed this out, because that child was Jamal, who had the ferocious pride of a child his age.

Mrs. Erickson crouched in front of the children. "Thank you. Thank you all so much. You've been my older siblings, my best friends, and even my children. I would have been so lonely without you—but you were here and you gave me purpose. Do you know where you have to go?"

Esme nodded. "I wish you could see it," she said, her eyes shining. "It looks like home—but *better*." Kaylin didn't ask which home; neither did Mrs. Erickson.

"You won't get lost, will you?"

"No. I don't think it's possible. But what about you?"

"I can't join you yet. I would, if I could."

"We don't want you to join us!" Jamal practically shouted. He then turned to Kaylin. "You have to take care of her."

Kaylin nodded.

"You have to promise to take care of her. She doesn't always remember to eat, you know. And she's a terrible sleeper. Sometimes she sleepwalks. And she is *way* too trusting."

Kaylin nodded again. Jamal held up one hand and crooked his pinky.

Kaylin lifted hers in response. "I don't think the neighbor will bother her anymore," she told the children.

"It's not about that jerk. It's about everything else. She's never lived alone. You heard her—she'll be lonely without us. She won't know what to do with herself."

"Jamal."

"I won't leave if you don't promise."

"Jamal!" Mrs. Erickson's voice now contained an edge of either anger or panic. Or both.

He ignored her; his gaze focused entirely on Kaylin. Kaylin looked at the other three, content, as they had been for their existence here, to let Jamal do the talking for them, when the talking was difficult. He hadn't said they would all stay; she was certain they wouldn't. But she was also certain that Jamal would, somehow.

"Jamal, after all Corporal Neya has done to allow you all to be free, this is unacceptable," Mrs. Erickson said, her voice firm. "It's a very, very poor expression of gratitude."

"We're grateful," Callis whispered.

So was Jamal. But his concern for, his protectiveness of, Mrs. Erickson had always given his presence a strength the others hadn't achieved. She had no doubt that he would keep his word. If he did, would he wait until Mrs. Erickson passed on? Could they then go wherever it was the dead went together?

She considered it, but she was afraid that Mrs. Erickson's resulting guilt might cause her to pass on early. Mrs. Erickson had the ability to force Jamal to go—but she would never use it against Jamal. Everything else relied on persuasion, and Jamal was not in a mood to be persuaded.

"I promise," she said, thinking of Helen. "I promise that I will take care of Mrs. Erickson."

"Will you live here?" The edge in his voice was so sharp it should have cut him.

"I'm not sure Mrs. Erickson would enjoy that; I tend to get mirrored at all hours of the night if there's an emergency. And it's her house—it's not your offer to make."

"Then how?" He was such a suspicious child.

"I have a home. It's not the home Mrs. Erickson grew up in, and she might refuse, but I will offer her rooms in my house." Kaylin hesitated, and then said, "My house isn't like yours. It's not like Azoria's, either. But it is a sentient building. Mrs. Erickson has already met Helen, the core of my house, and Helen approved of her.

"If Mrs. Erickson was willing, we'd both be delighted if she came to live with us. Would that be enough for you?"

Jamal nodded, and turned to Mrs. Erickson, whose disapproval had been replaced by anxiety and guilt. "Same deal," he said. "I'm not leaving you alone."

"Jamal, I'm—"

"Younger than we are, even if you don't look it. I trust Kaylin. She cares about you. You have to trust her, too." When Mrs. Erickson failed to answer, he said, in a slightly gentler tone of voice, "It's not only the dead who are capable of loving you as you are."

Kaylin was beginning to understand why Jamal could get away with breaking random things when he lost his temper; he was just one side of manipulative. The wrong side. Nor did he seem to care.

But she understood his fear, his concern, and the reason he was being a demanding little extortionist. If he looked— and mostly acted—like a jealous child, he had seen her born. He had seen her crawl, walk, learn to speak. The reason he had come to her side didn't matter, either to Mrs. Erickson or Jamal himself. He had grown to love her, just as she had always loved him. If the love changed with time on both sides, it nonetheless existed.

In his position, Kaylin thought she would have been the same. But…she *wasn't* a child; she wasn't a lifelong friend. If pressure was going to be brought to bear, it was Jamal's pressure: he was family. She therefore said nothing.

Mrs. Erickson looked at Kaylin in mute appeal.

"You're thinking we don't really want you?" Kaylin asked. She held out both of her hands. "Helen is old. She genuinely liked you. Her first tenant liked to bustle about the kitchen, and I think Helen misses that; I don't really touch the kitchen much. Helen gets lonely, and right now, she has a houseful of children. I mean, you met Terrano. He's a lot like Jamal."

"I try—but I'm not quite the company her earlier tenants were. I might become that as I get older, but I doubt it."

"I would have doubted it at your age," Mrs. Erickson said.

"Did you find Helen intimidating?"

"No, of course not!"

"Did you find her company unpleasant?"

"No. She reminded me of..." Mrs. Erickson didn't finish the sentence.

Kaylin surrendered then. Maybe she *was* too much like Jamal. "It's partly for Helen's sake that I'm asking. She's trapped in herself; she can't leave the building because it's her body now. It wasn't always. She once housed Arcanists, possibly Sorcerers, but she had no choice in that. The first tenant she chose was an older woman who had been brought in as a servant. A woman without power, without obvious ambition, and with no desire to control a living entity. She was, according to Helen, gentle. And tidy. She liked to garden. She liked to cook. She liked to take care of the house.

"Helen doesn't *need* a housekeeper; she can clean without a second thought. Or practically a first one. She doesn't need tenants, either. But she gets lonely.

"I think she'd be less lonely if you agreed to live with us."

Jamal's glint of approval made Kaylin feel guilty. Yes, definitely too much like Jamal, but nothing she had said was a lie.

"Jamal," Mrs. Erickson said, voice firm. "If I promise to speak to Helen to make *certain* Helen wants me to stay, will you leave?"

Jamal looked past her to Kaylin; Kaylin nodded.

"Yes."

"You could follow her if you wanted to be sure," Kaylin

told him, before she could shut her mouth and bite back the words.

Jamal frowned, brow creasing. "I can leave."

"You can leave. I'm not like you. I don't know if there are natural limits—I mean, I thought ghosts were supposed to haunt the places in which they'd died."

"I'll go." He turned to the other three. "I'll see her off. You don't have to wait for me."

At least one wouldn't, in Kaylin's opinion. Katie was already almost gone, her body a shimmering transparency, quivering as if in intense joy.

"You're sure?" Callis asked.

Jamal nodded. "I want you to go on ahead of me. Someone has to." He held out one hand to Mrs. Erickson. "You don't have to move all the stuff right now, but…I want to meet this Helen."

Mrs. Erickson nodded.

Severn was silent. Kaylin paused on the porch to really look at him. *You're injured.*

It's minor. If it were serious, I wouldn't have stayed. He smiled. *Good work, there.*

You don't think I was being a bit pushy?

You were, but you were pushing her in a direction I think she wanted to go. It's hard to lose companions of a lifetime—it's hard to lose family you know. And there are ghosts in your house that no one but Mrs. Erickson can touch.

Kaylin had almost forgotten about them.

I think it would be best for Mrs. Erickson for other reasons, among them the Dragon Court. Her power is dangerous. Had Azoria fully absorbed it…

Kaylin thought of the Ancient then, and shuddered.

EPILOGUE

Helen was waiting in the open door when Kaylin crossed the fence line. Mrs. Erickson had fallen back nervously; had she not been leading Jamal, Kaylin thought she might have remained standing there, looking at Helen's exterior. Jamal, however, was a concern, as he had been for so much of her life.

Kaylin turned to Mrs. Erickson and offered her a hand; Mrs. Erickson missed it the first time. Helen, smiling softly, waited at the door, watching their slow progress up the walk. Only when Kaylin reached her did Helen move; she opened her arms to offer Kaylin what Kaylin thought of as the *welcome home* hug. It was a bit more awkward than usual because Mrs. Erickson hadn't let go of her hand.

"Imelda," Helen said, as she released her primary tenant, "I'm delighted to see you. Will you come in?"

Mrs. Erickson nodded. Kaylin knew her name was Imelda, but doubted she'd ever feel comfortable actually using it.

"We've come to ask you a question," Kaylin said, although Helen already knew what it was.

"Yes, I see that." Helen's smile was soft, almost radiant.

It made truth out of what Kaylin had feared were exaggerations. "Come in. Come in, all three of you."

Jamal's brows rose.

"No, dear," Helen said softly, "I can't see you. But I believe that you're there because both Imelda and Kaylin can. Thank you for giving me this opportunity." Although she had invited Mrs. Erickson—and Jamal—in, Jamal shook his head.

"You are worried for Imelda, and I find that commendable. Please, come in. You can look at the house, and you can decide whether or not you think this would be suitably safe for the woman you have protected for so long. I do wish I could see you," she added, her voice almost familiar. It took a moment for Kaylin to realize why: Helen had chosen to subtly mimic Mrs. Erickson's speech habits.

Jamal didn't seem to notice, but that made sense: this sounded natural to him. Although he had observed other people, they didn't speak to him; they couldn't see him. Helen was the edge case—but Helen's acknowledgment made clear that she respected Mrs. Erickson's ability.

"Come in. If you are not satisfied by the end of the tour, you may offer Mrs. Erickson your advice. I am not a prison. I hope, in time, to be a friend."

Jamal hesitantly slid one foot across the threshold. When nothing happened, he slid the other across it. Helen then led them away from the door before it closed—quietly—at their backs.

The tour that Helen gave Mrs. Erickson and Jamal was unlike the tour that Kaylin had received—but nothing was trying to kill them at the moment, and there were no pressing emergencies. Mrs. Erickson inspected the kitchen with delight, not judgment; she asked questions about storage, about cupboards, about the operation of the stove—and received answers that were a bit too technical for Kaylin's taste. They included a history of Imperial stoves.

They entered the dining room, and Helen apologetically explained that the dining room tended to be where the cohort gathered, and the dimension of the table tended to change to accommodate the number of guests. The parlor, she explained, was similar. The cohort didn't use it, but on occasion Kaylin had Imperial guests, and when she did, Helen arranged a sitting room worthy of those visitors. Kaylin disliked the "worthy" part, because she saw nothing wrong with the parlor into which Mrs. Erickson entered.

While they walked, Helen explained—largely for Jamal's benefit—the defenses erected against intruders, be they mortal, Immortal, or otherwise. This impressed Jamal, who asked Mrs. Erickson about *Dragons*.

"Yes, even against Dragons, should they decide to enter without permission. I believe it's the reason Kaylin felt Imelda would be safest here."

"She thinks the Dragons will try to hurt her?" He was skeptical. Mrs. Erickson had clearly chosen not to share the events of the day that might prompt that dire interest.

"You're quite aware that Imelda has talents that other people don't. Those talents, used in the wrong place or the wrong way, could be deadly to the living, and hell for the dead. But you know this; you know what Azoria wanted."

"What about Barrani?"

"She will be absolutely safe from Barrani, even the ones who live here should they lose their tempers. I do not allow my guests or my tenants to harm each other."

"What about the spiders?"

"I believe you mean the Wevaran, and yes, I can prevent Wevaran from entering my home. I admit I've never had one try, but I understand how their portals work."

"Azoria?"

In a very gentle voice, Helen said, "She is dead. And unlike you, she doesn't have Imelda as a friend. I do not believe she will come here—or anywhere—again."

"What are your neighbors like?"

"I am uncertain. I cannot leave my house, so I have never met them. But if you look out the window, you'll see how far away the nearest neighbor is. Our properties are not connected in any way, and I'm sorry to say, the guard patrols are quite frequent in this part of town."

"Why sorry?"

"This isn't really where they're needed, in my opinion. It's just where the money resides."

"Don't get me started," Kaylin muttered.

Jamal nodded. And then insisted on seeing the other tenants. Helen didn't correct his use of the word, but apologetically said every tenant was entitled to privacy, and she wasn't certain she could demand they come out to be inspected by a person they couldn't see.

Far from upsetting Jamal, this seemed to comfort him. He did ask for information about each tenant, and Helen complied, adding that until very recently, one of the residents had been a Dragon. His eyes nearly fell out of his head, and he demanded details with the excitement of a boy his apparent age.

"Wait'll I tell the others!" His smile froze then.

It was Mrs. Erickson who knelt beside him. "I'm sure they'll love it—they might even be a bit envious."

"They're not here anymore."

"No. But you can join them now. You don't have to worry about me anymore. I'll be fine here, and…it's a long time since I had a living friend. A very long time."

Jamal looked at Helen. Although he knew Helen couldn't

see him, it was to Jamal she had been speaking. Helen could see what Kaylin could see with a tiny bit of effort.

"Promise you'll protect her until it won't make a difference." His expression was every bit as serious as it had been when he made the same demand of Kaylin. He had less leverage here, and knew it. He didn't threaten to remain. He knew, with Helen, it wouldn't matter.

"I promise I will protect her as well as I protect Kaylin, unless she attempts to harm her."

Jamal bristled instantly. "She would never do that!"

"No. I don't believe she would. And if she did, she might have good reason. But I am what I am, and my imperative should that ever occur is to protect Kaylin. Can you accept that?"

Jamal considered this with as much care as an annoyed child could. He made the effort not to let annoyance make any decisions for him, but it was clearly work. "Yes. Yes, I can accept that."

"Imelda," Helen said, turning to the woman Jamal was afraid to leave behind. "I would very much love it if you would accept the hospitality of our house. You will not be imprisoned here; you are free to leave should you decide the house is too loud or too hectic. Choice in these things will always be yours. But I would value and appreciate your company, should you care to accept our offer."

Mrs. Erickson's smile was gentle and almost beatific. She held out one hand; Helen took it carefully. "I would. I would love to live here."

"I want to see her rooms," Jamal said. "I want to see where she'll be staying first."

"You're adding conditions after the fact," Kaylin told him. "That's poor sportsmanship."

"Jamal, be reasonable," Mrs. Erickson added, in the tone

of a woman who has no hope whatsoever that her request will be granted.

He ignored her, focusing on Kaylin. "Who cares about sports?"

Helen, however, smiled. "You may see her rooms, if it will comfort you. She cares very much for you, and she does not want you to worry in any way."

"It's all right?" Mrs. Erickson asked, with a trace of anxiety.

"Of course it is. They will be your rooms, and Jamal has always been part of your home." Helen then turned and led Mrs. Erickson to the foyer, to the wide staircase, and up it, to the second floor. She turned down the hall in which all of the tenants—except one—had their rooms. Those rooms were adorned by silhouettes that spoke to or about the inhabitants.

Kaylin noted the new door down the hall; it was beside her own room. On it was something that looked suspiciously like the basket in which Mrs. Erickson put the baking she brought to the Halls of Law. Kaylin wondered if baking would still be done, still be brought in, when she no longer had the children to entertain; she wouldn't need stories of her daily life to bring back to them.

"This is your room," Helen told Mrs. Erickson. "I am always present; if you call me, I will answer. Kaylin's is next door, if you feel calling me will cause discomfort."

Mrs. Erickson nodded, and then reached out for the door's handle. She opened the door slowly. "This...isn't a room," she whispered. Kaylin looked over her shoulder; she could see grass and wildflowers, a blend of white and green and violet.

"It is one of *my* rooms, Imelda. Just beyond the field—you can see it from here—is where you would be living should you choose to stay."

Kaylin did not expect tears, but Mrs. Erickson shed them,

as if unaware that they were falling. She turned to Helen. "You knew?"

"No. Not until you opened the door."

"This was the home we wanted, when we were young. A home of our own, not a home that was only mine. My mother said—she always said—that no matter how much we loved the homes of our birth, we would outgrow them; we would need to stretch and experience life before we could make a home of our own."

"You have experienced much of life—and death—Imelda. If the dream does not live up to those you had in your youth, this room will change; it will accommodate you. It always will. That is my gift and my responsibility."

Jamal watched in silence, and then a smile graced his face, a moment of deep and abiding joy.

Mrs. Erickson turned to him; a deeper, older joy had transformed her features. That and tears. She knelt in front of Jamal, and for only this moment, he seemed to Kaylin to be the older of the two—as if his apparent youth had somehow transmuted her apparent age into something lighter, something precious.

She held out her arms, and he came to her, although she couldn't touch him.

"Goodbye, Jamal, my dearest friend, my brother, my child."

"We'll wait for you," he said. "We'll wait. Bring us *lots* of stories. But not too quickly, okay? This is your time now. Yours."

She nodded.

The door closed as Kaylin watched.

"Let them have this moment on their own," Helen said. "We'll have moments of our own in the future. It is how history is built." She paused, and then added, "Thank you. You were, of course, right."

Kaylin didn't pretend to misunderstand.

"I have always been grateful that you came to me—but even I did not expect so much. You have been a tenant, yes, but a gift as well. When you at last depart, I will always remember you. And now I will go inform the cohort—and consider a welcome dinner."

★ ★ ★ ★ ★